Julie Miller is an award-winning *USA TODAY* selling author of breathtaking romantic suspense, Readers' Choice Award and Award, among other prizes. an *RT Book Reviews* Career Achievement Award. For complete list of her books, monthly newsletter and more, go to www.juliemiller.org.

Debbie Herbert writes paranormal and romantic suspense novels reflecting her belief that love, like magic, casts its own spell of enchantment. A 2017 Rita finalist, she's always been fascinated by magic, romance and gothic stories. Married and living in Alabama, she roots for the Crimson Tide football team. Her eldest son, like many of her characters, has autism. Her youngest son is in the US Army. A past Maggie Award finalist in both young adult and paranormal romance, she loves to hear from readers!

Discover more at millsandboon.co.uk

KANSAS CITY COP

JULIE MILLER

APPALACHIAN ABDUCTION

DEBBIE HERBERT

MILLS & BOON

First Published in Great Britain 2018
By Mills & Boon, an imprint of HarperCollins*Publishers*
1 London Bridge Street, London, SE1 9GF

Kansas City Cop © 2018 Julie Miller
Appalachian Abduction © 2018 Debbie Herbert

ISBN: 978-0-263-26561-3

39-0318

MIX
Paper from responsible sources
FSC
www.fsc.org
FSC™ C007454

MILLS & BOON

KANSAS CITY COP

JULIE MILLER

To Edna Castillo, reader and bookseller extraordinaire.

A fellow *The Wizard of Oz* fan, too! Thanks for your help with the Spanish. Any mistakes are my own.

Chapter One

The bright sunlight glaring off the fresh February snow through the police cruiser's windshield was as blinding as the headache forming behind Officer Gina Galvan's dark brown eyes.

"No, Tia Mami, I can't." She glanced across the front seat to her partner, Derek Johnson, and silently mouthed an apology for yet another family crisis infringing on their shift time with KCPD. "I don't get off until seven. And that's if our paperwork's done. That's why I left my car at home and took the bus this morning—so Sylvie could drive you and Tio Papi to his doctor's appointment."

"Sylvie no come home from school," her great-aunt Lupe replied quietly, as though apologizing for the news.

"What? Where is she?"

"Javi said he saw her riding with that boyfriend of hers we don't like."

"Seriously?" Anger and concern flooded Gina's cheeks with heat. The boyfriend they didn't like had too much money to have gotten it in the old neighborhood by any legal means. But Bobby Estes's flashy cars and devilish good looks were too much for Gina's dreamy, dissatisfied baby sister to resist. And if Bobby was a teenager, as he claimed, then Gina was Santa Claus.

Clearly, her last conversation with Sylvie, about the definition of statutory rape and learning to act like an adult if she wanted to be treated like one, had not made a memorable impact. "I'm going to have to ground her. That's all there is to it."

But dealing with her sister's rash choices didn't get Tio Papi to the doctor's office. Gina slipped her fingers beneath the base of her wavy brunette ponytail to massage the tension gathering at the nape of her neck.

Derek nudged her with his elbow. "Need a ride home tonight?"

Missing the point! Although, in his defense, Derek was only hearing half the conversation. Gina summoned a smile for the friend she'd been riding a squad car with for almost two years now. "It's okay. Just a miscommunication at home."

"Gotta love our families, right?" Derek teased. She knew he had a strained relationship with his father. And there was no love lost for Derek's mother, who'd divorced his father and moved away, leaving her teenage son behind to be raised by an aging hippie who had trouble keeping a job and staying out of jail.

A difficult upbringing was part of the common ground they shared, and had helped solidify their working relationship and understanding of each other. Gina gave the sarcasm right back, whispering so her great-aunt couldn't hear. "Do we really have to?"

Derek grinned and directed her back to her phone. "Tell Aunt Lupe hi for me, okay?"

"I will. Tia Mami, Derek says hi."

"You teach that young man to say *hola*, and bring him to dinner sometime."

"I'm working on it." Gina continued the conversation with appropriate responses while her great-aunt rattled on about other concerns she'd have to deal with once she got home. While Lupe talked, Gina concentrated on the scenery as they drove past, partly because it was her job to observe the neighborhood and take note of anything that looked suspicious or unsafe, and partly because she'd already heard the same worried speech too many times before about fast cars and traffic accidents, young men who didn't come to the door to pick up a date and Uncle Rollo's deteriorating health.

Now *there* was something different. Gina lifted her chin for a better look. A tall man in silver and black running gear came around the corner off Pennsylvania Avenue and ran down the narrow side street. A jogger in this neighborhood was unusual. Maybe he was one of those yuppie business owners who'd opened an office in this part of town for a song, or he'd bought a loft in one of the area's abandoned warehouses, thinking he could revitalize a little part of Kansas City. Not for the first time, she considered the irony of people with money moving into this part of the city, while the natives like her were doing all they could to raise enough money to move out.

But irony quickly gave way to other thoughts. The runner was tall, lean and muscular. Although the stocking cap and wraparound sunglasses he wore masked the top half of his head, the well-trimmed scruff of brown beard on his golden skin was like catnip to her. Plus, she could tell he was fit by the rhythmic clouds of his breath in the cold air. He wasn't struggling to maintain that pace and, for a woman who worked hard to stay physically fit, she appreciated his athleticism.

As they passed each other, he offered her a polite wave, and Gina nodded in return. Since he already knew she'd been staring, she shifted her gaze to the side mirror to watch him run another block. Long legs and a tight butt. Gina's lips curved into a smile. They probably had a lot of scenery like that in the suburbs. A relationship was one thing she didn't have time for at this point in her life. And no way did she want to tie herself to anyone from the neighborhood who might want her to stay. But there was no harm in looking and getting her blood circulating a little faster. After all, it was only twenty-two degrees out, and a woman had to do whatever was necessary to stay warm.

Gina glanced over at her partner. Derek was handsome in his own way. He, too, had brown hair, but his smooth baby face was doing nary a thing for her circulation.

"Do we need to take a detour to your house and have a conversation with your sister? I'd be happy to um, have a word, with that boyfriend of hers." He took his hands off the steering wheel to make air quotes around *have a word*, as if he had ideas about roughing up Bobby on her behalf. As if she couldn't take care of her family's issues herself.

Since the car was moving, Gina guided one hand back to the steering wheel and changed the subject. She covered the speaker on her phone and whispered, "Hey, since things are quiet right now, why don't you swing by a coffee shop and get us something hot to drink. I haven't been able to shake this chill since that first snow back in October."

Although the remembered impression of Sexy Jogger Guy made that last sentence a lie, her request had the desired effect of diverting Derek's interest in her family problems.

"That I can do. One skinny mocha latte coming up."

Distracted with his new mission, Derek turned the squad car onto a cross street, plowing through a dip filled with dirty slush as they continued their daily patrol through the aging neighborhood. With houses and duplexes so close together that a person could barely walk between them, vehicles parked bumper-to-bumper against the curb and junk piling on porches and spilling into yards, this was a part of the city she knew far too well. Add in the branches of tall, denuded maple trees heavy with three months' worth of snow arching over the yards and narrow streets, and Gina felt claustrophobic. As much as she loved Kansas City and her job as a police officer, she secretly wondered if she was the reincarnation of some Central American ancestor and was meant for living on the high, arid plains of her people with plenty of blue sky and wide-open space, without a single snowflake in sight.

Setting aside her own restless need to escape, Gina turned toward the passenger door to find some privacy for this personal conversation. "Did you call Sylvie?" she asked her great-aunt, once the older woman's need to vent had subsided.

"She don't answer."

"What about Javi?" Her brother, Javier, was twenty-one, although that didn't necessarily mean he was making better choices than Sylvie. She kept hoping for the day when he would step up as the man of the family and allow their great-uncle to truly enjoy his retirement. "Can he drive you?"

"He's already gone. He's picking up some extra hours at work."

Well, that was one plus in the ongoing drama that was Gina's life. Maybe so long as Javi was intent on saving up to buy a truck, he would focus on this job and avoid the influence of his former friends who'd made some less productive choices with their lives, like stealing cars, selling drugs and running with gangs. "Good."

"Papi says he can drive," Lupe Molina offered in a hushed, uncertain tone.

Gina sat up as straight as her seat belt and protective vest allowed. "No. Absolutely not. The whole reason he's going for these checkups is because he passed out the last time his blood pressure spiked. He can't be behind the wheel."

"What do I do?" Lupe asked quietly.

As much as she loved her great-aunt and -uncle who'd taken in the three Galvan siblings and raised them after their mother had died, Lupe and Rollo Molina were now both close to eighty and didn't need the hassle of dealing with an attention-craving teenager. Especially not with Rollo's health issues. "I'll call Sylvie. See if I can get her home to help like she promised. If you don't hear from her or me in ten minutes, call the doctor's office and reschedule the appointment for tomorrow. I'll be off except for practicing for my next SWAT test on the shooting range. I'll make sure you get there."

"All right. I can do that. You see? This is where having a young man to help you would be a good thing."

Gina rolled her eyes at the not-so-subtle hint. There was more than one path to success besides getting married and making babies. "I love you, Tia Mami. *Adios.*"

"*Te amo,* Gina. You're always my good girl."

By the time she disconnected the call, Derek had pulled the black-and-white into the coffee shop's tiny parking lot but was making no effort to get out and let her deal with her family on her own. Instead, he rested the long black sleeve of his uniform on the steering wheel and grinned at her. "Sylvie off on another one of her escapades?"

Gina might as well fill in the blanks for him. "She's supposed to be driving my uncle to the doctor. Instead, she's cruising around the city with a young man who's too old for her."

Derek shook his head. "She does look older than seventeen when she puts on all her makeup." He dropped his green-eyed gaze to her black laced-up work boots. "She's got the family legs, too."

Ignoring the gibe at her five-foot-three-inch height, Gina punched in Sylvie's number. Then she punched Derek's shoulder, giving back the teasing camaraderie they shared. "You're eyeballing my little sister?"

"Hey, when you decorate the Christmas tree, you're supposed to celebrate it."

"Well, you don't get to hang any ornaments on my sister, understand? She's seventeen. You could get into all kinds of trouble with the department. And me."

Derek raised his hands in surrender. "Forget the department. You're the one who scares me. You're about to become one of SWAT's finest. I'm not messing with anyone in your family."

The call went straight to Sylvie's voice mail. "Damn it." Gina tucked her phone back into her vest and held her hand out for Derek's. "Could I borrow yours? Maybe if she doesn't recognize the number, she'll pick up."

"That means I'll have her number in my phone, you know. And Sylvie *is* a hottie."

"Seven. Teen." Gina repeated the warning with a smile and typed in her wayward sister's number.

She'd barely been a teenager herself when her mother had passed away and their long-absent father had willingly signed away his parental rights, leaving the three Galvans orphans in No-Man's Land, one of the toughest neighborhoods in downtown Kansas City. They'd moved out of their cramped apartment into a slightly less cramped house. Instead of prostitutes, drug dealers and gangbangers doing business beneath Gina's bed-room window, they'd graduated to the vicinity of a meth lab, which KCPD had eventually closed down, at the end of the block. Naturalized citizens who were proud to call themselves Americans, her great-aunt and -uncle had stressed the values of education and hard work, and they'd grown up proud but poor. With her diminutive stature, Gina had quickly learned how to handle herself in a fight and project an attitude so that no one would mess with her family or take advantage of her. That hardwired drive to protect her loved ones had morphed into a desire to protect any innocent who needed her help, including this neighborhood and her entire city. But she couldn't forget which side of the tracks the Galvans and Molinas had come from—and just how far she had to go to secure something better for them.

"Hey, don't jinx the SWAT thing for me, okay?" A lit-tle bit of her great-aunt and -uncle's superstitious nature buzzed through her thoughts like an annoying gnat she thought she'd gotten rid of. If she made Special Weapons and Tactics, the rise in status with the department and subsequent raise in pay would finally allow her to move her whole family into a house with a real yard in a safer suburb. She wasn't afraid of setting goals and working hard to achieve them, but it was rare that she allowed any-thing so personal as wanting some open space to plant a proper garden or get a dog or owning a bathroom she didn't have to share with four other people to motivate her. "I'm not the only recruit on Captain Cutler's list of candidates for the new SWAT team he's forming. There are ten people on a list for five spots. Including you."

"Yeah, but you're the toughest."

"Jinxing, remember?" Gina crossed her fingers and kissed her knuckles before touching them to her heart, a throwback from her childhood to cootie shots and negating bad karma. "We all have our talents."

"I'm just repeating what Cutler said at the last training meeting. McBride scored the highest at the shooting range. And you, my kickass little partner, are the one he said he'd least like to face one-on-one in a fight. Take the compliment."

It was on the tip of her tongue to remind Derek that she wasn't his *little* anything, but she was dealing with enough conflict already today. "You're doing well, too, or you'd have been eliminated already. Captain Cutler announces things like that so we stay competitive."

"Hey, I'm not quittin' anything until those new promotions are posted. I only have to be fifth best and I'll still make the team."

"Fifth best?" Gina laughed. "Way to aim high, Johnson."

"It's too bad about Cho, though. He's been acing all the written tests and procedure evaluations."

Gina agreed. Colin Cho was a fellow SWAT candidate who'd suffered three cracked ribs when he'd been shot twice while directing traffic around a stalled car on the North Broadway Freeway in the middle of the night two weeks ago. Only his body armor had prevented the incident from becoming a fatality. "Any idea how he's doing?"

"I heard he's up and around, but he won't be running any races soon. He's restricted to desk duty for the time being. I wonder if they'll replace him on the candidate list or just shorten it to nine potential SWAT officers."

"Cho's too good an officer to remove from contention," Gina reasoned, hitting the phone icon on the screen to connect the call.

"But there *is* a deadline," Derek reminded her. "If he can't pass the physical…"

The number rang several times before her sister finally picked up. "Sylvie Galvan's phone," a man answered.

Not her sister but that slimy lothario who struck Gina as a mobster wannabe—if he wasn't already running errands and doing small jobs for some of the bigger criminals in town. Gina swallowed the curse on her tongue. She needed to keep this civil if she wanted to get her great-aunt and -uncle the help they needed. "Bobby, put Sylvie on."

"It's your wicked big sister," he announced. The sounds of horns honking and traffic moving in the background told her they were in his car. Hopefully, in the front seat and not stretched out together in the back. "What will you give me to hand you this phone?"

That teasing request was for her sister.

Gina cringed at the high-pitched sound of her sister's giggles. She groaned at the wet, smacking sound of a kiss. Or two. So much for keeping it civil. "Bobby Estes, you keep your hands off my sister or I will—"

"Blah, blah, blah." Sylvie was on the line now. Finally. She could live without the breathless gasps and giggles and the picture the noises created of a practically grown man making out with her innocent sister. "What do you want?"

"You forgot Tio Papi's doctor's appointment." Better to stick to the purpose of the phone call than to get into another lecture about the bad choices Sylvie was making. "You promised me you would drive him today."

"Javi can do it."

"He's at work. Besides, it was your responsibility." Her fingers curled into a fist at the sound of her sister's gasp. Really? Bobby couldn't keep his hands to himself for the ten seconds it would take to finish this call? "Do you want me to treat you like a grown-up or not?"

"I just got home from school."

"A half hour ago. I was counting on you. This isn't about me. It's about helping Rollo and Lupe. Do you want to explain to them why you've forgotten them?"

Bobby purred against her sister's mouth, and the offensive noise crawled over Gina's skin. "Is big sis being a downer again? You know she's jealous of us. Hang up, baby."

"Bobby, stop." Sylvie sounded a little irritated with her boyfriend. For once. The shuffling noises and protests made her think Sylvie was pushing him away. Gina suppressed a cheer. "When is the appointment?"

"Four forty-five. Can you do it?"

"Yeah. I can help." Thank goodness Sylvie still had enough little girl in her to idolize her pseudo grandparents. She'd do for them what she wouldn't do for Gina. Or herself, unfortunately. Her tone shifted to Bobby. "I need to go home."

"I said I was taking you out to dinner. I was gonna show you my friend's club," he whined. "Just because Gina's a cop, she doesn't make the rules. She sure as hell isn't in charge of what I do."

"Don't get mad, Bobby. Just drive me home." Sylvie was doing some purring of her own. "I'll make it up to you later."

"Promise?"

"Promise."

"Ooh, I like it when you do that, baby."

Gina wished she could reach through the phone and yank her sister out of Bobby's car before she got into the kind of trouble that even a big sister with a badge couldn't help her with. "Sylvie?"

"I'll call Tia Mami and tell her we're on our way."

"Bobby doesn't need to go with you." A powerful car engine revved in the background. "Seeing him will only upset—"

"Bye."

Bobby shouted an unwanted goodbye. "Bye-bye, big sis."

She groaned when her sister's phone went silent. Gina cursed. "Have I ever mentioned how much I want to use Bobby Estes as one of the dummies in our fight-training classes?"

Derek laughed as he put away his phone. "Once or twice." He opened his door, and Gina shivered at the blast of wintry wind. "I keep telling you that I'd be happy to help run him in."

At least the chill helped some of her temper dissipate, as did Derek's unflinching support. "Bobby's too squeaky clean for that. He does just enough to annoy me, but not enough that I can prove he's committing any kind of crime. And Sylvie isn't about to rat him out."

"Just say the word, and I'm there for you, G." He turned to climb out. "I'll leave the car running so you stay warm."

But the dispatch radio beeped, and he settled back behind the wheel to listen to the details of the all-call. "So much for coffee."

Derek closed the door as the dispatch repeated. "Attention all units in the Westport area. We have a 10-52 reported. Repeat, domestic dispute report. Approach with caution. Suspect believed to be armed with a knife."

"That's the Bismarck place." Derek frowned as he shifted the cruiser into Drive and pulled out onto the street. "I thought Vicki Bismarck took out a restraining order against her ex."

"She did." This wasn't the first time they'd answered a call at the Bismarcks' home. The address was just a couple of blocks from their location. Gina picked up the radio while Derek flipped on the siren and raced through the beginnings of rush-hour traffic. "Unit 4-13 responding."

Her family troubles were forgotten as she pulled up the suspect's name on the laptop mounted on the dashboard. Domestic-disturbance calls were her least favorite kind of call. The situations were unpredictable, and there were usually innocent parties involved. This one was no different.

"Gordon Bismarck. I don't think he's handling the divorce very well." Gina let out a low whistle. "He's got so many D&Ds and domestic-violence calls the list goes on to a second page. No outstanding warrants, though, so we can't just run him in." She glanced over at Derek as they careened around a corner. "Looks like he's not afraid to hurt somebody. You ready for this?"

"I know you've got my back. And I've got yours."

She hoped he meant it because when they pulled up in front of the Bismarck house, they weren't alone. And the men belonging to a trio of motorcycles and a beat-up van didn't look like curiosity seekers who'd gathered to see what all the shouting coming from inside the bungalow was about.

Derek turned off the engine and swore. "How many thugs does it take to terrorize one woman? I hope Vicki's okay. Should I call for reinforcements?"

"Not yet." Gina tracked the men as they put out cigarettes and split up to block the end of the driveway and the sidewalk leading to the front door. Middle-aged.

A couple with potbellies. One had prison tats on his neck. Another took a leisurely drink from a flask before tucking it inside the sheepskin-lined jacket he wore. Their bikes were in better shape than they were. But any one of them could be armed. And she could guess that the guy with the flask wasn't the only one who'd been drinking. Judging by what she'd read on the cruiser's computer screen, these were friends, if not former cell mates, of Gordon Bismarck's. Gina's blood boiled in her veins at the lopsided odds. She reached for the door handle. "But keep your radio at the ready."

Gina pushed open the cruiser door and climbed out. "Gentlemen." She rested her hand on the butt of her holstered Glock. "I need you to disperse."

"You *need* us, *querida*?" Flask Man's leer and air kisses weren't even close to intimidating, and she certainly wasn't his *darling* anything.

Derek circled the cruiser, positioning himself closer to the two in the driveway while she faced off against the two on the sidewalk. "In case you don't understand the big word, you need to get on your bikes and ride away."

"We gave Gordy a ride home," Potbelly #1 said, thumbing over his shoulder just as something made of glass shattered inside the house.

A woman's voice cried out, "Gordon, stop it!"

"I paid for this damn house. And I'll—"

Gina needed to get inside to help Vicki Bismarck. But she wasn't going to leave these four aging gangbangers out here where they could surround the house or lie in wait for her and Derek to come back outside. "We're not interested in you boys today," she articulated in a sharp, authoritative tone. "But if you make me check the registrations on your bikes or van, or I get close enough to think any of you need a Breathalyzer test, then it *will* be about you."

Prison Tat Guy was the first to head toward his bike. "Hey, I can't have my parole officer gettin' wind of this."

Potbelly #2 quickly followed suit. "I'm out of here, man. Gordy doesn't need us to handle Vic. My old lady's already ticked that I stayed out all night."

Potbelly #1 clomped the snow off his boots before climbing inside the van. But he sat with the door open, looking toward the man with the flask. "What do you want me to do, Denny? I told Gordy I'd give him a ride back to his place."

Flask Man's watery brown eyes never left Gina's. "We ain't doin' nothing illegal here, *querida*. We're just a bunch of pals hangin' out at a friend's place."

"It's *Officer Galvan* to you." She had to bite down on the urge to tell him in two languages exactly what kind of man he was. But she wasn't about to give this patronizing lowlife the satisfaction of losing her temper. She was a cop. Proud of it. And this guy was about to get a lesson in understanding exactly who was in charge here. "Mr. Bismarck isn't going to need a ride." Potbelly #1 slammed his door and started the van's engine. Gina smiled at Flask Man and pulled out her handcuffs. "Denny, is it? I've got plenty of room in the backseat for both you and good ol' Gordy." She moved toward him, dangling the cuffs in a taunt to emphasize her words. "How do impeding an officer in the performance of her duty, aiding and abetting a known criminal, public intoxication and operating a vehicle under the influence sound to you?"

"You can't arrest me for all that."

"I wouldn't test that theory if I were you." Derek stepped out of the way of the van as it backed out of the driveway and sped after the two men on motorcycles. "Not with her."

Gina was close enough to see Flask Man's nostrils flaring with rage. "Handcuffs or goodbye?"

"I don't like a woman telling me what to do," he muttered, striding toward his bike. "Especially one like you." Once he was astraddle, he revved the engine, yelling something at Derek that sounded a lot like a warning to keep his woman in check. The roar of the bike's motor drowned out his last parting threat as he raced down the street, but Gina was pretty sure it had something to do with her parentage and how their next meeting would have a very different ending.

"Make sure they stay gone," Gina said, hooking her cuffs back onto her belt and running to the front door. She opened the glass storm door and knocked against the inside door. "KCPD!" she announced. The woman screamed, and the man yelled all kinds of vile curses. "Vicki Bismarck, are you all right? This is the police, answering a call to this address. I'm coming inside."

Twenty minutes later, Gina and Derek had Gordon Bismarck and his former wife, Vicki, separated into two rooms of their tiny, trashed home. Gina had bagged the box cutter Gordon had dropped when she'd pulled her gun and blinked her watery eyes at the stench of alcohol, vomit and sweat coming off Gordon's body. Either Gordy and his buddies had been beefing up their courage for this confrontation or they'd partied hard and gotten stupid enough to think violating a restraining order was a good idea.

Although the slurred epithets were still flying from the living room where Derek had taken Gordon to put a winter coat on over his undershirt, and Vicki was bawling in the kitchen while Gina tried to assess the woman's injuries, Gina was already wrapping up this case in her head. Even if Vicki refused to press charges, she could book Gordon on breaking and entering, violating his restraining order and public intoxication— all of which should keep him out of Vicki's life long enough for her to get the help she needed. If she'd ask for it. Clearly, this wasn't the Bismarcks' first rodeo with KCPD. That probably explained why Gordon had brought his friends.

Although she hadn't noted any stab wounds on Vicki, the woman was cradling her left arm as if it had been yanked or twisted hard enough to do some internal damage. Gina glanced around at the slashed curtains and overturned chairs in the kitchen, her gaze landing on the shattered cell phone in the corner that had been crushed beneath a boot or hurled across the room. Clearly, there'd been a substantial altercation here.

Gina righted one of the chairs and urged the skinny woman to sit. "Will you let me look at that arm?" Gina asked, tearing off a fresh paper towel for the woman to dab at her tears. When Vicki nodded, Gina knelt beside her. Bruise marks that fit the span of a man's hand were already turning purple around her elbow. But there didn't seem to be any apparent deformity suggesting a broken bone. Didn't mean it hadn't been twisted savagely, spraining muscles and tendons. Gina pushed to her feet and headed toward the refrigerator-freezer. "An ice pack should help with the swelling."

She heard a crash from the living room and spun around as Derek cursed. "Gina—heads up!"

"Are you turnin' me in, you bitch? My boys are gonna kill you!"

"Gordy!" Vicki screamed as Gordon charged into the kitchen.

Chapter Two

Gina simply reacted, putting herself between the frightened woman and the red-faced man. There was no time to wonder how the drunk had gotten away from Derek. She ducked beneath the attacker's fist, kicked out with her leg, tripped the big brute, then caught his arm and twisted it behind his back, following him down to the floor. Before his chin smacked the linoleum, she had her knee in his back, pinning him in place.

"He's too big for the damn cuffs," Derek shouted, running in behind the perp. He knelt on the opposite side, catching the loose chain that was only connected to one wrist.

Gordon Bismarck writhed beneath her, trying to wrestle himself free. His curses switched from Vicki to Gina to women in general. Locking her own handcuffs around his free arm, Gina twisted his wrist and arm another notch until he yelped. "Don't make me mad, Mr. Bismarck. Your buddies outside already put me in a mood."

The mention of his friends sparked a new protest. "Denny! Al! Jim! I need—"

"Uh-uh." She pushed his cheek back to the floor. "They went bye-bye. Now you be a good boy while my partner walks you out to the squad car so you can sober up and chill that temper."

"My boys left?"

"That's right, Gordy." Derek wiped a dribble of blood from beneath his nose while Gina locked the ends of both cuffs together, securing him. "You're on your own."

"I don't want him touchin' me," Gordy protested. "I don't want him in my house."

"Not your choice." Gina stayed on top of the captive, her muscles straining to subdue him until he gave up the fight. She glanced up at Derek, assessing his injury. Other than the carpet lint clinging to his dark uniform from a tussle of some kind, he wasn't seriously hurt. Still, she kept her voice calm and firm, trying to reassure Vicki that they could keep her safe. "You got him okay?"

"I got him. Thanks for the save. I didn't realize the cuff wasn't completely closed around his fat wrist, and I ended up with an elbow in my face." Derek pulled the man to his feet, his bruised ego making him a little rough as he shoved Bismarck toward the front door. "Forget the coat. Now we can add assaulting a police officer to your charges. Come on, you lousy son of a..."

The door banged shut as Derek muscled Bismarck outside. Gina inhaled several deep breaths, cooling her own adrenaline rush. She watched from the foyer until she saw her partner open the cruiser and unceremoniously dump the perp into the backseat. Only after Derek had closed the door and turned to lean his hip against the fender did she breathe a sigh of relief. The situation was finally secure.

When he pulled out a cigarette and started to light it, Gina muttered a curse beneath her breath. She immediately thumbed the radio clipped to the shoulder of her uniform. "Derek," she chided, wanting to warn him it was too soon to let down his guard. "Call the sit-rep in to Dispatch, and tell them we'll be bringing in the suspect. I'll finish getting the victim's statement."

"Chill, G. Let a man catch his breath." He lit the cigarette and exhaled a puff before answering. "Roger that."

Gina shook her head. She supposed that losing control of the perp had not only dinged his ego but also rattled him. Maybe she should have a low-key chat with her partner. Aiming for fifth place wasn't going to get the job done. If he didn't light a fire under his butt and start showing all the ways he could excel at being a cop, Captain Cutler might cut him from the SWAT candidate list altogether.

But she had more pressing responsibilities to attend to right now than to play the bossy big sister role with her partner and nudge Derek toward success. After softly closing the front door on the cold and the visual of Gordon Bismarck spewing vitriol in the backseat of the cruiser while Derek smacked the window and warned him to be quiet, Gina pulled out her phone again and returned to the kitchen. She found Vicki making a token effort to clean up some of the mess.

"Is he gone?" the woman asked in a tired voice. Although the tears had stopped, her eyes were an unnaturally bright shade of green from all her crying.

"He's locked in the back of the police cruiser, and I sent his friends away. He won't get to you again. Not today. Not while I'm here."

"Thank you." Vicki dropped a broken plate into the trash. "And Derek's okay?"

"'Derek'?"

"Officer Johnson." A blush tinted Vicki's pale

cheeks. "I thought maybe Gordy thought...having another man in the house..." She shrugged off the rambling explanation. "I remember you two from the last time you were here. So does Gordy."

"I'm sure Officer Johnson will be fine. May I?" Gina held up her phone and, at Vicki's nod, snapped a couple of photos of the woman's injuries and sent them to her computer at work. "I'll need them to file my report."

"What if I refuse to press charges?" Vicki asked. "Gordy's friends might come back, even if he's not here. Denny's his big brother. He looks out for him."

Reminding herself that she hadn't lived Vicki Bismarck's life, and that the other woman probably had had the skills and confidence to cope with a situation like this beaten and terrorized out of her by now, Gina took a towel and filled it with some ice from the freezer. "I still have to take Mr. Bismarck in because he resisted arrest and assaulted an officer. And he's clearly violated his restraining order." She pressed the ice pack to Vicki's elbow and nodded toward the abrasion on her cheek. "You should get those injuries checked out by a doctor. Would you like me to call an ambulance?"

Vicki shook her head. "I can't afford that."

"How about I call another officer to take you to the ER? Or I can come back once we get your husband processed."

"No. No more cops, please." Vicki sank into a chair and rested her elbow on the table. "It just makes Gordy mad."

"What set him off this time?" Not that it mattered. Violence like this was never acceptable. But if Gina could get the victim talking, she might get some useful information to help get the repeat offender off the street and out of his wife's life. "I could smell the alcohol on him."

"He's been sleeping at Denny's house." Gina pulled out her notepad and jotted the name and information. "Gordy's been out of work for a while. Got laid off at the fertilizer plant. And I haven't been working long enough to get paid yet. I asked him if he'd picked up his unemployment check. He said he'd help me with groceries."

"And that set him off?"

"He doesn't like to talk about money. But no, as soon as I opened the door, he started yelling at me. Denny had said he saw me talking to another man." Vicki shrugged, then winced at the movement. "I just started a job at the convenience store a couple blocks from here. Guys come in, you know. I have to talk to them when I ring them up. I guess Denny told Gordy I was flirting."

Gina bit back her opinion of Gordy's obsession and maintained a cool facade. "When was the last time you ate?" If the woman needed money for groceries, Gina guessed it had been a while. She unzipped another pocket in her vest and pulled out an energy bar, pushing it into the woman's hand. "Here." She pulled out a business card for the local women's shelter as well, and handed it to Vicky. "You get hungry again, you go here, not to Gordy. They'll help you get groceries at the food pantry. Mention my name and they'll even sneak you an extra chocolate bar."

Finally, that coaxed a smile from the frightened woman. "I haven't eaten real chocolate in months. Sounds heavenly."

After getting a few more details about Vicki's relationship with Gordon and her injuries, Gina wrapped up the interview. "You need to be checked out by a doctor," she reiterated. "Sooner rather than later. Do you have a friend who can take you to the hospital or your regular doctor?"

"I can call my sister. She keeps nagging me to move in with her and her husband."

"Good." Gina handed Vicki her phone. "Why don't you go ahead and do that while I'm here?"

Vicki hesitated. "Will Gordy be back when I get home?"

"I can keep him locked up for up to forty-eight hours—longer if he doesn't make bail." Gina had a feeling Vicki's husband would be locked up for considerably longer than that but didn't want to guarantee anything she couldn't back up. "We can send a car through the neighborhood periodically to watch if his brother and friends come back. See a doctor. Go to your sister's, and get a good night's sleep. Call the shelter, and get the help you need."

"Thank you." Vicki punched in her sister's phone number and smiled again. "That was sweet to see you take Gordy down—and you aren't any bigger than I am. Maybe I should learn some of those moves."

Gina smiled back and pulled out her own business card. "It's all about attitude. Here. Call me when you're feeling up to it. A few other officers and I teach free self-defense training sessions."

Although Vicki didn't look entirely convinced that she could learn to stand up for herself, at least she had made arrangements with her sister and brother-in-law to stay with them for a few nights by the time Gina was closing the front door behind her and heading down the front walk toward the street. What passed for sunshine on the wintry day was fading behind the evening clouds that rolled across the sky and promised another dusting of snow. Despite the layers of the sweater, flak vest and long-sleeved uniform she wore, Gina shivered at the prospect of spring feeling so far out of reach.

Ignoring the glare of blurry-eyed contempt aimed at her from the backseat of the cruiser, Gina arched a questioning eyebrow at Derek. "Bismarck didn't hurt you, did he?"

Derek massaged the bridge of his nose that was already bruising and circled around the car as she approached. "Just my pride. I don't even know if the guy meant to clock me. But I was on the floor, and he was on his way to the kitchen before my eyes stopped watering."

"Ouch."

"Just don't tell anybody that a drunk got the upper hand on me and you had to save my ass. I don't imagine that would impress Captain Cutler."

"We're a team, Derek. We help each other out."

"And keep each other's secrets?"

"Something like that."

His laughter obscured his face with a cloud of warm breath in the chilly air. "Now I really owe you that cup of coffee." Her aversion to the cold weather was hardly a secret compared to his possible incompetence in handling the suspect. Maybe her partner wasn't ready for the demands of the promotion. He pulled open his door. "Come on. Let's get you warmed up—"

The sharp crack of gunfire exploded in the cold air.

Derek's green eyes widened with shock for a split second before he crumpled to the pavement. "Derek!"

A second bullet thwacked against the shatterproof glass of the windshield. A third whizzed past her ear and shattered the glass in Vicki Bismarck's storm door. Gina pulled the Glock at her hip and dove the last few feet toward the relative shelter of the car. A stinging shot of lead or shrapnel burned through her calf, and she stumbled into the snow beside the curb.

Where were the damn shots coming from? Who was shooting? Had Denny Bismarck come back? She hadn't heard a motorcycle on the street. But then, he hadn't been alone, either.

"Derek? I need you to talk to me." There was still no answer. Bullets hit the cruiser and a tree trunk in the front yard. Several more shots scuffed through the snow with such rapidity that she knew the shooter either had an automatic weapon or several weapons that he could drop and keep firing. Gina crouched beside the wheel well, listening for the source of the ambush, praying there were no innocent bystanders in the line of fire. The bullets were coming from across the street. But from a house? An alley? A car?

"Derek?" The amount of blood seeping down her leg into her shoe told her the shooter was using something large caliber, meant to inflict maximum damage. But her wound was just a graze. She could still do her job. Before she sidled around the car to pull her partner to safety, Gina got on her radio and called it in. "This is Officer Galvan. Unit 4-13. Officers need assistance. Shots fired." She gave the street address and approximation of where she thought the shooter might be before repeating the urgent request, "Officers need assistance."

Gina stilled her breath and heard Gordon Bismarck cussing up a blue streak inside the cruiser. She'd heard Vicki screaming inside the house. What she didn't hear was her partner. Guilt and fear punched her in the stomach. She hadn't done job one and kept him safe. She hadn't had his back when he needed her most.

"Derek?" she called out one more time before cradling the gun in her hands. When she heard the unexpected pause between gunshots, she crept around the trunk of the car, aiming her weapon toward the vague target of the shooter. "Police! Throw down your weapon!" she warned.

A quick scan revealed empty house, empty alley, empty house…bingo! Driver in a rusty old SUV parked half a block down. Gina straightened. "Throw down your weapon, and get out of the vehicle!"

The man's face was obscured by the barrel of the rifle pointed at her.

There was no mistaking his intent.

Gina squeezed off a shot and dove for cover, but it was too late.

A bullet struck her in the arm, tearing through her right shoulder, piercing the narrow gap between her arm and her protective vest. She hit the ground, and her gun skittered from her grip. Unlike the graze along the back of her leg, she knew this wound was a bad one. The path of the bullet burned through her shoulder.

She clawed her fingers into the hardened layers of snow and crawled back into the yard, away from the shooter. It was hard to catch her breath, hard to orient herself in a sea of clouds and snow. She rolled onto her back, praying she wasn't imagining the sound of sirens in the distance, hating that she was certain of the grinding noise of the SUV's engine turning over.

She saw Vicki Bismarck hovering at her broken front door. When Gina turned her head the other direction, she looked beneath the car and saw Derek on the ground, unmoving. Was he even alive? "Derek?"

Did someone have a grudge against him? Against her? Against cops? She hadn't made any friends among

Denny Bismarck and his crew. Was this payback for arresting his brother? For being bested by a woman?

Her shoulder ached, and her right arm was numb. Her chest felt like a boulder sat on it. Still, she managed to reach her radio with her other hand and tug it off her vest. The shooter's car was speeding away. She couldn't see much from her vantage point, couldn't read the license plate or confirm a make of vehicle. The leg wound stung like a hot poker through her calf, but the wound to her shoulder—the injury she could no longer feel—worried her even more. Finding that one spot beneath her armor was either one hell of a lucky shot or the work of a sharpshooter. Gina's vision blurred as a chill pervaded her body.

"Stay inside the house!" a man yelled. "Away from the windows."

She saw silver running pants and black shoes stomping through the snow toward her. Gina tried to find her gun.

"Officer?" The tall jogger with the sexy beard scruff came into view as he knelt in the snow beside her. "It's okay, ma'am." His eyes were hidden behind reflective sunglasses, and he clutched a cell phone to his ear, allowing her few details as to what he looked like. He picked up her Glock from the snow where it had landed and showed it to her before tucking it into the back of his waistband. "Your weapon is secure."

She slapped her left hand against his knee and pulled at the insulated material there. "You have to stay down. Shooter—"

"He's driving away," the man said. She wasn't exactly following the conversation, but then he was talking on his cell phone as he leaned over her, running his free hand up and down her arms and legs. "No, I couldn't read the license. It was covered with mud and slush. Yes, just the driver. Look, I'll answer your questions later. Just get an ambulance here. Now!" He disconnected the call and stuffed the phone inside his pocket. He tossed aside his sunglasses and looked down into her eyes. Wow. He was just as good-looking up close as he'd been from a distance. "You hit twice?"

Gina nodded, thinking more about her observation than her answer. She reached up and touched her shaking fingertips to the sandpapery stubble that shadowed his jaw. "I know you." Before her jellified brain could place why he looked so familiar to her, he grabbed her keys off her belt and bolted to his feet. She turned her head to watch him unlock the trunk to get the med kit. How did he know it was stored there? He was acting like a cop—he'd provided the squad car number and street address on that phone call. He knew KCPD lingo and where her gear was stowed. "Captain Cutler?" That wasn't right. But the blue eyes and chiseled features were the same. But she'd never seen the SWAT captain with that scruffy catnip on his face.

She wasn't any closer to understanding what she was seeing when he knelt beside her again, opening the kit and pulling out a compress. She winced as he slipped the pad beneath her vest and pressed his hand against her wound to stanch the bleeding. The deep, sure tone of voice was a little like catnip to her groggy senses, too. "I'm Mike Cutler. I've had paramedic training. Lie still."

Why were her hormones involved in any of this conversation? She squeezed her eyes shut to concentrate. She was a KCPD police officer. She'd been shot. The perp had gotten away. There was protocol to follow. She had a job to do. Gina opened her eyes, gritting her teeth against the pressure on her chest and the fog inside her head. "Check my partner. He's hit."

"You're losing blood too fast. I'm not going anywhere until I slow the bleeding." The brief burst of clarity quickly waned. The Good Samaritan trying to save her life tugged on her vest the moment her eyes closed. "Officer Galvan? No, no, keep your eyes open. What's your first name?"

"Gina."

"Gina?" He was smiling when she blinked her eyes open. "That's better. Pretty brown eyes. Like a good cup of coffee. I want to keep seeing them, okay?" She nodded. His eyes were such a pretty color. No, not pretty. There wasn't anything *pretty* about the angles of his cheekbones and jaw. He certainly wasn't from this part of town. She'd have remembered a face like that. A face that was still talking. "Trust me. I'm on your side. If I look familiar, it's because you're a cop, and you probably know my dad."

Mike Cutler. My dad. Gina's foggy brain cleared with a moment of recognition. "Captain Cutler? Oh, God. I'm interviewing with him… Don't tell him I got shot, okay?" But he'd left her. Gina called out in a panic. "Cutler?"

"I'm here." Her instinct to exhale with relief ended up in a painful fit of coughing. "Easy. I was just checking your partner."

"How is he?"

"Unconscious. As far as I can tell, he has a gunshot wound to the arm. But he may have hit his head on the door frame or pavement. His nose is bruised."

"That was…before." She tried to point to the house.

"Before what?"

The words to explain the incident with Gordon Bismarck were lost in the fog of her thoughts. But her training was clear. Derek was shot. And she had a job to do.

"The prisoner?" Gina tried to roll over and push herself up, but she couldn't seem to get her arm beneath her. The snow and clouds and black running shoes all swirled together inside her head.

"Easy, Gina. I need you to lie still. An ambulance is on its way. You've injured your shoulder, and I don't see an exit wound. If that bullet is still inside you, I don't want it traveling anywhere." He unzipped his jacket and shrugged out of it. He draped the thin, insulated material over her body, gently but securely tucking her in, surrounding her with the residual warmth from his body and the faint, musky scent of his workout. "The guy in the backseat is loud, but unharmed. The lady at the front door looks scared, but she isn't shot. Lie down. You're going into shock." He pulled her radio from beneath the jacket and pressed the call button. "Get that bus to…" Gina's vision blurred as he rattled off the address. "Stay with me. Gina?" His warm hand cupped her face, and she realized just how cold she was. She wished she could wrap her whole body up in that kind of heat. She looked up into his stern expression. "Stay with me."

"Catnip."

"What?" Her eyelids drifted shut. "Gina!"

The last thing she saw was her blood seeping into the snow. The last thing she felt was the man's strong hands pressing against her breast and shoulder. The last thing she heard was his voice on her radio.

"Officer down! I repeat: officer down!"

Chapter Three

Six weeks later

"He shoots! He scores!" The basketball sailed through the hoop, hitting nothing but net. Troy Anthony spun his wheelchair on the polished wood of the physical therapy center's minicourt. His ebony braids flew around the mocha skin of his bare, muscular shoulders, and one fist was raised in a triumphant gloat before he pointed to Mike. "You are buying the beers."

"How do you figure that?" Mike Cutler caught the ball as it bounced past him, dribbled it once and shoved a chest pass at his smirking competitor. It was impossible not to grin as his best friend and business partner, Troy, schooled him in the twenty-minute pickup game. "I thought we were playing to cheer *me* up."

Troy easily caught the basketball and shoved it right back. "I was playing to win, my friend. Your head's not in the game."

Mike's hands stung, forgetting to catch the pass with his fingertips instead of his palms. He *was* distracted. "Fine. Tonight at the Shamrock. Beers are on me."

He tucked the ball under his arm as he climbed out of the wheelchair he'd been using. Once his legs unkinked and the electric jolts of random nerves firing across his hips and lower back subsided, he pushed the chair across the polished wood floor to stow the basketball in the PT center's equipment locker. At least he didn't have to wear those joint pinching leg braces or a body cast anymore.

But he wasn't about to complain. Twelve years ago, he hadn't been able to walk at all, following a car accident that had shattered his legs from the pelvis on down, so he never griped about the damaged nerves or aches in his mended bones or stiff muscles that protested the changing weather and an early morning workout. As teenagers, Mike and Troy had bonded over wheelchair basketball and months of physical rehabilitation therapy with the woman who had eventually become Mike's stepmother. Unlike Mike, because of a gunshot wound he'd sustained in a neighborhood shooting, Troy would never regain the use of his legs. But the friendship had stuck, and now, at age twenty-eight, they'd both earned college degrees and had opened their own physical therapy center near downtown Kansas City.

"C'mon, man. Don't make me feel like I'm beatin' up on ya. I said you didn't have to go back to the chair to play me. I could beat you standing on your two feet. Today, at any rate." Troy pushed his wheels once and coasted over to the edge of the court beside Mike. His omnipresent smile and smart-ass attitude had disappeared. "Losing that funding really got to you, huh? Or is this mood about a woman?"

He hadn't put his heart on the line and gotten it stomped on by anyone of the female persuasion lately. Not since Caroline. "No. No woman."

Troy picked up a towel off the supply cart and handed one to Mike, grinning as he wiped the perspiration from his chest. "No woman? That would sure put *me* in a mood."

"You're a funny guy, you know that," Mike deadpanned, appreciating his friend's efforts to improve his disposition. But he couldn't quite shake the miasma of frustration that had plagued his thoughts since opening that rejection letter in the mail yesterday. "I had a brilliant idea, writing that grant proposal." Mike toweled the dampness from his skin before tossing Troy his gray uniform polo shirt. "We had enough money from the bank loan and our own savings to get this place built. But it's hardly going to sustain itself with the handful of patients we have coming in. If we were attached to a hospital—"

"We specifically decided against that." Troy didn't have to remind him of their determination to give back to the community. Mike opened the laundry compartment on the supply cart and Troy tossed both towels inside. "We wanted to be here in the city where the people who needed us most could have access to our services."

"I still believe in that." Mike stared at the CAPT logo for the Cutler-Anthony Physical Therapy Center embroidered on the chest of his own shirt before pulling it over his head and tugging the hem down to cover his long torso. "But those are the same people who don't always have insurance and can't always pay. I was certain that urban development grant for small businesses would help us."

"There'll be other grants." Troy donned his shirt and peeled off the fingerless gloves he wore when he played anything competitive in his wheelchair. "Caroline said she'd fund a grant for us. To thank you for being there when she needed you."

"And that would be right up until the night she turned

down my proposal?" The fact that he could talk about it now told Mike that his ego had taken a bigger blow than his heart had. But that blow had been the third strike in the relationship game. He had no plans to step up to the plate and put his heart on the line anymore. If he couldn't tell the difference between a friends-with-benefits package and a connection that was leading to forever, he'd do well to steer clear of anything serious. He'd been the shoulder to cry on, the protective big brother and the best friend too many times to risk it. He could rely on his principles, his family and friends like Troy. But he wasn't about to rely on his heart again. "No. No asking Caroline. I didn't propose because I wanted her money, and I'm not going to take it now as a consolation prize."

Troy knew just how far he could push the relationship button before he made a joke. "Maybe you could hock the engagement ring. That'd keep us open another month."

Mike glared down at his friend for a moment before laughter shook through his chest. "More like a day and a half."

"Dude, no wonder she said no."

The shared laughter carried them through the rest of putting away the equipment they'd used and prepping for their first—and, as far as Mike knew, their only—appointment of the morning. But even Troy's mood had sobered by the time they headed toward the door leading into the entry area and hallway that led to a row of offices and locker rooms. "You're a smart guy, Mikey. You'll figure out a way to keep us solvent."

"Without losing your apartment or my house?"

"I'd be happy to go out and recruit us more female

clientele. It's Ladies' Night at the Shamrock tonight. I can pour on some of that legendary Anthony charm."

"Creeper."

"You got a better plan?"

"Not at the moment."

"You're thinkin' too hard on this, Mike. We haven't even been open a year. We'll get more paying customers soon. I feel it in my bones." He held up a fist and waited for Mike to absorb some of his positive thinking.

Trusting his friend's outlook more than his own, Mike bumped his fist against Troy's. "I just have to be patient, right?"

"Nobody waits out trouble better than you."

Mike shook his head. "Is that supposed to be a compli—?" The door opened before they reached it, and the center's office manager, Frannie Mesner, stepped into the gym. "Good morning."

"Hey, Sun…shine." Troy's effusive greeting fell flat when they saw the puffy, red-rimmed eyes behind Frannie's glasses. He rolled his chair over to get a box of tissues off the supply cart and take them to her. She sniffed back a sob as she took the box.

Was she hurt? Had she gotten some bad news? Mike moved in beside her and dropped a comforting arm around her trembling shoulders. "Frannie?"

The flush of distress on Frannie's pale cheeks made her freckles disappear. She pulled out a handful of tissues and dabbed her eyes before blowing her nose. "Leo gets released on parole today."

Her ex. She wasn't hurt. But definitely bad news.

"Has he contacted you?" Mike asked.

"He's not supposed to."

"Has he contacted you?" he repeated, articulating the protective concern in his voice. Frannie shook her head, stirring short wisps of copper hair over her damp cheeks.

Troy set the tissue box in his lap. "Is the restraining order still in effect?"

Mike watched the confidence she'd built over the past few months disappear in the span of a few heartbeats.

When she didn't answer, Mike pulled away to face her. "Take a few minutes to call your attorney and make sure it is. If not, make an appointment to get it reinstated. Troy or I can go with you, if you want."

Troy slid Frannie a worried glance before spinning away from the conversation to return the box to its shelf. "Yeah. I can do that. We'd have to take my van, though. If you don't mind riding shotgun. And you trust my driving."

What happened to that legendary Anthony charm? The Troy he knew was all mouth and swagger 99 percent of the time. Except when it came to the office manager Mike had hired for their fledgling physical therapy center. Frannie had been their first client. But more than rebuilding her physical strength after a beatdown from her ex that had cost her the sight in one eye, she had needed a job, and Mike and Troy had provided it. He suspected she also appreciated the office's predictable routine and the haven of a well-built workplace run by the son of a cop and a paraplegic, whose friends were also cops.

Mike might not carry a gun but, because of his dad and friends at KCPD, he knew how to keep a woman safe. Avoiding dangerous situations in the first place was rule one. "You know we'll give you the time off for personal business like that. Make sure that protection order is in place. Beyond that, Troy or I will escort you to your car and follow you home. You notify the police if he calls or you see his face anywhere close to you."

"I can swing by your place and double check the locks on the windows and door," Troy offered.

Mike nodded. "Sounds like a plan."

"My building isn't handicapped accessible." Frannie sniffed away the last of her tears and dabbed at the pink tip of her nose. "I'm sorry."

Troy shrugged, then reached for her hand. There was definitely something going on with him where Frannie was concerned. "Don't you apologize for that."

Mike wasn't sure how to help his friend, other than alleviate his concern about Frannie. "I'll stop by after work, then."

At least she felt safe here at the clinic. She tucked the used tissues into the pocket of her khaki slacks and dredged up a shy smile. "You guys are the best bosses ever. Thank you." Although she'd started the job with no secretarial experience, Frannie had eventually found her feet and her own system of organization that worked—for her. And, when she wasn't afraid for her life like she was this morning, she was a friendly, quiet presence who made their patients feel welcome at the clinic. She wound her arm around Mike's waist and squeezed him in a shy hug. "Thanks." She turned toward Troy with her arms outstretched and leaned over to give him a hug, too. "Thank you."

Troy turned his nose into her hair, breathing deeply. "No sweat, Sunshine."

Either sensing Troy's interest or feeling a similar longing herself, Frannie quickly pulled away and tipped her face to Mike. "Your eight o'clock appointment is here. He's already changing in the locker room."

Chaz Kelly, a retired firefighter with a new knee,

opened the door behind Frannie, startling her. "Hey, pretty lady. You weren't at your desk to greet me this morning when I checked in." Bald and blustery, his gaze darted over to Troy and Mike. "Morning, boys. Ready to put this fat old man through his paces?"

Frannie's body visibly contracted away from Chaz's pat on her shoulder. Uh-huh. So much for feeling safe. She scooted closer to Troy's chair and didn't look any more comfortable there. "Your dad is here, too, Mike."

"Here?" It was rarely a good thing for the supervisor of KCPD's SWAT teams to make a surprise visit. Mike's concern instantly went to his stepmother and much younger half brother. "Is everything okay? Jillian? Will?"

"He didn't say. But I think it's work related. He's in uniform. There's someone with him. I put them in your office. I'll go start a pot of coffee." Her hand went self-consciously to one tear-stained cheek. "And wash my face."

As Frannie left, Mike pulled his phone from his pocket, wondering if he'd missed a text or call during the basketball game. The lack of messages altered his concern into curiosity.

Troy tapped his fist against Mike's arm and pointed at the door. "I got this. Better not keep the captain waiting." Troy spun his chair around toward the door on the far side of the half gym that led to the equipment room and treatment tables. "Come on, Chaz. Let's get you on the treadmill and get you warmed up. Did you stick to that diet we gave you?"

Their conversation faded as Mike hurried down the outer hallway to his office. "Dad?" Michael Cutler Sr. was on his feet to greet him with a handshake and a hug when Mike rounded the corner into his office. "Hey. Everything okay?"

"Not to worry. I'm fine. The family's fine."

Both standing at six-four, father and son looked each other in the eye as Mike pulled away. "What's up?" His eyes widened when he saw the petite woman waiting behind his father. "Officer Galvan."

Her dark eyes shared his surprise. "Catnip…" Mike arched his brows at her stunned whisper. She blinked away the revelation of emotion. "It *was* you."

"Excuse me?"

Gina Galvan was shorter than he remembered. Of course, his perspective was a little different, standing upright versus kneeling over her supine body. Without the hazards of gunfire or a medical emergency to focus on, Mike stole a few seconds to take in details about his visitor. She'd changed her hair. Instead of a long ponytail spilling over the snow, short, loose waves danced against the smooth line of her jaw. She wore a black sling over her right shoulder, keeping her arm immobile against her stomach. And he shouldn't have noticed the athletic curves arcing beneath the narrow waist of her jeans. But he did.

"The day I got shot—you were the runner who stopped to help us." Her gaze shifted between Mike and his father. "You two look so much alike, I guess I convinced myself I'd hallucinated you."

Mike chuckled at her admission. Although there was a peppering of gray in his dad's dark brown hair and Mike didn't shave as closely as KCPD regulations required, it wasn't the first time he'd been mistaken for his father. "I don't think I've ever been anyone's hallucination before. Fantasy, maybe, but…"

She frowned as if she didn't get the joke. His father

looked away, embarrassed at his lame attempt at humor. Right. Leave the jokes to Troy.

The proud tilt of her chin and intense study from her dark eyes warned him that Gina Galvan wasn't inclined to laugh at much of anything. Which was a pity because he suddenly wondered what those pink lips would look like softened with a smile.

Reel it in, Cutler. Clearly, this wasn't a social call. And he already had enough on his plate without letting his errant hormones steer him into another misguided relationship.

Starched and pressed and always in charge of the room, Michael Sr. turned to include them both. "I wasn't sure you two would remember each other after a meeting like that. I guess there's no need for introductions."

"No, sir." Off-duty and out of uniform, she still talked like a cop.

"Nah." Mike invited them both to sit in the guest chairs in front of his desk before circling around to pull out his own chair. "How's the recovery going?" Gina's gaze drilled into his. He interpreted that as a *Don't ask.* "Did they catch the guy who did it?"

"No."

He'd suspected that was the case, or else a detective or investigator from the DA's office would have been back to question him on his account of the incident. "Sorry to hear that. And I'm sorry I couldn't give KCPD a better description of the shooter's SUV or license plate. The whole back end was covered in frozen mud and slush."

She nodded. "He probably went straight to a car wash afterward so we couldn't even look for a dirty vehicle."

"Probably. How's your partner?"

"Back on active duty."

"That's good news." Or not, judging by the scowl that darkened her expression. Even with a frown like that, Mike had a hard time calling Gina Galvan anything but pretty. High cheekbones. Full lips. Dark, sensuous eyes. Hair the color of dark-roast coffee. "You cut your hair since I saw you last."

"I was bleeding in the snow when you saw me last." The subtle warmth of an accent made an intriguing contrast to the crisp snap of her words.

"I like it—the hair, not the blood. I didn't realize how wavy your hair was."

"Well, long hair is hardly practical with—" she gestured at her arm in the sling "—this. And I am not going to rely on my aunt or my sister to put my hair up every day."

"Sounds smart."

"Why are we talking about my hair?" The accent grew a little more pronounced as a hint of acid entered her tone. Was that anger? Frustration? A clear message that she wasn't interested in his compliments or flirtations—idle or otherwise. She froze for a moment before inhaling a deep breath. Then, oddly, she crossed her fingers and brushed them against her lips and heart before settling her hand back into her lap. He thought it must be some kind of calming ritual·because her posture relaxed a fraction and the tension left her voice. "I owe you for saving my life, Mr. Cutler. Thank you."

He'd heard the gunshots on his morning run through the neighborhood just a mile or so from the clinic. What else was he supposed to do besides try to help? "It's just Mike. And you're welcome."

Was that what this visit was about? A proud woman wanting to thank him? But she'd indicated that she hadn't remembered him.

Mike's father clearly had a purpose for coming to the clinic. "Could you give us a few minutes, Galvan?"

Gina popped to her feet, eager to please the captain or simply eager to escape the uncomfortable conversation. "Yes, sir."

Mike stood, too, as Frannie stepped into the room carrying a tray of steaming coffee mugs with packets of sugar and creamer. He scooted aside a stack of bills for her to set the tray on his desk. "Thanks. Why don't you give Officer Galvan a tour of the facility while Dad and I talk."

"Okay." Frannie's eyes were still puffy behind her glasses, but the pale skin beneath her freckles and pixie haircut was back to normal. She smiled at Gina and led her into the hallway. "We can start with the women's locker room."

Mike closed the door and returned to his seat, looking across the desk as his father picked up a mug and blew the steam off the top. "How worried should I be about this impromptu visit?"

Chapter Four

His father pursed his lips and made a rare face before swallowing. "Um..."

Mike took a sip and spit the sour brew back into his mug. "Sorry about that. Frannie must have cleaned the coffeemaker out with vinegar again."

"Did she rinse it afterward?"

"I'll sneak in there and make a new pot later this morning while she's busy." Mike spun his chair and emptied his mug into the potted fern beside the door. "She's a little distracted. Her ex gets out on parole today."

"Leo Mesner?" Mike nodded, returning his mug to the tray. Michael Sr. followed his lead, dumping out his coffee. "I'll find out who Leo's parole officer will be so we can keep tabs on him for her."

"Thanks. After that last assault, he shouldn't have any contact with her, but you never know if prison sobered him up and made him rethink hurting his ex-wife or just made him even angrier and bent on revenge. We'll do what we can to keep her safe from this end, too."

"I know you will, son. You're too kindhearted for your own good."

"You know it's not all kindness, Dad." His father's blue eyes pierced right into Mike's soul, under-standing his need to atone for the damage he'd done in his youth—and wishing his older son would for-give himself already. Mike smiled a reassurance to ease his father's concern. "But you didn't come here to talk about my problems. I'm assuming this visit has to do with Officer Galvan?"

His dad nodded. "I'm bringing you a new client."

He pointed briefly to his own shoulder. "She had surgery?"

"Stitches in her leg to seal up the bullet graze there. Emergency surgery to repair a nicked lung. She's recov-ered from those without incident." His dad's expression turned grim. "But the second bullet went through her shoulder and tore it up. The doctors had to rebuild the joint. The PT is for muscle and nerve damage there."

"What kind of nerve damage?"

"You're the expert. But I know it has affected her hand. She can't hold a gun."

"Only six weeks after getting shot? She shouldn't be trying."

"You don't know Gina." His dad leaned forward, sharing a confidence. "She's nobody's pretty princess. Not the easiest person to get along with, especially since the shooting. She's already quit one therapist, and an-other refused to work with her after the first session."

"But I'm so desperate for patients, you think I'll take her on?"

"No." He leaned back, his features carved with an astute paternal smile. "I know how tough you are. All you've survived and been through. I know how re-sourceful you can be. If anybody can stand up to Gina, it's you."

There was a compliment in there somewhere, one

that ranked right up there with Troy's claim that he could outlast trouble. Maybe his dad and friend were subtly trying to tell him that he was too hardheaded for his own good. "What was the issue with the other therapists? She wouldn't do the work?"

"Just the opposite. She pushed herself too hard."

Mike nodded. "Did more damage than helped her recovery. You think Troy and I want to risk that kind of liability?"

"She's an ambitious woman. Trying to do better for herself and her family. Other than her great-uncle's disability and social security, she's their sole support. But she's a good cop. Good instincts. Well trained. Gina can think on her feet. Once the bad guys realize they've underestimated her, they discover they don't want to mess with her. I was ready to put her on my new SWAT team until the shooting. I've still got a spot for her." His dad's shoulders lifted with a wry apology. "But if she can't handle the physical demands of the job, I can't use her."

"You want me to fix her so she can make the team?"

"I want you to fix her so we don't lose her to No-Man's Land." Just a few city blocks north of the clinic. Poverty, gangs, drugs, prostitution, homelessness—it was a tough place to grow up. His dad's second wife, Jillian, had barely survived her time in one of Kansas City's most dangerous neighborhoods. Troy had almost lost his life there. Mike knew his father and his SWAT team had answered several calls there over the years. There was a lot to admire about a woman who held down a good job and took care of her family in the No-Man's Land neighborhood. In *this* neighborhood, where he and Troy were determined to make a difference. Michael Cutler Sr. was a professional hostage negotiator. He knew what buttons to push to ensure Mike's cooperation, and helping someone deserving in this part of the city was a big one. "Help her realize her potential. KCPD needs her. She needs the job, and I want her if she can do it."

Mike scrubbed his hand over the stubble shading his jaw before deciding to swallow a little pride. "Can she pay?"

"I'll cover whatever her department insurance doesn't."

"You believe in her that much?"

"I do."

"Then I will, too." Appreciating the faith his father had always had in him, Mike rolled his chair back and stood. "I'll get the job done for you, Dad."

"Thanks. I knew I could count on you." With their business completed, Michael Sr. stood as well, adjusting the gun at his hip and pulling the black SWAT cap from his back pocket. He tipped his head toward the unpaid bills that Mike had pushed aside earlier. "Did you get the grant?"

"No."

"I suppose applying to Caroline's foundation is out of the question."

"Yes."

He shook his head as he crossed to the door. "To be honest, I think you dodged a bullet there, son. Caroline was a nice girl. But Jillian and I were never so bored out of our minds that night we had dinner with her parents. And, of course, if she can't appreciate you for who you are and not who she wants you to be—"

"Yeah, yeah." Mike grinned, patting his dad's shoulder to stop that line of well-meaning conversation. "Nice Dad Speech."

"I'm really good at 'em, aren't I?" They shared a

laugh until Michael Sr. paused with his hand on the door knob to ask, "Say, what was that 'catnip' thing about with Gina?"

"Beats me. She said it to me before she lost consciousness the day of the shooting. Maybe she was delirious and thinking about her pet."

They both suspected there was more to the story than that but Mike didn't have the answer. His dad paused before opening the door. "You'll give me regular reports on Gina's progress?"

"Does she know you're setting this up for her?"

"She knows I want her on my team and that I was happy to give her a ride this morning. She still can't drive for another two weeks."

"And she knows this is her last chance to get her recovery right in time for you to name the new SWAT team?"

"Very astute. You got your mother's brains." They stepped into the hallway and Michael Sr. pulled his SWAT cap on. "See you at Will's science fair presentation Thursday night?"

"I already told the squirt I'd be there."

A small parade, led by a grinning Troy, stopped them before they reached the clinic's entrance. Troy held out his hand. "Hey, Captain C. I wanted to make sure I said hi before you left."

"Troy." The two men exchanged a solid handshake. "Good to see you."

"You, too, sir."

Frannie and Gina waited behind Troy's chair. The two women were a stark contrast in coloring and demeanor—pale and dark, subdued and vibrant.

"How's Dex doing in med school?" Unaware of Mike's distracted gaze, Michael Sr. asked about Troy's younger brother. Since Mike and Troy had practically grown up together, Dexter Anthony and their grandmother who'd raised the boys were like extended family.

"Long hours. But he's killin' it."

"I knew he would. Jillian wants to know when you're coming over for dinner. More for the games afterward than the food."

"Just give me a time, and I'll be there. And tell her I've been reading the dictionary every night. I'm not losing that word game to her again."

"Will do." The two men shook hands again before his dad nodded to Gina over the top of Troy's head. "You sure you don't want me to stay and give you a ride home?"

"No, sir. Thank you, but you need to get to work. Besides, I've been getting home all by myself for a lot of years now."

"I'll make sure she gets home, Dad."

"Son." Michael traded one last nod with Mike before he left.

There was an awkward moment between the four of them in the congested hallway before Mike stepped to one side. Gina politely followed suit, giving Troy room to spin his chair around and head back to his patient in the workout room. Frannie quietly excused herself and slipped into her office, leaving Mike and Gina standing side by side with their backs against the wall. The woman didn't even come up to his shoulder. But he appreciated the view of dark waves capping her head and the tight, round bump of her bottom farther down.

One by one, doors closed behind Frannie, Troy and Mike's dad. The second her potential boss had gone and they were alone, Gina turned on him. "I didn't ask you to be my chauffeur."

Forget the raw attraction simmering in his veins. Her hushed, chiding tone gave Mike an idea of what the next few weeks were going to be like, and it wasn't going to involve fun or easy. But he'd been rising to one challenge or another his entire life. Five feet and a few inches or so of attitude wasn't about to scare him off. She might as well get used to how he intended to run things with her. "You didn't ask me to be your physical therapist, either. But it looks like *that's* going to happen." He took her into his office and closed the door. "Have a seat. I need to do an informal assessment before we get started."

She eyed the chair where she'd sat earlier, and obstinately remained in place. "I've already had two evaluations, three if you count the orthopedist who sent me to PT in the first place."

"Well, none of them reported to me, and I've got no paperwork on you, so have a seat." Mike sat and pulled up a new intake file on his computer screen.

She poked a finger at the corner of his desk. "Listen, Choir Boy. Your father outranks me and can give me orders. But you can't."

Choir Boy? What happened to *Catnip?*

And why couldn't the woman just call him Mike? "Fine. Stand. I'm still asking questions."

He typed in her name as she snatched her hand away. "Are you making fun of me now? You don't know me. You don't know my life."

If he recalled correctly, he'd saved that life.

"Age? Address? Phone number? Surgeon?" He typed in the answers as she rattled them off. "What are your goals?"

She puffed up like a banty hen, swearing a couple of words in Spanish, before perching on the chair across from him. "My goals? Isn't it obvious? I want to be a cop again. And not just some face sitting behind a desk, either. I want to be able to pick up my gun and take down a perp and be the first Latina on one of your father's SWAT teams."

"You want me to put in a good word for you?" He met her gaze across the desk. "You're going to have to earn that. I warn you, Dad and I are close, but he doesn't let anybody tell him what to do when it comes to the job." Mike leaned back in his chair. "But I have a feeling you're familiar with that kind of attitude."

"Are you trying to make me angry?"

"Apparently I don't have to work very hard at it."

Her eyes widened and the tight lines around her mouth vanished. "Things have been a little tense…" She parted her lips to continue, closed them again, processed a thought, then leaned forward to ask. "Can you make me whole again? If I can't be a cop, I don't know… My family is counting on me… I'm used to dealing with problems myself. But this…" She tilted her chin, as if the proud stance could erase the vulnerability that had softened everything about her for a few moments. "I need this to happen."

In other words, *Rescue me.* He'd just taken a hit to his Achilles' heel. Not that this woman looked like she wanted a knight in shining armor, but a woman in need had always been a problem for Mike. Caroline had needed him to build her confidence and stand up to her parents. Frannie had needed him to feel safe. They weren't the first, and he had a feeling they wouldn't be the last. Maybe it had something to do with atoning for the mistakes of his rebellious youth after his mother had died of cancer. Maybe it had something to do with finding a purpose for his life the day he helped rescue his stepmother, Jillian, and Troy from a bomber. Maybe it had something to do with that lonesome need to be needed—to be the one man that a woman had to have in her life.

And maybe he *was* too hardheaded to accept defeat because he heard himself saying, "I can help it happen if you let me. You're going to have to take orders from someone besides my dad. Can you do that? Do what I tell you? *Not* do more than I tell you?" he emphasized, suspecting that *slow* and *easy* weren't in Gina's vocabulary. "You can do as much damage by pushing too hard too soon as the original injury inflicted."

"I can do more than those other therapists were letting me. I can handle pain. And training is something I've done in sports since middle school, and certainly at the police academy. I'll do my job if you do yours."

Not exactly the clear-cut agreement he'd been looking for. But he'd take it. If Gina saw this as a competition, he'd give her a run for her money—and then make sure she won. He reached across the desk with his right hand, purposely challenging her to respond with the hand that rested limply in the sling.

A light flashed in her eyes, like a sprinkling of sugar dissolving in rich, warm coffee. Not the sour kind Frannie made, either. Then she thrust her hand out of the end of the sling. Her thumb and forefinger latched on to his hand with a decent grip, but the last three fingers simply batted against the back of his knuckles. Mike stretched each limp finger back, checking the muscle tone, before he finished the informal assessment and gave her hand a reassuring squeeze. Then he pulled away and pushed to his feet. "You accept that I'm in charge of your recovery? That when it comes to your health, I'm the boss?"

He towered over her, but there wasn't any backing down to this woman. Gina stood as well, adjusting her arm in the sling. "You want to be the boss, Choir Boy? Let's do this."

An hour later, she had a sheen of perspiration dotting her forehead and neck, and her left arm was shaking with the extra exertion of compensating for her damaged right shoulder and weak arm. Mike had a pretty good idea of why Gina had run into issues with her previous physical therapists. The woman was as fit as any athlete he'd ever worked with, and her frustration with the limited use of her hand and arm was obvious. Her assessment session had been a battle of wills, with Gina determined to perform any task Mike asked of her, even when the purpose of the exercise was to give him a clear idea of her limitations.

His dad had been right. Gina's recovery was going to be a mental challenge as much as a physical one. He walked her to the door, suggesting she wear something besides jeans for the next session and giving her a list of dos and don'ts for her recovery.

Since he'd been raised to be a gentleman, he lifted the denim jacket hanging from her left wrist as she struggled to put it on and slipped it up her arm before tucking it securely around her healing shoulder. He wasn't sure if that grunt was a protest of independence or a flash of pain. It certainly wasn't a *thank you*. Still, he helped her pull the ends of her hair from beneath the collar, sifting the damp waves through his fingers and learning their silky texture before he leaned in to whisper, "You're welcome." She grunted a second time, and Mike chuckled as he reached around her to push open the door and follow her out into the sunshine that warmed the springtime air. "How are you going to get home?"

She eyed the scattering of cars in the parking lot, between the reclaimed warehouses that had been converted into various businesses and lofts, and the busy street beyond. "If there's no snow on the ground, I can walk."

Mike thumbed over his shoulder at his black pickup truck. "I'll give you a ride."

"You're going to leave work in the middle of the day to drive me home?"

The gusting breeze blew her hair across her cheek, and he curled his fingers into his palms against the urge to touch those dark waves again. "It's not that far. My next appointment isn't until after lunch. Troy can cover any emergencies that crop up."

"Therapist, not chauffeur," she reminded him.

"Suit yourself. I'll see you tomorrow?"

"I'll be here."

"No working out between now and then, understand? You can do the hand exercises, but no running and no lifting weights."

She smoothed the fluttering hair behind her ear and held it in place there. "What about the yoga stretches?"

"Lower half of your body? Sure. But nothing that could create a balance issue. If you fall and catch yourself with that arm, you'll set your recovery back another two weeks, if not permanently."

"Understood." She stepped off the sidewalk and headed across the parking lot.

"Really?" he challenged. Promising to obey his directives was different from hearing the words and understanding them.

Her sigh was audible as she turned back to face him. "Are you always this stubborn?"

"You bring it out in me."

"I won't apologize for being a strong woman."

"I wouldn't want you to." However, that acceptance and respect needed to go both ways. "I won't apologize for being a nice guy."

"Who says you're—?"

"'Choir Boy'?"

She snapped her lips shut on the next retort, perhaps conceding that he knew exactly what the reverse prejudice of that nickname meant to her. Nice guys didn't cut it in her world. Too bad she hadn't known him back in the day. Of course, teenage bad-boy reputation aside, if he hadn't gotten his act together, he might still be in a wheelchair or even dead. He sure wouldn't have sobriety, a college degree, his own business, nor would he be in a position to help her.

He watched the debate on what she should say next play over her features. *That's right, sweetheart. There's a difference between nice and naive.* "My apologies, Mr. Cutler."

Without so much as a smile, she turned and walked out to the street, where she changed direction to follow traffic along the sidewalk toward the lights and crosswalk at the corner. Fine. So friendship wasn't going to happen between them anytime soon. And those curious, lustful urges she triggered in him were never going to be assuaged. But maybe, just maybe, they could learn how to get along.

Mike tucked his hands into the pockets of his gray nylon running pants. He mentally calculated how many blocks she'd have to walk and how many busy streets she'd have to cross before she got home. He'd cover two or three times that distance on his morning runs. But he didn't have two recent gunshot wounds or the muscle fatigue of a therapy session to slow him down.

She'd be on her feet for another thirty minutes before she got the chance to rest.

Maybe he should have insisted on driving her home. He fingered the keys in his pocket, wondering how much Gina would protest if he pulled up beside her and...

That was weird.

Mike's eyes narrowed as Gina's steps stuttered and she suddenly darted toward the curb. She pulled up sharply, swiveling her gaze, looking everywhere except straight back at him. Mike's balance shifted to the balls of his feet. Had she seen or heard something that had alarmed her? Maybe she'd simply recognized a familiar face driving past.

Gina dodged a pair of businesswomen hurrying by in their suits and walking shoes, clearly unaware of whatever had caught her attention. Three more pedestrians passed her before she shook her head, as if dismissing what she'd seen or heard, and turned toward the intersection again.

By that time, Mike was already across the parking lot, jogging toward her. He fell into step about a half block behind her, following her through the intersection before the traffic light changed. Although the number of pedestrians heading to work or running to the periodic transit stops to catch the next city bus filled the sidewalk between them, he had no problem keeping Gina in sight, simply because of his height.

Her posture had subtly changed after that original reaction. There was less of the defiance she'd shown him at the clinic and more of a wary alertness. Judging by the occasional glimpses of either cheekbone, he could see she was scanning from side to side as she walked.

Who was she looking for? What had she seen or heard that put her on guard like that?

She pulled out her cell phone, glancing over her left shoulder at the traffic as she placed a call, before Mike noticed what might have gotten her attention. A tan luxury sedan zipped across two lanes before it slowed dramatically, pulling even with Gina and matching her pace. He moved toward the curb, trying to read the license plate of the car. Other vehicles ran up behind the car, then swerved around it. He quickened his own pace to see the silhouette of a ball cap above the driver's seat headrest. That wasn't any little old lady driving it, poking along at her own pace. Was that car following Gina?

And then Mike saw something that hastened his feet into a dead run. The driver raised his arm over the passenger seat, his fingers holding a gun. "Gina!"

She spun around. The instant he shouted her name, the driver floored it, swinging into the next lane, darting around a bus and speeding through a yellow light. Horns honked, brakes screeched.

Mike snaked his arm around Gina's waist, lifting her off her feet and hauling her away from the car. At the last second, he could see the driver hadn't held a weapon, after all, but had made that crass gesture with two outstretched fingers and a flick of his thumb, imitating firing a gun.

"What the hell, Choir Boy?" Gina's phone flew from her grasp, skittering across the sidewalk and getting kicked once before a helpful soul picked it up.

Mike set her down in front of the yellow brick facade of a bail bondsman's office, keeping his body between her and the street. The other man handed Gina her cell phone, pausing to eye Mike suspiciously, as if the guy thought he was assaulting her. Mike's hand was still at

Gina's waist, the adrenaline of taking instinctive action to protect her still vibrating through his grip. He nearly bit out a warning for the other guy to move on when Gina smiled and waved him on his way.

Interesting how she managed a polite thank you and a reassurance that she was all right for the young man, but she'd cursed at Mike. Even more interesting how quickly the mix of concern and the remembered sensation of her body snugged against his made him vividly aware of every tight curve of her petite frame. He was so not thinking of her as a patient right now. But the sexual awareness burned through him as quickly as the shove against his chest separated them again. "Let go of me."

"Are you okay?"

"Are you following me?" Her question overlapped his.

"Somebody is." Mike splayed his fingers apart, releasing his grip without giving her space to move away from the wall. Those fractious nerves from his teenage injury tingled through his hips and the small of his back, protesting the abrupt movements and tension running through him. But he ignored the familiar shards of pain. "What the hell is going on?"

Although the casing on her phone was scratched, he could see on the screen between them that her call was still connected. Her focus was there instead of answering his questions. "I'm fine. Just let me do my job." She put the phone back to her ear, reporting a license plate number. "I didn't get the last two digits."

"Thirty-six," Mike answered, reciting the number he'd seen.

Her dark eyes tilted up to his. "Tan Mercedes?" He nodded. "Three six, Derek," she reported into the phone, holding Mike's gaze while she talked. "Yeah, it circled around the block. Let me know what you find out. Thanks." She disconnected the call and tucked the phone into the back pocket of her jeans. "What are you doing here? And don't you ever pick me up like that again."

"I want to know why that guy threatened you."

Her dark eyes narrowed as she studied his face. "Are you hurt?"

Yeah, a sharp twist of a pinched nerve had just made his left thigh go numb, so she must have noticed the tight clench of his jaw. But that injury was old news. He needed to understand what was going on now. "Answer the question."

Dismissing her concern because he had dismissed it, she glanced around him at the next stream of pedestrians getting off the bus and dropped her voice to a terse whisper. "I'm a cop."

Shifting to the side, Mike braced one hand on the bricks beside her head and created a barrier between Gina and anyone who might accidently bump into her shoulder. "You're not in uniform. Either we have some random whack-job roaming the streets of Kansas City or that was personal. Did you recognize him? Is he the man who shot you?"

She put her hand in the middle of his chest to hush him when a couple of people turned their heads and slowed, catching wind of the conversation. "You saw it. The driver was acting suspiciously. I was doing my duty by calling it in." When she tried to dismiss the conversation and move around him, Mike dropped his hand back to the cinch of her waist, refusing to budge. She muttered something in Spanish, then tipped her face up to his. "I was probably staring at him too long, and he mimicked shooting me instead of flipping me off. Thought he was being funny."

Mike wasn't laughing. "Okay, so you're a tough chick. I get that. Didn't anybody ever teach you how to answer a polite question? I grew up around cops— I know the signs of somebody going into alert mode. You're not armed. You're injured. You don't have backup. I'm not going to think any less of you if you tell me that guy spooked you."

Her pinpoint gaze dodged his for an instant, revealing a chink in her armor. Mike summoned every bit of his patience to wait her out before she finally told him something that wasn't a flippant excuse, meant to dismiss his concern. "I've seen that car before—driving by my house at night the past couple of weeks. And now…" She curled her fingers into his shirt, pulling him half a step closer as a group of pedestrians strolled behind him. Sure, she was avoiding foot traffic, but she'd also moved him closer to whisper, "Do you remember the vehicle from the shooting?"

"Yeah, but it wasn't a car. Certainly not anything top-of-the-line like that. Did you recognize the driver? He could have ditched the truck I saw." Although he doubted the man who owned that piece of junk would also own a Mercedes.

"The man who shot me—I never saw his face." Mike dipped his head to hear her over the noise of the crowd and traffic. "I thought it might be someone else I'd recognize."

"Like who?"

"My sister's boyfriend. He doesn't like me, and the feeling's mutual. Or one of a group of bikers I ticked off a few weeks back…the day I got shot. That can't be a coincidence, can it?" One thing he had to give Gina credit for—whether she was venting her temper, discussing a case or admitting her fear—she looked him straight in the eye. He had to admire a woman with that kind of confidence. But it also gave Mike a chance to read the real emotions behind her words. "I couldn't see this guy's face, either. He had dark glasses on and a ball cap pulled low over his forehead. I couldn't even give you a hair color or age. I don't suppose you got a description of him?"

She was afraid, and it didn't take a rocket scientist to guess that fear wasn't an emotion she was used to feeling. Mike moved his fingers from her waist to stroke the sleek muscles of her arm, wanting to reassure her somehow. But he had an idea she wasn't used to accepting comfort, either. "No. But you think that car has been following you? Is that why you're running the plate number?"

"My partner is. Technically, I'm on medical leave. He's doing me a favor."

Knowing the shooter was still out there, and that she wouldn't be able to identify the man if he came back to finish the job until she saw a gun pointed at her would rattle anybody. Even an experienced cop like Gina. "Come back to the clinic. I'll drive you home."

"No." She started to push him away, but the tips of her fingers curled into the cotton knit of his polo, lightly clinging to the skin and muscle underneath. "No, thank you," she added, apologizing for the abruptness of her answer. "It's probably someone who lives or works in the neighborhood. There are gangbangers in my part of town. They know I'm a cop. Maybe one of them recognized me. And maybe it was nothing. After the shooting, I'm overly suspicious of any vehicle that slows down or stops when it shouldn't."

He was surprised to feel her reaching out to him, even more surprised to realize how every cell leaped beneath her touch, even one as casual as her hold on him now. This wild attraction he was feeling was unexpected—and most likely unreciprocated, if his track record for following his hormones and heart was any indication. Gina had had her entire life turned upside down, and she was learning how to cope with the changes. All she needed from him right now was a steady presence she could hold on to for a few seconds while she regrouped. He could give her that. "I wouldn't rationalize away your suspicions, Gina. Sounds to me like survival skills, not paranoia."

Her gaze finally dropped from his to study the line of his jaw. She smiled when she murmured, "Physical therapist, not counselor. *Not* bodyguard."

"How about friend?" he offered. Because this pseudo embrace against the brick wall was starting to feel a lot like something more than a therapist–patient relationship was happening between them.

"Maybe it *is* a little far to walk." But she wasn't asking for a ride. Another bus pulled up behind him, her phone rang and she pulled away to take out her cell and join the line waiting to board the bus. "I'll see you tomorrow morning…Mike."

She paused before his name, as if it was hard to pronounce.

Maybe it was just hard to accept his offer. "Do you need me to pick you up?"

"*Not* my chauffeur." She raised her voice to be heard above the bus's idling engine.

He raised his, too. "I'm not being nice. I'm being practical."

But she was already climbing on, taking her call.

Mike backed away as the bus door closed and the big vehicle hissed and growled, spewing fumes that blocked out the spicy scent he was learning to identify as Gina's.

Mike watched the bus chug up to speed and sail through the intersection before he turned back toward the PT clinic. He scanned the traffic as he walked, trying to spot the car again. Maybe the driver had circled around the block a third time. Maybe the tan sedan was long gone. Maybe it had nothing to do with Gina or the shooting.

Erring on the side of caution, he pulled out his own phone and texted himself the license plate number before he forgot it. He'd ask his dad or one of his buddies at the police department to see what they could find out about the car and its owner.

He hadn't gotten a look at the shooter who'd sped away that day, either. He'd been too focused on helping the cops who'd been wounded. Had the car triggered a memory in Gina's subconscious mind, reminding her of something she'd seen? Or was all that bravado she spouted the protective armor of a woman who'd had her confidence ripped out from under her feet?

Mike wasn't a cop. But he was thinking like one, and he needed answers.

Was the shooter tracking her down, learning her routine so he could come back and finish the job? If so, did that mean the shooting was personal? Not a random attack on cops?

Was Gina still in danger?

What kind of backup did a cop on medical leave have? Maybe she didn't need Mike to protect her. But, injured as she was, without the ability to use her gun, how would the woman protect herself?

Chapter Five

"Not my chauffeur, Choir Boy," Gina insisted, catching the towel Mike tossed her way with her left hand. Slightly breathless after a duel on side-by-side treadmills that she suspected he'd let her win, she dabbed at the perspiration at her neck and at the cleavage of the gray tank top she wore. "I can get to KCPD headquarters on my own."

After a week of physical therapy sessions with Mike Cutler, she had to give him grief, or else he might begin to think his jokes amused her—and that his efforts to be a gentleman and push her toward recovery with the same mix of authority and restraint his dad used at KCPD might result in her actually liking the guy.

At least he had the sense to respect her fitness level. He allowed her to push hard with her legs and left arm, in addition to the far gentler stretches and coordination exercises he did with her right hand and arm. "I suspect your legs are like jelly, so you're not walking. And I can't wait for you to get there by bus. How much time do you think I can spare for you out of my busy day?" he teased. He picked up his own towel to wipe his face. "I'm driving."

Busy day? Gina picked up the sling he'd let her remove before that last running challenge and swung her gaze over to where Troy was working with a retired firefighter with knee issues. She hadn't seen many other patients. And she'd overheard a conversation between Mike and Frannie on Monday about moving money from his personal account to make a payment on an expensive piece of equipment.

They might come from two different worlds, but growing up in suburbia hadn't guaranteed that a person could make ends meet. Still, the fact that he drove into this part of the city from somewhere else and probably lived in a house big enough to stretch out those long, muscular legs of his made her a little jealous. Heck, he no doubt had more bathrooms in that house than any one man could use, while she intended to take a quick shower here so that she wouldn't have to let her workout scent marinate while she waited in line to use the bathtub at home.

His tone grew serious as he sat down on the bench, facing her. "Are you worried about going back to Precinct headquarters? I'd rather evaluate the status of your grip at the shooting range than bring a gun here."

"No. That's fine. While we're there I can check in with my partner—see if there are any developments in the shooting investigation. Not that I can do anything about it officially, but…" Maybe she should take Mike up on his offer of a ride, in case being back in the building where she could no longer work stirred up her frustrations again—or embarrassment if she discovered she was no better at handling a firearm today than she'd been seven weeks ago. She'd hate to be waiting for the bus if she wanted to make a quick escape.

Those piercing blue eyes studied every nuance of her expression, trying to read her thoughts. "But you want to regain a little control over what you're going through?"

Funny how she'd lost control of everything during those few seconds in the street outside Vicki Bismarck's house.

Not funny how well this man could read her fears and insecurities. But she wasn't about to admit those vulnerabilities to Mike or anyone else. Better a chauffeur than a therapist. "All right, then. You can drive me."

He arced an eyebrow, looking as surprised by the one-time concession as she'd meant him to be. But her plan to catch him off guard and stop him from analyzing her emotions backfired when Mike pushed to his feet. Suddenly, she was nose-to-chest with Mike's lanky frame. His broad shoulders blocked her peripheral vision and she could feel the heat coming off his body. "Give me fifteen minutes to shower and change, and we'll go."

Catnip. She retreated a step when she realized she was inhaling the earthy smells of sweat and soap and man, and savoring the elemental response his scent triggered inside her. "Make it ten," she challenged, denying her body's feminine reaction. "How much time do you think I can spare for you out of my busy day?"

Mike laughed at her mimicking comeback, and she smiled for a moment before mumbling one of her great-uncle's curses and spinning away to march toward the women's locker room. When had his silly sense of humor started rubbing off on her? She wasn't supposed to like a man like Mike Cutler. At least, she wasn't supposed to like him as anything other than a physical therapist and maybe a friend. Besides, she already had enough responsibilities demanding her time and energy. When did she think she was going to squeeze in dating?

Mike was right about one thing. She needed to be in control of her life, in control of her future, again. She'd be smart to ignore any fluttering of her pulse, any urge to laugh at their banter, and that relentless pull to the heat of his body.

"Ten minutes, Choir Boy."

Gina had learned long ago how to get in and out of the bathroom quickly and came out of the shower five minutes later, her skin cooled and fresh, her libido firmly in check. She towel-dried her hair and finger-combed the chin-length waves into place before she started to dress. After the shooting, she'd switched to a front hook bra and button-up blouses so she could dress herself. But, though she'd taken Mike's advice and worn her KCPD sweats for their therapy sessions, she wasn't about to show up at Precinct headquarters looking like she'd just come from the gym. It would be hard enough to be there out of uniform, sending the obvious message to her coworkers and superior officers that this was just a visit. Looking like a bum might also give them the impression that she wasn't coming back.

But the fitted jeans she took from her bag were a little tricky when she had to pull them up, especially when her skin was still dewy from the shower. The twinge in her shoulder and resulting tingling in her fingers when she gave them a tug warned her she needed to swallow her pride and ask someone to help her. When she heard a woman's voice out in the locker area, Gina gave a mental prayer of thanks that she wouldn't have to leave the locker room with her jeans hanging on her hips to go get Mike.

"Hey, could you help…?" Gina's question died when she saw Frannie dabbing at her red-tipped nose as she folded towels from a laundry basket and stacked them on a shelf. The woman with hair the color of a penny kept muttering something that sounded like *stupid ninny*. Gina cleared her throat to announce her presence. "Are you okay?"

Frannie spun around, hugging a fluffy towel to her chest. "I'm sorry. Did you need something?"

Gina pointed to her jeans. "I'm stuck."

"Oh, right." Frannie dropped the towel into the basket and hurried over to give the black pants a final tug. "Mike said you needed to be careful with that arm."

"Thanks." Gina took over buttoning the waistband and pulling up the zipper. "I guess I need to stick to sweats." But Frannie had gone back to folding. Maybe this wasn't any of her business, but the woman had just helped her pull up her pants, so there was a bit of a connection there. Moving closer, Gina plucked a hand towel from the basket and held it out to the taller woman. "What happened? And don't say *nothing* because you've been crying for a while."

Frannie took the towel and pulled off her glasses to dry her eyes. "I got a phone call."

"From your ex?" Even the eye that didn't seem to focus looked startled. When the other woman backed away, Gina reached for her hand. "I eavesdrop. I'm a cop. I like to know who the people around me are. You and Troy were arguing about a restraining order for your ex yesterday."

Frannie put her glasses back on and sort of smiled. "We were arguing about Troy's van. He drove me to the judge's office to reinstate the order. Troy can't use his legs, you know, so he has this special van where he uses a hand brake and accelerator to drive. I mentioned one thing about how fast he was going before a jerky stop at a red light, and he started yelling about the van falling apart, and that he hadn't had a chance to clean it up before I rode in it. I thought he was mad at me. I don't deal with confrontation very well."

"Have you ridden with Troy before?"

Frannie shook her head.

Sounded like wounded male pride. She thought she'd detected a few stolen glances between the two coworkers. Maybe Troy wasn't keen on Frannie seeing the extent of his handicap. "Not everyone who argues with you is going to hurt you."

"I know. Troy's usually really sweet and funny. I probably caught him on a bad day." That sounded like a woman who'd been victimized making excuses for a man who'd yelled at her or hurt her.

This whole conversation—and all the other interactions she'd had with the skittish Frannie—reminded her of Vicki Bismarck. She wondered if that last call she'd been working on before the shooting had been resolved. Was Gordon Bismarck still in jail? Had his big brother, Denny, and his friends retaliated against Vicki in any way? Had Vicki gotten the medical treatment she'd needed? Moved in with her sister? Pressed charges against Gordon?

Or were Denny and his biker boys more interested in retaliating against the police officers who'd arrested Gordon? Had he been the man in the rusty SUV the day she'd been shot? Gina's fingers drifted to her right shoulder—not feeling a physical or even phantom pain, but remembering with vivid detail the bullet tearing through her body, the multiple gunshots exploding all around her and the snow soaking up her blood and body heat.

Gina realized she was shivering before she pulled herself from the memories. The Bismarcks weren't her case anymore. And everyone at KCPD was working on finding out who'd shot one of their own. Everyone but her, that is. She wasn't used to being the victim. She didn't like being out of the investigative loop or being taken off the front line of protecting her city, her family and herself.

But the situation right in front of her was one she could handle. Gina sat and patted the bench beside her. She had a feeling Frannie's tears weren't really about the argument with Troy. "Tell me about the phone call."

"From Leo?" Frannie hesitated for a moment before sitting. "I was getting ready for work this morning. I didn't pick up. As soon as I heard his voice, I let it go straight to my machine. He said he missed me. That he still loved me. That he always would." She paused a moment before adding, "He wants to see me."

"Is he supposed to have any contact with you?" When Frannie shook her head, Gina's first instinct was to pull out her own phone and file a report. But she wasn't a cop right now. She couldn't take action, but she could give advice. "Polite or not—even if Leo pulled at your heartstrings—you need to call the police and report it." The jerk had probably just been served with the restraining order and thought he could talk her out of it. "Keep a record of any contact he makes with you—by phone, email, certainly in person. Do you know his parole officer's name? He needs to know about the call, too."

The other woman straightened her shoulders and nodded. "I know that's what I'm supposed to do. I can ask Mike to help. He said his dad was looking into it." Frannie offered Gina a smile that quickly faded. "I'm such a ninny. Have you ever been so scared of a person that you can't even think when he's around?" She stood abruptly and carried the hand towel to the clothes hamper near the shower room. "Look who I'm talking to. You're not scared of anything."

Gina was thinking that never regaining the full use of her hand and arm was a pretty terrifying thing to contemplate. Losing her job. Letting her family down. Never getting the life she wanted for all of them. "Maybe not people," she confessed.

Although there was one faceless shooter who'd put her on guard from the moment she'd regained consciousness in the hospital. Like nearly every other waking moment,

Gina wondered if there'd ever be an arrest of the man who'd targeted her and her partner. They weren't on Gordon Bismarck's good side after arresting him. There'd certainly been plenty of time for Denny to switch vehicles and come back to the house to shoot her and Derek. According to Mike, the SUV's plates had been unreadable. A citywide search for a rusted SUV matching the description he'd given the police had turned up nothing useful. Even the license number on the tan sedan she and Mike had seen wasn't any help. The plates were stolen, according to Derek. The car they'd been registered to belonged to an elderly man who rarely drove it and didn't even know the plates were missing.

Could the Bismarck brothers and their friends be running a stolen-car ring? Or even have legitimate access to a variety of vehicles? In her mind, Bobby Estes was a viable suspect, too. She wouldn't put it past Bobby to try something like that. From what she knew of her sister's smarmy boyfriend, his driving a stolen car, or one with a falsified registration and plates like the Mercedes she'd seen following her, wouldn't surprise her. Shooting the woman who stood in the way of getting what he wanted wouldn't surprise her, either.

Surely someone at KCPD had looked into the background of the prime suspects who'd been at the scene right before the shooting or lived in the same neighborhood. She certainly would. If she was on the case. But she wasn't. And until someone else found the answers, identifying a suspect and a motive, the shooter remained at large—and had the advantage of knowing her, while she remained clueless to his face and name and whether he was coming after her to finish the job he'd started.

"I know what fear is." Gina stood when Frannie resumed folding the towels, probably thinking the long pause meant the conversation was over. "You just have to decide you're not going to let it rule your life."

"That's easier said than done."

"I know. You have to keep trying—every day—to be stronger than the fear. If it gets you one day, then you wake up the next and you try harder." Frannie hugged a towel to her chest again and nodded, trying to internalize the hard-won advice that Gina had learned in No-Man's Land. Gina smiled and added a little practical advice to that philosophical wisdom. "If Leo does come to see you, call 9-1-1. If he physically threatens you, fight back. As hard as you can." She gestured as she gave each instruction. "Stomp on his instep. Gouge his eyes. Ram your hand against the bottom of his nose. And, of course, there's always the old goodie—kicking him where it counts." Frannie silently repeated each hand movement. Gina repeated them for her, encouraging her to use more force. "Scream your head off, too. Help will come running. At least around here. Either Troy or Mike has his eyes on you whenever I'm here. Probably when I'm not, too. Those two have a good-guy streak in them a mile wide."

Frannie nodded. "I know. They've been through so much, and they're still so nice. Any girl would be lucky to..." Her cheeks turned pink as she swallowed whatever emotion she'd been about to share. "Mike's like a big brother to me."

Gina wasn't forgetting where this conversation had started. "And Troy?"

Frannie's blush intensified. Interesting. Maybe she wasn't so keen on Troy seeing her shortcomings, either. "They're the best. I'll talk to Mike and call Leo's parole officer." She divvied up the clean towels and put half away before carrying the basket to the locker room door.

She paused there, looking to Gina before repeating her advice. "Feet. Eyes. Nose. Family jewels."

Gina grinned. "And scream like crazy."

"Thanks."

For what? All she'd done was give the woman a few tools to use if she ever needed to defend herself against her ex. It was what any cop would do. Acknowledging that it felt good to do something that made her feel useful again, Gina quickly finished dressing. No doubt Mike would have some comment about missing her ten-minute challenge to be ready. He'd expect her to laugh. And if she wasn't careful, she probably would.

They've been through so much...

What had Frannie meant by that comment? What could Troy and Mike, especially Mike, have endured that would make the other woman sound surprised—almost awestruck—that the two men would end up being such nice guys? Such hero figures to her?

And why was Gina so curious to find out the answer to that question?

"I'D LIKE TO check in with my partner first." Gina stepped into the elevator and pushed the 3 button on the panel, taking her and Mike upstairs instead of down to the shooting range in the basement. "Our desks..." Hopefully hers hadn't been filled yet, but she knew her partner had been temporarily reassigned to ride with someone else until she could get back to patrol duty. "Derek's desk," she corrected, "is on the third floor." She checked the time on her phone before tucking it into her back pocket. "They're probably getting out of morning roll call about now."

"Not a problem. My schedule's flexible." Mike joined her at the back railing. "Today is all about taking your recovery to the next level. Making that hand usable again."

Gina inhaled a deep breath. "I hope there's a level after that. *Usable* doesn't sound like it'll get me the job I want."

"The healing part I can't control. But I'll teach your body to do everything it's capable of. I promise. It's just a matter of time and training." Even leaning against the car's back wall, Mike was a head taller than she was.

Gina was used to being shorter than most men, often shorter than anyone in the room except for her great-aunt. But her bulky uniform vest, gun and determined attitude usually beefed up her presence. Yet there was something about Mike Cutler that seemed to fill up the limited space of the elevator and make her feel tiny, fragile, more feminine than usual. Perhaps it was the lack of the uniform and gear she usually wore. Or perhaps it was the protective way he opened doors for her and stood on her right side, shielding her injured arm now that she didn't have to wear the sling around the clock anymore. Although she might be vertically challenged, Gina had never considered herself delicate in any way. Not since she was a child had she needed anyone to protect her. Back then, an absent father and an ailing mother had forced her to grow some tough emotional armor and learn to fight and stay smarter than any adversary. Gina took care of herself and her family all on her own. She didn't need a man taking care of her.

Even if he did smell good and generate the kind of heat she fantasized about on chilly spring mornings like this.

"Am I your only patient today?" she asked, needing to start a conversation before she did something damsel-like and leaned into that body heat.

He tucked his fingers into the pockets of his jeans and answered. "Yeah. Business has been slow."

She wasn't blind to the lack of company at the CAPT Center in the mornings. "You didn't exactly pick the most lucrative area of the city to set up shop. Have you ever thought of affiliating with a hospital? Even moving the center a couple of blocks over to Westport would make it appealing to a broader audience. Not everyone feels safe spending a lot of time that close to No-Man's Land. You know, that part of the city where urban renewal hasn't quite reached—"

"I know what No-Man's Land is. Son of a cop, remember?" He tilted his face down to hers. "I've done the hospital thing. We're exactly where we want to be, offering physical therapy services to an underserved part of the city. We're our own bosses now. Troy grew up in the neighborhood, and I've had my share of experience there."

"Your share of experience?" Gina scoffed. "You're telling me you've been on the mean streets of the city? You've broken the law? I pegged you for a middle-class suburbia guy all the way."

Was that a scowl? Did Mr. Good Guy have a secret sore spot she'd just poked? He straightened away from the railing. "I'm not the *choir boy* you think I am. I've done things."

"Like what? Cheat on a test? Run a red light?"

The scowl deepened. Gina felt a stab of guilt, thinking back to Frannie's comment about Mike going through something terrible in his past. Had her smart mouth just crossed a line?

"You don't live in the suburbs? Have enough land that you can't touch your house and the neighbor's at the same time?" Good grief. Was she actually making light of the topic to try and restore that goofball smile to his face? "I was really hoping you had three bathrooms because I was totally going to come for a visit and spend the afternoon soaking in one of those tubs."

She heard an exhale of breath that sounded like a wry laugh.

"You want to get in my bathtub?" There was the glimpse of white teeth amid the sexy dusting of his beard. His voice dropped to a throaty whisper as he leaned in. "I wouldn't object to that."

Gina couldn't remember the last time she'd blushed hard enough to feel heat in her cheeks. "I meant…our house is small. I share one bathroom with four… I can't take my time…" She growled at her flummoxed reaction to his teasing innuendo.

Not a boyfriend. *Not* a lover. *Not* a man who should be getting under her skin.

Thankfully the elevator doors slid open, and she could escape the sound of Mike's laughter.

But she never got the chance to get her armor fully in place again. A trio of SWAT cops waited just outside the elevator, greeting Mike with a chorus of "Mikey," handshakes and a ribbing about an upcoming barbecue contest.

Gina knew the three officers, dressed in solid black, except for the white SWAT logo she coveted embroidered on their chest pockets. These were her trainers. Members of KCPD's elite SWAT Team One, led by Captain Cutler. The one with the black hair, Sergeant Rafe Delgado, was even slated to lead the new tactical team she wanted to be a part of.

Clearly, they were all longtime friends, with Mike giving the jokes right back, teasing Holden Kincaid, the team's sharpshooter, about the dogs living at his house who were all smarter than him. He asked about Sergeant Delgado's son, Aaron, and pointed to the baby bump just beginning to show on the woman with the long ponytail, Miranda Gallagher. "They're not letting you out into the field, are they, Randy?"

Gina admired the tall blonde who had been KCPD's first female SWAT officer. She'd shared a couple of private conversations with Gina about the challenges and rewards of being a woman with her specialized training. Officer Gallagher cradled her hand against her belly. "For now, these bozos are letting me drive the van. Pretty soon, though, I'll be relegated to equipment maintenance, and then it's maternity leave."

Gina felt like an afterthought, and considered ducking back into the elevator with the two detectives who snuck in behind her to go downstairs. She hadn't even realized she'd been backing away from the animated reunion until she felt Mike's hand at the small of her back, pulling her forward to stand beside him. "You all know Gina Galvan, right?"

Sergeant Delgado nodded. "Of course, we know our star recruit. We miss you at training."

Holden agreed. "She keeps us on our toes."

"Hi, Gina." Miranda Gallagher smiled down at her.

Apparently, she was going to be a part of this conversation after all. "Officer Gallagher."

Miranda tilted her head. "We talked about that."

Gina nodded. "Randy."

Sergeant Delgado pointed to her arm. "I heard you were at Mike's clinic. How's the recovery going?"

"Fine." She glanced up at Mike. *Was* she getting any better?

Mike's hand rubbed a subtle circle beneath her denim jacket, and she nearly startled at the unexpected tendrils of warmth webbing out across her skin and into the muscles beneath. "She's progressing nicely. Slowly but surely, I'm seeing improvement every day."

"That's good to hear." Holden tapped his thigh. "You willing to give out some free advice to the guy who once saved your life?"

Saved his life?

"What's up?" Mike asked. "And I thought I saved myself."

Saved himself? *I'm not the* choir boy *you think I am, Gina. I've done things.* She still couldn't get her head around what kind of secrets a guy like Mike might have.

"You wish," Holden teased before getting serious. "My knee hasn't been right since I took a tumble off a roof doing sniper duty last week. Anything I can do besides load up on ibuprofen?"

"You should go to Mike's clinic." Gina wasn't sure where the suggestion had come from, other than a deep-seated need to keep things even between them. If Mike was supporting her in a moment of social discomfort, then she'd support him. "The location's not that far from headquarters. You could stop in over lunch or right after work."

"I'll do that." Holden smiled at Gina. "He's obviously doing something right with you, so that's a good recommendation."

Mike's fingers pressed into her back. The tension flowing from him into her didn't exactly feel like a thank you. "Call for an appointment. My assistant will make sure we squeeze you in."

"I'll do that. Thanks."

Sergeant Delgado checked his watch and hurried the conversation along. "I hate to break up the party, but we've got an inspection this morning. We'd better get down to the garage and secure the van."

"Good to see you guys."

"You, too, Mikey."

There was another round of handshakes, and a hug with Miranda before the three uniformed officers got on the elevator and Mike pulled Gina aside to whisper, "I don't need you to drum up business for me."

"And I don't need you to stand up for me."

He shrugged. "It's what people do. Make everyone feel included. What is your hang-up with me being nice to you?"

She propped her hands at her hips and tilted her face to his. "You know those are my superior officers, right? I shouldn't be socializing with them."

"I practically grew up with those guys. That was running into family, not socializing."

"You weren't including me in the conversation to curry favor with them, were you? I want to earn my spot on the new team on merit, not because I'm friends with the captain's son."

Suddenly, the hushed argument was over. He straightened. "So, we're friends now? And here I thought you were going to fight me every step of the way."

She stared at his hand when he reached for hers, overriding the instinctive urge to close the short distance and lace her fingers together with his. No, she couldn't start leaning on Mike just because he made it so easy to do so.

Gina heard a wry chuckle, although she didn't see a smile, as he curled his fingers into his palm and turned toward the desk sergeant's station to check in and get visitor badges. "Right. Just friends. Come on. Let's find your partner."

Chapter Six

"Did you talk to the man who had his plates stolen?" Gina asked, scrolling through the sketchy details of the report on Derek's computer screen. Had he always been this lax about following up with paperwork on the calls they handled? Had she been too obsessive about her own A+ work ethic to notice his borderline incompetence? Or was he skating by on minimal effort without her at his side every day to push him into being the best cop he could be? "Could you tie him to the Bismarck brothers or Bobby Estes?"

Derek perched on the corner of his desk, looking over her shoulder at the screen. "It was just me running a plate for you. I didn't follow up because there wasn't any crime."

Gina shook her head, closing down the page. At least a mouse was easy to control with just her thumb and index finger. It wasn't frontline action, but she could make herself useful doing a little research. "Um, theft? Maybe tell one of the detectives working that stolen-car ring? You know I think Bobby is involved with something like that. How else could he afford the different cars he drives? And, clearly, Denny Bismarck is a motor head. You saw that bike he was riding. Does he work in auto repair? A guy like that could easily lift plates off another vehicle."

Speaking of detectives, her gaze slid across the maze of desks and cubicles to spot Mike chatting with a plainclothes officer she recognized as one of the department's veterans, Atticus Kincaid. Was he related to Holden Kincaid, the SWAT sharpshooter? From senior officers down to the administrative assistant in the chief's office, they'd all said hi or waved or nodded or smiled. He was a law-enforcement legacy more at home at Precinct headquarters because of his father's seniority than she was after six years of scratching her way up through the ranks. If she needed any more evidence that they came from different parts of the city, from virtually two different worlds, that comfortable-in-his-own-skin, one-of-the-boys conversation was it.

"You're right." Derek interrupted thoughts that felt melancholy rather than envious, as she would have had seven weeks ago. Either Mike had social skills she could never hope to possess or she truly was an outsider fighting to find her place among an elite group of cops. "I did mention it to a detective."

Gina spun the chair to face her partner. "What did they say?"

Derek shrugged his broad shoulders. "I just gave him the message."

Gina combed her fingers through her hair and clasped the nape of her neck, biting down on her frustration. "Well, has there been any progress on the shooting investigation?"

Surely, he'd be right on top of the case that was so personal for both of them. He nodded, moving off the desk to open the bottom drawer and pull out a file folder. "Detective Grove and his partner brought Denny Bismarck and his biker buddies in for questioning. Other than the verbal threats they made at the house, we can't get them on anything. They all alibi each other. Said they left the Bismarck house and went straight to the Sin City Bar."

"Can anyone at the bar confirm that?" Gina picked up a notepad and copied names and contact information. Holding a pen was a skill she'd worked on with Mike. The handwriting wasn't pretty, but it was legible, and learning these details was making her feel like a cop again.

"You'd have to ask Grove. Whatever he found out is in that file."

"You didn't follow up?"

"I was in the hospital."

"I know. But after that?"

"No."

"Four suspects accounting for each other's whereabouts is hardly a solid alibi. And that wasn't the first time we stopped Gordon Bismarck from hurting his ex-wife. What if that call was a setup to get us shot all along?"

"What's with all the questions?" he snapped, lowering his voice when the officers at the nearby desks looked his direction. "Look, G, I'm not trying to be a detective. My goal is SWAT."

"Your goal should be being the best cop you can be." Gina stood, tucking the notes into the pocket of her jeans. There had to be something else going on here. "Don't you want to find out who shot you? I want to see that guy behind bars."

"I just want to put it behind me." Derek skimmed his hand over the top of his light brown hair, a look of anguish lining his face. "I can't solve the case for you. Hell, G, I don't remember anything of that afternoon after being shot. The doctors said I hit my head. I remember getting shot, going down, and then…" He shook his head, his frustration evident. "You're not the only one who lost something that day."

"Why didn't you tell me?" She squeezed her hand around his forearm, offering the support she hadn't realized he needed. "I'm so sorry. I didn't know. I'm not criticizing. You must be as frustrated as I am. But I want answers. Justice. For both of us."

"I know." Derek patted her hand. "I didn't want to do anything that would get Vicki hurt either, so I kind of let things slide."

"Vicki Bismarck?" Gina frowned as she remembered a detail from the moments before they'd been shot. "You two were calling each other by your first names that day. Is there something personal going on between you two?"

He shrugged and pulled away to shuffle some papers on his desk. "We may have gone out a couple of times. Nothing came of it."

"You dated a victim you met on a call? A domestic-violence victim? Was that before or after someone tried to end us?"

"Vic is really sweet. Once you get past the shyness."

Gina's mouth opened. Shut. Opened again. "Derek— you know what a jealous idiot Gordon Bismarck is. Going out with his ex-wife could have been the motive to make him go ballistic and target us."

Derek spun around, his tone hushed but angry. "We don't know if that's what happened."

Gina pushed the papers back to the desktop, wanting some concrete answers. "Did you follow up on Gordon? Find out if he saw the two of you together?"

"No. And if I make a stink of it, he might take it out on her."

"Does Vicki mean something to you?"

"I haven't seen her since that day. Let it go, G."

"I'm not blaming you, especially if you're trying to protect her. I just want answers. I want to put someone away for trying to end our lives. Don't you?"

"Sure." Derek dropped his head to stare at the spot where her hand rested on his desk beside his. "Don't you think I feel guilty? I don't remember enough about what happened that day to ID the guy—and now you're suggesting I may have triggered the incident in the first place? I just thought some crazy was targeting cops."

And maybe that *was* the answer. But how could he not be using every spare moment to find the truth? Would guilt, amnesia and worry about a victim's well-being be enough to stop her from pursuing every possible lead?

The telephone on his desk rang. He inhaled a steadying breath before picking up after the second ring. "Officer Johnson. What? Right now? Just what I need," he muttered sarcastically. "No, that's fine."

"Is something wrong?" she asked once he'd hung up.

Derek smoothed the long black sleeves of his uniform and straightened his belt. "Let's drop this conversation for now, okay? I've got a visitor. They're sending him back." He made an apologetic face. "Fair warning."

"Huh?"

And then she understood the cryptic comment. A man wearing a visitor's badge, looking like a hippie version of Derek, with faded jeans, a stained fringed jacket and a graying, stringy ponytail hanging down the middle of his back, came around the cubicle wall. "Dad? What are you doing here?"

"There's my boy." The two shook hands before Harold Johnson pulled Derek in for a black-slapping hug. When he pushed away, he was grinning down at Gina. "Senorita Galvan. What are you doing here?"

Gina remembered the ruddy cheeks, leathered skin and inappropriate comments from her earlier encounters with Derek's father. All the years he'd spent outdoors working at a junkyard between stays in jail or rehab seemed to be aging him quickly but hadn't put a dent in his oily charm. "It's *Officer* Galvan, Harold. Or Gina. Remember?"

"My apologies. But you remind me so much of that *chica bonita* who used to serve me tequila shots at Alvarez's outside Fort Bliss." He chuckled at the memory of the pretty girl who used to wait on his table. "And she was just as insistent I call her Senorita."

Derek shook his head at the tired old joke. "You said that was because she didn't want you calling her after hours."

Harold swatted Derek on the shoulder and told him to get a sense of humor. "Forgive an old man. I know it's not politically correct, but some habits are hard to change. Come here, honey."

Honey? Like that was any better. Gina went stiff as the older man leaned in for an unexpected hug.

"I'm just glad you and my boy are okay. Scariest moment of my life was when I got that phone call that he'd been shot. I'm glad his mama didn't live to see…"

A hand came over Gina's shoulder, palming Harold's chest and pushing him out of the hug and out of her space. "Easy. She's injured."

Gina didn't need to hear Mike's low voice to know who'd rescued her from the unwanted squeeze. She recognized his scent and the heat of his body against her back. Her breath came out in a huff of relief. She hadn't even been thinking about her rebuilt shoulder. She'd been bothered by the same overly familiar discomfort she got when Derek talked about her sister, Sylvie, as if he wanted to date her. But, not wanting to insult her partner's father and drive a rift between her and Derek, she was glad for the physical excuse. "Sorry, Harold. I've got to watch the arm while it's still healing."

He settled for a loose handshake that extended the awkward moment when he pointed out her limp fingers. "That's too bad about your hand. I guess you didn't see the man who shot you, either. Derek had his back to him but said you were facing him."

Pulling away, Gina tucked her hand inside her jacket against her stomach, surprised by the indirect accusation. Of course, a father would want his child to be safe. Even if that child was a grown man, a good father would want to know why his son had gotten hurt. "I heard the shots. I didn't see—"

"Of course you didn't. Otherwise, you would have warned my boy. He wouldn't have gotten hurt."

"Dad," Derek warned.

Mike moved to Gina's side, positioning his body in a way that forced Harold back another step. He was shielding her again, even as he thrust out his hand. "I'm Mike Cutler."

Harold's bushy brows knotted with confusion as they shook hands. "Harold Johnson. I'm Derek's daddy. You a cop?"

"I'm a friend. And you're out of line."

Derek finished the introductions with an embarrassed sigh. "This is Captain Cutler's son, Dad."

"You're Captain Cutler's boy?" *Boy* wasn't a term Gina would ever use to refer to Mike, especially when he was a solid wall of defense between her and any perceived threat or insult as he was now. Harold's frown at Mike's intrusion flipped into a beaming smile. "I see the resemblance now. Your daddy's got my boy on a short list for his new SWAT team. That means a promotion and more money."

"Gina mentioned it." Mike nodded to Derek. "Congratulations. My dad doesn't make decisions lightly. I understand he's narrowed it down to ten good candidates."

Harold tilted his head to offer Gina a sympathetic frown. "Looks like it's down to nine, unfortunately."

"Harold," Gina chided, "Captain Cutler isn't making his final decision for another week. I have every intention of giving your son and everyone else a run for their money. And I'm as much a victim of that shooting as Derek was."

"Ooh, touched a nerve there, didn't I?" Harold laughed, elbowing Derek's arm before apologizing. "I'm sorry, honey. I just assumed—"

"'I'm sorry, *Officer* Galvan,'" she corrected with the most precise articulation her subtle accent allowed. How had Derek grown up to have any charm at all with a father who didn't possess an ounce of empathy or respect for personal boundaries?

Harold retreated a step as Mike leaned toward him. "Watch your mouth, Johnson."

But Derek had it handled. After sliding Gina an apologetic look, he pulled his father around the corner of the desk. "Why are you here, anyway? What do you need?"

"A place we can talk in private? Family business." Derek seemed relieved to usher his father toward an interview room. "I've been talkin' to a lawyer…"

That's when she discovered she'd latched on to the

back of Mike's shirt. Tightly enough to feel the flex of muscle through the cotton knit. Had she really thought Mr. Nice Guy was going after Harold and she'd have to stop him? Or had she subconsciously realized she needed the anchor of his solid presence to get through this difficult visit to Precinct headquarters after all?

She quickly released him and tilted her face to meet Mike's sharp blue gaze when he turned. "You ready to go?"

Gina patted her pocket with the folded notes. "I got enough information that I can follow up a few leads myself."

He arched an eyebrow that was as sleekly handsome as Harold's had been a bushy mess. "Need I remind you that you're on medical leave?"

"It doesn't hurt to make a few phone calls."

"What if you stir up the wrong kind of interest—like that driver who threatened you last week? What if he's the shooter, trying to figure out whether you recognize him? If you start poking the bear, he might stop the next time and finish what he started. You don't have a gun or a badge right now."

"You don't have to remind me of *that*," she snapped, turning toward the elevators. He followed in that long, loose stride that forced her to take two steps for every one of his to beat him to the elevator's call button. "I can't stand by and do nothing. I can at least make a pest of myself with the detectives investigating the shooting."

They had to wait long enough that logic had the chance to sneak past Gina's flare of temper. Mike was right about starting something she couldn't finish. What if she did manage to identify the man who'd shot her? She wouldn't be able to do anything more than call someone else at KCPD to make the arrest. If she confronted him herself, she'd be at a disadvantage. She hadn't been able to protect her partner back when she'd been at 100 percent. What did she think she could do now? Not only could he hurt her again, he could hurt the people around her—her family, innocent bystanders, this tall drink of annoyingly right catnip standing beside her—and she couldn't do anything to stop him.

She was worse than useless as a cop right now. She might well be a danger to everyone around her.

The elevators were busy enough that Gina and Mike were standing there when Derek came around the corner of the last cubicle wall, pulling his father by the arm, hurrying him toward the exit. Whatever *family business* Harold had wanted to discuss, it wasn't going over well with Derek. Words like *lawsuit* and *easy money* popped out of the hushed argument. Was he suggesting that Derek sue the department? The city? Her? To make a profit off getting shot?

Although she was getting used to Mike positioning himself between her and anyone who might accidentally bump into her arm, his protective stance couldn't stop Harold from tugging free of his son's grip and addressing her. "Talk some sense into my boy, *chica*. Do the right thing."

"What are you talking about?"

"Leave her out of this, Dad. You've embarrassed me enough with your get-rich quick schemes. I'm sorry, G. Are we good?"

Gina nodded. Derek was her partner and a friend. He needed her support—not someone grilling him for answers or blaming him for whatever nutso scheme his dad had come up with.

"Come on." Derek snatched Harold by the shoulder

of his jacket and pushed him toward the stairwell door. He shoved the door open and pulled his father inside, for privacy to continue the argument as much as the apparent need for speed in making an exit.

She was still staring after them when the elevator arrived and Mike's hand at the small of her back nudged her inside. She crossed to the back of the car and leaned against it, feeling her energy ebbing from the unexpected emotional onslaught of this morning's visit to the Precinct building. "That man is stuck in the Dark Ages. I suspect feminism and ethnic equality aren't part of his vocabulary."

"Derek's dad?"

"The only other Hispanic woman he knows is a bartender from a cantina during his army days? That's how he thinks of me? He blames me for Derek getting shot. No way could a *little woman*, much less one from my part of town, be a good cop and a good partner who could protect his son."

Mike pushed the button for the basement level before resting his hip against the back railing beside her. "He got to you. You don't blame yourself for getting shot, do you?"

Did she? Gina shook off the misguided guilt. "No. I know there's only one person to blame—a wannabe cop killer I can't identify."

"But Johnson made you *feel* guilty." The elevator lurched as it began its descent. "From the way that conversation started, I assumed he must always be a jerk and you were accustomed to blowing him off."

"Usually, I do. But…" Her mood descended right along with the elevator. "I feel out of step here today. Like I don't belong anymore. I don't know the facts of the most important cases. I can't maintain a conversation with people I've worked with for six years. Harold is always going to say something that gets under my skin, but I try to be civil about correcting him for Derek's sake. Yet today, I let him get to me. For a few seconds there, I thought you were going to do what I wanted to."

"Punch him in the mouth?" Gina groaned at his deadpan response. Besides lifting her spirits, the heat of his body standing close to hers was comforting, even though she hated to admit it. She watched as he slid his finger across the brass railing until his pinkie was brushing against hers. She couldn't feel that lightest of touches with her fingertip, but she felt the connection deeper inside. She felt his strength, his easy confidence, his caring. "Have you been back to HQ since the shooting?" he asked.

"Only to sign my incident report and fill out some insurance forms in the administrative offices. A few of the guys stopped by the hospital to see how I was doing. But I haven't done much to keep in touch since then. I've just been so focused…" She looked down at their hands, studying the differences in size and strength, the contrasts of male and female, the olive sheen of her skin next to his paler color. Mike Cutler was different from any man she'd ever taken the time to get to know. Not just on the outside. Somehow, her physical therapist had become her friend. A good friend. Her savior had become a trusted confidant who'd seen her at her worst and motivated her to be her best. He was honest and funny and strong in ways that went beyond his obvious athleticism. "I used to go toe-to-toe with those guys. Today, I feel like a rookie. Like I have to prove myself all over again just to keep my badge."

His pinkie brushed over the top of hers and hooked

between her fingers, holding on in the subtlest of ways and deepening the connection she felt. "I bet there's not a one of those guys who could handle what you've been through and come back the way you are."

"They're KCPD's best."

"They're men. Men are terrible patients."

"I'm a terrible patient," she admitted.

"Yeah, but you're cute." Mike's voice had dropped to a husky timbre that skittered along her spine.

"*Cute?* No one has ever called me *cute*. Except maybe Harold Johnson." Although she'd never developed her flirting skills the way her sister had, Gina could hear the huskier notes in her own voice. "Strong. Stubborn. Temperamental. But not *cute*."

"I figured you'd punch me if I called you *sexy* or *built like a fine piece of art*. And I don't want you to injure that arm."

Gina felt herself blushing for the second time that day. But with an infusion of Mike's humor and compassion and that delicious heat she craved, she could also feel her strength coming back. "Stick with *cute*, Choir Boy. That may be the best I can do for a while."

"I'll take that bet." Mike slipped his broad hand beneath her smaller one, turning his palm up to meet hers. "Squeeze my hand. Hard as you can."

Gina straightened at the challenge. "Another exercise?"

"I'm warming you up for the shooting range. Just hold on to me." Her thumb and forefinger easily latched on, but she had to concentrate to move the other fingers. She wasn't sure if it was simple gravity or her own effort, but the last three fingers trembled into place, curling against the side of his hand. When she would have pulled away, he tightened his hand around hers. "Do you feel that?"

"I feel the heat coming off your skin." His grip pulsed around hers. Gina straightened as a renewed sense of hope surged through her. "I felt that." His deep blue eyes were watching her excitement, smiling. So was she. "Does that mean I'm getting the sensation back in my fingers? Am I improving?"

He squeezed her hand again. "Baby steps, Gina. I saw you writing with that pen. Picked it up without hesitation. That's definite improvement."

A dose of reality tempered her enthusiasm. "A gun is going to be a lot heavier than a pen. Losing control of a weapon is far more serious than making a scribble on a page."

One by one, Mike laced his fingers between hers. "My money's on you, Tiger."

He raised her hand to his lips and kissed her knuckles. She gasped at the surprising tickle of his beard stubble brushing across her skin. Were her nerves finding new pathways to bring sensation back to her hand? Or was that flush of warmth heating her blood a sign that Mike was starting to mean more to her than just a friend?

Gina knew the strangest urge to stretch up on her tiptoes and feel the ticklish sensation of his lips on her own. The elevator jostled them as it slowed its descent, and the tiny shake reminded Gina that this man was all kinds of wrong for her. Any relationship was, at this point in her life. But she could appreciate his friendship and support. "You didn't have to defend me against Derek's dad."

"Maybe I was protecting him from you."

A long-absent smile relaxed her lips as she leaned back, letting her shoulder rest against his arm. "You're a good man, Mike Cutler."

He shrugged. "It's what nice guys do."

Chapter Seven

The following Monday afternoon, Gina was back in training. After her regular session at the CAPT clinic, Mike took her back to the Precinct offices for another round at the shooting range. He was a taskmaster, and she loved the challenges he set up for her. Running. Light weights. Flexibility. Although she still didn't believe they had much in common beyond these sessions, she enjoyed the time they were spending together—Mike the physical therapist putting her through her paces, Mike the friend making her laugh, Mike the protector watching her every move to make sure she didn't injure herself, even as he pushed her to do more.

Today, her hard work and his patience were going to pay off. She was going to shoot her gun, instead of merely manipulating the weapon as she had during last week's session. This time Mike was giving her a baseline test to see how much progress she was making toward returning to active duty.

Other than the officer manning the door to the shooting range, she and Mike were alone and could take their time going through the dexterity exercises they'd practiced last week. She cleared and unloaded, then reloaded her gun twice—once using both hands, and a second time that took several frustrating minutes, while

Mike held her left hand down on the counter, forcing her to do more of the work with her right. Now, with their noise-cancelling headphones hanging around their necks, Mike picked up her service weapon.

"You're sure you know what you're doing?" she asked. "It's loaded today."

With an efficiency she envied and respected, he demonstrated that he knew exactly what to do with a Glock 9 mil. "I'm the son of a cop and grew up with guns in the house. Dad always made sure my brother and I knew gun safety and how to handle a weapon."

She put on her ear protection when he did and stepped to the side of the booth as he fired off five rounds. And, if she wasn't mistaken at this distance, he placed all but one of the bullets center mass of the target.

"Show-off," she teased, when he caught her staring in openmouthed admiration.

He grinned, unloading the Glock and setting the gun and magazine on the counter. "Your turn."

He pulled her in front of him, in that protective stance that surrounded her with his warmth. But this wasn't an embrace. It was a physical therapist supporting his patient. She needed to focus on her physical training.

Still, it was hard to miss the intimacy of their positions when her hip brushed against his thigh and his arm reached around her to tap the weapon. "I don't want you to fire any rounds yet. Let's practice raising and aiming the weapon."

Before last week, Gina hadn't handled her weapon since an embarrassing fiasco shortly after she returned home from the hospital. She'd thought she could suit up like any ordinary day and resume the chaos of her life without missing another step. But the heavy Glock had slipped from her grip and bounced across her bedroom floor. Thank goodness the safety had been on. That humbling morning when she realized that all of her cop armor, both figurative and literal, had been stripped away from her by a gunshot was the day she started her determined journey to return to the job and to the protector and provider her family needed her to be.

Realizing the extent of her impediment had been a shock to her sense of self that morning. Today, she knew better than to expect a miracle. But she didn't intend to humiliate herself, either.

She'd ask for a little backup before she put her hand on that weapon again. Crossing her fingers, she raised them to her lips before brushing them across her heart.

"You superstitious?" Mike asked.

"It doesn't hurt to ask for a little luck before doing something new or difficult." She closed her thumb and finger around the grip of the gun before wrapping her left hand around that to seal her grip.

Feeling a gentle pressure at the crown of her hair, Gina paused before lifting the weapon.

"For luck." Mike's gentle kiss and the husky tremor of his deep voice vibrated across her skin and eardrums, seeping inside her like the warmth of his body. Any trepidation she felt was under control, thanks to the support of this unexpected ally. "Let's do this."

She raised the weapon, tilting her head slightly to line up the sight and aim it at the paper target at the end of the firing lane. The gun dipped slightly when she moved her finger to the trigger guard, but she stabilized it with her left hand. The gun clicked when she pulled the trigger.

"Again," Mike instructed, sliding his hand beneath her elbow to steady her arm.

Gina aimed the empty weapon. *Click.*

"Again. Control it."

Click.

"Now use your left hand just to steady it, not to keep your fingers on the grip." Her right hand shook as she made the adjustment. Mike's fingers stroked along her arm as he pulled away. "This one's all you."

Gina pressed her lips together, willing her grip to remain fixed as she took the whole weight of the weapon on her own. "Bang."

Steady. Her strength hadn't flagged.

"There you go." Mike praised her, setting the new clip of bullets on the counter. "Clear it and load it while I bring up a new target."

With Mike's hand at her shoulder to support the extra kickback of firing real ammo, Gina took aim at the target and fired off six shots. By the fourth bullet, she could feel the strain in her shoulder. By the sixth one, her hands were shaking.

"Easy," Mike warned, catching her right arm beneath the elbow to control the weapon as her hands slumped down to the counter.

But she kept hold of the gun, kept it pointed safely away from them. She batted his helpful fingers away to expel the magazine and clear the firing chamber herself before setting the gun aside. Gina exhaled an elated sigh as she pulled off her earphones. "I did it."

"That you did." Mike's hand settled at her hip, his long fingers slipping beneath her jacket, spanning her waist with a familiar ease while he nudged her to one side to secure the Glock. Whether casually or with a purpose, he touched her often, as if he had the right to do so, and she wasn't complaining. "Have you considered using a lighter weapon?"

She shook her head as she removed her goggles and set them on the shelf beneath the counter. "I need one with stopping power." When she straightened, she asked, "So how did I do? I was six for six, center mass before I was injured."

Mike laughed as he pushed the button to bring the target up to the counter. "Give me a minute to check, Annie Oakley."

"I could learn to shoot left-handed if I have to."

But Mike pointed out the challenge in that solution. "How would you steady your grip and secure your aim? It's smarter for the strong to support the weak."

Was that supposed to be a metaphor? That he was strong and she was weak? Or that he believed she had the strength to overcome this setback? Mike was too nice a guy to give her a veiled put-down, so she chose to believe the latter.

Mike stowed his earphones, his body brushing against hers in the tight quarters of the booth. This was crazy, this distracted feeling she got whenever Mike was around. From the first moment she'd seen his long, powerful stride eating up the sidewalk on his afternoon run, there'd been something about him that pulled her attention away from the laser-sharp focus that had ruled most of her life. He was still a little too Dudley Do-Right compared to her streetwise bad girl persona for her to think they'd have any chance at making a relationship work—or even surviving a regular date. But she couldn't deny that he'd been a solid and dependable teammate since he'd taken over her recovery program. And for a woman who'd had very little *solid and dependable* in her life, Mike Cutler seemed an awful lot like that dream of peace and space and security she'd been chasing for so long.

She could count the individual holes in the target

before it stopped in front of them, and some of her excitement waned. "I'm not six for six, anymore, am I?"

There was one hole right through the heart, the ultimate target for stopping a perp when cops fired their weapons. There were two more holes in the stomach area, two more in the left thigh and one completely off the map beneath the target's elbow. But the goal was to stop the assailant when threatened, not just to slow him down or give him a bellyache.

"At least they're all on the paper, and you didn't put a bullet in me or you." His humor eased some of her disappointment.

"You're right. Seven weeks ago, I couldn't even hold that gun." She tilted her gaze to Mike's clear blue eyes, his optimism feeding her own. "I am getting better. I just have to be patient."

"*Patient?* I didn't know that word was in your vocabulary."

"Ha. Ha. After all my hard work—*our* hard work—" she admitted, "I feel like celebrating."

"Celebrating?"

Gina reached up to stroke her fingertips along the chiseled line of his jaw, her hormones enjoying the perfect blend of ticklish stubble and warm skin. His eyes darkened to a deep cobalt at her touch. "Catnip." He shook his head slightly, his lips thinning into a smile. But before that smile fully formed, Gina's fingers were there, tracing the supple, masculine arc of his mouth. She heard a low-pitched rumble in his throat. Or maybe that visceral sound was coming from her. "Thank you."

She was stretching up on tiptoe as his mouth was coming down to meet hers. His lips closed over hers, and Gina slipped her left hand behind his neck, holding on as they dueled for control of the kiss. She delighted in the rasp of his beard against her softer skin as his mouth traveled leisurely across hers, pausing to nip at her bottom lip. When she mewed at the tingling stab of heat warming her blood, he grazed his tongue across the sensitive spot, soothing the sting of the gentle assault. But *leisurely* was frustrating, and *gentle* only made her hungry for something more.

When his tongue teased the curve of her mouth again, Gina parted her lips and thrust her tongue out to meet and dance with his. She slipped her right hand up around his neck as well, her sensitive thumb and finger learning the crisp edge of his short hair. When his fingers tunneled into her hair to press against her scalp and angle her mouth more fully against his, she didn't protest. When her hips hit the countertop and Mike's thighs trapped her there, she reveled in the feel of him surrounding her, consuming her. He tasted of rich coffee and man and desire, and Gina demanded the liberty to explore his mouth and learn his textures and delight in the chemistry firing between them.

"I like the way you celebrate," Mike growled against her lips before slipping his hands beneath her denim jacket to skim the length of her back and the curve of each hip through the cotton of her blouse. When his thumbs spanned her rib cage to catch beneath her breasts and tease the subtle swell there, she moaned in a mix of pleasure and frustration. What would it be like to feel his hands on her bare skin? To eliminate the barriers of clothing that kept her from touching him?

But even as she clutched at his shoulders, relishing the rare satisfaction of feeling warmth in every part of her body, from her taut, aching breasts to the tips of her toes, she knew this was a mistake. This kiss was moving too fast. Moving them in the wrong direction.

Changing their relationship and jeopardizing every goal on her life list. "Mike…"

She made a token effort to push him away and ended up curling her fingers into the front of his polo shirt, latching on to the skin and muscle underneath.

"Tell me what *catnip* means." He reclaimed her mouth.

She helplessly answered his kiss.

"Hey, G. You in here?" A familiar voice shouted from the doorway, followed by the noise of heavy boots and other voices.

Gina shoved Mike back, abruptly ending the kiss. Even as his hands closed around her hips to steady her, she was twisting from his grasp.

"Gina?" Although he must hear the footsteps approaching, too, Mike's hoarse, throaty whisper demanded an explanation. Did he want an apology for cutting short that ill-advised make-out session? A reassurance that she had no regrets the kiss had happened? She wasn't sure what her honest answer would be. He tugged her jacket back into place and smoothed the wrinkles she'd made in the front of his shirt. "I get that the timing sucks, but we need to talk about this."

"What *this*? There is no *this*." With the walls of the booth granting them a few precious seconds of privacy, Gina wiped her copper lip gloss from his mouth, regretting the defined line her hasty withdrawal had put there. She swiped her knuckles across her own mouth, willing the nerve endings that were still firing with the magnetic need to reconnect with his lips to be still. "You're not my…" Boyfriend? Temptation? Best decision? He had to understand that she'd never meant her thank-you kiss to go that far. "I have to focus on me right now. On taking care of my family. I—"

He cut her off with a tilt of his head, warning her that they were no longer alone.

"There you are." Derek appeared around the corner of the booth. His gaze glanced off Mike and landed on her, his eyes narrowed as if he suspected something more than firing a gun had happened here. "Everything okay?"

"Of course," she answered a little too quickly. Although she could feel Mike's blue eyes drilling a hole through her, Derek seemed to buy it. She needed to change the subject before she admitted something she might never want to. "What are you doing here? Did you get things straightened out with your dad last week?"

"Yeah. He had another harebrained scheme to make easy money. I told him to stick with restoring the junk he finds in the scrapyard. I talked some sense into him. Sorry that he was being such a jerk." Grinning, he rattled on. "I heard you were down here, training with the captain's son. Brought you a surprise."

"A surprise?" she echoed.

Derek stepped aside to usher two other men, dressed in their distinct black SWAT uniforms, over to join them. "She's here, guys."

Mike moved out of the booth as a compactly built man with black hair joined them. Alex Taylor, one of her SWAT team trainers, grinned. "Hey, Galvan, we heard you were on the premises. Thought we'd stop in and say hi, see how you're doing."

As he stepped aside, another SWAT officer appeared. Despite the blond man's intimidating facade, she knew Trip Jones was a gentle giant until he went into SWAT mode. And then he was all serious business. His big hand swallowed up hers in a light grip as he smiled. "Look what the cat dragged in. Good to see you without the sling and hospital gown."

"Good to be seen. Thanks."

By the time she'd stepped out of the booth to join the minireunion, Alex was shaking hands with Mike. "Michael Cutler Jr. How'd you get involved with this fireball?"

"I'm her physical therapist." Apparently, Mike *did* know everybody at KCPD. Although the tension from that kiss and the guilt she felt at ending it so quickly still vibrated through her, making it difficult to think of what to say to these men she hoped to serve with one day, Mike didn't seem to have any problem joking with them as equals. "We're getting her back into fighting form."

"Don't do too good a job," Alex teased, including Gina in his smile. He swatted the big man beside him. "Trip's been practicing that takedown maneuver you used on him in training so you can't knock him over again."

Trip gave the teasing right back. "I stumbled over her. Didn't see her down there. Same problem I have when I'm sparring with you, Shrimp."

"You know I can take you out at the knees," Alex challenged.

Trip didn't bat an eye. "You know I can take you out, period."

Mike and Derek laughed, although both responses seemed forced to her. Mike wasn't in a laughing mood, and Derek was trying too hard to fit in as one of the team.

Gina inhaled a deep breath, determined to be a part of this camaraderie the men all seemed to share. "How do you all know Mike? Captain Cutler's summer barbecues?"

Trip splayed his hands at his waist, considering the answer. "Well, let's see. We first met when that creep had a bomb at Jillian's clinic. SWAT Team One was deployed, and Mikey here got up out of his wheelchair to get us inside to defuse the situation."

"Bomb?" Derek asked.

Gina looked up at Mike. "Wheelchair?"

She felt the sharp dismissal of Mike's blue eyes. He'd claimed she didn't know him, that he'd chosen to embrace his nice-guy persona *despite* his background, not because of it. What had confined him to a wheelchair and put him in the middle of a Bravo-Tango, or bomb threat?

Alex snapped his fingers. "No, wait. It was before that. We had to clear a building in No-Man's Land. Remember? There were a couple of druggies, and we were off the clock, but the captain called us in." Alex swatted Mike's arm. "You and Troy were outside in Captain Cutler's truck. Hey, how is Troy, anyway? The new business taking off for you two?"

"We could use a few more patients," Mike confessed, ignoring her silent questions. "As Gina pointed out to me—we didn't exactly set up shop in the most profitable part of the city. But we're making do. We'll turn the corner soon."

While they chatted, Derek stepped into the booth to pick up the discarded target paper on the floor. He let out a low whistle of appreciation. "Whoa, G. Is this your score? Looks like you're ready to come back to work."

"No. That's Mike's." Swallowing her pride in front of her peers, she pointed to the mutilated paper still hanging in the firing lane. "That guy's mine."

"Oh." Derek was at a loss for words. Alex covered the awkward moment with a cough.

Trip Jones, ever the practical one, stated the obvious. "You're going to have to do better than that to make SWAT."

Mike interrupted before she could acknowledge that she knew that score probably wouldn't qualify her to wear a sidearm for even regular duty. "Gina's improving every day. This is only her second time on the shooting range. Give it a couple more weeks and she'll be beating your scores."

"No doubt." Alex smiled, and Gina's spirits lifted a little. "This woman can do anything she puts her mind to."

Trip extended his hand to shake Mike's, bringing the brief reunion to an end. "You do good work, Mikey." He glanced down at Gina. "Heal fast," Trip said with an encouraging smile. "We need more good cops like you."

The door to the shooting range swung open at the same time as the radios clipped to Alex's and Trip's shoulders crackled to life.

"Taylor. Trip." SWAT Team Captain Michael Cutler strode across the room, the clip of authority in his tone and demeanor making Gina snap to attention. "Time to roll. We need to clear a neighborhood. Armed suspect at large."

"Yes, sir." Alex and Trip muted the same information coming over their radios, nodded their goodbyes and jogged from the room, heading toward the Precinct garage, where their SWAT van was located.

"You're the one I've been looking for, Johnson. Why aren't you at your desk?"

Derek pulled his shoulders back, too, at the direct address. "I was just heading up when I ran into Alex and Trip in the locker room."

"You're up to do a trainee ride on this call. You want to join us?"

"Definitely."

Gina's hand fisted with the same anticipation charging through Derek's posture.

"Gear up on the van. We're leaving as soon as I get there. This is an observation opportunity only," the captain reminded him. "You stay behind the front lines unless I tell you otherwise. Understood?"

"Yes, sir." Derek jogged off after the others, and the impulse to follow the action jolted through Gina's legs.

The older man backed toward the door. "Gina. Son."

Gina took half a step after him. "Any chance I'll get the opportunity to ride on a call with you again, sir? Keep my tactics skills fresh?"

Captain Cutler halted, his face lined with an apology. "I'm sorry, but you're a liability right now. Until you're declared fit for duty…"

"I understand." She nodded toward the door. "I'll let you go."

Mike's fingers curled around hers, down at her side between them. Holding her back from embarrassing herself? Or comforting her obvious disappointment over yet another reminder that right now she wasn't good enough? "What's up?" Mike asked.

The captain's pointed gaze landed on her, sending a silent message. "Somebody shot another cop. Frank McBride."

Gina's blood ran cold. First Colin Cho was shot. Then she and Derek were hit. And now this? With each incident, the injuries had grown more severe. "Is Frank…?"

"Ambulance is on the scene. No report yet."

"Go." The urgency of Mike's command matched her own sentiment. "Keep us posted. And be safe."

Captain Cutler's expression was grim as he hurried out behind his men.

Three assaults on police officers since the beginning of the year. Gina drew her hand away from Mike's, pacing several steps toward the door, needing to do something more than accept his comfort. She should be out there, protecting her brethren on the police force.

"Who's shooting cops?" she wondered out loud.

"I don't know," Mike answered. "But it sounds to me like KCPD is under attack."

Chapter Eight

"Could these incidents be related?" Mike speculated on the phone with his father. "They're all Kansas City cops."

His visit with Gina to the KCPD shooting range had stretched into the evening as they waited at headquarters for word on the injured officer. Once the news that Frank McBride had come out of surgery in fair condition, triggering a collective sigh around the Precinct offices, she'd agreed to let him drive her home. Troy would escort Frannie to her car and lock up the clinic, freeing Mike to stay with Gina. Now the city lights were coming on and streets were clogging with rush-hour traffic as the sun warmed into a glowing orange ball in the western sky. And though he hadn't followed his father's footsteps into the police force, Mike was just as eager as the woman sitting across from him in the cab of his truck to find out who the shooter might be and put a stop to these crimes against cops.

Gina leaned against the center console, following his half of the conversation. "Not just KCPD," she whispered. "The victims—Cho, Derek, McBride and me—we're all candidates for the new SWAT team."

Michael Sr. continued. "It sure feels personal to me. Every person hit since the beginning of the year has been one of the candidates we've been training for the new SWAT team. Maybe he's challenging himself to take down the best of the best."

"Gina was just mentioning that connection."

His dad's voice hushed. "She's with you now?"

Mike slowed for a stoplight. "I'm giving her a ride home."

"Good. I've put my team on alert and am in the process of notifying all the candidates to keep their guards up. Keep an eye on her for me, will you, son? This guy might just be toying with us, taking potshots at random cops. But I'm guessing there's something else at work here we don't understand yet. I'd like to think he can't bring himself to actually kill a cop. But more likely, he's working up his nerve and fine-tuning his MO. Once he's made one kill, he might decide he has a taste for it and come back to finish what he started."

The sunset warmed Gina's cheeks as Mike glanced across the seat at her. He didn't have to wonder at the twisting in his gut at the thought of the shooter making another attempt on her life. He had feelings for her. And her giving him the cold shoulder after that kiss wasn't making them go away. "Thanks for the update, Dad. Give Frank and Mrs. McBride my best."

Mike disconnected the call and placed the phone in the cup holder in the center console. "Dad noticed the same thing you did. The victims aren't just cops, they're all SWAT contenders."

She sat back in her seat with a deep sigh, giving him a rare glimpse of fatigue. "That has to be a coincidence. We're all uniformed officers. We haven't earned our SWAT caps and vests yet, so there's no way to distinguish us from anyone else at KCPD. How would this guy know?"

Mike shrugged as the light changed. He could think of several possibilities. "What about the car you've seen following you? Could be he's staked out the training center or Precinct headquarters. Maybe he's in the crowd when you go on observation calls with SWAT Team One and has seen you in action. Or he's hacked the KCPD computer system? There are a lot of ways he could get that information."

She grunted a sound that could have been a reluctant laugh. "You're not making me feel better."

"I'm not trying to. You're not the only one who wants to nail this guy and put a stop to the assaults on cops. It's personal to me, too."

Reaching across the center console, she patted his arm, as if she thought *he* needed comforting. "Your dad is too high-profile of a police officer. A highly trained veteran, to boot. I'm sure the perp wouldn't go after him."

Unless a high-profile officer like his father *was* the ultimate target, and Gina, Derek and the others were a diversion to make KCPD think the attacker was hunting cops, in general, and not a specific target. Mike captured her hand against the warmth of his thigh. "I hate to think of someone hurting you as simple target practice until he works up the nerve or the skill to make an actual kill shot."

Gina pulled her small, supple hand from his, as if even that small intimacy made her as uncomfortable as that kiss they'd shared. At least she wasn't discounting the attraction simmering between them, but she sure as hell didn't want to be feeling that way about him. Or maybe the aversion to the growing closeness was about something else. Bad luck with relationships. No interest in relationships. Or maybe the vulnerability that naturally arose when two people cared for each other was the thing she wanted to avoid.

The petite beauty studiously ignoring Mike was turning out to be as complex a mystery as the recent spate of attacks they both wanted to solve.

She pointed out the next intersection where he needed to turn and watched out the window as they entered the older neighborhood. The street narrowed and the houses got closer together and more run-down. The arching maple trees littered the small yards and sidewalks with their messy buds as leaves started to sprout. Gina shivered, and Mike discreetly turned on the truck's heater, although he suspected it was something mental, not physical, that had given her that chill.

Just as he thought they might reach her house in silence, Gina spoke again. "If the other incidents have all been a misdirection to throw the investigators off track, then who's his real target? Or if he just hates cops, why hasn't he killed any of us?"

"Thank God for that small favor."

"Seriously. Is it ineptitude? Is he toying with us?" Her shoulders lifted with a deep breath as she continued to speculate about the possibilities. "What if this has nothing to do with us being cops at all? What if it's something personal—that there's something besides a badge that connects all four victims? Or they're not connected at all? What if he's going after cops to make us think it's the uniform he's targeting and not a specific individual? How do we figure out who to warn? Who to protect?"

"Right now, we protect you."

"I can take care of myself."

"Right. While you're busy trying to find answers to these attacks, taking care of your family, vying to make the new SWAT team, and, oh, yeah—healing—you really think you have the capacity to watch your back, as well?"

She shook her head, stirring her dark hair around her face. "*Not* my bodyguard, Choir Boy."

Mike exhaled an irritated sigh. "That tough-chick shtick is getting pretty old."

"Look around you." She nodded toward the trio of young men hanging around a jacked-up car. "I have to be tough."

The young men, smoking cigarettes, all wore ball caps with the same telltale color underneath the brim, labeling them as gang members rather than a baseball team. Their souped-up car and air of conceit reminded Mike of his dangerous forays into No-Man's Land half a lifetime ago, when he'd sought out teens like that, instead of hanging with his true friends. He hoped it wouldn't take a tragedy like the ones he'd faced to convince them to make better choices and see the hope in their future. If Gina was the real target, and the other assaults were planned diversions, could the real threat be from someone close to home, like these guys?

"Gangbangers," Gina pointed out unnecessarily. She waved as they passed. Two of the boys waved back. One flipped them off.

Mike's hands fisted around the steering wheel as he remembered the faceless driver who'd pantomimed shooting Gina that morning outside the physical therapy clinic. "I assume they know you're a cop?"

"Uh-huh." He noticed her good hand fisting in her lap, too. "The one with the rude salute is in my sister's high-school class. My brother used to run with the other two. They're low-level members of the Westside Warriors, more bark than any real bite. I doubt they'll try anything unless their captain gives them the order to do so."

"Are they a threat to your brother or sister?"

"Not them." But someone else was? Gina's mouth twisted with a wry smile. "Can you see why I need that promotion at KCPD? It's so I can get my family out of this place."

Mike didn't have any platitude to offer. This *was* a dangerous part of the city. But it hurt to see that brave tilt of her chin and how all her responsibilities and the danger surrounding her day and night changed her posture. If he could make that smile a genuine one, for a moment, at least, he'd feel as though he was easing her burden. "And here I thought you just wanted a private bathtub."

Her dark eyes snapped to his before he heard the laughter bubbling up from her throat. "I'm a very serious woman with a very serious set of troubles. I don't have time for laughing with you."

Mike grinned. Fortunately, she'd said *with* him and not *at* him. "That's officially part of my recovery prescription for you. Laughing at least once a day."

She settled back into her seat and pointed out the window. "Turn here. It's the brick house with white trim and black shutters in the next block."

Mike spotted a row of three small houses whose owners seemed determined to maintain a clean, respectable appearance. The lawns were greening up, and there was a lack of junk or old cars sitting on the grass or at the curb. Gina's home was the one in the middle.

But the respite from worry and wariness was short-lived. "Did Captain Cutler say anything else about today's shooting?" she asked.

Mike nodded. "SWAT One did a building-to-building

search in that block. Stopped traffic and checked vehicles. No sign of him."

"Any leads?"

Obliquely, Mike wondered if Gina had ever considered aiming for her detective's badge rather than SWAT. Although he suspected, with her position as the major breadwinner for her family, she didn't have a college degree yet, a prerequisite for becoming a detective. However, she was a natural at asking questions and observing the world around her. "It was an ambush from an unidentified vehicle, just like with you and Derek. McBride was answering a call on a fight at a bar and grill downtown. Not far from Precinct HQ. Still, the shooter was gone before backup got there."

"No description of the shooter or vehicle either, I bet."

"The only witnesses were a drunk still sobering up from last night and the bouncer. He was busy breaking up the fight. The two perps, of course."

When there was no empty spot to pull up in front of the house, Gina pointed him into the driveway. "Any bystanders hurt?"

Mike pulled his truck up to the garage door. "The only casualty was Officer McBride. Looks like the man in uniform was specifically targeted."

Unhooking her seat belt, Gina sat forward, facing him. "Wait a minute. Was the incident at the Sin City Bar and Grill?"

"Yeah. How'd you know?"

She pounded her fist on the console. "That's the bar where the bikers we chased away from the Bismarck house allegedly went before Derek and I were shot. I'd love to talk to the patrons there. See if the Bismarck brothers and their buddies were there today—maybe even part of that fight. They don't like cops. Maybe the whole fight was staged."

"How would they know Frank McBride would respond?"

"Maybe the guy was willing to shoot at any cop who responded to the call. Or maybe he scouted the place out and knew that was Frank's beat." Her voice trailed away as she thought out loud. "Did he know the streets Derek and I patrolled? Or Colin Cho?" She was in full voice again as she turned to the door. "I need to see if anyone's followed up on this."

She tugged on the door handle and muttered a curse in Spanish when her recovering hand didn't cooperate quickly enough.

Mike caught her left wrist before she could reach across to open the door with both hands. "I know what you're thinking."

She tugged on his grip. "No, you don't."

Mike tightened his hold on her. "You aren't talking about making a phone call. You're planning on going to the bar yourself to investigate. Not tonight. You're home. You're staying put."

The tension left her arm and she smiled for a split second before forcing her right hand to fumble with the handle. "You're not the only means of transportation available to me. I can call a cab."

"The bar will either be closed or the cops investigating the shooting will have already talked to everyone."

"I'd be in the way. No help to anyone. Is that what you're saying?"

"What I'm saying is that it'd be a fool's mission right now. Plus, you need your rest and some dinner because I know you missed lunch."

"Not my nursemaid, Cutler."

"Not your chauffeur—yet here I am driving you. Not your friend—yet I'm the one thinking of your best interests. Not your lover." Her head snapped toward him, her startled eyes wide and dark as midnight. "And yet you kissed me like—"

She jerked her arm from his grasp. "Forget that kiss. I got carried away. I just wanted to thank you."

"A tough chick like you couldn't be interested in a nice guy like me, huh?" Why was he pushing this sore spot? Probably because his heart and ego had been battered one time too many. And a little of that rebel he used to be was getting tired of taking hit after hit. He reached across her, ignoring the clean, citrusy scent coming off her hair and skin, and pushed open the door. "Run if you want. You'll face down anything except what's happening between us."

Gina climbed out and circled around the hood of the pickup. But Mike was there to block her path.

She propped her hands at her hips and tilted her chin to face him. "Fine. Let's hash this out, Choir Boy. Is this where you tell me why you hung out in No-Man's Land as a teenager? Why you were in a wheelchair? Where you prove to me you're not so nice and that the two of us have enough in common to make something work after all?"

An image of his teenage friend Josh's mangled body flashed through Mike's thoughts, followed by the familiar upwelling of guilt he'd known since he was sixteen years old. The grief of his mother's death to cancer had sent him spiraling out of control, and the boozy haze of those wild months had cost him a football scholarship, the use of his legs and his best friend's life.

But the pricks of fear and grief and guilt were manageable now. He could acknowledge those feelings and lock them away before he did damage to anyone else's life. Or he allowed anyone else to be hurt when he could damn well do something about it. Including the stubborn Latina facing off against him. Gina needed to see him as her equal, as a partner who could help her if she'd only let him beneath that proud, protective armor of hers. "Let's just say I made some bad choices after my mother died. I found the solace I needed in No-Man's Land."

That took her aback. The sparks of defensive anger in her eyes sputtered out. "You did drugs? You had a dealer here?"

Alcohol had been his drug of choice. "I had *friends* willing to sell liquor to an underage drinker. I was happy to take them up on the offer. Defied my dad's rules, trashed my chance at a football scholarship, got a friend killed."

Gina's gaze dropped to the middle of his chest as she reassessed her opinion of him. Was she trying to realign her image of Mr. Nice Guy Choir Boy with an out-of-control teen who lived with baggage from No-Man's Land the same way she did? Was the real Mike Cutler someone she could relate to and admire for getting his act together and making amends to the world for his mistakes every day of his life? Or did she now see him as the very kind of thing she was trying to get away from?

But Gina Galvan was nothing if not boldly direct. She tilted her gaze back to his. "How did your mother die? My mother had cancer."

All the no-one-can-hurt-me attitude had left her posture. Her voice warmed with compassion and understanding.

At the balm of that hushed, seductively accented

tone, Mike wanted to reach out to her. He rested his hand on the hood of his truck, mere inches from where her fingers now rested. He stretched out his fingers, brushing the calloused tips against hers. When she feathered her fingers between his to hold on, something eased inside him. There were some understandings that crossed the barriers of backgrounds and economics and skin color. "Cancer. It was long and painful, and I didn't handle it well."

"Is that where you met Troy? Was he in a gang?"

"Nope. But that's where he got shot. In the wrong place at the wrong time during a drive-by shooting in the old neighborhood."

Her fingers danced against his palm, spinning tendrils of warmth, desire and healing into his blood with even that gentlest of connections. "How did you end up in a wheelchair? And why aren't you in one now?"

Gina's persistence would make her a fine detective. But Mike hadn't forgotten where this conversation had started. "If I answer all your questions, will you answer one of mine?"

She held his gaze expectantly, considering his request. Then she pulled her hand away and squared off her shoulders. Even without her flak vest, that woman's armor was locked down tight. "All right. What's your question?"

"Will you go to the Sin City bar on your own tonight after I leave?" She didn't need to say the word *yes*. He could read the guilty truth all over her face. Mike angled his gaze toward the orange glow of sunset on the horizon, shaking his head at the symbolism of his chances of making a relationship work with Gina going down right along with it. He'd better reel in his emotions like the champ here, and settle for finding answers and keeping her safe. "How about I pick you up in the morning and we go to Sin City together after your training session. Somebody should be there setting up by ten. And you won't be stepping on anybody's toes at KCPD then."

"Are you going to park outside my house tonight to make sure I stay put?" She'd barely uttered the flippant accusation before her expression changed. "Oh, my God, you are. You do know a truck this nice could get stripped in this neighborhood."

"I'm not leaving."

"Fine." Her cheeks flushed with irritation that he could be just as stubborn as she. "I promise to wait until you drive me in the morning if you promise to go home and not put yourself in danger because of me."

He couldn't make that deal. Mike planted his feet, tucking his hands into the pockets of his jeans and standing fast. If she was going into a dangerous situation, then he wasn't letting her do it alone.

"I'm going inside." She nudged his shoulder brushing past him, and Mike turned to follow her to the porch. "What are you doing?"

"Making sure you get inside safely."

"Nothing's going to happen to me between the curb and the front door."

He waited for the import of what she'd just said to sink in. A quick glance out to the street and he knew she was reliving the day she'd been shot. That short distance between the safety of her police cruiser and Vicki Bismarck's front door was exactly where she'd gotten hurt.

One look at the color leaving her cheeks and Mike turned her to the front door of her own home, sliding his fingers beneath the hem of her jacket and resting a supportive hand at the small of her back. He scanned up and down the block and through the neighboring yards, ensuring they were safe before nudging her forward. "Indulge a nice guy the manners his mama taught him, okay?"

Gina shivered at the polite touch but fell into step beside him as they climbed the single step onto the porch. "And here you are insisting over and over that you aren't so nice. Which Mike Cutler am I supposed to believe?"

"Both." Mike was grinning as they reached the door.

Gina pulled her keys from her pocket, but the door swung open before she could insert them into the lock.

A portly man with a strip of gray hair circling from his temples to the back of his head leaned heavily on his walker as he backed out of the doorway. "Gina, *la niña*. You are so late. We were getting worried." The elderly man raised his dark gaze to Mike. "You bring us a friend?"

"Tio Papi." Gina stepped inside to kiss the man's pudgy cheek while Mike waited in the doorway. A tiny woman with snow white hair that curled like Gina's dark mane tottered up behind the man, drying her hands on a dish towel. She gently chastised Gina's tardiness in Spanish before the two women exchanged a hug. Keeping her arm around the older woman's waist, Gina made the introductions. "This is Mike Cutler. My great-uncle, Rollo Molina. My great-aunt, Lupe."

Mike nodded a smile to each. "Ma'am. Sir."

"*The* Mike Cutler?" In addition to being overweight, Rollo Molina was a tad sallow-skinned. The man must be struggling with circulation or heart issues. But that didn't stop him from grinning from ear to ear and extending his beefy hand. "I like to meet the man who saved my girl's life. Now you see her every day. More than we do. We worry, but not when she's with you."

Mike accepted the vigorous handshake. "She's mentioned me, huh?" Why did that surprise him? More importantly, why did knowing that she'd talked about him with her family fill him with a warmth and sense of connection that eased the lingering sharpness of that argument they'd had outside? Gina's dark eyes bored into his, as if daring him to make something out of knowing she thought enough of him to tell her family about him. Oh, he was making something of it, all right. He'd been recognized as *"The* Mike Cutler," so she must have done more than simply mention his name. Mike winked at Gina. "I imagine she's a hard one to keep track of."

Rollo laughed, pulling Mike into the entryway and shutting the door behind him. "She has a mind of her own, *sí*?"

"Yes, she does."

Those dark eyes rolled heavenward. "Tio Papi…"

Gina started to explain something, but diminutive Lupe, a good three to four inches shorter than her greatniece, pushed past Gina to stand in front of Mike. She grabbed hold of his forearm, her body swaying slightly as she tilted her head back to study him through narrowed dark eyes. "You are Gina's friend? The young man who makes her well?" She tugged on the sleeve of Mike's jacket and he instinctively grasped her shoulders to steady her balance. "*¡Dios mio!* You are so tall. Your eyes are so *azul*, er, blue. Very handsome."

Mike glanced past her to Gina. *She* was the one blushing at her great-aunt's compliments. "Tia Mami… Mike was giving me a ride home. He can't stay."

"He doesn't eat dinner?" The fragile woman's grip on his arm tightened as if he'd imagined Lupe's balance issues. "I made chicken pozole soup. I put on a fresh pot of decaf coffee. And I have cheesecake empanadas for dessert. You like empanadas?"

"Yes, ma'am. But I don't want to intrude—"

"Come in, come in. You join us." A twenty-something man with a curling black ponytail strolled out of the kitchen, munching on an empanada. With her fingers latched on to the sleeve of Mike's jacket, Lupe pulled him past Gina and Rollo to swat the young man's arm. "Javi, those are for dessert."

"I'm hungry," he whined around the doughy sweetness in his mouth. "Who's the big dude?"

"This is Gina's friend, Mike."

He glanced up, then down at the white-haired woman. "*The* Mike Cutler?"

"My brother, Javier," Gina explained. "Where's Sylvie?"

"Yo, Mike."

Mike chuckled. "Yo."

Javier stuffed the last bite into his mouth and looked to his sister. "She's out."

Gina came up beside Mike, tension radiating from her posture. "Out as in running an errand? Or…out?"

Between Javier's darting glance at his great-aunt and Rollo's weary sigh as he shut the door, Mike could guess that, wherever Sylvie Galvan had gone, it didn't meet with the family's approval. Gina pulled out her cell phone. "Maybe I should go," Mike offered.

"Put that away." Lupe touched Gina's phone. "We have a guest. Sylvie makes her choices. She can eat without us." Then she shooed her great-nephew out of her path. "Go wash up. You need good food before you go to work. Not sweets." When she looped her arm through Mike's and pulled him into the kitchen, he re-thought his first impression that she was a fragile grandmother. Lupe Molina ran this home in a way that made it easy to see why Gina was such a determined woman.

"Tia Mami—"

"Senora Molina, really, you don't have to—"

"You saved my Gina's life." Lupe patted a chair at one side of a rectangular white table. "You sit. I feed."

Short of wrestling all one hundred pounds of the elderly woman out of his way, Mike had no choice but to do as she asked.

Once he took a seat as the honored guest, Lupe bustled around the kitchen. By the time she'd set an extra place setting and the fragrant, steaming food was on the table, Rollo, Javier and Gina had joined them.

Mike enjoyed Gina's family as much as he enjoyed the spicy, hearty soup. Although his understanding of Spanish was limited to the classes he'd taken back in high school, he had little trouble following the mix of English and Spanish and the teasing, loving conversation. Lupe and Rollo were animated and charming. Javier was interested in Mike's truck and Chiefs football. Gina was quiet in the chair beside him and, though Mike suspected that wasn't typical, at least she'd stopped glaring a silent warning that he needed to leave as soon as possible.

If anything, she seemed to be assessing his response to her family and circumstances. He could understand her concern for her family's well-being. He could also understand her devotion to this tightly knit group. Maybe she was chalking up the apparent success of this dinner to him being a nice, polite guy, or maybe she was finally beginning to believe that he was more complex and able to relate to her and her background than she'd given him credit for.

Javier popped a third empanada into his mouth and took off for the bus stop a couple of blocks from the house to get to his job as an overnight custodian at a downtown office building. In between, Mike answered a barrage of questions: no, he wasn't married; yes, his father was the man Gina wanted to work for at KCPD; no, he didn't live with his dad and stepmom and brother; and, yes, he owned his own home off Blue Ridge Boulevard. Yes, he thought Gina was making a good recovery that would get her back on the police force, although he wouldn't promise how long it might take or if he could guarantee her a place on a new SWAT team.

They answered a few of his questions, too. He heard a bit about how Gina, Javier and Sylvie had come to live with their great-aunt and -uncle, and a lot about how proud they were of each of them. Gina had gladly taken on the job of supporting them, in addition to Rollo's pension check. Javi had enrolled in tech classes at one of the city's junior colleges. And Sylvie, who was as pretty as their late mother and prone to being late, was set to graduate from high school in just a couple of months.

Mike was sipping a cup of coffee that was richer and smoother than anything Frannie brewed at work and bemoaning the fact that he'd eaten that second empanada, when he heard the screech of tires braking on the street in front of the house.

He couldn't miss the instant bracing of alarm around the table, or the exchange of worried looks between Rollo and Lupe. Gina shoved her chair away from the table and hurried out of the kitchen.

"Gina," Rollo warned, reaching for his walker.

Mike stood, putting up a cautionary hand to keep the elderly couple in their seats. "I'll keep an eye on her."

The older couple reached for each other's hands across the corner of the table and muttered a prayer as he went after Gina. Not good.

He heard the slam of a car door and raised voices outside and saw Gina's curvy backside storming out the front door. Even worse.

"Gina?" Concern lengthened Mike's stride, and he caught the storm door before it closed in his face.

Ignoring him, Gina stepped off the porch and marched down the walk toward a cream-colored luxury sedan parked catty-cornered across the end of the driveway. Outside the front passenger door of the slick, pricey car, a black-haired man was kissing a young woman with long, curling dark hair.

"Sylvie!" Gina called.

Sylvie? *That* was Gina's younger sister? The ankle boots and mini skirt showed so much leg that he'd question a grown woman wearing that outfit out of the house—much less a teenage girl.

Although the man who'd mimicked shooting Gina outside the clinic had driven a darker tan car, Mike found himself checking the license plate for a familiar 3-6. No match. Different car, different plate number— didn't mean Loverboy there wasn't a threat. And judging by the money invested in that car, he could afford more than one vehicle. "Gina, stop."

She didn't. Mike doubled his pace to catch up to her.

"I'll call you tomorrow," the would-be lothario murmured, looking over the girl's head to note their approach before adding an endearment in Spanish.

The teen pushed away from her adult boyfriend and hurried up the driveway. Although the sun had set and the street's tall maple trees blocked the moonlight, the glare of a nearby streetlamp cast a harsh glow across Sylvie Galvan's pretty face. The streaks of mascara running down her cheeks indicated she'd been crying.

The smudge of violet on her cheek bone hinted that she'd been hurt, too.

Gina noticed the mark, too, and caught her sister by the arms. She looked up into Sylvie's face, brushing the long hair away from the tears and the bruise. "Did he hit you?"

Sylvie sniffled. "I'm fine."

"Tell me what happened."

"Let it go, okay?" Then she tilted her gaze up to Mike. The young woman wiped her nose on a tissue and smiled, dismissing Gina's maternal concern and cop-like probing. "Who's this? You've been holding out on me. I thought you didn't have time for a man." She shrugged off Gina's grasp and circled around her older sister. "Wait. You've only talked about one guy lately—are you Mike Cutler? *The* Mike Cutler?"

"Guilty as charged." He took the hand Sylvie offered, noting the bruises on her wrist that were only slightly smaller than the span of his own fingers before turning her toward the yellowish streetlight to inspect the injury to her face. Although he kept his smile friendly, he was fuming inside. He'd seen marks like that on Frannie, courtesy of her ex, when she'd started working for him. "You hurt anywhere else?"

Sylvie tucked her hands inside the cuffs of her jacket, avoiding his questions, too. "You're cuter than Gina told us."

And Gina was angrier than Mike had ever seen her.

"Bobby Estes!" Gina whirled around and charged at the compact, muscular man in the black leather jacket. She spewed out a stream of Spanish Mike couldn't follow, but he could guess it had something to do with accusation and condemnation.

"Get inside the house," Mike ordered Sylvie before running after Gina. "Go."

When Sylvie started to protest, he glared her toward the front door, throwing out any essence of Mr. Nice Guy and replacing him with the stern taskmaster who wouldn't take no for an answer. With Gina's protective instincts raging like a mama bear protecting her cub, Mike had a sick feeling this confrontation was going to escalate into something a lot more serious than a lovers' quarrel.

The black-haired man leaned against his spotless car, laughing at Gina's approach. "You want a piece of me, Big Sister?"

That's when Mike spotted the telltale bulge beneath Bobby Estes's black leather jacket. Aw, hell. "Gun!"

Gina wisely backed off a step, her hand at her waist where her own weapon had once been. "I see it. Keep your hands where I can see them, Bobby."

While Bobby raised his hands into the air with a smug grin, the situation skipped from bad to worse and went straight to hell when a second man climbed out of the back of the car. He was armed, too. Mike shifted in front of Gina.

Gina shifted right back. "Hands on top of the car," she ordered. "Who's he?"

"A friend," Bobby answered. "I have a lot of friends. They protect me when I need it."

"Protect you from what?"

"People who threaten me?" With a gesture from Bobby, the second man held his position on the far side of the car, but did as she'd commanded, resting his hands on top of the car. "They're jealous of my success, or they want what I have."

Mike's stomach knotted right along with his fists at the obvious taunt.

But Gina kept her cool. "Like my sister? She's not a possession. If you really cared about her you'd leave her alone."

Bobby's arrogant amusement turned smarmy with a purse of his lips. "Maybe she's not the Galvan I want."

"You're using her to get to me?"

"Is it working?" he mocked, brushing his fingers against her hair.

This was a neighborhood power struggle, not a romantic foray. Still, it stuck in Mike's craw that the other man was putting his hands on her. He was already moving forward when Gina grabbed Bobby's wrist and flipped him against the car. "Stay away from Sylvie. Stay away from my family."

"See? Can't keep your hands off me." Bobby laughed. Mike turned his attention to the young man on the far side of the car, who looked more alarmed than amused by the wrestling match.

Gina bent Bobby's arm into the middle of his back, shoving him against the vehicle. That spike of jealousy instantly switched to concern that she would get hurt if this physical altercation escalated any further. "Get in your car and drive away," she warned, twisting his arm. "Lose Sylvie's number. Get out of our lives."

She pinched his wrist tightly enough for Bobby to curse in pain and, suddenly, the joke was over. "*My* neighborhood. *My* girl. Get your damn cop hands off me."

Bobby jerked his hips, knocking Gina back a step. Then he swung back with his free arm, the point of his elbow connecting squarely with her bad shoulder. Gina grunted with pain, grabbing her arm as she stumbled to the sidewalk.

Mike was right there to shove Bobby back against the car, his forearm pressed against the bully's neck as he reached inside the leather jacket to pull the gun from Bobby's belt. "Leave. Now." With the smooth ease his father had taught him, Mike pointed the weapon over the roof of car at his buddy, who was reaching for his own gun. "Put it on the ground."

From the corner of his eye, he saw Gina scrambling to her feet and hurrying around the car to pick up the gun. Was she hurt? How badly? And just how much trouble would he get in if he pressed his arm more tightly against this sleazeball's windpipe?

Once Gina had the weapon trained on the other man and he'd wisely linked his hands over his head in surrender, Mike pulled back the Smith & Wesson pistol he was holding and leaned into Bobby's ruddy, angry face. "You got a license for this?"

"You a cop, white boy?" When Bobby shoved against him, Mike shoved right back.

The tendons in his back and legs strained as he kept the shorter man wedged in place. A zap of electricity shot down his leg as one of the old nerves pinched. Pain gave way to numbness in his right hip and thigh and would eventually settle into a dull, bruising ache if the injuries he'd lived with for more than a decade followed their usual pattern.

Mike gritted his teeth against any discomfort and kept Bobby a prisoner while he watched Gina cover the second man. "You okay?" he asked.

"I'm fine," she ground out, grimacing with the strain of keeping the gun pointed at Bobby's friend. She needed both hands to keep the weapon from shaking, but there was no mistaking the authority in her tone. "Get back in the car. Get in!" The man didn't need a nod from Bobby to obey the order this time. Once he was in the backseat, with his hands out the window as she'd instructed, Gina lowered the weapon and circled around into the driveway again. "Let him go, Mike."

"You're sure?"

"Keep the gun, and let him go."

Bobby was laughing again as Mike released him and stepped beyond his reach. "You sure you can handle Officer Gina?" The neighborhood thug straightened his shirt and jacket as if this had been a civilized encounter. "I know how feisty Sylvie can be. All the Galvan women have fire in them."

"If you're so good at *handling* women, why did you need to hit a teenage girl?"

"Prove that I did." Bobby winked at Gina before circling around the hood and climbing behind the wheel of the car. He leaned toward the open passenger door. "May I have my weapon back, Officer?" When Gina hesitated, he added, "If you arrest me, I'll file assault charges against your boyfriend here."

As far as Mike was concerned, anything he'd done to Estes was justified. Hitting a girl? Assaulting a police officer? But he wasn't the cop here, and he'd defer to however Gina wanted to play this. He was right beside her as she dumped the bullets from each gun into her palm and tossed the empty weapons back into the front seat before Mike closed the door.

"You'll be seeing me again, Gina," he promised before backing out into the street and speeding away.

The car veered around the corner and out of sight before Gina moved again. She stuffed the bullets into her jeans and turned back to the house. "I want to get these to the crime lab. See if they match the bullets from any of the police shootings. Bobby might have been targeting me and using the other incidents as decoys to throw the investigation off track."

Checking one last time to make sure Estes and his buddy stayed gone, Mike followed, wincing at the nerves still sparking through his hip and thigh. A hot shower or a long run would ease the kinks out of those muscles and tone down the minijolts. It had been a lot of years since he'd gotten mixed up in a physical confrontation that twisted his body like that, and he'd be paying for it later.

But he wasn't the only one in pain here. Although Gina was booking it up the driveway, he could hear the soft grunts with every other step and see her rubbing her shoulder.

"Are you all right?" he asked, catching up to her.

"Bruised my shoulder. My fingers are a little tingly. At least I'm feeling them, right? I'll be fine. I want to talk to Sylvie and find out what happened. If she presses charges, I'll serve the warrant on Bobby myself." She jumped onto the porch and reached for the storm door. "Could you drive me to the lab tonight? I don't want to have any issues with chain of custody—"

"Gina. Stop." Mike put a hand on her arm. "Take a breath. Everyone is safe."

"Are they?" Gina whirled around on him, and he spied something he'd never expected to see in her beautiful eyes. Fear. "I couldn't protect my family, Mike. I couldn't defend myself tonight. How the hell am I ever going to be a cop again?"

Chapter Nine

Mike closed the door to Lupe and Rollo's dimly lit room and moved down the hallway toward the bedroom Gina and Sylvie shared. It had been a long night at the Molina house. The family had gone through a second pot of decaf coffee, a phone call to Rollo's doctor, plus lots of tears, terse words and hugs. He peeked through the open doorway to see Sylvie perched on the corner of her daybed, dressed in black-and-gold sweats from her school, while Gina stood behind her, arranging her damp hair into a long braid.

As soon as her dark eyes made contact with his, Sylvie set down the ice pack she'd been holding against her swollen cheek and sprang to her feet. "How is Tio Papi?"

Leaning his shoulder against the doorjamb, Mike crossed his arms, hoping the relaxed stance would ease some of the worry and regret from her young face. "I checked his BP on the monitor again. He's resting comfortably now."

"But his pressure *was* elevated," she confirmed with a woeful sigh. "That's why he got dizzy."

Gina followed behind, winding a rubber band around the end of the braid. "His heart can't take much more of this kind of stress."

"I'm sorry, Gina. I never meant to upset him. Or Tia Mami," Sylvie apologized. "Is she okay?"

Mike nodded. Nothing that a little less worry and a good night's sleep couldn't fix for any eighty-year-old. "I encouraged her to lie down, too. She's getting ready for bed now."

"But she's upset?" Sylvie looked more little girl than woman without the heavy liner and mascara she'd worn earlier.

"Those bruises and guns would scare anyone."

Gina hugged an arm around her sister's shoulders and guided her back to the bed. "Come on. You should rest, too."

"Do we need to call anyone?" Mike asked, knowing Gina had asked Sylvie some pointed personal questions about the nature of her assault while he'd helped their great-aunt and -uncle settle in for the night.

"We're good," Gina assured him, meaning there'd been no sexual assault. She cleared the ice pack and some first-aid supplies off the top of the purple comforter, while Sylvie stacked a rainbow of pillows against the wall. "I think the shower helped, but she hasn't shared many details yet."

Sylvie sat on the bed and reached for Gina's hand, pulling her to a seat beside her. Mike would have excused himself from the private conversation, but Sylvie's eyes filled with tears as she raised her gaze to his. "I love Bobby, but he… His friend Emanuel…"

Since she was including him in this conversation, Mike took a step into the room. "The other guy in the car?"

She nodded. "Emanuel said I was pretty and that he wanted to kiss me. Bobby said I had to let him." Gina's curse echoed the thought going through Mike's mind. "I didn't want to. But Emanuel grabbed me, and Bobby didn't try to stop him. Not at first. He laughed. I slapped Emanuel, and then Bobby…" She touched her cheek, and Mike's hands curled into fists. "He said I'd embarrassed him. That's when they got into an argument. Emanuel said the Lexus was his car, and if Bobby wanted to drive it then I had to… I was a bargaining chip," she sobbed. "I'm worth the price of a stupid car to him."

Gina wrapped her arms around Sylvie, rocking back and forth with her. "You can't see him again. You just can't."

How often had Bobby Estes promised Sylvie's affections in exchange for a fancy car? The image of a tan Mercedes circling around the PT clinic so that the driver could threaten Gina filled his thoughts. "Does Bobby borrow his friends' cars a lot?"

Although Gina shook her head, warning him away from asking questions related to *her* troubles, Sylvie answered, anyway. "Bobby has a different car about every week, I guess."

"Do you remember what he was driving two weeks ago?"

"Mike…" Gina chided. But the phone rang in her pocket, and she pulled away to check the number. "It's Derek calling me back. I need to take this." She wiped the tears from her sister's cheeks before standing and turning toward the door. Mike spotted the hint of moisture sparkling in her own eyes and started to reach for her. "No more questions," she mouthed before putting the phone to her ear and hurrying past him into the living room. "Hey, buddy, where were you? I called a couple of hours ago…Yeah, she's fine—or she will be. I need to ask a big favor…"

With a nod, Mike excused himself, too. "I'll let you get some sleep."

But the teenager popped to her feet. "Will you stay for a while?"

Mike supposed Sylvie didn't want to be alone until her sister returned. "Sure, kiddo."

She plucked a tissue from a box on the dresser and wiped away her tears. "I know Gina tries to be all bad-ass. But I think Bobby scares her. I know he scares Rollo and Lupe. But things are a little calmer with you here."

"He scares her because you got hurt and she couldn't stop it. Doesn't mean she's going to back down from any of his threats. Your sister's a brave woman."

"I know." She rolled her dark eyes. "And I know I'm…a headache for her. But we're all trying to find our own way out of this part of town."

"Bobby isn't your way out."

Sylvie shredded the tissue in her fingers before tossing it into the trash. "Maybe not. But I thought he cared about me. Until tonight. And there aren't many guys like you around here."

"White guys?"

She smiled at his teasing chuckle. "Nice guys." Maybe that was a compliment, after all, because she padded across the rug and wrapped her arms around Mike's waist, squeezing him in a hug. "Don't let Gina scare you off. She really likes you, you know."

He knew. But did Gina? And given the career and family priorities she pursued to the exclusion of anything personal, would it make any difference if she did?

He pressed a chaste kiss to the crown of Sylvie's head. "You're going to be okay."

"I know."

"I'll be out on the couch tonight. Don't worry about Bobby or your aunt and uncle or Gina. Sleep tight."

He patted her shoulder before she moved away and crawled onto the daybed, leaning back against the pillows. After pulling a fuzzy blanket over her lap, she grabbed her phone, plugged in her ear buds, turned on her music and tuned him out the way a normal teenager would.

Mike grinned as he pulled the door shut, liking this version of Sylvie Galvan a lot better than the frightened young woman who fancied herself in love with Bobby Estes.

He found Gina in the darkened living room, sticking her cell phone into the pocket of her jeans. She flipped on a lamp beside the sofa where Lupe had set out a pillow and a blanket. He recognized the tight set of her full, bow-shaped lips as she waged an internal battle between the urge to tell him to leave and the desire to give her family the reassurance his presence here seemed to provide. Although hushed, so as not to disturb anyone else in the house, her tone was strictly business. "Derek said he'll do the paperwork for the lab and file a report on the assault."

Mike whispered back. "The one on you? Or the one on your sister?"

"Both."

"Good."

Gina nodded as she circled around the couch and gestured for him to follow her toward the front door. "Thank you for staying so long, but it's late. You have work in the morning and need to get some sleep. I've checked the doors and windows twice already. Sylvie's not sneaking out, and I'm not letting anybody get in. We'll be all right."

"I know you've got your bases covered. I'm staying, anyway."

She tilted her proud chin to his. "Because I'm weak?"

"You're the strongest woman I know." He reached out to brush his knuckles across her soft cheek, not liking the chill he felt there. "I don't want anything to happen to this family. Another set of eyes and ears can't hurt. If I can help—"

"You have helped. You always help." She tipped her cheek into his hand, and the silky curls of her hair tickled his skin, waking the nerve endings that flared to life whenever she got close. "Sometimes I wonder if you're for real. You're just too damn—"

"Don't you dare say *nice* again, like it's some kind of plague." Gina's pupils dilated in the shadows, turning her eyes into rich pools of midnight. She fisted her hand in the front of his shirt, and Mike knew he was in for another argument as she tugged him toward the privacy of the kitchen. "What now? I swear, woman…"

Once his shoes reached the tile floor, she yanked harder, untucking the front of his shirt and pulling him off balance as she bumped into the lower cabinets. Mike braced his hands against the countertop on either side of her so he wouldn't crash into her. But before he could ask what this sudden escape from the living room was all about, she slipped her damaged hand behind his neck and pulled his mouth down to hers.

The unexpected contact shot a bolt of lightning through him, igniting an urgent heat. There was something purposeful, maybe a little angry, in the way she clung to him and fused her mouth to his. Where that anger was directed, Mike couldn't tell. And, at the moment, Mike didn't care. Instinctively, his mouth moved over Gina's, claiming what she offered. Her lips softened, parted. With a husky gasp that went straight to his groin, Gina swept her tongue between his lips. Her fingers clutched at the edge of his jaw, stroking across his beard stubble, holding their mouths together. This wasn't anger; this was need. This was attraction simmering out of control. This was the inevitable release of every emotion roiling through this house tonight.

Mike understood that fire. That desperation. That crazy need to connect to the one person who could ease the fear, the anger, the need and the passion that had grown too powerful to control anymore.

Slipping his hands to her waist and pulling her body into his, Mike took control of the kiss, suckling on her sweet bottom lip, soothing the trembling response with his tongue. She pulled at the hem of his polo until she could slip her hands inside to palm the skin of his chest and stomach, branding him with her desire. He returned the favor, tugging her blouse from her jeans and splaying his fingers over the smooth curve of her back.

He felt the chill of her skin as he explored the length of her spine and flare of her hips. He dropped gentle kisses against her eyebrows and cheeks and the rapid beat of her pulse beneath her ear. The woman was responsive in a way that made him feel powerful, male, whole. Gina warmed at every spot he touched and cooed soft, excited moans that hummed in her throat. Her fingers raked through his hair, roamed over his shoulders, traveled inside his shirt, kindling an incendiary response that made him want to reclaim her lips and loosen the snap of her jeans and tug down the zipper so he could dip his fingers beneath the elastic band of her panties and fill his hands with that irresistible backside.

"Is Sylvie okay?" she murmured against his mouth, running her fingers along the column of his throat, nip-ping at the point of his chin, turning his response into a hoarse growl.

"You want to talk *now*?"

"Yes." She tipped her head back as he trailed his lips down the arch of her throat, seeking out the source of those sexy hums. She whimpered when he found a particularly sensitive bundle of nerves. "No. Is she?"

Mike chuckled his response against her skin. "She'll be fine. The bruises on her cheek and wrist are superficial. It might not hurt to talk to a counselor, though."

"I'll arrange it." Gina stretched up on tiptoe, her small breasts pillowing against his chest as she guided his mouth back to hers for another hungry kiss.

Mike indulged himself in the pleasure firing throughout his body. He grabbed her sweet, round bottom and lifted her, thinking he was never going to get enough of this woman until he was buried deep inside her. His hard length pushed against the zipper of his jeans, seeking out the heat of her body.

This make-out session was going from zero to sixty in a matter of seconds. And while their bodies were definitely willing, Mike had to wonder if their brains were on board with where this was headed. He moved his hands up to feather his fingers into her hair and rested his forehead against Gina's, sucking in a deep breath of much-needed air. "I need to understand the rules here. There is no *this*, no *us,* yet it's all right for you to kiss me like I'm the only snack on a deserted island?"

"Forget the rules. Just…" She tipped her head to seal their lips together in brief kiss. "I don't like being scared or vulnerable."

"Tell me about it." He welcomed the cinch of her arms around his waist, as he took her mouth in a leisurely kiss. "Sounds like you've talked to your family about me. Maybe said a couple of nice things."

"Don't let it go to your head, Choir Boy."

Oh, but there were a lot of other things going straight to his head.

Her hands slipped beneath his shirt, singeing the skin on his back. "I don't like feeling as if I can't handle myself in a fight."

"You'll get there. I promise."

The kiss jockeyed back and forth with forays and acceptance, with tantalizing discovery and revisiting a favorite angle or caress. "I'm glad you were here, that you had my back."

"Anytime."

"No. Not any—" she gasped as his palm settled over her breast, squeezing the proud nipple between his thumb and palm through the lace of her bra. She buried her face against his chest, pushing the pert handful into his greedy hand, her soft gasps belying her breathless words. "I want this, but…I can't do a relationship. I don't have time. It wouldn't be fair to you…all my responsibilities—"

"Do you hear me complaining?" He squeezed her bottom and lifted her again. She wrapped her legs around his waist, and Mike's pulse thundered in his ears. He wanted her. She wanted him. "There's just now." He spun around, leaning against the sink. But her knees butted against the countertop. "We're both adults. We're safe." He spotted the chair sticking out from the table and carried her toward it. "Don't overthink this."

He sank onto the seat, pulling Gina into his lap. He couldn't help but push against her as her thighs squeezed around his hips. They kissed as their hands fumbled between them. Mike spread his thighs to ease the tightness in his jeans. But he'd miscalculated his position on the chair, and his right leg slipped off the seat. Gina shifted. Mike caught her, planting his foot to keep her in place. He moaned against her mouth, a blend of anticipation and frustration as the inevitable jolt of electricity sparked down his leg.

Hugging her tight to his body, Mike winced as he stood to alleviate the pressure on the pinched nerve. His broken body was betraying him. Just when Gina was letting him get close. Ah, hell. Now the leg had gone numb.

"Mike? Put me down." Gina scrambled out of his grasp, pushing away but clinging to his arms until she found her balance. No, she was steadying him. "Are you hurt? Do you need to sit down?"

"Standing is better." He pulled Gina back into his chest, dropping his chin to the crown of her hair. "I'm sorry. Nothing like a twinge of the old bursitis and my leg going numb to put a damper on things. Just let me hold you for a second, okay?"

But the woman couldn't keep still. Now he'd just added himself to the long list of things she had to worry about. "What happened? Did Bobby hurt you?"

"Be still for a sec. I'll be fine. It's an old war wound acting up."

"Huh?"

When she stilled and leaned into him, Mike pulled her arms back around his waist and breathed deeply against her dark, fragrant hair, willing the numbness and the lingering desire still firing through his system to abate. "I was in a car wreck when I was sixteen. A friend was driving me home because I was too drunk to be responsible for myself. He died. Helping me. Pretty much every bone below my waist was shattered. Tore up muscles and nerves. The doctors weren't sure I was going to walk again."

Her arms tightened around him. He felt both hands hooking into the back of his belt as she nestled her cheek against his heart. "Your friend died?"

"Leave it to you to pick up on the important detail." Mike distracted himself from the guilt and regret by sifting her hair through his fingers. Although this stance gave him a bird's-eye view of that sexy bottom he wanted to grab again, he ignored the impulse and savored her willingness to simply be close to him without any kind of protest. "There's some residual nerve damage I deal with. Regular exercise keeps the weight off the joints and the muscles strong, but sometimes I'll twist wrong or even sleep wrong and tweak a nerve. Or the weather changes and all the metal pins and wires inside let me know it. But I'm walking now, with no braces and no cane. I can make love to a beautiful woman again—on most nights." His wry comment only made her snuggle tighter. "I can run again. So I'm not complaining. Sorry to start something I couldn't finish."

She shook her head. "*I* started it. And I'm not complaining. I'm just glad you're here."

"Me, too."

"We're a pair, aren't we? Gimpy and Hopalong. Maybe between us there's a whole person who can take down the bad guys." She released his belt to rub her hands over the backside of his jeans. Whether consciously or unconsciously done, the tender strokes across the muscles at the small of his back and hips felt good. The physical tension in him eased and the air around them cooled, even as something warmer and more profound than the desire they shared took hold inside him. "I'm sorry for all of the trouble I've brought to your life."

"Trust me, Tiger. I know trouble. You ain't it." He leaned back against her arms, framing her face between his hands and tilting those rich brown eyes up to his. He dipped his head to press a firm kiss to her beautiful lips before reluctantly pulling away. "You need to go to bed. Alone." He pulled her hands from his hips and backed away before he couldn't leave her. "Do not sneak out of this house and go to that bar by yourself. Do not take on Bobby Estes by yourself. Take care of your family tonight. Rest. I'll be here in the morning when you wake up."

"You can't stay." Despite her words, she pawed at him, buttoning his shirt, smoothing down the spikes of his hair. If she kept touching him, they were going to end up right back where they'd been a few minutes ago. "You shouldn't."

Mike listened to what she needed, not what she wanted. He stopped her hands from their busywork and squeezed them in his grip. "This is moving too fast, and you're not comfortable with that. I get it. I don't want you to regret anything that happens between us."

She nodded. "I don't want you to regret anything, either. I'm kind of a mess tonight."

"Join the crowd. The timing sucks. That's all." He released her hands and brushed a thick curl off her cheek, tucking it behind her ear. "Mind if I call a couple of friends at KCPD and ask them to make a few extra passes through your neighborhood tonight?"

This time, she pulled his hand away. But she was smiling. "I'd appreciate it."

"Consider it done." He leaned in for one more peck on the lips, thought better of it considering his will-

power around Gina and turned her toward her bedroom. "I'd better go to that couch now, or I never will."

He followed her into the living room, pausing at
the couch as she quietly opened the bedroom door and
peeked in. Even through the shadows cast by the lone
lamp, he could see her smiling.

"Sylvie asleep?" he whispered.

Gina nodded before opening the door wider. Mike
glanced down at his wrinkled shirt, grinning at the
mismatched buttons and buttonhole Gina had missed
in her haste to redress him.

"Mike?"

He glanced up to see her padding back across the
hall to meet him. "Something wrong?"

She drew her shoulders back, steeling her posture before speaking. "It's the five o'clock shadow. The way it's
just enough beard to be interesting, but not so shaggy
that it obscures your face." He frowned in confusion.
She touched his face, running her fingertips along the
line of his jaw. "Catnip," she explained. "That's my catnip. What I find attractive on a man. Something about
the angles and the rawness is *muy masculino*. There's
something a little bad boy about it that I want to touch."

He didn't need to be fluent in Spanish to understand
that compliment. His face eased into a smile beneath
her touch. He turned to kiss her palm before she pulled
away. "Happy to oblige. Now get some sleep. I'll stay up
and keep an eye on things until the first black-and-white
drives by. See you in the morning."

Mike waited for the bedroom door to close behind
her before he went back into the kitchen to splash some
cold water on his face, tempering those last vestiges of
desire lingering from that kiss. He called a couple of
friends from his father's SWAT team and explained the

situation, needlessly promising a free lunch or work-out at the clinic in exchange for their help watching the house.

Once his friends Trip and Alex had arrived and parked their truck across the street from Gina's, Mike peeled off his shirt, belt and shoes and stretched out on the couch that was too short for him. It was after midnight when he heard the hushed sound of a door opening and closing. More curious than alarmed, he peeked around the end of the couch to see Gina in a long-sleeved T-shirt and pajama pants. Instead of heading for the bathroom, as both Lupe and Rollo had done earlier, she kissed her knuckles and rubbed them against her heart.

Mike remembered the superstitious action from the shooting range. "What do you need luck for at this time of night?"

She didn't startle at his teasing voice from the shadows. "Not luck. Courage."

He sat up, concerned by her answer. "Gina?"

"I saw the men out front. Thank you." She circled the sofa and sat beside him. "I don't want to have sex. I'm not ready to complicate us like that yet. But…could we snuggle for a little bit? I can't seem to get warm again, and I can't sleep when I'm cold, and…"

Relieved to know that Sylvie and everyone else in the house were safe, he wrapped the blanket around her and pulled her into his arms. "You don't have to be the strong one all the time. Take a breather tonight. I've got you."

Turning onto his side, he stretched out on the couch behind her, spooning his chest against her back. "This doesn't mean anything," she insisted. "I'm just cold."

"Understood." Grinning at the tough act he wasn't

buying, Mike draped his arm around her waist and tucked her as close as the blanket and dimensions of the couch allowed. "Warm enough?"

She nodded, resting her head on his arm. "This doesn't make your legs cramp or hurt, does it?"

"Nope. Your shoulder okay?"

"It doesn't hurt at all when I lie on this side." Several seconds passed before he felt her body relax against his. "Sylvie gets up at seven for school."

He ignored the bottom nestling against his groin and reached for his phone. "I'll set my alarm for six."

"You're driving me to the crime lab and Sin City Bar in the morning."

"Yes, ma'am."

"Could we do that before my therapy session?"

Mike's laugh was as hushed as the shadows surrounding them. "Only if you stop talking and get some rest."

"*Not* my mother, Choir Boy." Her answering laugh faded into a yawn.

He nudged aside the dark curls at the nape of her neck and pressed a kiss there. "How about your partner?"

She brushed her lips across the swell of his bicep. "Deal. For now."

The strong fingers of her right hand latched onto his. In a matter of minutes, the tension eased from her body, and her soft, even breath against his skin let him know that she'd finally fallen asleep. "I'll be your armor tonight, Tiger," he whispered.

Mike settled into the most comfortable position he could manage and drifted toward sleep himself, knowing three things. One, Gina liked to keep things even between them—he'd revealed a secret, so she had, too. Two, there was far more danger surrounding this woman than even he'd realized. And three, the attraction simmering in his veins, the unexpected caring that took them beyond therapist and patient, or even friends, was mutual, no matter how stubbornly independent she tried to be.

Logically, he could see the pattern of his life repeating itself: play Knight in Shining Armor to a woman who needed him. Stir up his hormones and get his heart involved. The next inevitable step would be her realizing she no longer had a use for the strength and support he provided, and him getting hurt again.

But he couldn't stay away from Gina. Out of all his relationships—Caroline, Frannie, others who'd grown tired of Mr. Nice Guy before anything real had started—none of them had gotten him twisted up inside as fast and feverishly as Officer Gina Galvan. Her bravery and vulnerability, her fierce determination to improve her standing and protect her family, her passionate impulses and the stubborn emotional shield she couldn't quite keep in place—all got under his skin and inside his head and into his heart, refusing to answer to caution or logic.

He was falling for Gina Galvan. Falling hard and fast. And the closer he got, the more he realized there were too many ways he could lose her.

Chapter Ten

Gina fingered the badge clipped to the belt of her jeans, trying not to feel as if she was impersonating an officer this morning, as she stared out the window of Mike's pickup at the heavy steel door below the Sin City Bar sign. Technically, although she was on medical leave, she was still a member of KCPD, and she'd earned the right to wear this badge. And, until that losing skirmish with Bobby Estes last night, she'd believed she was always going to be a working cop again. An elite cop. A SWAT cop.

Now she was feeling a bit like Sin City's fraudulent facade. At night, their sign lit up with red and yellow bulbs, bathing the entryway in a warm color, welcoming patrons. But the bright sunlight of a chilly spring morning revealed chipped white paint on the outside walls. Rust at each corner of their sign stained the painted brick and faded awning over the door. With the blinds drawn at every window, there was no promise of a party at a friendly bar to draw in customers.

Just like wearing the badge didn't mean she could do this job the way she wanted to again.

Looking at the row of motorcycles and the beat-up van in the parking lot beside the bar, she was certain she was about to get another opportunity to chat with Gordy and Denny Bismarck and their biker buddies. And she suspected them being here at this time of day meant they were either very good friends with the manager and bartenders she'd hoped would break their alibi— which meant that probably wasn't going to happen— or they had gotten wind of KCPD looking into them as the potential cop shooters and they were here to make sure that no one gave them up. Either way, she was on their turf. Asking questions and getting straight answers wouldn't be easy, even on her best day.

"You ready to go play good cop/bad cop?" Mike's angular features crooked into a teasing smile as he pulled in beside the van and turned off the engine.

Drawn from the doom and gloom of her thoughts, Gina smiled back. One more day and that sexy beard stubble of his would cross the line into scruffy.

But in the dark hours of last night, she'd admitted there were plenty of other reasons why Mike Cutler was her catnip. Her family had felt reassured by his presence at the house, and anyone who was that kind and patient with her family was a hero in her book. That long, hard, rebuilt body had been a furnace at her back, keeping her warm and secure enough to enjoy the best night's sleep she'd had since the shooting. His hands had awakened an answering need inside her with each purposeful touch. And she shouldn't even think about the gentle seduction and commanding firmness of his mouth moving over hers. Even his do-the-right-thing stubbornness that matched her own was becoming less of a frustration and more of a type of strength she respected. She'd lowered her guard with Mike last night, both physically and emotionally. She'd felt normal, free of all her burdens, for a few hours. Mike Cutler managed to be strong for her without making her feel weak or foolish or at any kind of disadvantage.

She'd never expected that a man could make her feel like that—like she could fall in love with him if she wasn't careful.

She reached over the console to brush her fingers across his jaw. *Sí*. She had definitely developed a craving for that handsome face. "Not a cop, Choir Boy."

The color of his eyes darkened like cobalt at her touch. Just like that, with a piercing look and the ticklish caress of his beard beneath her sensitive fingertips, her stomach tightened with desire.

But she was here to work. She hadn't been lying when she'd said she couldn't fit a relationship into her life right now. If she could, there would be only one candidate. But reality made falling in love low on her priority list. It made falling in love with Mike nearly impossible. She pulled her fingers away and unbuckled her seat belt. She eyed the officer stowing the last of the yellow crime scene tape from Frank McBride's shooting into the trunk of the black-and-white police cruiser already in the parking lot.

"Looks like Derek's ready for us." Having her partner here made this interview sanctioned, despite her own self-doubts. He'd met them at the crime lab earlier so she could deliver the bullets she'd taken from Bobby's and Emanuel's guns to the ballistics tech. He would run a comparison between them and the spent rounds recovered from the police shootings, including her own. "You wait in the truck."

Mike shook his head, pocketing his keys in his jacket. "I can't very well watch your back from here."

Gina paused with her hand on the door handle. "Derek will have my back. I'm guessing the Bismarck boys aren't going to cooperate, and I need you to stay safe."

"How about we double our efforts?" He pointed through the windshield to the garage on the opposite side of the bar's parking lot. "An auto-repair and customization shop right next door to their hangout? Want to bet that one or more of them works there? I can wander in and ask if anyone there remembers them from the day of your shooting, or if they saw them here yesterday when Frank was shot. Maybe I'll get an estimate on rotating my tires."

"And, while you're in there, see if you spot any familiar vehicles like the rusty old SUV the shooter used or the tan Mercedes that's been following me?"

"Is that a bad idea?"

"No. It's a smart one." Derek was out of the cruiser, heading toward the truck. As uneasy as the thought of Mike investigating on his own made her, she couldn't deny that he had inherited all the right instincts about being a cop from his father. Other than the fact he was unarmed. But then, so was she. "All right. You check out next door while Derek and I see if we can break anybody's alibi. But if the Bismarcks or their friends *are* there, I don't want you to engage any of them. Turn around and get out of there. I'll meet you back here."

"Ten minutes give you enough time?"

Gina nodded. "No heroics, okay? Just get information."

"Yes, ma'am."

Derek was waiting beside the truck when she shut the door. He rested an arm on the butt of the gun holstered at his waist, his eyebrows arched in confusion as Mike jogged across the parking lot and entered the automotive shop. "I thought Cutler was just driving you around until you're cleared to do it yourself. What's he up to?"

"Detective work." Kissing the back of her fingers and rubbing them against her heart, she sent up a silent prayer that Mike wasn't on a mission that could get him hurt. Then she butted her elbow against Derek's and headed for Sin City's front door. "Come on. We'd better do the same."

On a different day, if she was in uniform and back on patrol, Gina would have run in the bar's owner, Vince Goring. The myopic manager was already serving a drink to a dazed old man who, judging by his ratty appearance and eye-watering stench, had probably been sitting on the same barstool since closing time the night before. She wondered if he was the drunk who'd allegedly witnessed Frank McBride's shooting yesterday afternoon.

Nothing about this quest for answers was going smoothly. The deep voices and laughing conversation from the back of the bar fell silent by the time her eyes had adjusted to the dim lighting. She'd been hoping she could talk to the owner alone, find out who'd been tending bar that wintry afternoon when she'd gotten shot. But Vince was carrying a tray of coffee mugs to the back booth, where Gordon and Denny Bismarck, Al, Prison Tat Guy and one of their potbellied buddies were sitting. Denny pulled his flask from his pocket and doctored his coffee before passing the container around the table. Oddly enough, none of them seemed to be sporting a black eye or broken nose, or other signs that'd they'd been involved in the fight that had lured Frank McBride here. But in this dim lighting, it was hard to tell.

Still, she wasn't here about serving drinks to someone who'd already had too much, or citing a barkeep who allowed patrons to bring in their own alcohol. Letting the glare from Denny Bismarck's dark eyes fuel her resolve to conduct this interview, she ignored him and the whispered conversations at the table, while Vince shuffled back to the bar where she and Derek stood.

"Mr. Goring." Gina made no effort to whisper. If Bismarck and company knew she was here, then they had to suspect she was asking questions about them. "That group of men at the back table—are they regulars?"

Vince pushed his thick glasses up onto the bridge of his nose before answering. "Sure. Al and Jim work next door at the body shop."

Gina had done her homework. She pointed to her neck. "Jim Carlson is the guy with the tats?" She remembered Al Renken, the van driver. He was bald.

"Yep. You friends with them?"

The last man, Aldo Pitsaeli, was the guy who'd been worried that day about getting in trouble with his wife. Denny and the others had been with Gordy at the Bismarck house before the shooting. Did the five men always travel in a pack? Would they alibi any member of their group who wasn't there? Even if he left to go shoot a couple of cops? "We're acquainted."

That seemed good enough for the barkeep to start talking. "Gordy got his bike customized at the shop. Denny, too. Although they sometimes drive a '75 Bronco SUV they inherited from their daddy. If you ask me, they ought to take that wreck to the scrap-metal yard, or else get *it* customized. All painted up with a couple new fenders, folks might go for it."

She wasn't here for a lesson in auto mechanics, either. "They come in here a lot?"

He picked up a rag to wipe down the bar around the

drunk who never moved. In fact, she could hear him snoring. "They hang out with Al and Jim when they're workin'. Sometimes do odd jobs over there. They're all motor heads. They come over here a lot when Al or Jim go on break or have a day off."

Derek tapped her on the arm and straightened behind her. But Gina was already aware of Denny Bismarck standing up and his younger brother sliding out of the booth behind him. She doubted they'd do anything stupid like attack a uniformed officer so soon after yesterday's shooting, but she still felt the urgency to ask her questions faster. "Do they ever come into the bar in the afternoon?"

"I guess." He snapped his fingers. "Oh, you mean like those cops were asking yesterday?"

"I'm more interested in seven weeks ago, January twenty-sixth," she clarified. "Were you working the bar that day? Were they all here?"

Vince nodded. Then frowned and shook his head.

Gina's hand curled into a fist. "Yes or no? Were they here that afternoon?"

"Seven weeks is a long time to remember something."

As far as Gina was concerned, seven decades wouldn't be long enough for her to forget that day. "Well, can you remember yesterday? There was a fight in your bar. A black police officer responded. He was shot out front."

"Oh, yeah. That was real bad. I didn't know what was going on until I heard the shots. Thought it was an engine backfiring next door."

"Who was in the fight?" She pointed to the back of the bar. "Was it any of those guys?"

"G?" Derek's hand brushed the small of her back, alerting her to the group of men ambling their way.

Gina caught and held Denny's glare as she asked Vince a follow-up question. "Are they always here together? The brothers, their friends—in a group like this morning?"

"I guess."

"Was one of them missing?"

"Yesterday?" He looked at the group of approaching men, as if seeing their faces for the first time. "As I recall, they were out front by the time I got there. Fight was over. The officer was writin' folks up. Maybe they were in the bar. Guess they could have come out of the shop."

Gina bit down on her frustration and kept a friendly smile on her face. "All of them? What about seven weeks ago?"

Vince adjusted his glasses again. "Come to think of it, Gordy wasn't here that day."

No. He'd been sitting in the back of her police cruiser. "But the others were all here at the bar? Could you swear to that in court?"

Vince's eyes widened behind his glasses. "Am I going to court? Lady, I don't want to testify against anybody. That's bad for business."

Derek put up a warning hand. "You boys keep your distance. We don't want any trouble."

Denny snickered. "You're the only one making trouble, Johnson. Moving in on my brother's wife?"

"Ex-wife," Derek reminded him. "I only went out with Vicki twice."

Jim Carlson moved within chest-bumping distance. "That's two times too many as far as we're concerned.

You're taking advantage of my friend's unfortunate situation."

"Back off, Carlson," Derek warned. "Assaulting a police officer and impeding an investigation will land you back in jail."

"Were the others all here that afternoon, Mr. Goring?" Gina needed an answer. "Even Denny?"

Jim Carlson's skin reddened beneath the tats on his neck. But even as he wisely retreated a step, Denny slipped onto the barstool beside Gina, brushing his shoulder against hers. "You checking up on me, *querida*? I heard you weren't a cop no more."

Gina plucked her badge off her belt and slammed it on top of the bar in front of him. "Touch me one more time and I'll arrest you."

Derek held his ground behind her, but she heard the urgency in his tone. "G, we need to get moving."

Denny wiped his mouth, leaving a dot of spittle on his scraggly beard. "You think I shot you?"

"Doesn't seem like Vince here is much of an alibi. And I think your buddies are scared to say anything you don't want them to. Maybe you wanted revenge on us for arresting your brother? For me bossing you around? Or you were after Derek for dating Vicki, and I was collateral damage."

"And I shot all those other cops, too? Why would I do that?" Denny snorted and reached for his flask. "I watch the news. I know you ain't the only cop who got hurt. As far as I know, ain't none of them boinking my brother's wife."

"That's enough, Bismarck," Derek warned him.

Bobby Estes was more likely to have premeditated the shooting, setting up the diversion of attacking other cops before going after her. The Bismarcks were heat-of-the-moment types of criminals. But she and Derek had been to the Bismarck house before on previous calls. Were these bozos smart enough to stage another assault on Vicki to set her and Derek up as targets? They sure seemed to have plenty of time on their hands to follow her to the physical therapy clinic or drive by her home or hang out here.

Denny had taken a swallow and tucked the flask back inside his jacket before Gina realized the place had gone quiet, except for the snoring coming from the end of the bar.

Gina backed away from the bar and surveyed the rest of the interior. There was nothing but a circle of abandoned coffee mugs at that back table now. "Where are your friends?"

Denny shrugged. "Al had to go back to work."

And she hadn't seen him leave. She clipped her badge onto her belt and pointed to Vince. "Is there a back door to this place?"

"Yeah."

She didn't know if she was madder at Derek for not telling her the men had slipped out or at herself for not noticing. She was damn certain she was mad at Denny for setting up the diversion while his comrades snuck out, knowing her suspicions were centered on him. "You could have left here that afternoon and come back to shoot up the Bismarck house without anyone seeing you leave."

Denny wasn't fazed by her brewing temper. "You saw me leave on my bike that day. Did you see me come back?"

She remembered the rusty old SUV with frozen, dirty slush thrown up around the wheel wells and masking the license plate. "You could have dropped your bike off here and come back in your '75 Bronco."

Gina held her ground when Denny stood and towered over her. "I could have, *querida*."

It didn't feel like a confession so much as a taunting reminder that she still had no answers. Only too many suspects with motives and opportunities.

The front door banged opened, flooding the bar with light. Gina squinted Mike's tall frame into focus. "Your ten minutes are up. We need to go."

"Mike—"

"Now." He sounded as if he'd just run a wind sprint. He backed out the open door, letting her know this wasn't that overprotective streak kicking in but something else.

She was smart enough to follow him. "Did you find something out?"

Denny's laughter confirmed her suspicion that he'd been diverting her attention for a reason. While Derek shoved him back onto his barstool and warned him to shut up, Gina hurried outside and ran to Mike's truck as he climbed in behind the wheel. "Mike?"

"That guy who was in the backseat of your cruiser the day I rescued you is leaving in a mighty big hurry." He turned the key in the ignition and shifted the pickup into Drive.

She was climbing onto the running board between the open door and frame of the truck, when she heard the growl of an engine revving up to full speed. When a big motorcycle roared out of the garage next door and jumped the curb before skidding into a sharp turn, Gina dropped into the passenger seat and slammed the door. "Go! Don't lose him."

Derek ran out of the bar behind her, shouting through

the open window. "I'll call it in. If you get the plate number, let me know." Mike's tires spit up gravel before they found traction and they raced down the street after the motorcycle. "I suspect that place next door was a chop shop. They had an awful lot of car and motorcycle parts in the back room that belonged to high-end vehicles. Not the kind of stuff you see in this neighborhood."

Gina reached across the console to buckle him safely behind the wheel before sitting back to buckle herself in. "What were you doing in the back room?"

"Chasing the guy who ran in while you were next door asking questions."

"You were supposed to stick to getting your tires rotated." He was intent on dodging in and out of traffic and honking to warn pedestrians before they stepped into the street. Apparently, it was useless to argue the idea of staying away from danger with this man. "You're certain it was Gordon Bismarck? Big guy? Needs a haircut?"

He nodded, skidding his truck in a sharp right turn to follow the motorcycle around the corner. "The boss yelled 'Gordy' when he flew out of the garage. Thought that was a pretty good clue."

Gina frowned. Out of all the members of that aging biker gang, she'd figured Denny would be the one to come back and take potshots at the cops arresting his brother. She eyed the spinning lights of Derek's police car taking the corner behind them. Gina gripped the center console as Mike's truck sped through the next intersection. Denny was the one who should be running now. Was this chase the real diversion? Was Denny Bismarck slipping away into hiding right now?

"We should get back to the bar."

"You want me to turn this truck around?"

"Gordy Bismarck couldn't have shot me. He's the only one with an airtight alibi."

Mike skirted through another intersection as the light was turning red. "I'm staying on this guy's tail. Why run if he's got nothing to hide?"

Why wouldn't the answers she needed fall into place? "If that place was a chop shop for stolen car parts, then Gordy's violating his parole by being there. Maybe that's why he's running. It might not have anything to do with me."

"And it may have everything to do with you." Mike leaned on his horn and ran a second red light. "Maybe he knows who shot you and doesn't want you asking questions. Put a call through to my dad."

"I'm not calling in SWAT for a car chase." Gina's bottom left the seat as they bounced over a pothole. The motorcycle swerved around a delivery truck. Mike followed, nearly rear-ending the slow-moving car in front of it. "Look out!"

"I see it." He cut into the opposing lane of traffic, coming nose to nose with an oncoming bus.

"Mike!" He swerved at the last second, knocking Gina between the door and the console.

"You okay?"

"I'm fine. Just don't lose him." Her heart pounded against her ribs. "And don't do that again."

He steered his truck around another corner and sped up the hill, trying to catch the racing motorcycle before it disappeared over the crest. "Call Dad and tell him to send somebody back to Sin City. We'll stay on this guy. And I want someone to know that we're chasing down a suspect. We're flying through town in an unmarked truck. Why hasn't anyone stopped *us* yet?"

They shot over the top of the hill and veered down

the other side. Downtown traffic gave way to under-passes, railroad tracks and the warehouse district near the confluence of the Kansas and Missouri rivers. She should be seeing some neighborhood black-and-whites by now. Roads should be blocked off. A wary sense of unease that had nothing to do with the dangers of this daring thrill ride shivered down her spine. "Where's our backup?"

"Call Dad."

"Derek already called—"

"Your buddy Derek lost us after we nearly hit that bus. If we catch this guy, we'll need help. Call."

"What?!" But her partner's black-and-white wasn't in the rearview mirror. "Where…?"

"Call!"

She pulled out her phone and dialed Dispatch. "This is Officer Gina Galvan. I'm an off-duty cop." She gave her badge number and recited the partial license plate she'd gotten off the motorcycle, along with Gordon Bismarck's name and a description of the rider. "He's moving west on Twelfth. Suspect is in violation of his parole. I am in pursuit in a black pickup. Unit 4-13 has been notified of our intent and is also in pursuit. Although, I've lost sight of him. Please verify that he hasn't been in an accident."

"Acknowledged." The dispatcher's efficient mono-tone put out an APB over her headset before coming back on the line. "Notifying units in area of high-speed pursuit."

"No one's called this in yet?"

"I'm sending out a notification to all units now."

An all-call warning officers of the dangerous traffic situation in the area should have gone in five minutes ago. "What about sending a unit to the Sin City Bar?"

The dispatcher hesitated. "That's where Frank Mc-Bride was shot."

"Yes. I was questioning suspects there."

"My records show there's already a unit assigned to watch the bar."

"What?" She hadn't seen any police car in the area. "Then call them."

"Unit 4-13 was assigned that duty this morning. 10:00 a.m. to 2:00 p.m."

"4-13 is with me." Only he wasn't. Gina inhaled a deep breath, quashing her emotions. "I need you to send a new unit to Sin City Bar to round up Denny Bismarck, Al Renken, Jim Carlson and Aldo Pitsaeli for questioning. And send an alert to Michael Cutler of SWAT Team One that his son is with me."

"Copy that. Unit dispatched. Message sent."

"Galvan out." Gina's phone tumbled out of her hand as they bounced over a railroad crossing and followed the motorcycle into the West Bottoms area of the city. Once a teeming center of commerce, the monoliths of rusting metal and sagging brick walls stood like looming sentinels beside the river. Although much of the district had been bought by investors and was slowly being transformed into trendy art houses, antique shops and reception halls, the buildings were only open on weekends. In the middle of the week, there were only a few lone cars on the streets, and one small moving van backed up against a concrete loading dock.

It should have made it easy to spot Gordy. But he'd steered the more maneuverable motorcycle up and down side streets and alleys, and they'd lost him. Mike slowed his speed as they drove down Wyoming Street, each checking every alleyway and open warehouse door on their side of the street.

"Where did he go?" Gina heard the distant sound of police sirens a split second before she heard the familiar sound of an engine revving. When Gordy shot out of the cross street in front of them, Mike floored the accelerator. "There he is!"

"Hold on!" Mike's big pickup left the stink of burned rubber behind them as he took a hard turn to the left.

Gina spotted the wall of chain link fence and piles of plastic trash bags stacked between it and the food truck at the loading dock behind a café where two men were hauling out crates of produce. "Blind alley!"

Mike stomped on the brakes. Gina's shoulder protested bracing her hands against the dashboard. The truck skidded to an abrupt halt while Gordy gunned his bike up the concrete ramp to leap the security fence. But he hit a dolly loaded with lettuce and tomatoes and spun out. The bike crashed into the fence and Gordy rolled across the concrete, sliding off the edge into the bundles of trash.

Before Gina could get unbuckled, pull out her badge and warn the two workers to stay inside the café, Mike was out of the truck, racing down the alley toward Gordy Bismarck as he scrambled to his feet. But his limping gait didn't stand a chance against Mike's long legs. Gordy abandoned his bike and was halfway up the fence when Mike leaped up, grabbed the other man and pulled him down. They tumbled into a sea of restaurant waste, but Mike had Gordy's face pressed against the pavement by the time Gina caught up to them.

"KCPD!" she announced. "Stay on the ground!"

Mike was breathing hard from the exertion. But given Gordy's deep gasps, and pale, oxygen-deprived skin, she knew Mike clearly had the upper hand. Still, Gina wasn't about to trust any perp's cooperation at this point. After a quick assessment of their surroundings, she shut off the motorcycle's engine and pulled the strapping tape from one of the broken crates to wind it around Gordy's wrists, securing him and checking his pockets for any weapons before she gave Mike the okay to release him.

"I'm getting tired of arresting you, Gordy. Why did you run from us?" Gina demanded, stowing the pocketknife she'd found on him before rolling him over and showing him her badge.

When he didn't immediately answer, Mike grabbed him by the shoulders of his jacket and sat him up against the fence to face her. "Answer Officer Galvan's question."

"I'm not going back to prison," he answered on a toneless breath.

"You will if you shot a cop," Mike reminded him, his usually friendly voice low and menacing. "We were just there to ask questions. You look guilty making us chase you all over town."

Gordy tilted his gaze up to Mike, evaluating his younger, fitter, more ready-to-do-battle posture before deciding to talk to Gina. "I didn't shoot you, lady. You know I didn't. Hell, I was in the backseat of your car. I got shot at, too."

"But you didn't get hit. You were protected while my partner and I were out in the open. What about Officer McBride?"

"Who?"

"The cop who was wounded yesterday at Sin City." Silence.

Mike tugged Gordy forward by the collar of his jacket. "Do you know who shot Gina?"

Gordy glared at Mike but didn't answer.

Refusing to speak wasn't an option as far as Gina was concerned. "Did Denny come back to the house to shoot us? Is that why you ran? To protect your brother the way he protected you that day? Or are you just worried about you and your boys getting caught working in a chop shop?"

She must have struck a nerve with one of those questions because Gordy's gaze dropped to the pavement. "I want my attorney."

Gina turned at the blare of sirens at the end of the alley as two black-and-whites pulled up. Two officers climbed out of the first car, one radioing in the situation report, while the other hurried over with a proper pair of handcuffs to secure Bismarck and drag him to his feet.

Gordy looked down at Gina. "A man's got a right to protect what's his."

Was he confessing a motive for the shooting? Or was he defending his actions to protect his brother?

While the officer led Bismarck to the backseat of the cruiser, Derek jogged around the corner. "G? You all right?"

Her voice was sharp when he reached her. "Just how many times did you sleep with Vicki Bismarck?"

"Whoa." Derek put up his hands, stopping just short of touching her. "That came out of left field."

"Not really. Gordy and Denny seem to think you're a motive for their behavior. Beating up on Vicki. Threatening us. Maybe even firing a gun at us. Because you moved in on Gordy's woman."

Derek propped his hands at his waist, alternately smiling and looking as if he was about to cuss up a blue streak. "That is out of line, G. Bismarck's got no claim on her. They're divorced. And I told you, I went out with her twice."

"The Bismarcks seem to think it was more than that."

"The Bismarcks are wrong. Whose side are you on, anyway?"

Gina shook her head. "You should have recused yourself from that interview this morning."

The smile didn't win. "Hey, you were the one who called me for the favor."

"That was my mistake. My second mistake was counting on you to help me round up Bismarck." She took two steps toward Mike's truck and spun around to face Derek. "Where were you? What if he'd gotten away?"

"I circled around to Thirteenth to cut him off when I lost you. I thought he was heading for the interstate. How was I to know he'd do a U-ee and head toward the river?"

"What about sealing off traffic corridors and keeping everyone else safe while we were in pursuit of a suspect? I called Dispatch myself."

"I called it in," he insisted.

"When? Dispatch hadn't gotten your call yet."

"So it wasn't the first thing I did. I was focused on driving. Everybody has an off day."

An off day? She was done with him settling for being an average cop who lived by an ambiguous moral code.

"You should have stuck to stakeout duty at the bar." He'd have to be blind not to read the disappointment screaming from her body language. She marched back to Mike's truck, aware that Derek was hurrying after her.

"I'll go back to the bar and round the Bismarcks up for questioning."

Gina waved off the offer and kept walking. "Already taken care of. If they're not long gone."

"Did you want me to take care of *them*? Or take care of *you*?"

Gina whirled around on him. "I don't need to be taken care of. I need you to do your job."

He thumped his chest. "I'm the one still wearing a uniform."

Gina shoved her fingers through her hair, muttering a curse, before inhaling a deep breath so she could speak calmly. "Well then, Mr. Uniform, notify the auto-theft team that that place next door to Sin City may be housing stolen vehicle parts. If Denny and his gang haven't cleared them out already."

"Stop giving me orders, G. Look, it's not like we were chasing some piece-of-junk Chevy."

"Why would we—?"

"You were after a guy on a motorcycle. A wild-goose chase that steps on the toes of some other department's investigation. You've got me running errands and filing reports on KCPD time, when I'm supposed to be doing my job at the Precinct." He gestured to the empty belt at her waist. "You're not even cleared to wear your gun, much less run your own investigation. I'm the one trying to cover your backside so you don't get in trouble with the brass."

"Me?"

"Yeah. Haven't you heard? My dad talked to a lawyer about suing you and the department for allowing me to get shot."

"Allowing...?" She'd suspected as much. Didn't stop her temper from flaring. "He has no case. There is only one person responsible for you and me and Frank and Colin getting shot. I'm doing everything I can to find this guy before he shoots someone else—before he kills one of us. I thought that was what you wanted, too."

She turned toward the truck, then faced Derek one last time. "And why would you say 'piece-of-junk Chevy'? Are you remembering something from the shooting? Did you see the shooter's vehicle?"

That seemed to genuinely take him aback, knocking the anger out of his voice and posture. "What? I don't think so. It's just a figure of speech."

"No, it's not."

She was aware that Mike had followed them and spoken briefly to the officers in the first police cruiser to arrive on the scene. It wasn't the hole ripped into the knee of his jeans or the unidentifiable glop of food staining the sleeve of his shirt or even the subtle limp she detected in his stride that proved he'd gone above and beyond to protect her and help track down the man who might hold the key to the truth. Now he circled to his side of the truck, giving her some space to deal with her partner. But his watchful blue eyes never left her. He was ready to intervene if she needed him—and willing to step back if she didn't. *That* was the kind of backup she expected from anyone she called *partner*.

But Derek just didn't get it. He didn't understand fire and dedication and getting the job done the way she did. "G, you're a little obsessed. Maybe we're never going to catch the guy who shot us. Maybe we just need to move on. I can handle my dad. You need to go home and heal. We need to focus on keeping our noses clean and making SWAT."

She shrugged off his placating touch and climbed in beside Mike. "You quit if you want, Derek. I never will."

Chapter Eleven

"Here's a clean shirt from my locker, son." Mike caught the black KCPD polo his father tossed to him and straightened away from the wall outside the Fourth Precinct's third-floor conference room as several more officers, both uniformed and plainclothes, filed out of the room behind him and moved on down the hallway to their various work stations. Michael Sr. wrinkled his nose at the stain on Mike's shoulder, which could be the remnants of spoiled pasta sauce or a really old tomato. "You're a little fragrant."

"Thanks, Dad." Ignoring the protest from joints that weren't used to duking it out with armed bullies or tackling a man off a concrete loading dock, Mike unbuttoned his soiled shirt and shrugged into the clean one. "What's the verdict?"

Although the captain was just *Dad* to Mike, Gina hurried over from pacing up and down the hallway and practically snapped to attention. "What can you tell us, sir? Did Gordy Bismarck say anything else after lawyering up? No one else was hurt during that chase, were they? What about Denny Bismarck? Did we find him?"

The Precinct's top brass and investigators from various departments had been called in for a briefing on everything that had happened between the confrontation at Gina's home last night to the Sin City Bar and stopping Gordon Bismarck in a pile of trash near the river this morning. Michael Sr. splayed his fingers at the waist of his dark uniform, looking down at her with a boss-like seriousness. "Denny Bismarck has gone to ground, but there's a citywide APB out on him. We've got unis checking their regular haunts. We've arrested Al Renken on trafficking stolen goods and Gordy on his parole violation and resisting arrest."

"Even though I was the officer in pursuit?" A worried frown marred Gina's beautiful eyes. "Technically, I'm still on leave. The arrest is good? Am I going on report?"

Mike felt the same paternal, perhaps reprimanding, glare fixed on him for a moment before his father answered Gina's concern. "You're still KCPD. You identified yourself with your badge—Bismarck said as much. Your instincts were good about the Bismarcks and their buddies hiding something. The auto-theft team wants to buy you a drink down at the Shamrock for breaking one of their investigations wide open. I think I've got some competition for recruiting you."

The compliment didn't seem to register. "But I'm no closer to finding out who's shooting cops."

"None of us are." The grim pronouncement hung in the stuffy hallway air. "But there are a lot of officers in there who'd like to get Denny in an interrogation room. I'm confident we'll figure this out."

Gina rubbed her shoulder through her denim jacket. Mike wondered if she was in pain, or if that was becoming a habit of the self-doubts and second-guessing that were new to her. "Hopefully, before anyone else gets hurt."

He agreed with a nod. "We're all working this case, Gina. When you attack one cop, you attack all of us. You and Mike have given the detectives several leads to follow up on, including your buddy Bobby Estes. But you need to step back and let Detectives Grove and Kincaid take the lead on this. Go home. You've earned a good night's rest. We'll get this guy. I promise."

"Yes, sir."

Michael's face relaxed into a smile for Gina. "Mind if I borrow my son for a moment?"

Gina's dark gaze darted up to Mike's. "I didn't mean to get him into trouble, Captain. No one's issuing Mike a reckless driving ticket, are they? If I'd been able to drive myself—"

The captain raised a reassuring hand. "Mike's a grown man. It's kind of hard to reprimand him. But we decided not to issue any tickets since he was assisting a police officer." It probably didn't hurt that he was Michael Cutler's son, either. "We do, however, have some things to discuss. Personal things."

But Mike could see his father's explanation had only made Gina straighten to a more defensive posture. Defending him? Or worried that causing friction between father and son would further jeopardize her chances of making the new SWAT team?

"This is nothing for you to stress over," Mike assured her. "We're just two guys having a conversation."

"I'll give you some privacy then." Gina reached over to brush her limp fingers against his knuckles before turning her hand into his and squeezing it. The gesture was shyly hesitant—if he could believe anything about this brave, direct woman could be shy—but it meant the world to Mike. Was that an apology for getting him into any kind of trouble? A thank-you? Maybe her only hesitation was that she was confirming the connection between them in front of his father. "I want to read over my statement again before I sign it. I'll be downstairs in the lobby when you're finished."

"I'll find you there."

He watched her cross to her desk in the main room, pick up the printout of the statement she'd typed earlier and sit down to read it before his father nodded toward the break room. "Buy you a cup of coffee?"

Mike followed his dad inside and closed the door, although he questioned the privacy of this conversation since the walls on either side of the door were glass windows with open blinds hanging in front of them. "*Personal* things?"

When had his dad gone all touchy-feely?

His father pulled out a couple of insulated paper cups and poured them both some hot coffee. "The auto-theft team impounded Denny Bismarck's '75 Bronco. They'd like you to look at it to see if you recognize it from that day at the shooting."

"Not a problem." He took the cup from his dad. "Let's hear the real reason you wanted to talk without Gina around. You think I'm getting in too deep with this. Too deep with her."

"She's getting her grip back?"

He wasn't surprised that his dad had noticed the way Gina had reached for his hand. "I don't know if it'll ever be one hundred percent, probably not steady enough to hold a sniper rifle. But I still wouldn't count her out in a fight. She's already good enough to pass her competency exam on the shooting range."

"Have you told her that?" His dad arched a questioning brow. "I need better than competent for SWAT."

Mike took a sip of the steaming brew, thinking the bitter sludge beat Frannie's coffee but wasn't anywhere near the smooth delight Lupe Molina's coffee had been.

But he knew this conversation wasn't about father-son bonding or evaluating caffeinated drinks. This was Captain Michael Cutler, KCPD, asking for a report on the recovery of a wounded police officer he wanted to recruit. "She's still a good cop. You haven't seen her out in the field, Dad. She's fearless. Gina knows how to handle herself in an interview. She's got good instincts about protecting people. And she's kind and strong and inspiring with the victims I've seen her talk to."

"She wants to be SWAT. Not a victim's advocate."

"She wants to be a cop."

His father nodded, considering the update on Gina's progress. He took a drink before changing the subject. "How do you figure into all this? Are you looking to be a cop now, too?"

Mike chuckled, hearing the fatherly concern about risking his life, yet knowing exactly from what gene pool he'd inherited this strong urge to help others and protect the people he cared about. "That's your calling, Dad. Not mine. Business has been slow at the clinic, so I've had time on my hands. Gina's going to chase this guy down whether or not she has anyone watching her back. I prefer she not take on the whole world alone and aggravate her injury before she's completely healed." He shrugged, instantly regretting the twinge through the stretching muscles of his back. "I help out where I can."

"Driving eighty miles an hour through downtown Kansas City is your idea of helping out? I didn't know your big dream was to drive for NASCAR one day."

Nah. His big dream was to find the man who'd shot Gina so that she'd give up this crazy investigation and give them a chance at being a couple. "I couldn't lose that guy, Dad. He knows something that could help her. For all we know, he's the key to stopping whoever is

targeting cops. Or who might be targeting Gina specifically. That's a theory we're working on."

"A theory?" Those observant blue eyes, so like his
own, narrowed, no doubt suspecting the pain he was
in. "You look a little beat-up yourself. Fractured nerves
and steel pins doing okay?"

Mike admitted to the electric shocks sparking in-
termittently through his lower back and the ache in his
right leg that had been numb when they'd left the crime
scene earlier. "I've had better days. Some ibuprofen and
a hot shower ought to take care of it."

"I wanted you to help Gina get fit enough to come
back to KCPD—not for you to get caught in the cross
fire. I nearly lost you once." He wandered over to peer
through the blinds beside Mike. "Trip and Alex told me
about the run-in at Gina's place last night. Your truck
never left the driveway. Just how serious has it gotten
between you two?"

"We've become friends." Standing beside his father
and fingering the visitor's badge hanging around his
neck, Mike studied the main room. More accurately,
he studied the dark-haired woman at the far end of the
sea of desks between them. Gina methodically read
through the printout, making notations. "I was giving her a break from having to be responsible for her
family, her neighborhood, this whole city for one night.
She's such a tiny thing, and yet she carries the weight
of the world on her shoulders." Mike grinned, trying to
make light of the truth his father was no doubt reading
between the lines. "And her great-aunt Lupe sure can
cook. Her coffee's a damn sight better than this stuff."

The joke didn't work. He felt his father's hand on his
shoulder. "You are never going to be so old that I won't
worry about you. If she's using you to get into SWAT—"

"Gina wouldn't know how." Mike pulled away from his father's hand and poured out the last of his coffee into the sink before dropping the cup into the trash. "She's honest to a fault, Dad. Good, bad or ugly. She says what she means, and anything she gets she wants to earn on her own merit."

"I thought as much. But I had to ask."

Mike headed to the door, thinking this tête-à-tête was over. But before he turned the knob, he saw Derek Johnson perch on the corner of Gina's desk. She tipped her head up to her partner as they chatted, then pushed to her feet as the conversation grew heated. Derek pointed toward the break room, and Mike had to wonder if the disagreement had to do with him or his father. But whatever they were arguing about ended quickly. Gina tucked her report into a file folder and carried it over to Kevin Grove and Atticus Kincaid, the detectives leading the investigation, and dropped it on Grove's desk. Mike glanced back to her desk to see Derek watching her, too. When she excused herself and headed to the elevators, Derek sank into his chair, slumping like a pouting boy. He wasn't thrilled with whatever she'd said or written. Gina had disappeared around the last cubicle wall by the time he sat forward and picked up the phone on his desk, punching in a number as if an idea had suddenly entered his head.

Mike was about to overstep a line with his father, taking advantage of his KCPD connections. "Dad, I know you're not an investigator, but could you check out Derek Johnson for me?"

"Gina's partner?"

Mike wondered how much of that argument he'd just witnessed had to do with the accusations she'd made that morning after the car chase through downtown.

"I've seen rookies who make fewer dumb moves than that guy does. It's almost like he's sabotaging anything Gina tries to do. I wonder if he blames her for getting shot."

"That's a serious accusation. Not every partnership works out," his father conceded. "Maybe there is some tension between them—especially if someone was targeting her and he feels like collateral damage. Or vice versa. I heard about his fling with Bismarck's wife. But his work history is clean. He came recommended to me for SWAT training, so I know he hasn't been written up for anything."

"What kind of cop do you think he is?"

Michael Sr. considered his answer before speaking. "He's in the top half of every test I've given him. He takes orders. Does what I ask of him in training. He gets along with everybody on the team."

"What about his personal life?"

"I don't know him that well, but I can poke around. No one will question me looking more closely at any of the SWAT candidates. What am I looking for?"

They both watched the animated phone call as Derek smacked the desktop and argued with whoever was on the other end of the line. "I'm not sure. I can't put my finger on it. But something's hinky with that guy. I don't think Gina trusts him any more than I do. Maybe that's one reason she's so damn independent. She doesn't believe Johnson's got her back."

"But you do?" His father crumpled the empty coffee cup and tossed it into the trash. "Need I remind you, you don't wear a uniform? You've got no responsibility here. Gina has a whole police department she can call on for help. Last I checked, putting your life on the line for a woman in trouble isn't part of a physical therapist's job description. You took on Leo Mesner when he was hitting Frannie. Caroline's parents were controlling every aspect of her life until you…" He saw realization dawn in his father's sharp blue eyes. "You're in love with her. Mike, I wasn't matchmaking when I asked you to help—"

"This isn't like Caroline or Frannie, Dad." He didn't need to be reminded of his past mistakes. "They needed a support system—someone who would put their needs first."

"Isn't that what you're doing for Gina?"

"She won't let me half the time." He laughed, but there was no humor in the sound. "She was a fighter before I ever met her. Strong and confident. This injury is just a temporary setback until she figures out a new way to move forward. That spirit is still inside her. She doesn't need me to hold her hand or build up her ego, she just…needs me. For how long, I don't know yet, but—"

"I like Gina well enough." His father looked him straight in the eye, wanting him to really hear what he was saying. "Whatever you decide, you know I'll back you all the way. But I don't want to see you get hurt again."

Yeah, the pattern of Mike's woeful love life did seem to be repeating itself. Maybe he was the one who needed to be rescued from the mistakes he kept making. But not yet. He wasn't giving up on Gina or his feelings for her. "She says she doesn't have the time or space in her life for a relationship right now. But everything in me says that she's the one. That we could be really good together if she'd give us a chance."

"From what I've seen, she cares about you. But caring isn't the same as—"

"Just check Johnson out for me, okay? If his partner can't rely on him or his priorities are somewhere else besides his job… She doesn't need that right now."

"That kind of behavior is troubling when it comes to building a SWAT team, too." With a nod, his father became a cop again. "I hope you're wrong. But I'll see what I can find out. I'll give you a call the moment we take Denny Bismarck into custody, too. In the meantime, keep your head down. I'm not explaining it to Jillian and Will if you get hurt again."

"Thanks, Dad." He pushed open the break-room door to go after Gina and run interference between her and Derek if she needed it.

"Mike?" He stopped and turned as his dad caught the door behind him. He turned for one last piece of paternal advice. "Falling for your stepmother was a complete surprise for me. I thought I was done with love until Jillian came along. And then I nearly lost her."

"I know Jillian's been good for you, Dad. She's been good for all of us. Hell, she's the one who finally got me up out of that wheelchair. She made our family complete."

"If Gina's the one, you need to be a fighter, too." That was the voice of experience that Mike took to heart. "Fight for her with everything you've got."

"I intend to."

WHY THE HECK were they running the air conditioning this early in the spring? Maybe it was the cold marble walls of the Precinct's first-floor lobby that made Gina shiver. But looking through the reinforced glass and steel-framed doors, she still saw more brown than green in the grass outside. And even without a cloud in the sky, the afternoon sun couldn't quite seem to reach her skin through the glass.

She was practical enough to know the chill came from a place inside her. But as to its cause? Where to begin?

She worried that she'd gotten Mike into trouble with his dad by involving him in this private investigation into the cop shootings, along with the rest of her screwed-up life. Not that she'd invited him to be a part of any of it. But now she couldn't imagine *not* having Mike around as her chauffeur, friend, sounding board, protector and catnip. On paper, he was every kind of wrong for her. Wrong background. Wrong neighborhood. Wrong skin color.

But in reality, everything between them felt right. Gina shook her head. How could she ever make a reality with Mike work? Chemistry alone couldn't sustain a relationship. Their personalities clashed. Her family was a responsibility she would never give up. His father might be her boss one day. But the thought of Mike Cutler not holding her for another night, or never kissing her again or never even butting heads with her made her feel empty. And cold.

Maybe the lack of warmth stemmed from the fact that she'd probably irreparably damaged her relationship with Derek by promising to report his less-than-stellar performance on the job to their superior officer and Captain Cutler if he didn't get off his lazy butt and start doing his job the way they'd been trained at the academy. Today she'd been reminded that, technically, it wasn't her job to solve this case. But she knew they could find the shooter if they stayed sharp and ran down every lead. Maybe she'd called in one favor too many, and Derek was right to be angry about helping her. But why couldn't he have just told her *no* instead of stringing her along with his half-hearted assistance? When had they stopped being able to trust each other and communicate like partners should? Maybe Derek had moved on from the shooting. But she needed closure. She needed to know why someone had wanted to change her life so irreparably.

Maybe those answers would finally erase the sense that an enemy was watching, circling, drawing ever closer. And she wouldn't be able to recognize him until it was too late.

Gina moved closer to the rays of sunlight streaming in through the windows and rubbed her hand up and down the sleeve of her jacket while she waited for her great-aunt or -uncle to pick up the phone.

Knowing how slowly Lupe and Rollo moved, she waited patiently through several rings. Still, she breathed an audible sigh of relief when her great-aunt picked up. "*Hola*, Gina."

"*Hola*, Tia Mami." Some of the pervading chill left at the cheerful sound of Lupe's voice. She was glad to hear that someone in her family was having a good day. "I'm calling to see if you're all okay after last night. Mike and I had to leave before everyone was up. Did Sylvie get to school okay?"

"*Sí.* I let her drive the car so she wouldn't have to call Bobby. She wore blue jeans and looked like a teenage girl. So pretty."

"Good." Hopefully, her sister would be smart enough to come straight home after school, too, even if Bobby tried to contact her. "And Tio Papi? How's his blood pressure?"

"He is taking it easy today. He found the Royals playing a preseason game on television. Javier is watching with him." She could hear the laughter in Lupe's voice.

"In truth, they are both napping. They wake up when there's a big play."

The gentle normalcy of such a report made Gina smile, too. "And you're checking Papi's pressure every hour?"

"He fusses at me. But I remind him that Mike said to do so, and he stops arguing with me."

Gina's attention shifted and her smile faded when Harold Johnson, Derek's father, loped up the front steps. The fringe of his brown leather jacket bounced with every stride. Since they were both on their cell phones, intent on their own conversations, Gina turned away from the door, letting the people milling through the lobby and Harold's hurry to get to the elevators prevent him from seeing her. She'd already had enough unpleasant conversations today. Did he really think he had a legal case against her? Was the idea of suing her and the department on Derek's behalf just his way of showing his son he cared? Or were the accusations an idle man's latest idea on how to get some easy money, as Derek claimed? Should she be worried that he was running upstairs to see Derek now?

Gina gradually tuned back in to Lupe's list of errands she needed to run when Sylvie or she got home. "Will Mike be coming to the house again tonight? Should I set him a place for dinner? He has a good appetite, that one."

"Tia Mami…" Suddenly, Harold Johnson's reflection loomed up behind her in the front window. So much for avoiding unpleasant conversations.

"I know, I know. He is not your boyfriend. But he could be. You are being nice to him, yes?"

A shiver ran down her spine like a wintry omen. But having Derek's father intrude on her personal phone call only made Gina stand up straighter. She turned to face him, keeping her voice calm even as she felt the glass behind her back and knew she was trapped. "I have to go. I'll call you later. *Te amo.*"

Harold flipped his oily, gray ponytail behind his back and leaned in toward her. *"Hola, traidor."*

Traitor. Gina tilted her chin, refusing to be insulted or intimidated. "Mr. Johnson."

"I just got off the phone with Derek. Just because you got crippled up doesn't make it fair to file a complaint about my boy."

Crippled up? Is that how Harold saw her? Gina glanced around either side of his worn jacket, wondering if anyone else—maybe the two men coming off the elevators, maybe the elderly couple chatting with a public information officer at the front desk, maybe Derek or even Captain Cutler—saw her as crippled, too. Her damaged hand curled into a fist down at her side, the only outward sign that anything Harold Johnson said could get to her. "Mr. Johnson, you need to take a step back. You're in my personal space."

"Is that so?" If anything, he moved closer.

"Maybe you shouldn't be talking to me. Especially if you're filing a lawsuit. Derek told me. You know what part of town I live in. Even if you had a case, you wouldn't get any money out of me." More than anything, she wanted to shove him back a step. But she suspected turning this battle of wills into a physical confrontation would only add fuel to his irrational fire. "Maybe you should be supporting your son, encouraging him to be a better police officer, instead of making excuses for him or blaming other people when things go wrong."

"Ooh, now the pretty little *chica*'s got her dander up." Harold placed his hand on the window beside her

head, smudging the glass. His clothes smelled of grease
and dust and had the burnt odor of acetylene from the
blow torch he must use at the junkyard to disassemble cars, appliances and old construction materials into
scrap metal. Not that she had anything against a hard-working man, but she doubted this lifelong schemer
and champion of political incorrectness qualified. "I
talked to a lawyer. I'm going to prove my boy is a better cop than you are."

"You're doing it to make a buck and retire at the department's expense. Think about Derek's reputation.
No one is going to want to partner with him if they're
afraid you're going to sue them over any grievance or
mistake they make."

"You admit you made a mistake that got my boy shot?"

She was admitting nothing. Harold could twist the
truth any way he wanted, but Gina knew there was only
one person to blame for her and Derek's injuries—the
gunman who'd fired those bullets. "Your son will get
the job on SWAT if he earns it. If someone else is more
deserving, then they will be put on the new team."

"Like you?" He snorted and backed away. "You immigrants are all alike." *Immigrant?* She and her siblings
had been born right here in Kansas City. Not that it was
worth arguing that point with a man who wouldn't listen. "Thinking you're entitled to something just because
you're a girl or a minority. If you've done anything to
hurt Derek's chances of that promotion—"

"Dad." The stairwell door off to Gina's right closed
behind Derek as he strolled over to join them. "You
need to back off before you get me into more trouble."

Harold ignored his son's stern warning. "No. If she
can't do the job, she can't do it. She needs to step aside
and let a man take her place on the team."

The stairwell door opened a second time, and Mike entered the lobby. He strode straight to Gina, made no apology for nudging Derek aside, reached for her hand and pulled her away from the window and uncomfortable closeness of Derek's father. "Everything okay?"

He'd followed Derek. He'd probably been suspicious of her partner taking the stairs instead of coming down on the elevator. Why was Derek here, anyway? He should still be on duty. Was he following her? Did he know his dad had her cornered down here? Had he summoned his dad to do just that? Or was he truly worried about his father making his situation worse by showing up here?

Gina squeezed Mike's hand, glad for the subtle show of support. "I'm fine. Mr. Johnson was just expressing an opinion. I disagreed."

Derek propped his hand on his father's shoulder, uniting them as a team, too. "Gina never gives up, Dad. She made that perfectly clear." He turned that smug, mocking smile on her. "Well, you should know, G, that I don't, either. I deserve to be on that SWAT team. I'm the one who's still training with them every week. I'm the one going on calls with them." He cupped his arm where he'd been shot. "I'm the decorated cop who's returned to duty. When Captain Cutler posts the list, I'll be on it." He snorted through his nose, sounding just like his father. "You'll still be on medical leave. Unless you think sleeping with your boyfriend here will get you that SWAT badge. I can't compete with that."

Gina felt the instant tension of Mike moving forward. She latched on to him with both hands and held him back. "*Not* my bodyguard," she whispered against his shoulder. "If anybody's going to punch this guy, I want it to be me. You'd better get me out of here."

Chapter Twelve

Gina scooped up the last handful of bubbles in her wrinkled fingers and blew them across the top of the water. She should feel guilty for stepping away from her responsibilities for any length of time. But technically, she was following orders.

Captain Cutler had told her to take the night off. Give other officers a chance to do their job. Mike had told her she needed to rest, that she'd been pushing herself physically more than he thought wise at this stage of her recovery. And since that was the only thing he'd said during the first ten minutes of their drive after pulling out of the KCPD parking garage across from headquarters, she was quick to agree.

Mike's silence wasn't something she was accustomed to. No comment on her stowing her gun and badge in the glove compartment of his truck. No admonishment over pushing so hard on this investigation that they could have both been injured or killed more than once. No explanation for how she'd been ordered to stand down by a superior officer—Mike's own father—and then Mike was the one who'd been taken aside for a private conversation.

A few weeks ago, she would have relished not having him tell her what she could and couldn't do. She would have been more than happy for him to drop an argument when she suggested he do so. But now, after spending so much time together, after drawing on the strength and support of a true friend, after developing these feelings that went beyond friendship—feelings which she was certain would get her into trouble somewhere along the way—his silence worried her. Was Mike angry? Deep in thought? Worried about something he didn't want to share? Did this have to do with the insults Derek had slung at her? Frustration with the investigation? Was he in pain?

Why would the man who prodded her about everything suddenly go silent?

When she'd admitted that she'd like to wash up before dinner, Mike had responded with a simple, "Me, too." Although she hadn't taken the brunt of the garbage outside the West Bottoms café this morning, she felt soiled and slimy just from her conversations with Denny and Gordy Bismarck, and then with Derek and his father. A quick cleanup and fresh change of clothes sounded wonderful.

She thought he'd take her to her house. Or maybe once he'd charmed the socks off her great-aunt during a quick phone call, saying not to hold dinner for them but that they'd be there for dessert, she thought Mike was taking her out to eat someplace, making the break his father had ordered them to take sound very much like a date. She wouldn't have complained if that had been his plan.

But Mike Cutler knew her far better than she'd realized. They drove through a burger joint for takeout and ate in the truck before ending up at his ranch-style home in the suburbs. The neighborhood was quiet except for the kids playing a game of hide and seek across the street. Traffic was light. There weren't cars parked bumper-to-bumper at the curb. The yards were well tended and, though they had mature trees, the street itself was wide, allowing plenty of late afternoon sun through to warm her skin as she tipped her face up to the sky and breathed deeply.

The house itself needed a little work—probably why a single man struggling to make his fledgling business a success could afford to buy a home here—but the space was more than double the size of the home she shared with her family. The fenced-in backyard was made for barbecues and swing sets and gardens. And even though much of the house was stuck in the 1970s or was in the process of being remodeled, he showed her three different bathrooms where she could freshen up.

Three bathrooms. Heaven.

Other than the green and gold of the '70s decor, this place was everything she wanted for her family. It was as suburban and perfect and interestingly unexpected as Mike himself was.

When the tour was finished, Mike left her with a fresh towel and new bar of soap in the tiny powder room off the modern white kitchen. "Make yourself at home. I'll take a fast shower. If you get hungry or want something to drink, help yourself to whatever you can find in the fridge."

While she liked the retro look of the new black and white tiles and nickel-finish faucet, the pedestal sink just wasn't calling to her. "Do I have to use this bathroom?"

Mike shrugged. "I haven't had time or money to remodel the guest bathroom in the hallway yet."

"But it has a bathtub. Could I...?" She tilted her face up to his. "Instead of just washing my face here, would it be a horrible imposition if I took a bath?"

"And I thought *I* was your catnip." Mike smiled at her request. Really smiled. Then he dipped his head to capture her mouth in a kiss that heated her blood but left her little time to respond. Instead, he turned her around, gently swatting her bottom to nudge her down the hallway into the guest bathroom. "Towels are in the cabinet. Some of my little brother's bubble bath, too, if you want. Enjoy yourself."

"I'm sure I will. Thanks."

He closed the door. She heard the shower running in his own bathroom off the master bedroom before she turned on the faucets in the tub to let it fill while she quickly shed her clothes.

She was still lounging in the tub when the shower next door stopped. Gina checked the time on her phone on the towel shelf beside the tub where she'd stowed her folded clothes. Fifteen minutes. She sighed in contentment, closing her eyes and leaning her head back against the tub wall. She hadn't relaxed like this in weeks, months maybe.

This was no five-minute shower and dash to her bedroom to dry her hair so that someone else could get into the bathroom. This was fifteen minutes of pure heaven, soaking in a bubble bath. Even the fruity smell of the child's soap bubbles couldn't diminish the dreamy satisfaction of hot water turning every muscle into goo and the delicious quiet of long-term solitude, interrupted only by an occasional dribble of water as she shifted position.

Had anyone ever pampered her like this? She was a warrior. A protector in every sense of the word. No one ever saw the girly-girl inside her. Had anyone outside of her family ever cared enough to indulge her feminine side? Growing up in a life so full of need, had she ever opened herself up enough to allow an outsider to know her foolish secrets? It was a little unsettling to admit that Mike knew her like that. When had she allowed herself to become so vulnerable to a man? Why wasn't she more frightened by the inherent risk of allowing a man to see her as a woman? Not a cop. Not a big sister or neighborhood protector or family breadwinner. Not a patient or even a friend.

With Mike Cutler, aka Choir Boy and Mr. Nice Guy, of all people—she felt like a woman.

Gina heard a whisper of sound from the doorway behind her.

Make that a desirable woman.

She'd been so deep in thought that she hadn't heard Mike open the door. "I knocked. You've been in here so long and it was so quiet that, when you didn't answer, I'd thought I'd better check to see you hadn't fallen asleep in the tub and drowned."

"Sorry to worry you. But I'm fine." She crossed her arms over her chest, inhaling a satisfied breath. "More than fine, actually."

"Very fine, from this angle." Mike shifted, leaning his shoulder against the door jamb. From the corner of her eye, she could see he'd only been out of the shower long enough to towel off and pull on his jeans. Droplets of water still glistened in the dark spikes of his hair. He'd trimmed his beard back to sexy perfection.

The only bubbles that remained were clinging to the edge of the tub. Gina smiled, not feeling the water's cooling temperature at all. If anything, her temperature was rising. "A nice guy wouldn't stand there staring."

"Told you I wasn't a nice guy."

She found his gaze, dark blue and unabashedly focused on her, in the mirror. The message she read there was crystal clear, and it thrilled her down to her very core. Last night, the timing had been off. She'd been emotionally exhausted and worried about her family. But this evening was a different story. There weren't family members here they had to tiptoe around. Other cops were handling the bad guys tonight. And Mike had been so sullen earlier, to see him engaged and talking again like the man she'd gotten to know made her want to savor this charged moment. "How are your hips and legs? Did the hot shower help?"

"I'm okay."

"Okay enough to climb in this tub with me?" she invited.

Mike walked over to the tub, holding out his hand to her. "Okay enough to help you into my bed in the next room."

"Deal." She curled her fingers around his and stood, proudly showing her body as she stepped out of the tub. "Want to hand me a towel?"

"Nope."

Gina Galvan did not blush. She didn't embarrass easily or feel self-conscious beyond her injury. Yet this man, with a hungry look and a single word, could set her on fire from the inside out.

Gina Galvan *did* know how to go after what she wanted, though. Her skin flushed with heat from head to toe. For once in her life, she felt uncomfortably warm.

While Mike's hungry perusal dappled her skin with a riot of goose bumps, that long, leanly muscled chest beckoned to her like real catnip. His attentive blue eyes told her he wanted her as much as the bulge at the front of his jeans did. She slid her arms around his waist, pressing her naked, wet body against his. She nearly lost her breath as an intense awareness sparked through every cell of her body, lighting her up from the inside out.

The tips of her breasts pebbled with the teasing caresses of his wiry chest hair and solid muscle underneath moving against her as he swept his hands down her back. He paused a moment at her waist before he curved his shoulders around her and reached lower to squeeze her bottom. The soft denim of his worn jeans stroked against her thighs as he spread his legs slightly, lifting her onto her toes and pulling her into his body. The masculine swell of his desire filled the indention between her legs and Gina pressed her face into his chest, letting her body adjust to the ribbons of heat coursing through her from every spot he touched. Matching goose bumps pricked his chest and abdomen as the cooling water dripped from her skin onto his and rivulets of moisture soaked into his jeans. Gina pressed a kiss to one chill bump, and then another, inhaling the clean scents of spicy soap and man, following a path to the firm swell of pectoral muscle. She closed her lips around the taut peak of the nipple she found there. "Now show me how bad a guy like you can be."

His muscles jerked beneath the stroke of her tongue, and Gina felt powerful, sexy, loving that he wasn't afraid to respond to her overtures. But if she thought she was in charge of this seduction, Gina was mistaken.

"Only if you promise to show me how good you can be."

Mike reached beneath her chin and tilted her face up so he could claim her mouth. He tongued the seam of her lips before thrusting between them, telling her with every stroke of the deep, drugging kiss exactly what he wanted to do with her body. Gina released his waist to wind her arms around his neck and hang on as

he lapped up the droplets of water clinging to her face
and neck. She willingly tipped her head back, giving
his lips and tongue access to her throat and the mound
of her breast before he dug his fingers into her bottom,
lifted her off the floor and took the aching nipple into
his mouth. Gina cried out at the fiery arrow of need
that shot from the sensitive nipple deep into her core.

"Mike…" she hissed, clawing at his shoulders.
She'd thought the hot, sudsy water had turned her
bones to mush, but she knew if Mike let go of her now,
she wouldn't be able to stand. She wrapped her legs
around his waist, clinging to him as he turned his attention to the other breast. Between gasps of pleasure,
she dropped kisses anyplace she could reach. The point
of his chin. The strong column of his neck. She nibbled
her way along the perfect line of his stubbled jaw until
his hands and mouth made it impossible for her to think.
"Mike…I want… Can we…?"

His lips came back to smile against her mouth and
plant a kiss there. "Yes."

Despite her protests that she could walk and that she
didn't want to risk aggravating his injuries by carrying her, Mike tightened his hold on her and hauled her
down the hallway to his bedroom. Although he laid her
gently on top of the bedspread, Gina scrambled onto
her knees to maintain contact as he tossed his billfold
onto the bed and shucked out of his jeans.

"I hate that you got hurt." Her fingers tangled with
his, pushing the waistband of his shorts down over his
leanly muscled backside. She found the ridges of scar
tissue at his lower back, tracing them over his hips and
partway down each thigh. Her heart constricted with
compassion, then beat with admiration, over the pain
he must have endured and overcome. Leaning forward,

she pressed a kiss against one particularly wicked look-ing web of scars at the juncture of his back and hip. "I didn't fully understand how badly you'd been injured."

His skin jumped at the brush of her lips against the next scar and he turned. He grasped her by the arms and hunkered down to eye level. "This isn't pity, is it?"

"No." The intensity in those cobalt eyes was impos-sible to ignore. But she held that gaze, willing him to understand the depth of need and admiration she felt. "Is it for you?"

"Never." He dipped his head to kiss the newer, pinker scars on her shoulder before pushing her down on the bed and lying on the covers beside her. She trembled as he nudged his long thigh between hers to rub against that most sensitive place. He threaded his fingers into her hair and kissed her eyelids, her cheeks and the tip of her nose. "I hate that you got hurt, too. But we're not damaged goods, Gina. We're a man and a woman. Every part of me that counts is perfectly healthy. And if you can't tell how badly I want you…"

Gina pushed at his shoulders, turning him onto his back, bracing her hands against his chest, straddling his hips. "Like this?"

His answering laugh was more of a groan as she leaned over him to retrieve a condom from his billfold. His hands played with her breasts and tugged at her hair, making it difficult to concentrate on sheathing him. When his thumbs found the juncture of her thighs and pushed against her, a feverish riot of sensations bloomed like heat lightning. For a moment, she couldn't see, and her hands shook. She could barely stay upright.

Mike sat up, catching her in his arms as she tumbled into his lap. He nipped at the lobe of her ear, whispering against her skin as he lifted her slightly and slipped inside her. "Your secret is safe with me, Tiger."

"What secret?" she gasped, her body opening as he filled her, then tightening again to keep him intimately close.

He framed her face between his hands and claimed her mouth as he moved inside her. "That you're not always a tough chick. Let this happen." He kissed her again. "I've got you."

Gina nodded, believing him as she rocked over his lap in a matching rhythm that stoked the fire between them.

There were no more words. Only touches and kisses. Gasps and moans. Strokes and shivers. The friction between them turned to passion. The teasing words became an answer to every temptation. The understanding they shared transformed into a connection that bound them closer than she'd ever been to any man. Gina had never felt so deliciously warm. She'd never felt so thoroughly loved, so completely vulnerable without feeling afraid. She buried her face in Mike's shoulder as a consuming heat blossomed in her core and seeped with delicious abandon through every part of her. She was still riding the fiery waves of pleasure when he clutched her in an almost unbearably tight embrace and found his release inside her.

Then he fell back against the pillows, pulling Gina on top of him. As she rode the deep rise and fall of his chest, he pulled the edge of the bedspread over her back, securing her against the heat of his body.

"You okay?" he whispered, feathering his fingers into her hair and tucking it gently behind her ear.

"Very okay." Gina snuggled beneath his chin. "You?"

"Very." He kissed the crown of her hair before tugging loose the other edge of the bedspread and wrapping them up in a cocoon of heat and contentment. "I'm always good when you let me get close."

Sometime later, Gina was snuggled up against Mike's chest. His arm anchored her in place as he spooned behind her. He dozed, his soft snoring stirring the wisps of hair at her neck. Gina was wide awake as darkness fell over the city. She traced the dimensions of Mike's long, agile fingers that had brought her such pleasure and ran her tongue around the abraded skin of her mouth, remembering each and every kiss they'd shared.

What was she going to do if she fell in love with Mike? How was she ever going to fit this strong, funny, brave, stubborn, generous man into her life? How could she and her needy family and demanding job be good for Mike? She wanted to be a helpmate, not a hindrance, to any man who cared about her. How would they handle children? Where could they all live without him thinking that all she wanted from him was a house with three bathrooms? What if her hand never got any better than it was right now and she couldn't return to the job she loved? What if she couldn't contribute her fair share to a relationship? Knowing Mike, he would shoulder any burden. But she didn't want to be a burden. She wanted to be his equal, the way they were right now.

She should have a plan in place for falling in love with Mike.

Because Gina knew she already had.

MIKE KNEW GINA was awake the moment he opened his eyes. Even though she was facing away from him in the bed, he could tell by the repetitive circles she traced on the back of his hand that she was deep in thought. That couldn't be a good sign.

He brushed his lips against the nape of her neck so his words wouldn't startle her. "Having regrets?"

The circles stopped. She rolled over to face him, letting him see the troubles that formed shallow lines beside her beautiful eyes. "No, but..."

"A *but* can't be good."

She patted the middle of his chest, warning him he might not like what she had to say. "Where is this leading? What kind of future can you and I have?"

Mike inhaled deeply as the familiar hints at not being good enough or no longer being necessary to a woman chafed against his ears. He wondered at the irony of his guarded sigh pushing his heart against her hand. "What kind of future do you want?"

"I have so many responsibilities. I have plans."

"And they don't include me?" He wasn't particularly proud of the bitterness that crept into his voice. But some scars were slower to heal than others. He pulled his hand from the nip of her waist and rolled onto his back. "For what it's worth, I'm not sorry we made love. I'm only sorry you can't see the possibilities between us."

She pushed herself up onto her elbows beside him. "But you can? Derek said I would sleep with you to get closer to your father and improve my chances of making SWAT."

Mike's thoughts burned with the sick idea that her partner had put into her head. "He knows he screwed up. He was lashing out at you."

"Is that why you were so quiet on the ride here? Did you think his words had hurt me?"

"I didn't like the way the Johnsons talked to you." His hand fisted over his stomach, remembering the blinding urge to ram his fist down her partner's throat for saying such hateful, untrue things. "It's one thing to hear crap like that from a stranger. But from someone you're supposed to trust?"

Gina rested her hand over his fist, willing the tension in him to relax. "I know. I thought Derek was a better man than that—a better friend. Everyone reacts differently when they feel threatened. Fight. Flight. Meanness. Fear. But in one way, he was right." She shrugged, steeling herself for some unpleasant truth she was determined to share. "There are all kinds of advantages to me being with you. But what benefit could there possibly be for you to get involved in my life?"

Mike looked up into her beautiful dark eyes. "You're kidding, right?"

She didn't think a sense of being valued, shared understandings, her great-aunt's coffee, this undeniable attraction and filling the hole in his heart were good enough reasons for a relationship? He turned his palm into hers, lacing their fingers together, trying to convey how her straightforward words and these rare glimpses of tenderness were gifts he would always treasure.

"You're Michael Cutler's son. A fine man in your own right. You have a college degree, own your own business, possess an unshakable sense of right and wrong and could have any woman you wanted." That part clearly wasn't true. But he suspected he would be even less thrilled at what she'd say next. "I grew up in No-Man's Land. I can't afford the time or money to go to college. I've got crazy stress in my life, and I'm..." her gaze shifted away to study some nameless point on the headboard as her voice trailed away "...an immigrant."

He cupped the side of her face, forcing her gaze back to his. "That's Derek and his dad talking."

Infused with a sudden energy, she rolled over and sat up, pulling the bedspread up to cover herself. "Harold Johnson called me an immigrant."

Mike sat up beside her, not understanding why the insult was something to get excited about. "He's a classless SOB. Don't let him get to you."

"He doesn't." Her animated expression told Mike this conversation was no longer about them and their apparently lousy chance at a future. "That's another way all the cop shootings are connected. Colin Cho. Frank McBride. Gina Galvan. Other than Derek, the victims have all been minority cops." She tilted her gaze to his. "Is that a coincidence?"

He shifted gears back to work with her. "Or a sad statement about some of our world today." Apparently, the discussion about a future together had ended.

"So many possible motives. So many reasons one person would want to hurt so many others." When she linked her arm through his and rested her cheek against his shoulder, the edgy frustration he'd felt a moment earlier abated. "Mike?"

"Hmm?"

"I'm sorry I called you *Choir Boy*. That probably didn't feel any different than Harold or Bobby Etes or the Bismarcks calling me *chica* or *querida*. They're labels. Assumptions. Even in jest, those nicknames show a lack of respect. Men like that—they don't care enough to get to know me. I don't want you to think I feel that same way about you. I'm sorry."

He turned his head to kiss her temple. "Apology accepted."

Her soft, lyrical laugh vibrated against his skin. "You *are* too nice."

Mike was beginning to think that there could be a

way for the two of them to make this work, when Gina's phone rang.

"Sorry," she apologized, pulling away. "Hazard of the job."

But she got tangled in the covers. Mike pulled the quilt up to her neck and motioned for her to stay put, while he slipped out of bed. "I grew up with Michael Cutler. I understand interruptions. Dinners. Football games. Driving lessons." He grabbed his jeans and jogged down the hall to retrieve her phone from the guest bathroom. She followed right behind him, two silly grown-ups running naked through his house.

When he handed her the phone, Gina saw the number and frowned. "Hazard of my family," she corrected. She offered him a silent apology as she swiped the answer icon. "*Hola?* This is Gina."

Since he couldn't understand the frantic, high-pitched tones, he assumed the caller was speaking in Spanish. But there was no second-guessing the color draining from Gina's olive skin. Before Mike could ask what was wrong, she was moving, grabbing her clothes, sliding into her shoes, putting on that tough-chick armor that couldn't quite mask the stark fear in her eyes. "Call 9-1-1. Is anyone hurt?" She was visibly shaking by the time she responded to the answer. "Tell them to send an ambulance. Lock the doors, and stay inside. Stay away from the windows. I'm on my way."

Mike had already pulled on his shorts and jeans by the time the conversation had ended. "What's happened?"

Gina reached for his hand, holding on tightly, pulling him toward the front door. "Someone shot up my aunt and uncle's house."

Chapter Thirteen

For the second time in as many days, Gina raced across Kansas City with Mike at the wheel.

An ambulance was already pulling away from the scene by the time Mike screeched to a stop at the end of the block. Gina was already on the ground and running before the truck stopped rocking. *"Mami! Papi!"* She spotted her brother and sister just outside a strip of yellow crime scene tape, wrapping up a conversation with Detective Grove. The overbuilt detective thanked them and moved away to take a phone call. "Javi? Sylvie? What happened? Who's hurt? Is this Bobby's doing?"

"Whoa!" Javier caught her briefly against his stocky chest before she turned away to hug Sylvie. But Mike had followed right at her heels, and now Sylvie was attached to his waist, wrapped up in a brotherly hug. "Nobody got shot, sis. We were all back in the kitchen eating dinner. We heard the gunshots and dove for the floor."

She glanced over at the bullet-ridden front porch and shattered windows at the front of the house. "But the ambulance?"

Javier tightened his arm around her shoulders. "It's Tio Papi. He had a heart attack."

Gina's stomach fell. "Is he…?"

Suddenly, she felt Mike's warm hand slide beneath the curls at the nape of her neck. His tone was as grounding as his touch. "Let's get the facts before we react to anything."

Sylvie pulled away from the anchor of Mike's chest and sniffed back the tears she'd been crying. "The paramedics said he was alert and responsive."

"That's a good sign," Mike agreed.

Sylvie nodded. "He was so pale. He couldn't catch his breath. I gave him a baby aspirin, just like the 9-1-1 lady said."

Mike kept Sylvie turned away from the officers securing the chaotic scene. The CSI van had arrived, too, and the techs were gearing up to remove bullets and analyze any usable foot prints or tire tracks. Kevin Grove was still on his phone, while his partner directed two other officers to close off either end of the block with their cruisers. Neighbors were at their windows or peeking out front doors, too afraid to step out into the night.

"Good girl," Mike praised Sylvie. Gina appreciated that he was keeping her siblings calm and focused, while she was a roiling mass of suspicion and fear and protective anger. "A stressor like having his home attacked could certainly cause it. Are they taking him to St. Luke's?"

The nearest hospital made sense. Javier nodded. "I was just about to drive over there with Sylvie. They look Tia Lupe in the ambulance, too, to monitor her blood pressure, they said. She was sitting up."

"That's standard precautionary procedure once you reach a certain age," Mike said. "It's good for both of them to be together at a time like this." He clapped Javier on the shoulder. "It'll be even better once they're surrounded by their family. You two go on. We'll meet you there later."

Javier frowned at Gina. "You're not coming with us?"

Gina had only been half listening to the conversation. Her attention had shifted to the flashing lights of a criminologist snapping photo after photo of the bullet holes in the posts and siding and chipped bricks on the front porch. And to Detective Grove's clipped conversation that included words like *Bismarck* and *BOLO* or Be On the Lookout For. On the lookout for who?

"I think your sister is in cop mode right now." She was. Mike told Javier and Sylvie to call them as soon as they learned more about their great-aunt and -uncle, then shooed them toward the car. "Don't worry. I'll stay with her. We'll be there as soon as we can."

By the time Javier and Sylvie had taken off, Gina had done a complete 360. Every cell in her body was screaming on high alert. The street and yards were already crowded with cars and junk. There were too many people here. Too many distractions. Too many places to hide. "This is a setup. This whole thing is a trap." The moment Kevin Grove hung up the phone, she ducked beneath the crime scene tape and marched over to him. "Detective Grove? You need to get your men out of here."

He didn't seem fazed that she'd entered the crime scene without permission. "This is the home of a cop, Galvan. Another attempted murder. Of you."

Gina shook her head. "No one was shot here. Not yet." She could feel the truth in her bones as clearly as if she was reading the information off a computer screen. "Have you recovered any of the bullets yet?"

The detective pulled a plastic evidence bag from his pocket for her to examine.

"These aren't like the bullets we took from Bobby Estes. These are rifle caliber."

"Estes carries a hand gun?"

Gina nodded as he pocketed the slugs. "The shooter is here. I know it. This is exactly the kind of chaos he thrives on. The perfect cover. While you and your people are focused on doing their jobs, he's picking out his target." She scanned the chaos and shadows around them. "Whoever he's after this time, he already has them in his sights."

Kevin Grove might be as stubborn as they came, but he was one of the best detectives in all of KCPD. He listened to Gina's take on the situation and started shouting orders. "I want a car-to-car search of anything parked within targeting distance. Clear all nonessential personnel out of here. Everyone on the scene wears a flak vest." He pointed to the porch lights across the street. "Let's get these civilians away from the windows and kill some of these lights. I don't want this guy having any advantage we don't." After the uniformed officers and CSIs scrambled away to do his bidding, Detective Grove looked down at Gina. "You got your badge on you? We can use every available cop right now."

"She's ready." Gina turned to see Mike holding out her badge and holstered Glock that she'd stowed in his truck. His half grin belied the serious warning in his eyes. "I figured you were going to jump into the middle of this, even if you are still on medical leave. I'd rather have you armed and able to defend yourself than be a sitting duck."

"Works for me." Grove nodded toward one of the officers jogging to the house next door. "Since you know these people, why don't you make the rounds and warn your neighbors to keep their heads down until we're finished."

"Yes, sir." Gina took the badge and gun and slipped them onto her belt. Mike's understanding of who she was touched her. Strapping the Glock onto her hip for the first time in almost two months was both empowering—like putting on a favorite pair of jeans—and a little unnerving. This wasn't just a good luck charm she was wearing. It was a loaded lethal weapon. And she was responsible for her use of it.

"You can do this, Tiger." She tilted her gaze up to those piercing blue eyes. Mike Cutler believed in her. So she believed, too. When Gina nodded, Mike reached for her damaged hand and squeezed, reminding her that she could feel with those fingers, she could control her body. She could do this.

She quickly squeezed back. "Thank you."

"Let's go."

"Go? Where are you going?" she chided, hurrying her steps to catch up with his long stride. "Not a cop, Cutler. You need to go back to your truck and get out of here."

But once she slipped under the crime scene tape he held up for her, he fell into step right beside her. "We're partners, remember?"

"Not when it comes to something this dangerous."

"You're not getting rid of me," he insisted.

"Fine. Just keep up."

Gina coordinated the contact with and notification to the residents of the nearby houses with the other officer, taking the east end of the block. She knocked on the doors of two houses, asking the residents if they'd seen anything, then warning them back into interior rooms of the house until KCPD had fully cleared the scene.

She'd just headed up the next front walk when Mike stopped at the edge of the driveway. "Gina."

She followed the general direction of his gaze to the north–south side street. A familiar tan Mercedes cruised slowly through the intersection. The driver watched the police cars blocking the street and the officers still moving around her great-uncle's house.

"That's your stolen license plate."

She spotted the last two digits, 3-6, as the car passed beneath the glow of the streetlamp at the corner. A shiver ran down her spine. Along with a sense of finality and purpose.

Mike was already moving toward the slow-moving vehicle when she joined him. "That's Bobby Estes." What was he doing here? Could he have something to do with the attack on her family, after all? It wouldn't be that hard for him or one of his friends to get a different weapon. Gina tossed Mike her phone as she quickened her pace to keep the car in sight. "Detective Grove's number is in there. Call him and let him know. I'll track the car as long as I can."

By the time Gina reached the corner, Bobby picked up speed. She ran across the street, chasing him past Mike's truck and down the sidewalk to the next intersection. But Bobby gunned the powerful engine and careened out of sight, leaving her no chance of catching him on foot. She stopped at the curb, breathing hard at the full-out sprint, her mouth open, her nostrils flaring. Her only hope was that Mike had gotten through to Detective Grove and an APB on the car and license would stop him before he got too far away. "You son of a…"

As her breathing eased and the urge to curse faded, Gina realized that she'd just run past a piece-of-junk Chevy. She let go of her enmity toward Bobby Estes as a chilling suspicion took its place.

Piece-of-junk Chevy. Derek's particular choice of

words rang in her ears. He *had* remembered something
from the day of the shooting. Gina slowly turned as
the ghost of a forgotten image filled her head. There.
A dented 1500 pickup with a faded red side panel and
rusted wheel wells was parked up the street, lost among
the bumper-to-bumper heaps that littered the neighborhood. It was far enough away from her house not
to be caught in the grid of police officers blocking out
a crime scene, but it sat at an angle that gave its driver
a clear view of everything happening along the street.
Its unremarkable appearance had camouflaged it from
notice. But she saw it now. Saw it clearly. She took one
step toward it. Two. She saw the tip of the rifle balanced
through the open window. Aimed right at her.

"Gun!" Gina yelled a split second before she saw the
flash of gunpowder lighting up the night.

The boom of the big gun's report hit her a nano-
second later. Before she could react, a long, broad chest
slammed into her, tackling her to the ground. Mike. Of
course. Rescuing her. Again.

She heard a rare curse against her ear. A second gunshot split the air. With his long arms snaked around her,
they rolled, scraping across the unforgiving concrete
before they hit crinkly brown grass and slammed to a
stop against a fire hydrant. Mike's back took the brunt
of the impact, and he swore again.

"Mike! Are you hurt?"

But he was pushing her out of his arms. An engine
roared to life in the distance. He pushed her to her feet
as he sat up. "Go!" Tires squealing against the pavement, fighting for traction, drowned out the engine
noise. Mike shoved her away from him. "Go get him!"

Gina shook off the dizziness from their tumble and
started moving. By the time she saw the other offi-

cers running toward the intersection, the Chevy had already bashed in the bumper of the car in front of it and was flying down the street. He was getting away. He couldn't get away.

Gina unhooked her holster and stepped into the middle of the street.

"Gina!"

"KCPD!" she shouted. "Stop the car!" She pulled out her Glock. "Stop the car!"

It picked up speed and raced toward her in a deadly game of chicken. No more wounded cops. This guy wasn't winning. Not on her turf.

Gina raised the gun with both hands, willed her shaky fingers to be strong, slid her finger against the trigger. "Stop the damn car!"

When the driver answered by gunning the engine, Gina squeezed the trigger. She felt the kick in her shoulder and steadied her aim, firing again and again. She took out one headlight, shattered the windshield, popped a tire and kept firing until the truck spun out of control and crashed into a row of parked cars.

The other officers were on the scene in an instant. Kevin Grove pulled the driver out of the car and put him down on the ground, cuffing him. Several other officers had rushed in to turn off the Chevy's motor and assist Grove with dragging him up onto the sidewalk before Gina reached the wreck.

Gina's hand, still holding the gun, was shaking down at her side. She recognized the oily gray ponytail and interrupted the detective charging the perp with numerous crimes. "Harold? Harold Johnson?"

"I didn't kill anybody," Derek's father protested, spitting his anger at everyone around him. "I didn't kill anybody. You can't get me for murder."

Gina shook her head. The adrenaline that had charged through her system a moment ago was draining away, leaving her stunned by the discovery of the man who'd hurt her. "You shot four cops. You shot your own son."

"That was a decoy. A flesh wound. I knew he'd recover. You were the one I was aiming for. Maimed you good, didn't I? Turned you into a cripple."

"You son of a…"

She startled at Mike's touch on her arm, urging her to holster her weapon. "Why?" he asked. "What do you get out of this?"

"It's what Derek gets. What my boy deserves." Gina still didn't understand. "They were going to promote you and that—"

"Shut up, Johnson," Mike warned.

"—ahead of my boy. You immigrants don't deserve a better job. You get special treatment you haven't earned. Just because your skin's a different color or you got boobs instead of—"

"He said to shut up." Grove dragged him to his feet. "Did Derek know about this? Know how you were stacking the odds in his favor?"

"Not at first. But he figured it out." He pointed his nose at Gina since his hands were bound. "Because of all that poking around that you were doing, he figured it out. He knows where his loyalties are. Unlike his lousy partner, who files complaints on him." Harold's face had been cut by some broken glass. His cheek was already swelling from where he must have smacked into the window or steering wheel when he crashed. But his injuries didn't stop him from spewing his vile prejudice. "I screwed up a lot in Derek's life, but I could do this for him. Made it so you couldn't be a cop no more. I got rid of the competition." He snorted a curse. "I thought you couldn't handle a gun no more."

Gina looked right into those bloodshot green eyes without blinking. "I got better."

"Someone take this jackass off my hands. I want to see Officer Johnson at my desk before the night's over," Detective Grove ordered. "Call Impound. And let's contain this scene." While others hurried to carry out his orders, the burly detective smiled down at Gina. "Good work, Galvan. Welcome back. I'd put you on my team any day. I'll get a report from you later." Then he nodded up to Mike. "In the meantime, you'd better get him to the hospital."

"What? Mike!" Gina spun around. Mike was holding on to his left bicep and blood was oozing between his fingers. More than the shock of learning the identity of the man who'd shot her, more than the disappointment of knowing Derek had hidden the truth from her, seeing Mike bleeding because of her might be the one thing she couldn't handle. "You need to sit down." She slipped her arm around his waist and started walking toward his truck. "What were you thinking?"

"That you are the most magnificent woman I've ever known. Facing Johnson down like that."

"I don't mean that. Harold was shooting at *me*. At cops."

"I didn't want you to get hurt."

"It's not okay for you to get hurt, either."

"It's just a graze. A few stitches and a shot of antibiotics and I'll be good."

Even though he seemed to be walking fine under his own power, Gina kept a steadying arm around him. Maybe she was steadying herself because her vision was blurring and her heart was breaking and she couldn't stand that she was falling apart. He sat on the running board of the truck, while she rummaged beneath the front seat to find his first aid kit.

When she knelt in front of him, he captured the side of her face in his hand and wiped away the tears with the pad of his thumb. "Hey. What are these? I didn't think tough chicks cried."

She unbuttoned his shirt and gently peeled the cotton sleeve off his shoulder and away from the wound. "I hate you, Michael Cutler Jr. I hate you for making me cry."

"Um, okay?"

She dabbed at the blood with a wad of gauze, relieved to see it was just a flesh wound. "I'm crying because you're hurt and I'm in love with you."

"You're not selling me on this, Tiger." He pulled her hand away from stanching his wound and dipped his head to meet her gaze. "Does it help if I tell you I'm in love with you, too?"

"You are?" The man had such incredibly blue eyes.

"Has there been one moment when you doubted that I cared about you?"

Gina stretched up to press a hard kiss against his mouth. When she pulled away, his lips followed hers to claim another kiss. Then she caught his stubbled jaw in her hand and kissed him again, feeling the fear fading and the emotional strength this man inspired in her returning. "I don't know yet how we're going to make this work. But we are going to make it work. Understand? You know how good I am at fighting for what I want."

"Do you mind if I fight for us, too?"

"But no more jumping in front of bullets, okay? No more running down bad guys." She poked a finger in the middle of his chest. "Not a cop. Even if I don't make SWAT, I'm going back to a beat or working with domestic-violence victims or earning my detective's badge. That's my job."

"If we're going to be a partnership, what is my job?"

Those blue eyes mesmerized her. Treasured her. Believed in her. "To love me every day of your long and healthy life."

Mike wound his uninjured arm around her and pulled her in for a kiss. "Deal."

Epilogue

Two months later

Mike would never tire of seeing Gina in her starched KCPD uniform. She walked into the CAPT clinic with takeout and drinks to share lunch in his office and his heart did a familiar tumble of love and pride. She carried herself with confidence when she wore the blue-and-black with her badge, gear belt and holstered gun. And her sweet figure filled it out in a way that was anything but mannish.

He waited while she greeted Troy and leaned in to give him a hug. Mike dutifully raised his gaze to her dark eyes when she turned to include him in her announcement. "Did I tell you I've already got three people signed up to take my self-defense training class here? Vicki Bismarck, Frannie and Sylvie. Lupe said she's going to bake cookies and bring them down to watch. Says maybe she's not so old that she can't learn a thing or two."

"Lupe's baking cookies?" Troy raised his hand. "Anything I can do to help with your class?" When Mike and Gina laughed, Troy pressed his hand against his heart. "Hey, I'm serious. She's brought food to each of the sessions where I've been helping her work on her balance issues."

Mike took the bag from Gina before teasing his friend. "You know that's not how we get our bills paid around here, right?"

"Yeah, but don't tell her that. That woman can cook."

Although Gina smiled much more often these days, she was serious for a moment. "So, it's okay if I set up my class here? I know it's not physical therapy, but you are in the neighborhood."

Mike read the agreement on Troy's face and nodded. "I think feeling safe and building self-confidence all fits into that wellness goal we strive for. Just let me know when and I'll schedule the gym for you."

Frannie came out of her office carrying a computer pad. "As long as you leave Monday and Wednesday nights open. That's when Colin Cho and Frank Mc-Bride are coming in for their PT."

Mike couldn't deny the recent upturn in business. Or the credit Gina deserved for helping him. "I wouldn't have thought you'd be the best PR person. But you've brought in a half dozen new clients from KCPD."

Gina shrugged. "Cops have a lot of back and joint issues. I just suggested they come here."

Troy rolled his chair up beside Frannie. "Hey, you signed up for Gina's class? You gonna wear those tight shorts you had on the last time you worked out?"

"Troy!" Her freckles disappeared beneath a healthy blush.

"Like I'm not gonna notice." Troy grabbed Frannie around the waist and pulled her into his lap before wheeling them both into the gym. "C'mon, Sunshine. Let's get you warmed up."

Once they were alone in the hallway, Gina smiled. "They seem happy."

"They do." Mike led her into his office and set lunch

out on his desk while Gina closed the door. "What about you, Tiger? Are you happy?"

"What do you think?" Gina was right there when he faced her. She nudged him onto the edge of the desk, moved between his legs and kissed him very, very thoroughly.

Mike returned the favor, pulling her onto her toes and taking over the kiss. When she mewled that telltale hum in her throat that told him they were about to take this embrace past the point of no return, Mike set her back on her feet. He settled his hands at her waist, resting his forehead against hers as they both struggled to return their breathing to normal. "Do you like working the special victims unit? I know how badly you wanted SWAT."

"There'll be other SWAT teams. The guys who made it deserve the honor." She tilted her gaze up to his, sharing an honest, beautiful smile. "Maybe one day my shoulder will be good enough so I can make the cut. If not, I'm okay. I think I'm really good at what I'm doing now."

"You'd be good at anything you set your mind to."

"Your dad doesn't still feel guilty about not putting me on the new SWAT team, does he?"

"No. I think he's happier to know he's got you for a future daughter-in-law."

Resting her hand against his chest, Gina eyed the simple solitaire he'd given her. "Me, too."

They shared another kiss before sitting down to lunch. As it often did between them, the conversation turned to her work and family. By the time they'd finished, she'd updated him on the Bismarck brothers, who were both in jail now. Rollo Molina's health was still a concern, but his stress was more manageable now that

Mike had moved the family into his home. Lupe cooked, Javier helped with the yard and Gina had planted a garden. Bobby Estes was still trading favors for fast cars in No-Man's Land, but at least he'd stopped pestering Sylvie. "We'll have to catch him at something where we can make the arrest stick," Gina groused. "But I like a project."

"Just say the word and I will help you do whatever is necessary to get Estes off the streets." Mike stood as Gina circled the desk to meet him.

"Not a cop, Cutler."

"No, but *you* are, Gina Galvan." He leaned in to kiss the teasing reminder off her mouth. "You're my cop."

* * * * *

APPALACHIAN
ABDUCTION

DEBBIE HERBERT

This book is dedicated to all my author friends who help me, especially: Gwen Knight, Lexi George, Ash Fitzsimmons, Michelle Edwards, Tammy Lynn, Fran Holland and Audrey Jordan!

And, as always, to my husband, Tim, my dad, J.W. Gainey, and my sons, Byron and Jacob.

Chapter One

Only one road climbed Blood Mountain to the exclusive Falling Rock community and its luxury mansions. But Charlotte had no interest in accessing the gated community through the pretty lane lined with oaks and vistas of manicured lawns and gardens.

No, the backside view of the swanky neighborhood was where she'd find clues to the ugly mystery of Jenny's whereabouts. And to get to this precious vantage point in the hollow, she'd hiked a good two miles down from neighboring Lavender Mountain. She raised her binoculars and focused on the nearest cabin's massive wooden deck.

Nobody milling about there.

She slanted them to the cabin's impressive wall of windows, hoping to catch a glimpse of Jenny—or any other young teenage girl, for that matter. The bastards.

Still nothing.

But she wasn't discouraged. If nothing else, her career as an undercover cop had taught her patience. She waited and, after a few minutes, scanned the row of houses yet again before dropping the binoculars and taking a swig from her water bottle.

Faint voices rumbled through the air, low, deep and indecipherable. Quickly she raised the binoculars to search for the source. But the field glasses weren't necessary. Near the base of the cabin, only one hundred yards away, stood two men armed with shotguns and wearing walkie-talkies belted at their waists. Where had they come from?

Suddenly the muscular guy on the left raised an arm and pointed a pair of binoculars at *her*.

Oh, no.

She'd been spotted, despite the fact that she was dressed in camouflage and had tucked her red hair into an olive ski cap. The man on the right raised a shotgun to his shoulder and scanned the area. Charlotte dropped to the ground on her stomach, praying she was out of sight. Three deep breaths, and she raised her binoculars again. The men had disappeared.

Strangely, she wasn't comforted by that realization. They could be creeping their way downhill to find her. Time to get the heck out of Dodge. Charlotte tucked the binoculars and water bottle into her backpack and with-drew her pistol. Not the standard-issue one provided by the Atlanta Police Department—they'd forced her to turn that in—but the personal one she always kept stashed in her nightstand. If they found her, she'd be ready for them. The cool, hard wood snuggled in her right hand provided a surge of comfort, just as it always had on those nights when she'd been home alone and whispers of danger made her imagine some ex-con had discov-ered where she lived.

Charlotte eased the backpack onto her shoulders. Cocking her head to the side, she paused, listening for anything out of the ordinary.

Wind moaned through the trees, and dead leaves gusted in noisy spirals. Then she heard it: a methodical crunching of the forest underbrush that thickly carpeted the ground. At least one of the men was headed her way.

Damn it.

She jumped to her feet and ran, heart savagely skittering. Its pounding beat pulsed in her ears, loud as the echo of dynamite. A slug whistled high above her, and bark exploded from near the top of a pine sapling eight feet ahead.

Did they mean to kill her or merely frighten her off? Because if their aim was the latter, it was working. Charlotte kept running, this time darting behind trees every ten yards or so. No sense providing them with an easy target. The path seemed to stretch on forever, though, and a stitch in her side finally screamed in protest at the brisk pace. Charlotte stumbled behind a wide oak and sucked oxygen into her burning lungs.

Another shot rent the air, but she couldn't tell where the bullet landed. Hopefully not anywhere nearby. She pushed off and ran once more. Wind blasted her ears and cheeks, stinging her eyes as she sped down the trail, mentally calculating her best escape. If only she knew how close they were.

There were three options. One, return to the nearby abandoned cabin and hope they didn't see her sneak inside. Two, if there was enough time, hightail it to her truck hidden in a copse of trees and take off. The problem with the first two was that her cover might be compromised if she were spotted. The third option was riskier, but it would leave her free to continue her planned surveillance.

Another shot torpedoed by like an angry hornet, grazing the side of a nearby oak. This shot was much closer. Again, she ran. Gnarled roots gripped her right foot and she fell flat. A pained cry slipped past her lips. She stared down at her twisted knee and the ripped denim on the outside of her right thigh where brambles and rocks had cut deep. Blood oozed and created a widening stain on her pants. Her right temple throbbed and she knew a knot would form on her scalp. Charlotte swallowed hard, pushing back the sudden stab of dizziness that narrowed her vision. No allowing the blessed relief of unconsciousness to take hold. The things men like them could do... she'd seen way too many victims and knew a thousand ways evil people could inflict pain upon another.

Focus. You can't let them catch you.

Option three it was, then. Quickly she ripped off her jacket and pressed it against her wound. Couldn't let blood drip to the ground and become a trail that would lead the men to her. Not to mention the danger of passing out from blood loss.

She hissed at the wave of pain that slammed into her knee. It was as if someone had tripped a live wire inside her that burned through her veins and traveled up and down her body. Even her mouth had a metallic, coppery taste. Charlotte spit a mouthful of blood, clamped her teeth shut and crouched low. Plenty of time later to moan and groan. Right now she had to find cover.

It hurt like hell, but she managed a stumbling trot, forsaking the main path and stumbling through shrubs and bands of trees. Winter was a hell of a time to seek shelter in the Appalachian forest. The plants were practically stripped bare, their only foliage a few withered, stubborn leaves that had not yet broken loose. But there were patches of evergreen shrubs and small pine trees still to be found. She'd checked on that in her earlier recon of the area.

"Where'd he go?" one of the men shouted from afar.

The answering voice was much closer. "Lost sight of him."

She dove behind a clump of rhododendrons and curled into a tight ball. If they hadn't seen her, she had a chance. Her breath sawed in and out—to her ears, loud enough to doom any hope of going unnoticed. She crossed her left hand over her thigh and pressed down on the wound to staunch the bleeding. Those damn briars ripped flesh like tiny surgical knives. The pistol was in her right hand, loaded, with the safety off. If they came too close and found her hidey-hole, she might be able to fire at them first.

They tromped through the area and continued the search. Subtlety wasn't their strength.

"You go that way," one of them shouted, pointing in the opposite direction, "and I'll head this way."

A tide of relief whooshed through her body. One would be easier than two if it came to a showdown.

Footsteps approached, and she rounded into herself even tighter, not daring to breathe.

Please don't stop. Keep walking, she prayed as the nearest man stomped not twenty yards away. He wore black leather boots and dark denims—that much she could see—but she didn't dare lift her face and examine him further.

He stumbled on a rock and tumbled forward several steps, managing to catch his balance at the last minute. "Damn it," he snarled, then yelled, "Anyone out there?"

Right. Like she was going to raise her hand and pop up like a jack-in-the-box to answer him.

"If you can hear me, you were trespassing. Stay away from Falling Rock, got it? Hey, Ricky, let's get back to the house," he called to his fellow tracker, then walked back toward the main trail.

Another voice, deeper and more gravelly, spoke. "Probably just a hunter, anyway."

"I didn't see no shotgun on him, but he was wearing camouflage. Scrawny little fella."

"Might not have been hunting animals. Could be one of them 'sengers."

What the heck was a 'senger? Whatever they were, she was grateful they provided another plausible explanation for a person roaming the woods in camouflage attire.

Her breathing slowed at the sound of receding footsteps. Today had almost been disastrous, and she wasn't in the clear yet.

If those men were smart, they'd linger a bit, hoping that their prey would be cocky enough, or stupid enough, to reemerge on the trail, mistakenly believing the danger had passed. But six years on the force had honed her methods and instincts. *Never believe your opponent isn't as smart, or smarter, than yourself,* she'd been warned.

And so she waited. As shock and adrenaline faded, the pain in her knee and temple increased. As soon as she got to the cabin, she'd clean the wound and patch it up with the first aid kit she'd brought along. She also had Ace bandages to wrap her knee. It had to be a superficial injury, since she'd been able to put weight on her leg and run. The air chilled her skin, although not enough to counteract the burn of ripped flesh. Were the men still lying in wait? She wasn't sure how much longer she could stay. Every moment the wound went unattended increased the likelihood of infection, and she desperately wanted to take something for the building headache.

Gingerly Charlotte rose and tested putting weight on her right leg. A bolt of pain traveled up from her knee, and she bit her lip to keep from crying out. Hurt or not, she had to leave. Those men might return with a larger force. And even if her damn cell phone worked out here in the boonies, who could she call? Right now, she was a pariah to her coworkers, and if she called the local authorities, they'd pepper her with questions.

She gripped her pistol more tightly and set off toward the main trail. Once she got there, she'd walk along the outskirts until she was sure the men were truly gone.

The trail looked as forlorn and barren as when she'd first hiked it that morning. Charlotte ran a hand through her hair and then stopped cold. At some point, her hat had been blown away by the wind. Good thing the men were gone. Now she needed to push through the pain and walk. She could do that. There was no choice.

It appeared she'd survived this encounter. Sometimes the best option was to hide and live to fight another day. Justice delayed beat justice denied. Besides, it wasn't as if she harbored a death wish, though death would be preferable to what these men were capable of doing.

They might have succeeded in running her off for the day, but she wasn't giving up. She couldn't give up. Not today, not ever. She was the last, best hope for Jenny and the other lost girls.

THE NEAR-DESERTED roads suited James just fine. October, while beautiful in the Appalachians, had drawn crowds of tourists flocking to view the scenic foliage. But November's gray skies and biting wind meant that Lavender Mountain was back to its usual calmness—and he could sure use some peace and quiet. Returning from Afghanistan hadn't exactly led to the grand family homecoming he'd once envisioned. Instead, murder had wiped out half his family before he'd even set foot in Elmore County. That tragedy, combined with what the doctors deemed a mild case of PTSD, had left him edgy and filled with uncertainty about the future.

With no conscious plan, James meandered the deputy sheriff's cruiser up the mountain road, and he startled at the sudden sight of his father's old cabin. How often had he done this very thing on routine patrols? Ended up driving right here, precisely at the place he'd rather *not* be?

He shook his head in disgust and hit the accelerator. Memory Lane had zip appeal.

Twenty yards down the road, a flash of beige slashed through his peripheral vision. What was that? He did a U-turn and craned his neck, searching the brown-and-gray woods. *There*, he spotted it again. Curious, he pulled onto his father's old property and exited the cruiser, shrugging into his jacket. He strode along the tree line until he solved the riddle: someone had parked their truck toward the back of the property behind a couple of large trees. He retrieved his cell phone and hurried over on the off chance that someone might be injured or stranded.

It was locked, but he peered in the tinted windows. No clues there. The interior was practically empty and spotlessly clean. He headed to the back of the truck and took a photo of the license plate. He'd call in the numbers shortly.

No damn reason it should be here. No *good* reason, anyway. Frowning, he went to the cabin and pulled out his keys. Better make sure some squatter hadn't decided to take up free residence.

He inserted the key in the lock, but it wouldn't turn. James withdrew it and checked—yes, this was the correct key. Someone had changed the locks. He felt a prickle of unease mixed with anger, and the twin emotions churned in his gut. Anger won.

"Open up," he bellowed, rapping his knuckles on the old wooden door. "Sheriff's department."

Silence.

He stepped back on the porch and noticed for the first time that every window was taped up with plain brown wrapping paper. This was *his* place, damn it. He'd chosen not to live in the cabin he'd inherited, but that didn't mean just anyone could help themselves to it and move in. James rapped on the door again, louder. "Open up now, or I'll break down the door."

Still no answer.

With a quick burst of energy, he kicked the door. Splinters flew, and the frame rattled. He kicked again, and it burst open. James shuffled to the side and removed his sidearm, then proceeded cautiously inside with his gun raised. The room was abnormally dark from the taped windows, and only the light from the open doorway illuminated the den. At least his sister had gotten rid of most of the furniture. In this room, only an old couch remained. No place to hide.

James flicked the light switch, grateful he'd kept the power on. The Realtor had insisted on it so she could show the place to potential buyers. *That* was a laugh— the place had sat empty for months. Seemed fixer-upper cabins in remote Appalachia weren't a hot commodity. Hardly a shocker.

He made his way to the kitchen, gun still drawn. Like the truck and the den, it was pristine, and mostly empty.

No signs of forced entry or habitation. Three more rooms to check. He padded down the short hallway, gun at the ready. The guest bedroom and bathroom doors stood open, but the main bedroom door was shut.

Gotcha, he almost whispered aloud. He spared a cursory glance in the guest room that housed only a bed. Nothing was underneath the tucked comforter, so he eased toward the closed door. Spots of spilled liquid, still wet, stained the pine flooring leading from the bedroom into the bathroom. He flipped on the bathroom switch, careful to keep his gun aimed at the closed bedroom door.

Smeared blood and dirt formed a drag pattern on the floor and basin and continued their path to the side of the tub. A wet towel lay beside the tub, as well as strips of gauze and a bottle of rubbing alcohol. Someone had been hurt—and recently.

A grating metal sound came from behind the closed bedroom door, and James barreled into the room. A mattress lay on the floor, and food provisions and clothes were neatly stacked in plastic containers along the side wall. But it was the open window that drew his immediate focus. Oh, *hell* no, they weren't slipping away. He was going to get answers. James rushed to the window and stuck his head out.

Red hair whipped in the breeze. A petite woman wearing a camouflage shirt and black panties—no pants, no shoes—ran through the yard. Blood oozed from ripped flesh on her right leg, and she limped as she headed toward the truck.

Okay, that was far from the thug or drugged-out squatter he'd expected. "Halt," he ordered.

She didn't even bother looking back at him as she continued a gimpy run to the tree line.

"For Christ's sake," he muttered, tucking his sidearm back into its holster and rushing through the cabin. He exited the busted front door and stormed down the porch steps to the side yard. "Stop right now," he called out.

Again she ignored his command. Stubborn, foolish woman. He couldn't let her get in that truck. But as he ran toward her, she spun around, raising a pistol in both hands and aiming it straight at his heart.

James threw up his hands and cautiously walked forward before pointing at his badge. "Lady, you don't want to shoot an officer of the law." He nodded at her leg. "Looks like you need medical attention."

"You're a cop? Let me take a look at that badge." She approached and examined the badge on his uniform. The harsh glint in her eyes softened, and she lowered the gun. "Sorry. I didn't stop to see who broke in when I ran."

"I identified myself as from the *Sheriff's department*," he said grimly. She might be pretty as all get-out and pretend compliance, but people weren't always what they seemed. This job and his tour of duty had taught him those lessons well. "Now gently lay down the gun and step away from it," he ordered.

She kept her eyes on him as she bent her knees and placed her weapon on the ground. "No problem, Officer. I always—"

Her right leg gave out from underneath, and she swooned forward—which put her hands right by her gun, he couldn't help noticing. Quickly he crossed the distance between them and kicked it several yards away.

"Suspicious much?" she drawled.

"I'll call for an ambulance or drive you to the hospital in my vehicle. Do you have a preference?"

"Neither. I'm fine. It's not as bad as it looks."

"There's blood on the right side of your scalp. Not to mention your mangled leg. Might need stitches, at the very least. Antibiotics, too."

"I said no." She struggled to stand and then limped past him. "Just let me get dressed."

"Not until you explain how you got hurt and what you were doing in my cabin."

That got through to the woman, and she whirled around. "*Your* cabin?" She bit her lip and mumbled, "Of all the damn luck."

"You can explain on the way to the hospital."

"I don't need a doctor."

She hobbled to the door, and he scrambled to retrieve the fallen weapon before following her, trying to deduce this stranger's game. "You hiding from an abusive husband?" he guessed.

"No," she said flatly, grabbing onto the porch rail and wincing as she climbed the steps.

"There are shelters that can help, you know. In fact, there's one less than thirty miles—"

"I don't need a shelter. I can protect myself."

Like hell she could. "Fine. You want to clam up? Let's go down to the station. I'll run your license plate and clear up this mystery."

She sighed, resignation rounding her shoulders. "If you don't mind, I'd like to get my clothes on."

Woman was probably freezing her butt off. "Of course. Look, whatever kind of trouble you're in, we can help."

She blinked and nodded her head. "Thank you, Officer. I'm sorry about intruding and…and pulling that gun on you."

About time she saw sense. "Fine. I'll wait here." He

took in her pale face, and his eyes traveled down to her right leg. "Can you manage by yourself?" he asked gruffly.

"Of course. Any chance I can have my gun back now? After you unload it, of course."

What kind of fool did she think he was? "No, you may not."

She cast her eyes down in a demure manner. "Be back in a minute."

He watched as she made her faltering way down the hall, her back ramrod straight. What kind of man could hurt a woman that way? It looked as though she'd taken a hard tumble. Her ex was obviously dangerous. He'd see that whoever the man was, he'd get his due punishment.

James paced the empty den, thinking of his dad and sister Darla, both murdered at the hands of another family member. How sad that the ones we most loved were often our worst enemies and betrayers of our trust.

He shook his head and strode to the windows, stripping off the papers the woman had taped up to avoid detection. It shouldn't matter, but he hated the thought of the cabin being shrouded in darkness night and day. Bad enough he'd abandoned it to die a slow death from neglect.

What was taking her so long? Had she passed out from loss of blood?

A flash of red in the barren landscape caught his eye.

Damn it to hell. She was running away again, this time fully clothed and with a backpack strapped to her shoulders.

Should have known the minute he'd seen those teal eyes and titian-colored hair that this woman spelled trouble.

Chapter Two

Charlotte suppressed a wince as she collapsed into the seat across from his desk at the Lavender Mountain Sheriff's Office. She glanced at his nameplate. Officer James Tedder. The name had a familiar ring.

"Driver's license, please," he said matter-of-factly, firing up the computer on his battered wooden desk. He examined her gun and wrote down the serial number before opening his desk drawer and locking it away.

"License. Right." She made a show of rummaging through her backpack. "Shoot," she mumbled. "It's not here. Must have left it at the cabin. Sorry."

He quirked a brow. "How convenient. Tell me your name."

The officer was bound to get her real name from the truck's license plate numbers. No use lying. "Charlotte Helms."

He picked up his cell phone, and she saw a photo of the rental tag as he typed. But there was no need to panic just because he had her name. He'd run a standard background check and see she had no priors. No reason for him to look further and check out her employment record. A little fast talking on her part to avoid trespassing charges, and her cover would remain uncompromised.

"The truck's a rental," she volunteered. "Thought it would be easier to keep my ex-boyfriend off the trail that way." She trembled her lips and let her eyes fill with tears. This wouldn't be her first performance for getting out of a jam. And acting was so much easier when she actually felt like crying from pain. "You were right. I'm running from someone."

"How did you wind up in my cabin?"

Bad spot of luck there. It'd looked perfect when she'd scouted the area earlier—practically deserted but sturdy, and the location so close to Falling Rock. She'd figured it would be less conspicuous to camp there than to rent a room at a local motel. The tourist season was long over and she didn't want to attract attention.

"It...seemed safe," she hedged. "I was afraid if I stayed at a motel he'd track me down. I don't have much cash on me, only credit cards." She added a hitch to her voice. "I left in a bit of a hurry."

He paused a heartbeat, drumming his fingers on the desk. "How did he hurt you?"

His face and voice were neutral and she couldn't tell if he was buying her story or not. Charlotte thought fast.

"It wasn't my ex-boyfriend. I'd gone for a walk," she lied. "Got a little stir crazy holed up in the cabin. I must have ended up on someone's property because a shot came out of nowhere. Might have been an irate land owner. Or...maybe it was a hunter mistaking me for a deer? I didn't stick around to find out. In my hurry, I stumbled and took a hard fall."

"Exactly where were you when this incident occurred?"

"About a mile or two south of the cabin? I can't say. I was focused on getting the hell out of there."

A *ding* sounded on the computer and he turned to the screen. "Truck was rented from Atlanta," he read. "Two days ago. The contract states you've rented it for two weeks."

"That's right." Charlotte swiped at her eyes and sniffed. "I apologize for staying at your cabin. I'll be glad to pay for a new door and any other damages incurred."

He leaned back in his chair and steepled his fingers. "A crime's been committed here."

"Please don't arrest me for trespassing. I've never been in trouble with the law." Then she remembered. "And, um, sorry for that other incident, too."

"You drew a gun on me," he stated flatly, a muscle flexing in his jaw.

"I thought you were my ex."

"Again, I identified myself before entering the cabin. Fleeing an officer is a crime."

"But I didn't *see* you," she argued. "I couldn't be sure who you really were."

"And then there's the matter of someone taking pot-shots at you. I'm going to need more details on that."

She waved a hand in the air dismissively. "Why? I'm fine. I won't be pressing charges even if you find the one who fired. I just want to move on. I decided during that long walk today that I want to stay with my parents in South Carolina for a bit. Get my life together and put distance between me and my ex."

"Move on all you like, but I still have the problem of a rogue shooter in the woods. We're going back there and you're going to show me where you were when this happened."

"But...my leg."

"You claim the injury's not serious enough for medical attention."

Her temper rose. "But I can't walk a mile and go scouting around the wilderness."

"I have a four-wheeler. You won't have to walk."

"I see." She cleared her throat and pressed a hand to her head injury. "Could we do this tomorrow?"

His blank expression never wavered. "You have a permit to carry a weapon?"

Charlotte blinked at the sudden change of topic. The damn gun. Once he ran the serial numbers he'd have her employment history. And then her cover was blown.

"Of course I have a permit."

If only she could be sure he was a clean cop. It would be amazing to have assistance in saving Jenny. And he acted sincere with his direct manner. His face was rugged while at the same time maintaining a certain boyish charm. She couldn't deny that she found him appealing and his forthright air inexplicably tugged at her to confide everything. But this was a small town, one that Jenny Ashbury's kidnappers had chosen for a reason. And that reason might very well be that local law enforcement had been paid to turn a blind eye on the abductor's comings and goings.

She couldn't take that chance with Jenny's life.

A middle-aged lady with dark hair and bifocals stuck her head in the door. "Harlan needs to speak with you ASAP."

Officer Tedder frowned. "Can't it wait?"

"Nope."

Charlotte's paranoia radar activated. Harlan Sampson was the county sheriff. Was there any way he knew who she was and why she was here? Was that why he wanted to speak with Officer Tedder?

"Be right back," he said.

Alone, Charlotte leaned over the desk and peeked at the computer screen. Her not-so-flattering driver's license photo was on display. Feeling restless, she stood and strolled to the open window, wincing at the burst of pain.

Downtown Lavender Mountain was picturesque with its gift shops and cafés. From here she could see the local coffee shop and a gourmet cheese store. Despite the off season, a few people were out and about.

Leave. Just leave. Now.

Charlotte bit her lip, debating the wisdom of her inner voice. It's not like Officer Tedder had arrested her, right? And he didn't issue an order to stay when he left. If she could keep out of sight for a couple of hours and then hitch a ride back to her truck, maybe he'd give up on questioning her.

Yeah…but then what? Stay the next town over? It wouldn't be as convenient, but she could rent a different vehicle, find an inconspicuous place to park it near Falling Rock, and then continue on as before. All it took was one photograph of any of the lost girls by a window, one slip-up by the kidnappers transporting their captives, or one girl to escape their cabin and make a run for it. Then she'd have the needed proof to obtain a search warrant and rescue Jenny.

It was worth the risk. Hell, she'd already damaged her career by coming to Lavender Mountain anyway. So what if a local cop got angry with her and eventually charged her with trespassing? That was the least of her worries.

With a longing glance at the locked drawer housing her gun, Charlotte scooped up her backpack. She'd get another weapon. If nothing else, she was resourceful and a risk-taker. With that, and a whole lot of luck, she'd bring down that human trafficking ring.

SOMETHING ABOUT HER story didn't jibe. James hurried back to his office. More than anyone, he realized these mountains were as dangerous a place as any city. He need look no further than his own family for confirmation of that sad fact. But hunters shooting at a woman didn't sound right. Hunters around these parts knew you shot by sight, not sound. Was it an irate property owner? It was possible they'd fired a warning shot or two in the air. People 'round these parts didn't take kindly to trespassers on their land.

And what was she so afraid of? If Charlotte Helms could afford to rent a truck, she could afford a motel. No reason an ex from Atlanta would ever think to look in this area.

Time for answers.

Squaring his shoulders, he stepped back into his office. His empty office. No, surely she didn't run again. She wouldn't, would she?

"Sammy," he bellowed, scurrying down the hall.

"What's up?" Samuel Armstrong asked, not looking up from his computer.

"Did you see a woman leave the building a minute ago? A redhead limping on her right leg?"

"Nah," he drawled with a wry grin. "Saw y'all come in, though. You manage to lose her?"

"Maybe." James hurried over to Zelda's cubicle. "Did you see that woman in my office leave?"

Zelda laid down her pencil and crossword puzzle book. "No, my back's been to the door. Want me to check the ladies' room?"

"Please."

She rose from her chair with a sigh. He followed Harlan's secretary to the lobby restroom. But he guessed Zelda's answer before she emerged half a minute later.

"She's gone."

Aggravating woman. "Thanks," he mumbled, hurrying back to his office for his jacket. He pulled it on as he rushed out of the lobby. He'd spoken with Harlan about five minutes, tops. Charlotte couldn't have gone far with an injured leg and no vehicle. He glanced up and down the road, but no flash of red was in sight. James crossed the street and entered the coffee shop. This was as good a place to start as any.

Myrtle waved as he entered. "What'll it be, Jim Bob? Your regular with two sugars and one cream?"

His campaign to have people address him as James instead of his boyhood nickname was not a success. "No, I'm looking for a woman. A petite redhead. Seen her?"

"You have very particular tastes," Myrtle said with a wink. "Didn't know you were partial to redheads and leather."

He was *so* not in the mood for jokes. "Sheriff's business. Has she been here or not?"

"Touchy today, huh? Nope, haven't seen your mysterious lady."

"Call me if you do."

He exited the shop and tried half a dozen others. No one had seen Charlotte. He stood in the middle of town square, hands on hips. Every minute that went by increased the likelihood that she'd succeeded in giving him the slip. *Think.* Where would he go if he were in her shoes? Probably slink around the alleys and slip into a shop's back door if someone approached. He hustled behind the coffee shop and scanned the alley lined with garbage bins. Down at the far end, he spotted Charlotte rounding a corner, red hair flaming like a beacon.

I've got you now, he thought with grim satisfaction. He hurried to the end of the backstreet in time to see her slip into the Dixie Diner.

Now he'd get answers.

Inside the diner, the aroma of fried chicken, biscuits and gravy made his mouth water. Chasing Charlotte was hard work and it was past lunchtime. He scanned the tables filled with families.

No Charlotte.

He proceeded to the back exit and stuck his head out to check the alleyway.

Still no Charlotte.

Only one place left unchecked. He rapped on the ladies' room door once and then entered.

Lucille Bozeman, an elderly member of the local Red Hat Society, shrieked and clutched her pearls. "James Robert Tedder," she said breathlessly, "what on earth do you think you are doing?"

At least she'd used his full name instead of Jim Bob. Normally, he found her and the other members of the Red Hats a hoot—amusing older ladies with their red hats, purple attire and carefree spirit. But not today. Heat traveled up the nape of his neck. "Sorry, Mrs. Bozeman. I'm looking for a woman."

"You've come to the right place, but this is hardly appropriate behavior. I'll speak to Harlan Sampson about this. How dare you…"

But he tuned her out and bent over. No feet were visible under the stalls, but one door was closed. He knocked on it.

"Come on out, ma'am."

A long sigh, and then a dry voice answered. "You going to order me to put my hands up or you'll shoot?"

"I don't think that'll be necessary," he answered in kind. "Unless you try to flee from an officer of the law again."

Charlotte emerged with a wry smile and leaned against the wall, arms folded. "Sorry. You never arrested me so I'd assumed I was free to leave earlier."

Despite her flippant attitude, James noted that her face had paled and her eyes were slightly glazed. "Right. So that's why you ran and tried to give me the slip." He nodded at the bump on her head. "You might be concussed. Change your mind about going to the hospital to have that looked at?"

"Not at all. I'm fine."

"Are you in some kind of trouble, young lady?" Lucille walked over, the brim of her outlandish purple hat brushing against his shoulders. Her gaze swept Charlotte from head to toe. "You appear a mite peaked."

Charlotte's smile was tight. "Just a few superficial wounds."

"Jim Bob, you should take her to see Miss Glory. She's a sight better helping folks than any doctor."

Actually, that wasn't a bad idea—and the healer's shop was only two doors down.

He addressed Charlotte. "What do you say? No forms to fill out or insurance cards to process."

"All I need is over-the-counter pain medication. If you could point me in the direction of the local pharmacy?" She pushed past them both and made for the bathroom door.

James took her arm. "You're coming with me. Stop being so stubborn. It's obvious you're hurt. Miss Glory can fix you right up."

He caught a glimpse of Lucille gaping at them in the bathroom mirror. News of this bathroom encounter would be all over town in an hour.

"Thanks for the suggestion, Mrs. Bozeman." He leaned into Charlotte, whispering in her ear, "If you don't want your business common knowledge, let's continue this outside."

He stayed near her as they walked through the diner. Charlotte briefly glanced at every face in the crowd, as if taking their measure. She opened the door and stumbled, pitching forward a half step. The full weight of her body leaned against him. She smelled like some kind of flower—a rose, perhaps. It was as though a touch of spring had breathed life into a dreary November day.

Charlotte stiffened and drew back. A prickly rose, this one—beautiful but full of thorns. James clenched his jaw. Didn't matter how she looked or smelled or felt. This woman was a whole host of complications he didn't need or want. He'd get her medical attention, find out why she came to Lavender Mountain and then escort her to her truck and wish her well.

"If you're on the run as you claim, the last thing you want is an infection to set in that injury. Miss Glory really can help you."

"If I agree, will you give me a ride to my truck afterward and let me go?"

"You're in no position to negotiate. You trespassed on

my property and pointed a gun at me, as well. I believe I'm holding the trump card."

"Okay, okay," she muttered.

She hobbled beside him until they reached the store.

Miss Glory's shop, The Root Worker, was dark. Glory claimed the light deteriorated the herbs strung along the rafters. The placed smelled like chamomile and always reminded him of the time he and his sisters, Darla and Lilah, had all come down with the flu at the same time. Their mother had infused the small cabin with a medicinal tonic provided by Miss Glory.

"What brings you here today, Jim Bob?" Glory asked, grinding herbs with a mortar and pestle. She swiped at the gray fringe of hair on her forehead. Her deeply lined face focused on Charlotte. "And who's your friend?"

James quickly made introductions. "She's here because of a lump on her head, a twisted knee and cut skin on her right thigh. She refuses to see a doctor, so I thought I'd bring her to you."

Glory didn't even blink an eye. No telling how many strange stories she'd heard over the years.

"I've already cleaned it out and bandaged it," Charlotte said. "Don't see the need for anything else."

"How bad do your injuries hurt?" Glory asked gently.

"I wouldn't turn down some aspirin."

"Hope you're not so stubborn that you ignore any signs of a concussion or infection. You start runnin' a fever or see red streaks flame out from the flesh, you get to a doctor quick, ya hear?"

Surprisingly, Charlotte nodded her head slightly. "I will."

"You seein' double or got the collywobbles in yer tummy?"

"None of that."

Every moment he spent in her company, his doubts about her story grew. He remembered her steady aim and fierce eyes as she aimed a gun dead center on his chest. This wasn't a woman who ran away from danger. She'd confront it head-on.

"Tell you what I'm gonna do, darlin'. I'm sending you home with a gallon of my sassafras tea. You drink a big ole glass of it at least three times a day. That sassafras is my special tonic that'll clear up any nasty germs brewing in yer body."

Miss Glory went behind the counter and rummaged a few moments, returning with a couple of items.

"A little poultice to draw out infection," she said, pressing it into Charlotte's palm. "And a few capsules filled with feverfew, devil's claw and a couple other goodies. Much better than an ole aspirin."

Charlotte shook her head. "I don't—"

"Now don't you fight me on this, child. I see the pain in them eyes of yers. You'll need a sharp mind to be of any use to anyone and you can't have that without rest. Take it before you go to bed at night."

"Thank you," Charlotte murmured, stuffing the poultice and pain packet in her backpack.

"Jim Bob, grab a gallon jug of sassafras tea on yer way out. It's in the cooler by the door." Glory rested an arthritic-weathered hand on Charlotte's shoulder. "I see danger surrounding you, child. They's people wish you would go away from here and never come back."

James was used to Miss Glory's eerie predictions. He wasn't sure he believed in all that hocus-pocus, but people around here claimed she had the sight. Couldn't hurt to pick her brain. "What do you know?" he asked sharply.

"Me?" She threw up her hands and cackled. "I'm just an old woman who's been around too many years to remember, and can sense people's energy."

He was reading too much into the old lady's ramblings. Wouldn't have even bothered coming to her shop, but Lilah swore that Miss Glory was the only one who helped her get through a difficult pregnancy and then again helped with her colicky baby.

Charlotte backed away to the door, suspicion hardening her classical features. "Who am I in danger from?" she asked sharply.

"That's not for me to say. But I suspect you know the answer to your own question."

Charlotte nodded and continued edging to the door.

He wasn't going to let her run again. James plopped down a couple twenties on the counter. "Will that cover everything?"

Miss Glory nodded and leaned in, her breath a whisper against his ear. "Watch after her. She needs help whether she likes it or not."

James shook his head. "I'm no one's protector," he grumbled. He had his own demons to fight. His tour of duty overseas had left him unwilling to get involved in others' problems, beyond what was required as an officer. Lilah often fussed that he'd become too withdrawn. But whatever—all he wanted was to perform his duties and be left alone.

Charlotte gasped suddenly and flung herself against the side wall, away from the shop door. A couple of mason jars filled with herbs crashed to the floor. The scent of something earthy, like loam in a newly plowed field, wafted upward.

"What is it?" Instinctively, his right hand went to his

sidearm and he surveyed the scene outside. On Main Street, a sleek black sedan accelerated and turned out of sight from the town square.

"Are they gone?" Charlotte asked past stiff lips.

"Whoever was in that vehicle? Yes. What's this all about?"

Charlotte lifted her chin and carefully picked her way through the strewn herbs and glass shards. "Sorry, Miss Glory. I'll pay, of course. Where's your broom? I'll sweep up the mess."

Glory shooed her off, then bent over and whispered something in Charlotte's ear before addressing them both. "I'll take care of this. You go on, now, and do what you have to do."

Charlotte rummaged through the backpack and dug out a wad of bills. She lifted a hand at the sight of Glory's open mouth. "Take it. I insist. And thanks for your help."

James grabbed a jug of tea and followed Charlotte outside. He took her arm. "What really brings you to Lavender Mountain?"

Chapter Three

"Anyone ever tell you that you're stubborn as hell?" Charlotte grumbled. She climbed into James's truck, slowly swinging her injured leg into the cab, and then eased back onto the leather seat with a sigh. She wouldn't admit it for a month's salary, but running from his office had been a mistake. Her first instinct, born from years of busting street gangs and drug rings, was to flee until she'd formed a plan and was ready to strike.

James got in beside her and slammed his door shut. "Start talking."

"You're taking me back to my truck, right? I'll be out of your hair soon enough."

"That wasn't the deal. What's your game?"

She opened her mouth, and he started the engine. "Don't lie," he said. "You're not running from some ex."

She had no choice. Once he ran the gun paperwork, he'd know. "I'm an undercover cop. Atlanta PD Special Crimes Unit."

He shot her an assessing glance, then pulled the truck away from the station and into town. "What are you doing ninety miles from the big city? Anything going on around here, we should be part of the investigation.

Atlanta's urban area may sprawl for miles, but this is still our jurisdiction."

He might have her cornered, but she didn't have to tell him the whole truth. "I don't suppose you'd accept the proposition that the less you know, the better?"

James snorted.

"Right. Okay, I'm investigating a missing girl and have reason to believe she's being held in the Falling Rock community."

His brow furrowed. "Why? Give me details."

"How can I be sure you're trustworthy? Well, not necessarily *you*," she amended. "But what about your boss and coworkers? Any of them could compromise—"

"I trust the sheriff explicitly," he ground out. "Harlan Sampson is as honest as they come, and I'm not saying that because he's my brother-in-law. I've known him all my life. We've been friends since third grade."

"That's fine for you, but it doesn't assure me. Far as my research shows, the previous sheriff is doing time for twenty years of covering up moonshine and murders."

"And Harlan has been working for over a year now to clean up the force," James said with a scowl.

"Are you sure he's finished? Most criminals don't work in a vacuum."

"Two officers were fired. That's out of an office with a dozen employees. I have complete faith in the ones remaining."

"But you've only worked with them six months." She'd done a cursory background search on every officer.

He shot her a glance, eyes widened in surprise. "You've done your homework," he noted, driving away from the downtown area and starting the drive up a winding mountain road.

"I know you've done a couple tours in Afghanistan. Army Special Forces."

"You seem to have me at a disadvantage," he said coolly. "I know nothing about you. Yet."

"No doubt you'll check the gun paperwork and confirm my story. I'd do the same in your position."

"So why did you break into my cabin? Couldn't you survey the Falling Rock area more directly?"

Typical cop. A rookie one, no less. "That's the difference between working undercover versus running routine patrols and answering callouts. Direct isn't best in my line of work. I picked your cabin because it's within walking distance of where I can get a behind-the-scenes view of most of the Falling Rock houses."

"What do you expect to find? Are you hoping by some miracle that the missing girl is going to step outside? I don't foresee that happening."

Charlotte squirmed. Put that way, it did sound like a lame plan. But then, he didn't know all the particulars. He didn't know that she was investigating a ring, and as such, she hoped to observe vehicles pulling into backyards to hide the drivers' comings and goings. Even license plate numbers would provide worthwhile leads to pursue. So let him think she was foolish. The less she revealed, the less interference and lower possibility of word getting back to the traffickers that she was closing in on their operation.

"Don't make this hard," James warned. "Either voluntarily give us the information so we can help find this missing girl, or drag your feet until we force the information out of your supervisors. Your choice."

Damn it. If he contacted Atlanta, she'd be ordered—again—to stop searching. And that was the best-case scenario. Worst case, it was entirely possible she'd lose her job. But she'd weighed the risks from the start, and the decision had been easy. Jenny was her best friend's daughter. If she didn't try her best, how could she live with that knowledge? How would she be able to face her best friend for the rest of her days? She couldn't.

"If I tell you more, can we keep it between us?"

"No way. I can't keep this secret from Harlan and the others. Like you said, I'm pretty new here. Everyone else will have more experience. Don't you want the full resources the sheriff's office can provide?"

Hell, yeah. No question. Charlotte gazed out the passenger window, where shadows already lengthened with a hint of the coming twilight. To his credit, James didn't press her as she weighed the pros and cons of telling him everything. But it wasn't much of a choice, really. She had a bum leg now, and she'd been seen by the bodyguards who were obviously protecting the traffickers.

"I do need your help," she admitted. "But if you go to the sheriff, he'll contact my boss for verification of my story, and then all hell will break loose."

James's eyes narrowed. "If you're on the up-and-up, what's the problem?"

"I've been suspended." There, she'd said it. Six years of exemplary service, and now she was in the hot seat. James would think she was a total screwup.

He pulled into the cabin's driveway, shut off the engine and faced her, arms folded. "Why?"

She jerked her head from his piercing gaze and stared down at her folded hands. "Because I won't give up on this case. That's why. The official charge against me is insubordination."

"Go on," he urged at the beat of silence between them.

Charlotte lifted her head. Officer Tedder had been more than patient. He could have arrested her for trespassing, or even decided she was too much trouble and not searched for her after she'd fled. But he'd found her and coaxed her into getting help for her injury. A good man, she decided. Perhaps even a trustworthy one. She'd been burned before, but mostly, her gut and intuition had served her well in a dangerous profession.

"Can we talk somewhere other than here? Sitting in the open in your truck is an invitation for trouble." Her stomach churned as she remembered the black sedan with tinted windows that had cruised through town.

He countered with a question of his own. "Is this where you run from me again?"

"No running. You can follow me in my truck while I get a motel room, or we can go in your cabin to talk."

James drummed his fingers on the steering wheel. "My cabin. I'll park my truck behind yours. No casual observer passing by would notice it. Probably safer than you spending the night at the local motel with your vehicle in plain view, anyway."

"Agreed."

He drove across the yard and parked behind her rental truck. Charlotte opened her door and eased onto the ground, putting most of her weight on her left leg. If it came down to another chase by land, she was doomed.

They walked across the yard, but try as she might, a low hiss of pain escaped her lips as she started up the porch steps. James placed a hand on her right forearm, and she leaned into his strength, hobbling across the wooden porch.

Damn if it wasn't heaven to feel his strong muscles taut and solid against her. For the first time since arriving at Lavender Mountain, Charlotte felt safe and protected. Not an emotional luxury she often indulged in with her line of work.

James frowned at the broken door frame as he ushered her inside. "Stay here while I check the cabin," he murmured, setting down the jug of sassafras tea from Miss Glory.

She nodded, grateful. Ordinarily that kind of take-command attitude by male coworkers annoyed her, but he was the only one around with a gun and two good legs. And he was her best hope for rescuing Jenny.

"ALL'S CLEAR," JAMES ANNOUNCED, returning to the den and placing the gun in his holster. "And I closed the back bedroom window you opened earlier this morning. You remember, the one you crawled out to run from me."

Charlotte nodded, making no apologies, and limped to the couch. Instead of collapsing into an exhausted heap, she settled in primly, back straight and feet crossed at the ankles.

What a striking woman. In the dark shadows, her hair glowed like sun fire and her eyes gleamed with intelligence, determination and…sorry to say, still a trace of wariness. Not that he blamed her for the mistrust. She'd most likely seen the worst of human nature, just as he had in Afghanistan.

He picked up the jug of tea and strode to the kitchen, where he located a glass in the near-empty cabinets. Miss Glory's tonic was purported to do wonders, and he hoped it lived up to its hype. He added ice to the glass and poured the pale, caramel-colored drink. Charlotte was being damn foolish about treating her injuries, but he couldn't force her to accept medical attention. A wry smile twitched the edges of his mouth. He imagined Charlotte Helms could be mighty stubborn when it came to changing her mind.

That was okay—he could be as damn stubborn as

Charlotte, and he meant to draw out everything from her about this case. The greatest lesson he'd learned in the military was to work with others as a team. It enhanced the chance of success for any mission. He preferred a quiet, solitary life these days, but when it came to his new job, he was all about teamwork.

James returned to the den. "Drink up," he ordered, handing Charlotte the glass. "I'll be back in a minute."

"Where are you going?"

"To get my tool kit."

And his tablet, because he wasn't letting this woman out of sight again. While she slept tonight, he'd double-check her story. Insomnia came in handy every now and then.

James scanned the yard and then strode to his truck, retrieving the toolbox, the tablet, a box of crackers and a cooler packed with water bottles. Another thing the military had taught him was to be prepared. The water and crackers would satisfy their basic needs for the evening, but he longingly recalled the smell of fried chicken and mashed potatoes at the Dixie Diner. Tomorrow he'd go back and eat his fill at the lunch buffet.

Inside, Charlotte sipped tea and raised a brow. "Quite an armful. You must have been a Boy Scout."

"Lucky for you. What did Miss Glory whisper to you back at the shop?"

She blinked at the sudden question. "I couldn't understand what she muttered. Her Southern accent's pretty strong."

Again, he suspected she wasn't truthful, but in this instance, it didn't matter. Not in the grand scheme of things. He let it go. "What do you think of Miss Glory's tea?"

"Has a licorice taste. I like it. Either that, or I'm really thirsty. You believe in this stuff?"

"People who refuse standard medical treatment can hardly complain."

A surprised chuckle escaped her lips, and her eyes sparkled. "Touché."

James nearly dropped the supplies in his hand. He'd known she was attractive—that was plain to any fool— but when she smiled? Stunning.

Charlotte's eyes widened and their teal hue deepened. The space between them grew electric, humming with energy. He swallowed hard and turned away, setting down the supplies and then gripping his hammer like a lifeline. Sexual attraction was the last thing he needed in this sticky situation.

"I don't have replacement hardware, but I can nail up this door and make do for tonight. That is, if you still want to stay here?"

"You'll let me stay?" Her voice was husky, and she cleared her throat. "Thank you."

"For now. Unless your safety becomes compromised. First thing in the morning, we'll—"

"*We?* I don't need you to stay with me."

"You think I'd leave you alone out here?" He might be reluctant to get involved with people, but he always did the right thing. Or tried to. "As I was saying, at dawn, we'll get my four-wheeler, and you can show me where you were shot at."

She slowly nodded. "Like I said, I don't need your protection, but it's your cabin, after all. As far as returning to that place, it's a needle-in-a-haystack possibility, but if we can find those shell casings, it could be important down the road."

He set to work, quickly repairing the door. Satisfied, he returned to the kitchen with the cooler and put the water bottles in the fridge. The only thing edible in the refrigerator was a jar of peanut butter, and so James set the crackers and peanut butter on the table with two paper plates and a roll of paper towels.

"Dinner's served," he announced. "Basic protein and carbs."

Charlotte took a seat. "I'm used to it. If we want to get really fancy, there are some granola bars and apples and such in my—I mean *your*—bedroom."

She started to rise, but he motioned her to stop. "I'll get them."

It wasn't fried chicken, but her contribution would add a little variety to the meal. In the bedroom, a plastic crate against the back wall was stuffed with dried foods. He lifted it, ready to carry it to the kitchen, when he spotted the laptop on her mattress. Stifling a twinge of guilt— there was a missing girl in danger, after all—he hit the space bar, hoping she hadn't properly shut it down earlier.

The screen lit and filled with images of scantily clad young girls. And by young, he noted that most didn't even appear to be sixteen years old.

"For the discerning customer," he read.

James closed the computer, lips curled in disgust. What possible connection did it have to Lavender Mountain? This was no simple kidnapping.

Charlotte's soft voice drifted down the hallway as he made his way back. "I'm doing everything I can, Tanya. I promise I won't stop until I find her." A slight pause, and then, "We'll get her back. I know it's killing you, but remember to let me call you. Not the other way around. Okay?"

As if she had eyes in the back of her head, Charlotte spun around, cell phone at her ear, as James entered the room. "Gotta go, hon. Later."

"Sounds like this case is personal," he observed, taking a seat across from her. "Who's Tanya?"

Charlotte laid the phone down and sighed. "Why do I have the feeling you're going to pry every last detail from me?"

"Because I am," he said with a grin, spreading peanut butter on a cracker. But his amusement faded at the memory of the computer photos. "Is Tanya the mother of the missing Jenny?"

"Yes. And my best friend." Charlotte pushed away her plate. "You see why I can't quit, don't you? I mean, wouldn't you do the same for your best friend?"

He flashed back to that night in Bagram when he'd awakened in the barracks and realized the cot beside him was empty. He'd waited, figuring Steve might be in the bathroom, but the minutes had ticked by, and he knew something was wrong. Against orders, he'd sneaked out of the barracks and searched the compound until he'd found Steve—huddled behind the garbage dump, holding a gun next to his head.

It still haunted James. Another minute and his friend would have committed suicide. He'd carefully taken Steve's gun away and escorted him to the infirmary. To hell with alerting the sergeant first and following protocol for a missing soldier. He'd known in his gut that Steve was in danger. "You're not the only one with a black mark on your record," he admitted. "I understand that sometimes—"

A shot rang out.

James froze, his breathing labored. Had he imagined the sound? No, Charlotte's hands gripped the edges of the table—she'd heard it, too. This was real and in the here-and-now.

"They've found us," she whispered.

Chapter Four

Charlotte reached for her sidearm and felt nothing but bare denim at her hip. Damn. She kept forgetting James had confiscated her gun. Its absence made her feel vulnerable and powerless. First order of business in the morning was to get it back.

But that didn't help her now.

As if they'd done this together a dozen times before, she and James rose from the table and flattened their bodies against the side wall by the window.

"See anything?" she asked.

"Nothing but shadows."

"Still think it's nothing but a shot-happy hunter out there?"

"Getting a little too dark for a regular hunter," he admitted.

"As opposed to what—an irregular hunter?" she quipped. "Maybe now you'll believe me when I tell you it's Jenny's kidnappers."

James kept his gaze out the window. "Shooter's motives don't matter at the moment."

"Right. Sorry. So what's the plan?"

"We wait."

"That's it? We wait?"

"And watch."

To hell with that. "We could get on your four-wheeler and see who's out there."

"And what if that shot was meant to draw you out? You'd be a sitting duck. Stop acting like this is your first rodeo."

He was right. Damn it. This was her least favorite part of the job—stakeouts and waiting for someone else to make their next move.

"There could be more than one, you know. Maybe they're going to surround the cabin." Hugging the wall, Charlotte made her way over to the den window on the opposite side of the cabin. "I'll keep a lookout here."

Dusk settled on the woods that were wrapped in a gray mist. The outline of her rental truck at the tree line was barely visible. The vehicle was useless to her now that she suspected it had been spotted. If there was time, she'd exchange it for another one tomorrow. Her eyes and ears tingled with focus as she tried to find shifting patterns in the shadows, or the whisper of an out-of-the-ordinary snap of twigs.

"We hear another shot, call for backup," James commented.

The minutes stretched on in a tense silence, and she shifted all her weight onto her left foot.

"Knee bothering you?" he asked, his gaze still concentrated on the gathering darkness.

How did he know with his back to her? Probably a good cop to be so observant of the slightest shift in details. "Hurts a little," she admitted.

James stepped away from the window. "Let's go. If there's a stalker out there, I believe they'd have made a move by now. No sense standing around all night. We'll come back at first light and take a look around."

"Sounds like a plan." Frankly, she was relieved. Her leg hurt like hell, and there was no way she'd be able to sleep in this cabin again without worrying she'd awaken staring down the barrel of a gun.

"You stay inside while I start the truck."

"No way. We go together."

He opened his mouth to speak, but he must have read her determination. "Okay. Anything you need to bring with you?"

She'd almost forgotten. "Yeah, let me grab my stuff. I'll be quick."

Charlotte scurried to the bedroom and then stuffed her laptop in the large duffel bag already filled with clothes and toiletries, prepacked necessities in case she'd needed to leave in a hurry. She rushed back down the hall, and a chill draft from the open door blew over her body. A truck engine started outside, and headlights pierced the darkness. How dare he? But the anger was soon replaced by a seed of fear. Was he leaving her alone in this compromised location? An image of a dark alley flashed across her mind—her old partners, Roy and Danny, fading into the shadows as they ran from the drug dealer flashing his small but lethal-looking pistol. She'd run, too, but not as fast. Not near fast enough to outrun a bullet. A quick peek behind her shoulder and she saw the dealer had aimed his gun at her.

She'd turned and faced him then. Better to see the flash of gunfire and take it head-on than be hit in the back while running away.

The drug dealer unexpectedly laughed and dropped his weapon. "Some friends you got there. You ain't no coward, I give you that." His arm had lowered to his side. His features had hardened. "Get out of here," he'd growled. "And don't ever forget this is my turf."

She didn't forget. Not the dealer, nor the partners who'd left her an easy target.

Faster than she'd ever believe possible with a bum leg, Charlotte flew out of the cabin and onto the porch, duffel bag clunking across the wooden floorboards.

The truck engine rumbled in Park. James wasn't leaving without her. She climbed in the king cab, throwing the bag into the back seat, where it landed next to the gallon jug of sassafras tea he must have grabbed from the fridge.

"You tricked me," she commented. But her words held no bite.

James shifted the truck into Drive. "I don't know about the big city, but around here, we try and protect women."

"I'm a cop, not a woman."

His brow quirked.

"Well, you know what I mean."

"I'm well aware you're a woman," he said drily.

The air was charged with something other than danger this time—the space between them sparked. Charlotte cleared her dry throat. "And a cop," she insisted. "Don't forget that part."

The truck jostled along the dirt driveway. "Uh-huh, right," he muttered.

"Wait. I'm not thinking clearly." She dug into her jeans pocket for her keys. "I can drive my own truck and then exchange it for a new one in the morning. Take me back."

James pulled onto the county road. "We'll worry

about your truck in the morning when we come back. For now, I think it's best we leave it."

"Okay, then. I can't argue against your logic there." Charlotte stuffed the key in her pocket.

Heat blasted from the vents, and she held her hands up against the warm air.

"Cold?" James asked.

She shrugged. "My hands are always cold."

"No gloves?"

"Somewhere in my bag. I'll dig them out later."

James opened the console and pulled out a pair of black leather gloves. "Here."

"Thanks, but that's not nec—"

"Go on. No sense suffering." He laid them in her lap.

Charlotte slipped on the overlarge gloves. They were lined with fleece and felt comfy and toasty against her skin.

The truck sped through the night, and they were in town in ten minutes. Charlotte rubbed the passenger window, scrubbing away the condensation to peer at the street. "What motel do you recommend?"

"Neither of them. There's only two."

He turned the wheel sharply, and the lights of the Dixie Diner blazed in front of her. "Why are we stopping here?" she asked.

"I'm starving. I'll pick us up a couple plates to go."

She frowned. He could have got his own meal after he dropped her off, but the rumble in her stomach couldn't argue with the need for food. Real food. Eating nothing but crackers and apples and granola bars for two days had gotten old. Charlotte followed him in, and her knees went weak at the smell of fried chicken. James ordered a meat-and-three plate for each of them, and her mouth salivated. She couldn't wait to check into her room, eat and then enjoy a long bath with no fear of intruders.

Back in the truck, James turned sideways in the seat and didn't start the motor. "This Jenny you're looking for—was she caught up in some kind of pornography ring?"

"You could say that."

"How about being a little more specific?"

It might have been framed as a question, but she knew it was a demand. Hell, if he knew this much, he might as well know the rest.

"A human trafficking ring. She's one of many girls who have been caught in its trap."

James nodded, but he didn't say a word as he started the truck and backed out of the parking space. He retraced his route and kept driving until downtown was visible only in the rearview mirror. They were far from anyone, on a lonely backroad where anything could happen.

A small frisson of fear chased down her spine. *Stop, just stop*, she chided herself. If he were one of the bad guys, he would hardly have stopped for fried chicken before doing her in. Or loaned her his gloves. Still, her hand sought the passenger door handle. "Where are we going?"

"My place."

"Now, wait a minute," she protested. "If you think—"

James held up a hand. "I have a spare bedroom. It's just a precaution."

She studied him—the hard planes of his face and his aura of calm command. Okay, she *would* feel safer staying with him. But he could have at least asked before assuming she'd follow along.

"I can't read you," she admitted. "Half the time you act like there are other explanations for the shootings, and the other half, you're extremely cautious."

"Blame my army training. I imagine all possible scenarios and then prepare for the worst."

Curiosity sparked to learn more about James. "What was it like in Afghanistan?"

His fingers drummed the dashboard as he considered his answer. "Lot of extremes. Hot during the day, cold at night. Periods of boredom followed by bursts of danger."

"I understand the boredom–danger thing. Lots of that with undercover work." Charlotte wondered if the experience had left him scarred. "What did you do in the army?"

"IED patrol."

She gave a low whistle. The man had put his life on the line with every mission. Lucky for him, he'd returned home in one piece. "Must have been tough. Do the memories ever bother you, now that you're home?" Charlotte bit her lip. This was none of her business. "Never mind. I have no right to ask. I thank you for your service."

He was silent for so long, she didn't think he was going to respond, and she stretched her right leg, trying to find a position that didn't hurt.

"It only bothers me sometimes at night," James said quietly. "Insomnia's a bitch."

James shook out two of Miss Glory's herbal pills on the kitchen table along with a glass of sassafras tea. "Drink up."

"I'm fine. My leg's not—"

"Stop it. I've seen you wince whenever you stand up

or sit down. The way you favor your right leg. Are you always this stubborn?"

Charlotte picked up one of the pills and held it in her palm, frowning. "I don't like feeling out of control. Like I could fall asleep and not wake up when there's a possibility of an intruder lurking."

"Remember that insomnia I mentioned? I'll be up all night." He felt his mouth twitch. "Let my problem at least benefit you."

She bit her lip, obviously debating the wisdom of taking the pills. "What the hell." In one swift motion, she popped them in her mouth and washed them down with tea. "I don't have much faith they'll be that strong, anyway."

"Hope they work. Others swear by her herbs and roots." He knew how to make her see it his way. "Besides, get a good night's rest, and you can work longer and harder tomorrow."

"Every day Jenny spends with that ring is torture for Tanya and Jenny. I never forget that. Not for a minute."

"I don't doubt your dedication. One night's sleep will help you think clearer, and means you can bring her and the others home sooner. I saw the photos on your laptop. The ones of those girls for sale." Disgust roiled in his stomach. Hungry as he'd been, he started regretting the fried chicken and gravy.

"When did you look at my laptop? How did you—"

"When we were back at the cabin."

"Seems like I'm not the only one with a suspicious nature."

"Comes with the territory in our line of work. Never know when it might save our ass."

She shook her head, a bemused smile lighting her

green-blue eyes. "Next you'll have me thanking you for doubting me."

"Good. Now let me use my influence to get you to shower and then let me take a look at your injuries."

A tinge of red crept up her neck and face. "I can take care of myself."

"A little late for modesty. The first time we met, you weren't wearing pants."

Charlotte groaned and lifted her hands to her face. "I forgot about that."

He hadn't. Sure, at the time, he'd been a little distracted by the gun she'd aimed at him, but yeah, he'd noticed the bare, shapely legs. James rose from the table. "Go on. I'll see to cleaning up."

Charlotte rose, and again a slight wince crossed her face.

"I've got aspirin," he noted. "You don't have to strictly rely on Miss Glory's home remedies."

"Might as well give them time to work. I'll see how I feel after a bath."

Head held high, Charlotte left the kitchen, and then paused by the den's fireplace mantel. "What's this?" she asked, picking up a wooden carving of a deer and examining it closely.

"Something I whittled," he admitted, feeling self-conscious. "It's a hobby, kind of relaxing."

"This is beautiful," she murmured. "How long did it take you to make this?"

"Hard to say. I whittled on it here and there in the evenings."

"It would take me a lifetime," she said with a laugh, placing the wooden deer back on the mantel. "Besides having zero artistic talent, I'm never accused of being a patient person."

Charlotte headed to the hallway. Despite the stiff set of her back and shoulders, it was obvious that the injury bothered her.

Whether she was willing or not, if the cuts showed infection, he was taking her to a real doctor.

James stacked the paper plates and napkins, pausing at the sound of running water. Right now, Charlotte was stripping. In his house. Just down the hall. He pictured her curvy body stepping into the steamy tub and groaned. It had been way too long since he'd been with a woman.

All his nights were long, but this one might be the longest yet. Resolutely, he put up the leftover mashed potatoes and green beans. He'd get through it. He'd been through much worse.

James settled on the couch and fired up his laptop. Five minutes later, he'd confirmed that Charlotte worked for the Atlanta PD. By the time she emerged, he'd flipped on the television and attempted to watch a basketball game, but his mind was focused elsewhere.

Charlotte cleared her throat and entered the room. "This is silly, but if you must, you can see that the cuts are fine. And my knee's only a little swollen."

Her skin was damp and pink, and she tugged at the bottom of the oversize T-shirt that barely covered her underwear. James stifled his amusement. How could such a hard-ass cop be so shy?

"Come here," he said hoarsely.

She advanced to within a couple of feet and turned to the side. Slashes of jagged crimson marred the otherwise smooth, pink flesh of her leg.

James swallowed hard. "Doesn't appear to be infected. Have a seat. I'll apply some of Miss Glory's balm and put a bandage on it."

"I can do it myself."

He didn't bother arguing, just picked up the antiseptic from the coffee table and applied some to a pad of cotton. "I'll be gentle."

"You'd better be."

She sat down beside him and angled her body on her left hip, leaning her elbow on the sofa's arm. Although she hissed as he applied the antiseptic to her head wound and cuts, she didn't say a word in protest. He opened the jar of balm from Miss Glory and dabbed it on with his index finger, barely grazing the torn flesh. Quickly he put on the gauze bandage. "All done." Damn if his voice wasn't several octaves deeper.

Charlotte nodded and sat up straight. "Thank you," she said simply. "I feel better already. I can't believe it, but those herbal pills really work." She gave a lopsided, loopy grin. "I'm getting drowsy."

He wished he could say the same. Instead, every cell in his body pulsed with energy, acutely aware of the beautiful woman who stared at him with such gratitude.

"Not too early to go to bed," he suggested.

Bed. More images played in his head of Charlotte sleeping across the hall in his guest bedroom.

She scooted sideways and lay down. "I could fall asleep right here," she murmured, wiggling her toes. Even her pink-painted toenails were adorable. As if of their own volition, his hands wrapped around her arches and he massaged her feet.

"Um, that's so nice." Her voice was husky and deep, and her eyelids fluttered.

"You must be wiped out."

"That and the pills." Her eyes widened, and she struggled to a half-seated position. Her thin T-shirt twisted, revealing a pair of lacy panties.

James reached for the afghan and covered her bare legs. A man could only take so much temptation, but he hadn't sunk so low as to take advantage of a half-drugged stranger. Hard to believe he'd known her only a day. Charlotte Helms had stormed into his life like some badass angel of justice, shaking up his quiet, orderly world.

"Do you have a girlfriend or—" her face tightened "—a wife?"

"Nope." He'd had a fiancée this time last year, but Ashley had brushed him off with a Dear John letter while he was in Afghanistan. Not that he could blame her frustration with his absence, but it rankled. Last he'd heard, she was already engaged to another man.

"What about you?" He'd assumed she wasn't married, but what did he really know about her?

She snorted. "Hell, no."

Irrational relief flowed over him.

"My profession doesn't exactly lend itself to maintaining close personal relationships," she continued. "Haven't even seen my own parents in months."

"That must be hard."

"Yeah, it's tough." Charlotte sighed and ran a hand through her long hair. "It never used to bother me, but lately…"

"Lately what?" he prompted.

"After seeing the hell Tanya's going through with her missing daughter—it kind of makes you stop and think. You shouldn't take family for granted."

"I get it. My dad and one of my sisters died last year.

Made me appreciate Lilah—she's my younger sister."
Lately he'd even been talking more to his estranged
mother. Something he never thought he'd do after she'd
run off with another man when he was in high school
and had left them all high and dry.

"Lilah Tedder," she murmured, gently probing the
knot by her right temple.

"She's Lilah Sampson now. Married the sheriff."

Charlotte snapped her fingers. "Thought it sounded
familiar. There was a serial killer up here and—"

"Yeah, she was lucky to escape. My dad and Darla
weren't so fortunate."

James shut down. He never talked about the incident.
What good did it do to rehash old sorrow?

"Must have been tough," she whispered. "And then
to find out the real killer was—"

"I'd rather not discuss it," he said, removing her feet
from his lap and standing up.

"Of course, I understand. It's just that—"

Annoyed, James strode to the window and pushed
aside an inch of curtain. A strong whipping wind battered barren treetops.

"Sorry. I'm not normally one to pry. Let's blame it on
Miss Glory's herbs."

"I'm sure you read all about the case in the Atlanta
papers. Heard it made the national news for a whole fifteen minutes." Even he heard the bitterness in his own
voice. "Old news," he added dismissively.

Charlotte pushed aside the afghan and struggled to her
feet. "How about we make some coffee? I'm good to pull
my weight for a night shift. You've had a long day, too."

"Not necessary. We weren't followed. Besides, I never
sleep much. No sense in you staying up, too."

"I never sleep well, either," she admitted.

He fixed his gaze on her. She'd probably witnessed a lot of the dark side of life and had her own demons, as well.

"Go on to bed. I've got this."

She yawned and cocked her head to the side. "Wake me up in about four hours?"

"Sure." He wouldn't, but he feared she'd never agree to sleep otherwise.

"Okay, then. Good night."

Charlotte started to turn, and then hesitated. Instead of leaving him, she slowly walked toward him, an uncertain gleam in her teal eyes.

She wasn't…surely, no. But she kept walking until she stood close enough that he could smell the soap from her recent bath.

"Thank you," she breathed, standing on her tiptoes.

Her lips pressed under his jaw, along the side of his neck. Before he could react, it was over. Bemused, he watched as she left the room. It was as though her kiss had sealed his fate. He would do everything in his power to help her find the traffickers. Whether it was for Jenny and the other trapped children, or whether it was for this maddening woman—or some combination of both—James couldn't say. Indeed, such soul-searching was pointless. He'd thrown in his lot with the charismatic Charlotte.

It was going to be a long, long night.

Chapter Five

James surveyed her efforts with a critical eye. "You didn't quite get it all," he pronounced, tucking an errant lock of hair into the knitted hat. His nearness and touch made her breath hitch, although he appeared unfazed by the contact. "Don't need your flaming hair blowing in the wind like a red flag."

"Does it really matter? They're bound to hear your four-wheeler before they see anything."

"With any luck, the roar of the wind will drown out most of the noise."

Despite last night's intimacy, this morning, James was all business. Charlotte inwardly cringed, thinking of the unsolicited kiss she'd planted on him. Totally uncharacteristic of her. She recalled Miss Glory's whispered words at the shop yesterday. *"Open your heart."* Yeah, she'd understood the older woman. Probably fancied herself the local matchmaker.

James swung a long leg over the ATV and pointed to the back seat. "Hop on," he commanded.

Charlotte climbed onto it, grateful that her injuries had improved leaps and bounds overnight. Only a slight soreness remained. Once she brought Jenny home—and she would—she'd pay Miss Glory another visit and present her with a big tip.

With a lurch, James gassed the ATV, and she wrapped her arms around his waist to keep from falling. Lordy, he felt good—strong, and warm, and reliable. She resisted an impulse to bury her head against his broad back. What was it about him that drew her so? No sense falling for someone who appeared to temporarily be her partner. Emphasis on *temporarily*. She'd been burned before mixing business with pleasure. Danny had proven to be a rat bastard. Once this case was over, she'd return to Atlanta, and James Tedder would continue on with his relatively peaceful life here on Lavender Mountain. With no complications from her.

The wind was brutal in the early morning chill. Luckily James possessed more than one pair of gloves, and she'd donned the loaner ones. How cold must he be? His body shielded her from the worst of the wind.

The four-wheeler jostled and righted itself as they drove off his cabin's property and entered the main trail leading to Falling Creek.

Finding the exact spot where she'd been shot at and searching for the left-behind shell casings wasn't likely, but they had to try. She hoped the guards were still there at the house she'd spotted, although unarmed this time. If nothing else, this morning's excursion would prove she'd told the truth about the shooting, and that there was nothing accidental about it.

Charlotte kept her eyes glued to the passing trees and brush until she spotted the clearing where she'd run off the trail. Another thirty yards or so, and they'd be in the general area. She leaned to the side. "Slow down," she called out to James. "We're close."

Close enough to also see the line of mansions on the Falling Rock bluff.

He let up on the gas and swerved off the beaten path, parking the ATV in a copse of pines, right under a hand-made sign stapled to a tree. "Private Property. Trespassers will be shot on sight."

"These people are crazy," she commented, pointing to the sign.

"Yeah, you trespassed. That tends to get people shot."

She hopped off and pulled the binoculars from her backpack.

The two guards were there at the same house, but apparently hadn't heard their approach as they conversed with one another.

"See anything?" James asked.

Charlotte pointed to the mansion in question and handed him the binoculars.

"They could be gardeners," he commented. "One's holding a rake and the other a hoe."

"Bet you could watch them an hour and you wouldn't see either of them using those tools. They're props."

"We'll keep an eye out. Where should we start looking for the casing?"

She sighed. "Here's as good a spot as any."

They separated and began combing the grounds. Charlotte hugged her arms to her waist, eyes focused on finding the small object amid the dead leaves and brown twigs. You'd think it would stand out, but they were hampered by being unable to pinpoint the exact location of the shooting. Too bad she hadn't thought to leave some sort of mark behind. That way, they could estimate how far away the shooter was when he fired his weapon.

"Found one," James called.

"Really? Damn, you must have eagle eyes." She scurried over.

James held it up to the sun, squinting at it a moment before dropping the casing into a small plastic baggie.

"What now?" she asked through chattering teeth. "Keep watching the guards?" She lifted her binoculars. They were still talking, gesturing broadly with their hands, the garden implements dangling uselessly by their sides. The men started pushing and shoving. "We're in luck today. They're too busy fighting each other to notice us."

"Then let's push it. We'll ride down the trail—it turns and runs perpendicular to the houses."

"What if they see us?"

He shrugged. "They'll just think we're out on a joyride."

"In this weather?" she asked skeptically.

"I want to gauge their reaction for myself."

Some small part of him still had reservations about her story. "You're the one sitting in front. If they shoot—"

"Exactly." James stuffed the baggie in his coat pocket and climbed on the ATV.

Charlotte lifted the binoculars one last time. The guards were throwing actual punches. Good to know the idiot thugs were so easily distracted. She tilted the binoculars upward, scanning the windows.

A face appeared. A young girl with long blond hair, nose almost pressed to the windowpane. The look of misery and longing in her blue eyes punched Charlotte in the gut. "I see a possible victim," she whispered, the sound of her voice lost in the wind.

"What's that?" James asked, immediately by her side. "Let me see."

She passed him the binoculars and hurriedly dug into her backpack for the camera. "Top left window."

James peered through the lens. "I don't see anything."

"Give it here." Charlotte dropped the camera, grabbed the field glasses, and pinpointed the target.

Nothing. The blinds were drawn closed. She hadn't imagined it—Jenny had been there seconds ago. "Damn it! Jenny was just there. I promise you."

"Too bad. If she'd stayed thirty seconds longer, you could have snapped a photo. Would have been solid proof to justify a search warrant of the house."

"I know," she said with a groan. "Who knows when or if she'll appear again?"

He laid a warm, heavy hand on her shoulder and gave it a quick squeeze. "At least we know where to focus our efforts now if that particular household doesn't claim children."

Our efforts. The world went bleary through a thick haze of tears, and Charlotte angrily blinked them back. She cleared her throat. "Does this mean you believe me? You'll help bring those bastards down?"

James stared ahead. "I saw the pictures of those missing children." A muscle worked in his jaw. "If they're being held there—" he nodded at the house "—then I'll stop at nothing to get them out."

Something tight in her shoulders relaxed slightly—a tension she hadn't been aware she was carrying. "That's where they are. I know for sure now, even if I can't prove it to anyone else."

Again she felt for the missing gun at her side. Maybe it was a good thing that James had confiscated it. She wanted nothing more than to force her way inside and search the premises. But even armed, it would take more than one person to get the captives out alive. *Soon*, she silently promised Jenny.

"Let's take 'er for a spin," James said, hopping on the ATV.

Privately she was unconvinced of the wisdom of that particular move, but partnerships were a give-and-take. She'd voiced her concern, and he'd overridden it. Fair enough. He'd been accommodating in other matters.

Charlotte resumed her position on the back seat, and they blazed down the trail. At last they were close enough to the guards that the men must have heard the oncoming vehicle. They pulled apart, warily eying their approach. Both drew their right hands to their hips as if reaching for sidearms.

SURELY THEY WEREN'T so brazen as to shoot two people in broad daylight.

But perhaps he'd been a fool to count on that. He couldn't let anything happen to Charlotte. Coming out here had been his idea. James threw up his right hand in a friendly wave, as if he were merely passing through without a care in the world.

They didn't return the wave or the smile, but they didn't fire, either.

James turned to the left and followed the path that led away from the territory the men guarded. Might be best not to return the same way, just to be safe. Another half mile ahead, he could cut across Old Man Broward's field and return to the cabin in a more roundabout fashion.

Charlotte tugged violently on his right arm. "Stop!"

Had they been followed? James veered the ATV sideways, slamming on the brakes. His eyes cut to the path behind them. "What is it?"

Before the ATV completely sputtered to a stop, Charlotte hopped off and rushed to the side of the road, pointing. "Is that blood?"

Dark crimson dotted and swiped across dried leaves.

"The drag pattern indicates something was shot and dragged here," he mused.

"Or *someone*," Charlotte said, rubbing her arms. "Oh, God, I hope it's not Jenny. Not that I want anyone dead, of course. It's just, I couldn't ear for Tanya to lose her only child. Her marriage went south last year, and Jenny is her world."

"Every girl is somebody's daughter. Somebody's world, too. But I know what you mean."

He dug another plastic bag from his coat pocket and bent down to collect a sample. "An eventful morning," he said grimly.

"Wait. Let me take a photo of this before you start collecting."

He waited, studying the blood. No way to tell if it was animal or human without running tests. There was a lot of it. If it was from a human, chances were they were dead. The body—or possibly a deer carcass—had been dragged a couple of feet before being hauled off.

A few snaps and clicks later, James quickly gathered up enough blood for lab testing and then drove the meandering route back to the cabin.

During the truck ride to the sheriff's department, Charlotte was unusually quiet and withdrawn. James took her hand. "We're going to free Jenny and the others," he promised, parking the truck.

She squeezed his hand, and he withdrew it. James

stepped out of the vehicle, and she fell into place beside him as they entered the sheriff's office. Why did he always feel the need to touch Charlotte? Totally inappropriate and nothing he'd ever felt the urge to do on the few patrols he'd run with Jolene, the only female officer in the department. Must be because this case was personal for Charlotte and she was passionate about freeing the prisoners. She cared deeply about this assignment.

Hell, so did he. Hard to believe in America, and right here in his county, young girls were brutalized and sold to men like sides of beef. Made it damn hard to sleep at night, imagining their suffering.

The clatter and whir of printers and scanners abruptly stopped. Necks craned, and fingers stilled over keyboards. For a good five seconds, he and Charlotte were scrutinized by Elmore County's finest.

Sammy arose from his desk and walked over to greet them. "Wondered where you were this morning," he remarked. He extended a hand to Charlotte. "Sam Armstrong."

"Detective Helms." She gave a polite nod but volunteered nothing further about herself. Sammy turned back to James. "You're late this morning. Boss wants to see you. Pronto."

That sounded fairly ominous. As the newest officer, he had no authority deciding what cases to take, much less setting his own schedule.

"Shall I go with you?" Charlotte asked, squaring her shoulders.

"Later. Let me talk to him first." He'd sent Harlan a couple of brief texts stating only that he was investigating a trafficking ring with an Atlanta cop. No doubt Harlan was less than pleased at being left out.

"How about some coffee?" Sammy asked, steering Charlotte toward the back of the lobby.

"Sure. Just point me in the right direction."

Once she walked a few feet away, Sammy leaned in, amusement flickering in his eyes. "Want me to handcuff her to the desk this time? She appears to be a flight risk."

"You can try, but I have a suspicion you'd end up the one chained to my desk. Not Charlotte."

Sammy laughed. "I like her spirit."

"Guess I better go face the music with Harlan."

"He's in a rotten mood this morning," Sammy cheerily informed him.

James stifled a groan and strode the hallway to Harlan's office. The sheriff sat at his desk, a newspaper sprawled out in front of him.

"Sir?" James asked, always formal in the workplace. He didn't want Harlan or anyone else to think he courted favor because the sheriff was his brother-in-law.

Harlan scowled, impatiently waving for him to take a seat. "Cut the *sir* crap. You aren't in the army anymore."

A fact James never intended to use to his advantage. "Yes, s—"

"Call me Harlan like everybody else around here." He leaned back in his chair, steepling his fingers. "What the hell is this about a human trafficking ring, and who's working undercover in my county?"

"Yesterday I found a woman camped out in Dad's old cabin. Turns out she's an undercover cop with Atlanta's special crimes unit. Her name's Detective Helms." He tried not to grimace as Harlan punched her name into his computer.

"Might as well tell you," James said. "Char—Detective Helms—is currently on suspension with them for insubordination."

Harlan stopped typing and cast him a surprised scowl. "Why?"

"She was ordered to drop her search and was reassigned another case. She refused."

"Why?" Harlan barked again. It seemed to be his favorite word.

"Because one of the victims is the daughter of her best friend."

"An officer can't allow personal emotions to interfere with duty," Harlan objected. "If she was ordered to cease, then that's the end of the matter."

James quirked a brow. "Like you did when J.D. ordered you to mind your own business last year when Lilah was in danger?"

What an ass the former sheriff had been. He'd never cared for the guy and wasn't a bit surprised when he returned home and learned J.D. was in jail. Especially since he'd protected the identity of James's father and sister's killer. Mentally James shook off the memory of his own tragedy.

Harlan shifted in his seat. "If I had stopped my investigation, your sister might have been the next victim."

"I'm not complaining, merely pointing out that sometimes it's impossible to give up."

It was easy to read Harlan's discomfort as his boss realized the hypocrisy of the situation. James went in for the kill.

"What harm can it be to work with her for a time? Worst-case scenario, it's been a waste of one officer's time. Best case, we find the traffickers, and you get all the glory for the capture."

"You really think that's all I care about? What people will think of me?"

He'd overstepped his bounds. Of course Harlan cared how all this would reflect on him as sheriff. It was an elected position, after all. But he was also a decent man intent on keeping crime out of the county.

"I was out of line," James admitted. "But I know you. If young girls are being held against their will and sold into the sex slave market, you'll do your best to stop it."

"Damn right," Harlan grumbled.

"So you'll let me continue working the case with Detective Helms?"

Harlan regarded him silently for several heartbeats. "With reservations. I'm going to speak with her supervisor and get more information on this suspension. In the meantime, tell me what, if anything, you've discovered that validates her claim of a ring operating out of Lavender Mountain."

Quickly he filled Harlan in on the attempted shooting, being tailed by an unmarked sedan, the shot in the dark last night and Charlotte's claim of seeing a young girl's face at the window this morning. "And then there's this," he added, pulling out the baggie of bloody leaves. "Found them close to the Falling Rock subdivision."

Harlan leaned over his desk and picked up the evidence, holding it up to the light. "Could be from a deer."

"Or it could be human."

Harlan nodded. "I'll send it to the lab straightaway and pull strings. They should know in a day or two if it's animal or human, but the DNA tests to determine whose blood it is could take weeks. And even then, we can only match DNA if the person has a DNA sample on file."

Then he drummed his fingers against the wooden

desk. "So far, you haven't proven anything sinister is going on at Falling Rock, but I don't want to take chances, either. I'll get the lowdown on this Helms woman, but in the meantime, check out her story." Harlan narrowed his eyes. "Heard she's a real looker. You aren't getting sucked in by a pretty face, are you?"

"'Course not." James swallowed back his irritation. "She's sacrificing everything to rescue her friend's daughter and whoever else is held captive."

Harlan let out a sigh. "So she claims. How long does she plan on staying?"

"As long as it takes."

"And where's she staying?"

Heat blossomed on his neck and face. "I've offered her my place." That sounded bad. Really bad. But he hated the idea of Charlotte staying in town and being exposed to danger.

Thankfully Harlan let that pass. "Suspension or not, Atlanta should have informed me of suspicious activity in this area. We've got enough problems without being in the dark on any leads they have. It's an insult to this office. An insult to me."

"Don't take it personally. It's the nature of undercover work. And Elmore County's reputation is ruined after all the crap J.D. pulled as sheriff."

Harlan didn't appear the least mollified. "They're still going to hear my complaint. Are you still sure this Helms woman is on the up-and-up?"

James immediately leaped to her defense. "Yes. A bit reckless, but brave and determined."

"Reckless?" asked a high-pitched voice.

Charlotte stood in the doorway, arms folded and chin

lifted. "Nothing's ever been accomplished without taking action based on calculated risks."

Harlan stood and assessed her with narrow eyes. "I don't want my officer placed at risk with any wild plans you might harbor for accomplishing your mission. Got it? Any evidence you find, you run it by me, and I'll decide what action to take."

"Got it." Her lips tightened to a thin line, and James was willing to bet she told Harlan only what he wanted to hear. Obedience didn't appear to be her strong suit.

"Excellent," Harlan said crisply. "As long as we have that understanding, Officer Tedder can work with you a few days to see if you two can turn up evidence. We'll issue you a uniform and a cover story that you're our new employee on probation and learning the ropes. Not being undercover will allow you to freely explore the area. That sound fair?"

"Perfectly."

Harlan buzzed the intercom on his desk and his secretary, Zelda, appeared immediately. "Escort Detective Helms to inventory and see she's issued a suitable uniform," he told her. "If there's not one in her size, check around with a few of the neighboring sheriffs and see if they have a spare."

"I'm on it."

Zelda motioned for Charlotte to follow, and James was alone again with his boss.

"I appreciate this," James began. "I realize I'm still fairly new, and if it turns out—"

"We're already understaffed, and all my other officers have a huge workload as it is." Harlan relaxed and sat back down. "Besides, I wouldn't have hired you if

I didn't think you were up for the job, and any assignment, brother-in-law or not."

James had his doubts about that. Lilah had fussed over him ever since he'd returned from Afghanistan, convinced he needed to get out of the house more. No one seemed to understand that after all he'd seen overseas, living alone and keeping to himself was his idea of paradise. He wanted nothing more than peace and quiet, but he suspected that ship had sailed.

The phone rang, and Harlan glanced at the screen. "Got to take this. Keep me informed. And James…keep your guard up, okay?"

With that, Harlan lifted the phone's handset, and James returned to his desk, mulling over the conversation. His feelings were mixed. It *was* an interesting case and one he'd campaigned to stay on. One that beat the hell out of roaming the back roads on patrol. But Charlotte unsettled him. He couldn't stop thinking about her haunted eyes when she mentioned Jenny. The need to leap to her defense had been surprising—and not in a good way.

Was he being fooled by a pretty face, as Harlan suggested?

He'd take his brother-in-law's warning to heart. Proceed slow and easy. And for God's sake, he'd resist the impulse to touch her. Detective Charlotte Helms was temporarily his new partner—and nothing more.

Chapter Six

"May I have my gun back now—partner?" Charlotte self-consciously tugged at the front of her too-tight uniform blouse. First opportunity, she'd buy some dark brown tank tops to wear underneath the shirt. Pink skin on her chest and stomach peeked out in the gap between the buttons. She was a quarter-pound cheeseburger away from completely popping out.

James's eyes slid down her uniform, and she barely resisted the urge to squirm. The pants were as tight as the top, hugging her hips and ass in a way that made her feel exposed.

"Right. Your gun." He unlocked a desk drawer. "Zelda's made arrangements for better-fitting uniforms to be overnighted."

Was it her imagination, or had his voice deepened and slowed? Suddenly it wasn't just her uniform that felt tight. The very room felt compressed and the air thick with tension.

Sexual tension.

Might as well call it what it was. Charlotte swallowed hard, eyes focused on his large hands as they palmed her weapon—metal caressed by muscle. Mesmerizing. What would it be like to have his hands stroke her naked flesh?

"Here," James said, his hand reaching for hers.

Lifting her arm was like a magnetic pull through molasses—slow and steady and inevitable. Her fingers wrapped around the gun's barrel, and she fastened it to her belt clip. She didn't dare face James. Didn't dare trust her eyes not to betray the sudden passion.

"Thank you," she murmured. Damn if her voice wasn't as gruff as his.

Buck up. He's officially your partner now. Passion meant distraction. And they each needed all their wits to break the trafficking ring. Not to mention, they also needed focus to keep their hides intact in the face of flying bullets. No wonder romantic relationships were taboo in law enforcement—they could get you killed. And once you broke up with a coworker? The worst. Danny had taught her that.

"For you."

Her eyes snapped to the doorway as Sam entered the room waving a thick manila envelope, which he tossed in James's inbox. His forehead crinkled. "Something going on in here?"

"No, thanks for—" James began.

"Nope," she denied.

He glanced between them, realization dawning in his eyes. "Right. Whatever you say."

Charlotte rummaged through her backpack for her case files, ignoring Sam as he swept out of the room. The situation was awkward enough without the man's teasing. She cleared her throat and spread her files across his desk. "Let's get down to it, shall we? Here's a photo of Jenny."

The blown-up color print portrayed a smiling girl, her mother's arm slung across her shoulder. The girl's eyes and skin had that glow that came only with youth. Tanya's grin was carefree and proud—in contrast to the past two weeks, when her eyes had been practically swollen shut from crying and her face puffy with misery. As thankful as Tanya would be when her daughter returned home—and Charlotte vowed to make it so—she suspected that Tanya's carefree look was gone forever.

"Jenny Ashbury," she said softly. "I also have photos of other missing girls ages twelve to sixteen, although most are twelve to fourteen years old. We tried a sting operation using me as bait, but I only drew men wanting to hire me as a prostitute. I'm too old to be considered a prime target for trafficking."

"Too old?" James shook his head in disgust and looked over the mug shots.

"Anyone look familiar?" she asked.

"No."

"Well, that was a long shot, but it could be helpful if you familiarized yourself with their faces and names. Never know when they might slip up and one of the girls escapes."

"Will do. I'm printing out the owner names and information for all the houses at Falling Rock. In the meantime, fill me in on everything you have."

Charlotte settled into a seat. "We've known for some time that a woman is locating and luring vulnerable young girls—runaways, foster children, the homeless, you get the picture. We don't know her name, but our nickname for her is Piper, short for Pied Piper."

"Where are you getting your info?"

"Mostly from Karen Hicks, a thirteen-year-old runaway who managed to escape. Piper befriended her after discovering her roaming around on Peachtree Street.

Bought her a meal and offered to put her up for a night at a motel."

James frowned. "Your Piper's a class act. But I don't see the connection. Lavender Mountain's a long way from downtown Atlanta."

Charlotte couldn't mask her distaste. "According to Karen, two armed men forced her and three other girls into a van, bound and blindfolded them, then drove them around for a couple of hours. They were offloaded at a huge, luxurious house…and then they spent the next week being instructed in the finer points of sexual relations."

"Lovely," James muttered.

"Oh, it gets better. Karen found out that there was to be a party that weekend where Piper's clients could come and sample the goods. If they liked what they found, the girls were to be sold at a price—either as exclusive property to their new owner, or to a man who would pimp them out to others."

Charlotte shook her head. Poor Karen. At first glimpse, her prison must have seemed like a fairy-tale castle. But it hadn't taken long for the illusion to shatter—there would be no happily-ever-after on the horizon.

"How did she manage to escape?"

"Luckily for Karen, one of the rapists who visited there was not only excited but also stupid. He forgot to lock them up from the outside of the bedroom door before he asked her to tie him up and gag him. Karen happily complied, managed to slip out the back door, and then hitched rides back to Atlanta."

James tapped an index finger to his lips, a thoughtful expression in his eyes. "And Karen claims this happened at Falling Rock?"

"When she escaped, she noticed the entrance sign on the subdivision gate. Unfortunately, she never got the house address. She and the others were kept in the basement, and once she got free, she didn't stop running to look back."

"What about a description of the captors?"

"Middle-aged white couple of medium build. Man had gray hair and woman had brown hair. Both blue-eyed. In other words, generic."

"We can show Karen photos of the different property owners and have her identify which couple held—"

"Karen's long gone. I can only assume she's left the Atlanta area. No family or friends have heard from her in weeks." Charlotte feared the worst for her former informant.

James pulled the plat map of Falling Rock from the printer and circled one property in red. "Pretty sure this is the house we observed with the gardeners out back and where you saw the girl at the window. It belongs to Richard and Madeline Stowers, who have no children. We're in luck."

Her heartbeat quickened. "Why? Do you know them?"

"Barely. Not like we run in the same social circles. But next week, they're hosting the annual fund-raiser for the sheriff's office." He gave a grim smile. "And we're always invited to attend. Every officer—including new trainees."

Charlotte slapped her hands on the desk and grinned. Finally, an opportunity to access the grounds. "Bam. We can take advantage of that and sneak around." But as suddenly as elation surged through her body, it deflated. "Still, a whole week…they'll have moved the girls out by then. Sure, it's brazen enough that they're

holding y'all a fund-raiser, but to keep the girls locked
up for hours with a dozen lawmen in the same house? I
don't see it happening."

"Oh, the fund-raiser won't be at their house. They
hold it at the Falling Rock Community Clubhouse." He
pointed to the map. "The clubhouse is only three doors
down from the Stowerses' cabin, though. They plan on
trying to sell the girls practically right under our noses."

"Perfect cover," she pointed out. "Invite all the law enforcement officers to the ball—which leaves no one patrolling the streets." Charlotte stood, restless and hungry
with the need for action. "I want to see their home and
the clubhouse from the front. I couldn't do a safe drive-
by in my rental, but what if we took a patrol car for a
spin? We'd be providing a routine public service, right?"

"I'm all in." He pushed back his chair and grabbed his
jacket. "Don't forget your camera. With any luck, you'll
catch a glimpse of Jenny."

JAMES KEPT HIS gaze fixed on the winding mountain road.
Something had happened back there in the office—unspoken, unexpected and unwanted. Sure, there had been
a few flashes of heat before, but now their chemistry
crackled and burned with tension. Charlotte's presence
filled the vehicle, filled his mind and filled his senses.

"Fancy, shmancy," she commented as the Falling
Rock entrance came into view. By the gatehouse was a
large stone wall with a six-foot waterfall feature.

"Only the best for these folks." Despite all his years
away and his overseas stints, James's nerves were still
set on edge whenever he crossed into the exclusive community. Growing up as the son of a local moonshiner
hadn't been easy. Even by Lavender Mountain standards,

his family had been poor and looked down upon. In many ways, the situation was even worse since the Tedder name had been linked to a string of murders last year. The disparity between the rich and poor couldn't be more evident.

Charlotte's voice wrenched him out of his thoughts. "Do they keep this gate manned 24/7?"

"Yep. The guards are paid out of homeowner association fees. Must pay them fairly well, too—there's seldom any turnover. Then again," he admitted, "steady jobs are hard to come by around here."

"Could be the Stowerses pay them a little something extra to turn a blind eye to their comings and goings," she mused.

James pulled up to the gate and rolled down his window. Les Phelps leaned out the gatehouse window with a clipboard. "Afternoon, Officer Tedder. Cold day today."

"Hey, Les. Meet our new officer, Bailey Hanson. I'm showing her around the area. Letting her get a feel for the lay of the land."

His gaunt face lit on Charlotte with interest. "Howdy, ma'am. Pleasure to meet ya."

Charlotte leaned forward and gave a friendly wave. "You write down every vehicle that comes and goes here?"

"Yes, ma'am. Make, model, time of arrival and time of departure. Always take a quick glance at strangers' driver's licenses, too. All day, every day."

"Bet nothing gets by you," she said with a coy smile.

"No, ma'am. It surely don't." He blushed and continued staring at Charlotte. "I take my job seriously."

"I don't doubt it for a minute." Her voice practically purred.

Irritation spiked James's blood pressure. Charlotte never spoke to *him* that way. "Thanks, Les," he muttered, then rolled up the window and hit the gas pedal.

Charlotte eased back into her seat. "How well do you know that guy?"

"I've seen him around. He was a couple grades behind me in school."

"Trustworthy or no?"

"Never been in trouble with the law, as far as I know. Seemed an okay kid."

"Not exactly a ringing endorsement."

He shrugged. "How can you ever really know what goes on in other people's lives? We all wear a mask to some degree. For all I know, Les might be a serial killer."

And he wasn't being flippant. Even family members sometimes weren't what they seemed—as he well knew.

Charlotte snorted. "And here I thought *I* was jaded. You're just as bad."

The road climbed until they rounded a bend and faced the first behemoth of stone and wood and glass. Charlotte gave an appreciative whistle. "Sweet little mansions you've got here. I bet most of the owners don't even live here full-time."

"Most don't," he agreed. "We hardly ever see them during the cold months unless it's for the fund-raiser or a holiday." James slowed the car. "And here we are. Third house on the left belongs to the Stowerses."

"Nice digs," she commented, studying the house. "Would it be possible to get an architect's drawing of the floorplan? Could come in handy later."

"I'll check. Shouldn't be a problem since the architect lives in Falling Rock. He'll want to help keep his community safe and clean."

"I take it there's only one entrance to Falling Rock?"

"It's the only paved road, yes."

"Good point. I noticed the jeep and four-wheeler trails along the back of the properties on this side of the street. We'll need a lookout posted front and back to secure the neighborhood."

"Harlan would agree to the needed manpower if we could show some proof that the girls are trapped there."

"Proof?" Charlotte slapped the dashboard and huffed, "She's there. It's so frustrating trying to prove it."

"You're a cop. You know how this works."

"I know," she muttered, staring at the dashboard. "I'm just… I call Tanya every night and have to give her bad news."

"But tonight you'll have good news. You saw Jenny. As long as she's alive, there's hope."

She sighed and rubbed her temples. "You're right. I can't imagine what it's like for Tanya, though."

He didn't want to do it, damn it, but he couldn't resist. Couldn't bear to see the misery in her eyes. James reached across the console and took her hand. Her fingers encircled his and held on. They didn't speak as they left Falling Rock and traveled back down Blood Mountain.

Peace settled over James. It was inappropriate, ill-advised and one step closer to heartbreak. Charlotte was his partner—a temporary one, at that. Once this case was over, she'd return to her life in Atlanta and forget all about him, just as Ashley had forgotten him while he was in Afghanistan.

And yet he held on to her hand.

A black car slowly exited Falling Rock and fell into place behind their vehicle. Although darkness had not yet fallen, it was impossible to make out the driver through the tinted windows. Reluctantly James removed his hand from Charlotte's and placed it on the steering wheel.

She instantly sensed trouble. "What is it?"

"Black sedan behind us. Just keeping an eye out since you were followed by one in town."

She straightened in her seat and turned her neck. "Holy," she grunted. "I'm glad I have a gun this time. And you beside me."

The five-mile stretch between them and town was practically deserted. A growing unease prickled his scalp as the sedan picked up speed and drew closer. Close enough that if he came to a sudden stop, the vehicle would ram into theirs. Two men were in that car, but he couldn't make out their individual features. James hit the accelerator.

The sedan did the same. An arm emerged from its passenger-side window, and a gun took aim.

"Get down!" he shouted, and shoved Charlotte's head below the glass. "They've got a—"

The ping of gunfire erupted, followed immediately by the grate of metal against metal as a bullet connected with fender.

His mind cleared and narrowed to a crystallized focus. He had to get them to safety. His brain worked at warp speed, calculating his options. It was another four miles to town, and he was willing to bet that the snipers wouldn't shoot with eyewitnesses around. And he knew every hairpin twist on this road—advantage, him. So... his best bet was to drive fast and weave the cruiser so that the snipers would have a more difficult shot.

Charlotte turned on the walkie-talkie. "Come in. This is Officer Hanson. We're at mile marker three on County

Road 143. Officers needs help. Shots fired. All available backup needed *immediately*."

James rounded a curve and jerked the steering wheel to the left. Another bullet fired, missing them completely. Quickly he maneuvered back into the right lane. Paved road and faded lines of white paint rose to greet him at a dizzying speed.

Ping. Glass shards exploded from the back window. He slowed for an instant, ensuring Charlotte was unharmed.

"That's it, damn it!" Charlotte loaded her gun, unrolled the passenger window, and halfway leaned out.

"What are you—"

The roar of her shot exploded, and James tugged at her jacket. "Get down!"

"No way." She took aim and fired again. "Missed. At least they're slowing."

"How the hell am I supposed to drive? One sharp turn and your ass will fall out that window."

"Don't worry about me. You focus on the road."

James gritted his teeth. If they managed to survive the next five minutes, Charlotte was in for a tongue lashing of a magnitude she'd never experienced. He was the lead, and as such, he had the right to—

A red pickup truck swerved around the corner, and James jerked the car back into his own lane. Only inches of space separated their vehicles. There was barely time to register the man's shocked face, and then he heard him lay on his horn. No doubt Harlan would be getting a civilian complaint about his reckless driving. So be it.

Another mile and a half passed. A few sprinklings of barns and cabins dotted the wintry landscape. They were getting closer to safety.

Charlotte fired again. "Got 'em! Bullet went through their windshield, but I'm not sure if it hit one of them."

And her tone indicated she hoped that the bullet found its human mark. A surge of admiration, mixed with adrenaline, rushed through him. He'd take Charlotte Helms as a partner any day, every day.

His bubble of appreciation burst as their cruiser suddenly pitched to the left. The sniper had shot out his left rear tire. James fought to keep the cruiser from veering over the side of the mountain. The flimsy guardrails would never hold back over three tons of speeding metal. Soon the heat from the tire rim grinding on pavement might lock up his brakes.

And that would be it. They'd come to a dead halt and be a sitting target. Orange and red sparks tunneled upward from the rear of the cruiser.

From a distance, the whirring of sirens approached. Would it be too late?

The sedan surged forward, trying to pass him on the left. Its right front fender crashed into them, and the cruiser spun out of control.

Round and round they flew in a circus ride of terror. He caught glimpses of Charlotte's face, which was set, grim and determined, even if her voice shook. "I'm ready to face them," she declared, one hand on the dashboard to keep from flying about, the other gripping her weapon.

The cruiser slowed its spin, and James withdrew his gun. This was it.

Another burst of gunfire erupted from beside him. "I hit their front tire," Charlotte said. "Take *that*, you bastards!"

The sedan took a sudden dive to the right, flipping over the guardrail like dandelion seeds in the wind.

James slammed on the brakes, abandoned his vehicle and rushed to the rail, Charlotte one step ahead of him.

On and on it rolled. "Radio for an ambulance," he said.

"I'm going down." Charlotte hopped over the mangled guardrail and slowly walked down the steep incline, holstering her weapon.

"What the hell," he muttered. Backup was on the way. It was more important that he stay close to Charlotte. Bastards were like cats—they always seemed to have nine lives. No way would he risk letting one of them shoot at her. And she still favored her right leg after yesterday's flesh wound.

"Careful," he warned. "They might still be alive and dangerous."

"As if this is my first day as a cop," she muttered as she continued the slow descent. Rocks and roots marred the surface, and bits of gravel tumbled beneath his feet. *Oomph.* Charlotte went down, feet flying out from under her, and tumbled a good ten feet on her side. James stumbled and slid to a halt beside her. "You okay?"

"Hell, no." Her breathing was jagged and raspy, her forehead scratched and bleeding. "My side hurts."

No blood that he could observe. Gently he ran a hand down her left rib cage. "Here?"

Charlotte moaned and batted his hand away.

"Probably cracked ribs," he said. "And maybe even internal injury."

"Who cares? Just go. Don't let those guys get away."

"You sure?"

She waved a hand. "Go!"

The siren wails grew louder—the cavalry would arrive soon enough.

"I'll send the backup your way," she urged.

He nodded and scrambled down the incline. Two men dressed in black pants and navy T-shirts crawled out of the sedan. One ran for the tree line, cradling his arm, and the other tried to run, but clutched his right leg and limped along at a slower clip.

James picked up his pace, half sliding and half jogging downward. What rotten luck that a tree hadn't broken the sedan's fall. Instead, it had rolled to a stop twenty yards from the edge of the woods. Gray smoke from its engine spiraled upward. Damn, the sedan could go up in flames at any moment.

The smell of leaking fuel brought him to a standstill. A whoosh of dizziness descended and he was again sucked into that quicksand of a flashback. A merciless sun beat down on the top of his head and his skin gritted and stung from an Afghan sandstorm. The enemy jeep approached and he was powerless to escape. Brain, body and lungs tightened into paralysis. He couldn't move or think past the boa-constricting fear that wrapped around his chest and squeezed and squeezed and squeezed.

"Look out!" Charlotte called, the words barely audible in the heavy gusts. But her voice cut through the time and distance his mind had created. The constriction in his chest loosened and he ran to the side of the smoking sedan, keeping plenty of distance between the smoking vehicle and himself. A curl of fire arose, licking the engine.

He ran as fast as he could, yet when the sedan exploded, the heat from the conflagration scorched his body like a blast furnace. How long had he been standing there, body present but his mind a thousand miles away? Probably enough time for the men to escape. They were nowhere in sight. He couldn't let them disappear and perhaps ruin their best chance of cracking the ring.

He ran into the woods, the brightness of the day dropping away. James withdrew his gun, stepped behind a tree, and surveyed the area. The men could be standing behind one of the wider oaks or curled down behind dense shrubbery and foliage. "Drop your weapons and give yourselves up!" he shouted.

The wind whistled and tree limbs rattled, but no other sounds emerged. How far had they managed to run?

At the distant shouts from behind him, James turned to find several officers making a slow descent down the mountain. Once more backup arrived, they could all spread out and search the area, but the sinking despair in his stomach said it would be fruitless. He knew only too well that it was easy for a man to hide out in these parts. The land was wild and tangled, populated with caves and plenty of nooks and crannies for desperate— or lucky—fugitives.

Damn it to hell. When were they going to catch a break in this case?

Chapter Seven

A helicopter roared overhead in the almost black sky, making conversation difficult. Harlan gestured for James and Charlotte to follow him to his cruiser. Inside, James took the back seat with Charlotte while Harlan started the engine and cranked up the heater. He took off his gloves and warmed his hands over the vent.

"Sure you don't want to go to the hospital and have your injuries looked at?" he asked, spinning around and addressing Charlotte.

"For the last time, *no*. All I've got is a scratch on the forehead and some bruised ribs."

Despite his misery of self-disgust over the PTSD issues, James's lips quirked upward. The woman obviously had a thing against doctors.

"No point in you both hanging around all night," Harlan said. "I'm keeping an officer on patrol at Falling Rock in case the men return there on foot. And I'm sending the rest of the search party home, helicopter included. I'll deploy men again at first light. For now, we've done all we can do."

James ran a hand through his close-cropped hair. "How about we question Les one more time—"

"Forget it. He's told us all he knows. Thanks to him, we have the sedan's tag number, at least."

"For all the good that did," Charlotte grumbled.

Another dead end in the case. The sedan was rented from an Atlanta company, but the driver had provided a fake ID. Shame lanced through him yet again. That damn PTSD. So far, Charlotte hadn't brought up today's failure, but he couldn't let it go.

"More bad news," Harlan continued. "Sammy got ahold of the Stowerses. He and his wife are still in Atlanta, and he claims no knowledge of who the men could be. I tend to believe him. Listen, y'all go ahead and crash for the evening. You've had enough excitement for one day. And you're bound to be bruised and sore come morning."

James was fine and wound-up enough to work all night, to make up for his lapse. But despite her bravado, Charlotte's eyes sported half moons of dark shadows, and she kept rubbing her temples as if trying to ward off a headache.

"I agree." Charlotte's mouth opened to object, and James sped up to stop her argument. "The best course is for us to get a good night's sleep and start fresh in the morning." He ached to reach an arm around Charlotte, but if Harlan saw the attraction between them, he'd more than likely assign another officer to work with her.

James wasn't about to let that happen.

Harlan nodded approval and pulled out onto the road. "I'll give you a lift home. Come to the station as soon as you're able in the morning, and we'll work out a plan of attack."

They left behind the strobing blue lights of a dozen cop cars and entered the thick blackness of unlit country roads. In the crystal coldness, the stars and moon were lit like a jeweled candelabra. At the edge of town, Harlan pulled into James's driveway. A familiar red car was parked outside, and the lights inside were on.

"Lilah's here," Harlan explained. "Soon as she heard you were okay after the accident, she insisted on cooking y'all a hearty dinner. You know how she is."

And Lilah was no doubt dying to meet his new, live-in partner. He and Harlan exchanged an amused glance. She was curious as a cat, and nothing deterred her from exploring the unknown. A trait that had almost cost Lilah her life.

"Here's something for you to think about, Sheriff," Charlotte suddenly said. "Those men who chased us were tipped off that we were exploring Falling Rock. Soon as we announced at the office that we were going to patrol the area, the men were lying in wait. It's time you considered whether one of your own officers alerted them."

Harlan's spine straightened, and his jaw clenched. Oh, hell, he took those kinds of remarks personally and was about to flip. After the corruption of the previous sheriff, he was hypersensitive to criticism. "Could have been the gatekeeper or just plain bad luck," James said quickly, hoping to diffuse the bomb before it went off.

Charlotte shot him a thanks-for-backing-me-up smirk. "Sticking your head in the sand never helps the situation."

"Don't be so quick to judge," Harlan said, snapping his fingers. "I run a clean operation and personally vetted every officer when I became sheriff."

"Still doesn't mean one of your staff isn't on the take," Charlotte said.

Harlan jerked the car to an abrupt halt.

James opened the back door, eager to forestall the argument. "Thanks for the lift. We'll see you in the morning."

Charlotte shot Harlan another sharp glance but climbed out without further comment.

Before James could follow her, Harlan muttered, "Like to speak to you a moment. In private."

Great. Just what he needed after this long, hellacious day. "Be there in a minute," he called to Charlotte. She continued walking to the porch without bothering to turn around and acknowledge him.

"No wonder she's been suspended for insubordination," Harlan remarked drily.

He leaped to her defense. "Look, she's got trust issues, okay? Probably had a few rats and sour deals go down after all those years working undercover. Their lives depend on suspecting the worst of everyone."

"I don't give a damn about her attitude. It's her...state of mind that concerns me. I spoke with her boss today in Atlanta. He insinuated Detective Helms has emotional issues. Her behavior has been erratic of late—refusing to be reassigned new duties, anger with a couple of other cops she claimed abandoned her during a drug bust, and taking an interest in one particular victim way too personally."

"Her best friend's daughter is one of the kidnapped children. You can't blame her for refusing to give up and taking it to heart. Didn't you take it personally when Lilah was in danger?"

Harlan blew out a deep breath. "Yeah, that's true. You don't have to keep bringing that up."

"And you broke every rule J.D. laid down during his

past few weeks as sheriff. You even managed to get yourself fired. Imagine if another agency looked at your record during that time to evaluate your trustworthiness as a potential employee."

"Point taken."

James stuck his hands in his jacket and stared ahead. "There's something you should know. I messed up today. I was in pursuit of those men, but when I got near their vehicle and smelled gasoline...well, I froze."

"The PTSD got to you?"

"Yeah. I warned you about it before I took the job. If you want my badge, it's yours."

Harlan stared straight ahead, as well. "Still seeing that counselor?"

"Twice a month."

He nodded. "If it gets worse, or you want out, let me know. Until then, I have no complaints about your job performance. The men probably would have escaped no matter what."

"We'll never know. But I wanted to set the record straight. I'm the screwup around here, not Charlotte."

Harlan gave him a considering appraisal. "Don't think I haven't noticed the way you've been looking at her. Just remember that she's only here temporarily."

He knew that, but Harlan's warning still twisted his gut.

"She might as well be from across the country," Harlan continued. "The differences between here and Atlanta couldn't be greater."

"I *know*," he said wearily. "I'm not stupid enough to think she'd ever want to stay in Lavender Mountain." Unless one was born and raised in Appalachia, it wasn't an area one often wanted to move *to*—usually, people want to move *out*. He understood this. And Charlotte wasn't seeing the mountains at their greenest and proudest time of year, either.

"This is ridiculous," he muttered, more to himself than Harlan. "I barely know her."

"That's the spirit," Harlan said as James headed to the porch. "Tell my wife not to stay too long, ya hear?"

As if Lilah would listen to either one of them. She pretty much did as she pleased.

He waved a hand in dismissal and entered the house. The scent of chicken and dumplings almost made him weak in the knees. He hadn't even realized he was hungry.

Charlotte was already seated at the kitchen table and blowing on a spoon to cool the dumplings. "I'm starving," she admitted. "Your sister is an angel."

"You might be the first to ever call her that," he said with a snort. "Where's Ellie?" Lilah was almost never without his niece on her hip.

"With the babysitter," said Lilah. "She's under the weather, so I didn't want to take her out."

"What's wrong?" he asked quickly. He hated that little Ellie wasn't her usual bright, babbling self. He'd never figured himself for the liking-kids type, but since the day she was born, Ellie had enchanted him.

"A bit of a cold and sore throat. She'll be fine."

Assured Ellie was going to be okay, he fixed a bowl of dumplings and sat across from Charlotte. Under the kitchen light, her red hair shone with a heat that his fingers itched to stroke. The bright warmth of the kitchen and intimacy of the home-cooked meal loosened the tension of the day.

He could get used to this.

And that scared him more than any high-speed chase.

"WE NEED TO do something about this. James told me your red hair really stood out. It's beautiful, but not practical for undercover work, huh?" Lilah reached across the table and twirled a strand of Charlotte's hair. "Picked up some temporary hair dye for you in town, the brown tank tops you requested and a few little extra somethings."

If by "a few little somethings" she meant underwear, Charlotte would be eternally grateful. She hadn't packed enough clothes, and there'd been no time to do laundry, which landed her in a desperate situation. Going commando wasn't her style.

James stood and peeked in the store bags on the counter, then pulled out a box. "Are you going blond or brunette?"

Charlotte eyed it warily. "Appears I'm going brunette." A wig would have been simpler and less fuss, but this wouldn't be her first dye job to go under the radar.

James continued rustling about in the bag.

"There's nothing in there for you," Lilah said. "Stop—"

He pulled out a six-pack of women's panties and a box of tampons. He dropped both items back into the bag as if it'd scalded his fingers and handed the purchases to Charlotte. "For you," he said drily.

"There's a peach pie for dessert," Lilah commented. "Why don't you get some and go watch television or something?"

"You don't have to tell me twice to get out of the way," he mumbled.

Charlotte suppressed a giggle before a wave of nostalgia washed over her. How long had it been since she'd enjoyed sparring with her two brothers? She did a quick mental calculation. It'd been two Christmases ago.

Way too long.

"Shall we get started?" Lilah asked, opening the hair color box and eyeing the directions.

"No need. I've done this before."

Disappointed blue eyes nailed her. "But I want to help. I've been shut in with a sick baby for two days and could use some serious girl time."

Dang. James's sister was as easy to like as he was. But Harlan's scowling face came to mind. "Your husband probably wants you to head on home."

"Harlan? Nah." She flicked her wrist. "His supper's in the oven, and he can fend for himself for one evening."

Was it wrong that she took a little pleasure in Harlan's forced solitude? She rose and headed to the bathroom. "Let's do this."

Ten minutes later, Charlotte cracked the bathroom window to air out the peroxide fumes. She wrinkled her nose at the mirrored reflection. The dye looked like shellacked tar coating her locks. This couldn't be good. "Maybe we should rinse this out in twenty minutes instead of thirty," she said, dubiously eyeing the mess.

Lilah bit her lip. "The saleslady helped me pick out the color. Made it sound real easy, too."

"It'll be fine," Charlotte reassured her, adjusting the towel around her neck. "It's just hair. It can always be fixed."

"If you say so."

Her tone did not inspire confidence.

Charlotte emptied out the shopping bag, glad to see all the essentials—panties, tampons, shampoo, conditioner, body wash. "Thanks so much."

"You need anything else, let me know. Do you already have a dress for the fund-raiser party?"

"I've got one in my Atlanta apartment I can fetch later. You going?"

"As the sheriff's wife, it's expected. Besides the cash infusion for Harlan's office, those property owners wield lots of political power. Much as my husband hates politics, it'd be foolish not to hobnob with them."

No wonder everyone was so cautious about descending on Falling Rock. "Wouldn't want to tick them off in any way," she slowly agreed.

Lilah nodded. "Not unless absolutely necessary. But Harlan will do whatever it takes to solve this case. Even if it means angering the wrong people."

"He's told you about the trafficking ring?"

"Of course. The whole thought of something so evil happening close by makes me sick." Lilah shrugged and took a deep breath. "I didn't come to talk shop. Y'all have enough of that on the job. Honestly, I'm looking forward to the fund-raising ball. Wouldn't miss it for the world. I've never gone before. Last year, I had the baby the night before the ball."

"They hire musicians?"

"Only the best. Or so I've heard." Her eyes grew dreamy. "I've always wanted to go inside one of the mansions on Blood Mountain. When I was a little girl, I thought the whole neighborhood was a fairyland of castles."

"Surprised you've never had the opportunity to go in one over the years."

The dreamy expression vanished. "Me? Not hardly."

"Why?"

Lilah let out a long sigh. "You're not from around here, so you wouldn't know. But you've seen the tiny cabin where I grew up. For a whole lot of reasons, the

Tedder name isn't one to land you a ticket to a fancy ball."

"Sounds like class bias is everywhere."

"It wasn't just the poverty," Lilah explained. "James hasn't told you our illustrious family history? I thought you two were close."

"He hasn't said much." Charlotte hesitated to bring up the past, but Lilah had broached it first. "I do read the papers, though. The serial killer incident made the Atlanta news."

Lilah's blue eyes darkened, but in spite of the painful memory, she seemed to quickly shrug it off. "Growing up in our household wasn't easy. My dad was a moonshiner with a monster temper, and my parents argued constantly until Mom moved out."

"I'm sorry. James hasn't mentioned any of that to me. Look, I don't want you to get the wrong idea about us. We're business partners. And I'm grateful to him for helping me with this case, of course."

Lilah raised a brow. "That's all there is to it?"

She flushed, thinking of his kisses. "What has he told you about me?"

"Nothing. But anyone can see the sparks between you two. And it's more than that. I've seen the way he looks at you."

She couldn't stop the warm glow that lit her belly or the smile that lifted her lips. "Really?"

"Positive. I've worried about James since he returned from Afghanistan. He's been withdrawn and alone for too long."

The warm glow faded. "You know I work undercover. Our living together is temporary. I won't be staying long."

"Atlanta's not so far you can't visit on weekends," Lilah said. "You have to come back to Lavender Mountain in the spring, when the whole forest comes alive. Or the fall, when the leaves are changing color. Right now, we're not at our best."

Lilah sounded as if she worked at the local tourist office. "I'm sure it's beautiful. But working undercover isn't like being a regular cop. I can't always come and go as I please. It's not a job. It's a lifestyle."

"Sounds extremely demanding and not much fun."

Fun? No. The fun had worn off years ago. Charlotte couldn't remember the last time she found it even remotely pleasurable. But she did important work. Work that few others wanted to take on.

Ding. The portable kitchen timer startled them both.

That time had gone by quickly. After rinsing the dye, Charlotte realized she'd have to eat her earlier words about it being "just hair" that could always "be fixed."

Lilah let out a startled wail.

Charlotte's formerly auburn locks were now a mess of tangled black straw. All she needed was a hawk of a nose and a wart on her chin for a perfect Halloween witch disguise.

Too bad it was November.

A knock rapped the bathroom door. "Everything okay in there?" James asked.

Quickly she wrapped her ruined hair up in a turban. The guy was probably impatient for a shower. "One minute," she called out.

"Sorry," Lilah breathed.

"No big deal. During work hours, I always wear it in a ponytail anyway."

Lilah washed and dried her hands and opened the

door. "Guess I'll be heading home now. Ellie might wake up feeling miserable and want me." Her face lit up. "Have I showed you her picture?" Without waiting for an answer, Lilah lifted her purse from the table and pulled out a cell phone.

James groaned. "Here we go."

"Just one quick look," his sister promised, holding out the phone to Charlotte.

Ellie's toothless grin and folds of baby fat were typical, but the crystal blue eyes were not. They were the startling blue shared by James and Lilah. She'd recognize that shade anywhere.

The towel slipped from her hair and dropped to the floor.

James stared at her, eyes wide and jaw slack. "What happened to your hair?" he asked, voice booming.

Lilah poked her brother in the side and scowled.

"I mean… I'm sure it'll look better when it dries," he amended.

"Sure." Like hell it would. She sat down at the table and felt the tangled tumbleweed of hair. The damage might be beyond repair. Maybe she should cut it supershort. Absently she said goodbye to Lilah, and the door opened and closed.

James sat down beside her. "So…you got some conditioner? Darla—my other sister—once had a dye job disaster. She went around the house slathered in hair conditioner for a week to repair the damage."

Charlotte sucked in her breath at the mention of Darla. That sister's name had been all over the news last year. She couldn't imagine how much it would hurt if something tragic happened with her brothers—no matter how big of a pain in the ass they could be. "Yeah, Lilah bought a bottle. It's in the bathroom."

He rose from the table and returned with it in hand. "Let's see what we can do."

Before she could protest, he poured half the bottle in her hair and gently ran his fingers over the knots.

"You don't have to—"

"Shhh…relax," he whispered.

His fingers pressed into her scalp and neck, massaging and caressing. She closed her eyes and gave herself up to the pleasure of the moment. Not even cold glops of conditioner running down her face and nape deterred from the comfort of his touch.

A vision of Ellie's blue eyes flashed through her mind, and a primitive urge to procreate clenched her gut. Hell, she hadn't known she had a biological clock. That wasn't anywhere on her radar.

Until now.

That realization almost made her want to run from the hills.

Chapter Eight

"The bloodwork came in," James announced at his office the next morning, slamming the phone down. "That was no deer killed in the woods. The blood was human."

Charlotte's face paled, and panic lit her eyes. "It wasn't... It can't be Jenny's. Maybe someone's just been injured—"

He hastened to reassure her. "We won't have the DNA results for weeks. And it's not necessarily from any of the captive girls. Anyone could have had an accident on a four-wheeler."

"We checked the hospitals and clinics. No serious accidents were reported near the vicinity. It *has* to be one of those girls."

Privately he agreed, but kept his mouth shut. "We'll find out soon enough. Harlan wants us and Sammy in his office right now to work out a plan."

As they scurried down the hall, their coworker joined them midway. "What the hell?" Sammy asked, pointing to Charlotte's hair.

"Red hair is a little too conspicuous," she answered stiffly. "I took corrective measures."

James stifled a grin at her tight French braid. But

Charlotte could dye her hair green and purple, and it wouldn't detract from her beauty one iota.

Zelda was seated by Harlan's desk, taking notes. "Subpoena the gatekeeper's records," Harlan ordered.

She adjusted the glasses on the bridge of her nose. "How far back ya want me to go?"

"At least a year."

Zelda nodded and left the room.

"Let's hit the ground running today," Harlan announced, slapping his hands on the desk. "I won't have my officers blindsided again like y'all were yesterday." He slid a pair of car keys across the table. "Here's your new vehicle. A temporary loaner from Floyd County until the destroyed cruiser is replaced. James and Detective Helms will canvass the Falling Rock neighborhood today, show photos of the Ashbury girl, and see if anyone's spotted her, or if their reaction is suspicious. Sammy, I want you to—"

Charlotte abruptly stood. "No. This isn't a good idea."

James shook his head. She never ceased to surprise him. "I thought you'd want to take action. You've been champing at the bit ever since you got here."

"If we do this, the traffickers will know something's up, and they'll find a way to transport the girls out."

"We can have an officer watch the gate to search any suspicious vehicles that leave," he suggested.

"What about the dirt path out back? If we give them any wiggle room, we can kiss the whole operation goodbye. I've been tracking them for over a damn year, and I won't have the girls' lives jeopardized."

He stood as well, standing toe to toe with her. So much for last night's détente. "Nobody wants that. But we can't just sit on our asses and do nothing."

Charlotte turned to Harlan. "Can't you do something to speed up those DNA results? All we need is one concrete piece of evidence for a judge."

"So, what's your great plan?" James interrupted, stung at her quick dismissal of him. "Keep sitting out in the woods every day and hoping Jenny or one of the others happens to look out the window again?"

Her face flushed, staining her cheeks crimson.

"Simmer down, you two," Harlan said.

They breathed hard, staring at one another. Sammy gave a low, amused whistle.

"I said sit *down*," Harlan thundered. "Last I checked, I'm the one running this show, and I'll decide what strategy to take."

James felt like a chastened schoolboy as he settled back in his chair.

"Now, here's what we're going to do. Sammy will guard the back of the Stowerses' property to make sure no one leaves via four-wheelers or a jeep on those back roads. He'll let us know at once if there's any suspicious activity."

"There are lives at stake here," Charlotte cautioned. "I know we all want to rush in and rescue them." Her fists clenched and unclenched by her sides. "But they're in a volatile situation. We can't make it worse for them by arousing premature suspicion. I say we keep an eye out from afar until the fund-raiser. Monitor the gate to make sure no one enters or exits Falling Rock to ensure that the captives stay where they are. Then, at the fund-raiser, we all spread out and find what we can inside the Stowerses' house."

"Search without a warrant? Highly illegal," James pointed out. "And how are we supposed to get in there?"

"You said they always had lots of out-of-town guests staying over for the event. There's bound to be lots of foot traffic between their place and the clubhouse. We'll try and blend in with the crowd."

"And we don't have to exactly call it a search," Harlan said slowly. "I'd phrase it more like *keeping our eyes open*. If you know what I mean."

"You can call it what you want. I won't leave until I've gone through every room in that house," Charlotte retorted.

"Ditto," James agreed. "Although I still don't see the harm in questioning the neighborhood today about who might have been driving that black sedan and if anyone's seen Jenny Ashbury. Only good can come when a community is alerted. Plus, it'll make future trafficking that much harder to slip by unnoticed if residents are on the lookout for unusual activity." James turned to Sammy. "What do you think?"

"I say let's head out there now." Sammy gave Charlotte an apologetic smile. "Sorry, Detective. Looks like you're in the minority."

She ran a hand over the black wisps of hair that had escaped her braid. "At least let me be the one to question the Stowerses. That is, if they even answer the door."

"Not alone, you aren't," James said quickly. Did she think she could brush aside their partnership so easily? Hurt, mixed equally with anger, coursed through his body.

"I can handle it," she said curtly. "I've been doing this kind of work for years. Much longer than you have."

Ouch. Bitten in the ass by his own logic.

"You'll go together," Harlan ordered. "It shouldn't be me. The Stowerses would view a personal visit by the sheriff as more threatening and suspicious. They might be more open with James."

"Doubt that," James muttered. "If you're hoping they'll invite me in for coffee and cookies, then you've forgotten what the Tedder name means around here."

Harlan shrugged. "Times are changing." His eyes and face softened. "A lot of that is thanks to Lilah. She has a real way with people."

Sammy stood. "Shall we get started?"

They all rose, and Harlan passed out copies of Jenny's photo. "Zelda got copies ready for us this morning. I'll form a blockade by the gatehouse and personally check every vehicle that passes by. Everyone all set?"

They nodded and left his office. It was a tense walk to their new department-issued vehicle. James opened the door and Charlotte edged up to him.

"Why don't I drive today?"

"I'm more familiar with the area. An advantage if another vehicle tails us again."

She didn't look happy about his answer, but walked over to the passenger side and got in. He faced Charlotte before starting the car. "Why all the hostility in there? Thought we were a team."

"That doesn't mean I quietly accept ideas that I think are wrong."

"I can't believe you're opposed to this questioning. You've been raring for action."

"I've already expressed my reservations. No need to rehash the issue. Let me do the talking when we get to the Stowerses'."

"No way," he said, starting the engine and backing out of the parking space. "The cover story is that you're a new trainee. It'll look suspicious if you take the lead."

"Oh, alright," she conceded in a huff. "I can admit when I'm wrong. You take the lead."

"Thank you."

They didn't speak again until the Falling Rock gatehouse came into view. Charlotte placed a hand on his arm. "Sorry you felt attacked in there," she said quietly. "I just… I can't screw this up."

He took her hand and gave it a quick squeeze. "I know what this case means to you and to Jenny's mother. I'd never do anything to jeopardize the girl's safety."

Charlotte nodded. "And James, there's no one I'd rather do this with than you."

SHE MIGHT HAVE been opposed to the plan, but Charlotte's heart skipped with excitement as they walked up the stone pathway to the Stowerses' house. Most of the neighbors hadn't been home today, but the few that were claimed no knowledge of a black sedan and said they didn't recognize Jenny's photo. But that was what they'd expected, anyway.

This was it. The real reason for questioning Falling Rock residents. She was walking on the very ground where Jenny was being held against her will.

James quirked a brow. "I'm lead. Right?"

"Right," she said grudgingly, stuffing her hands in the brown uniform jacket. Besides the fact that it would look suspicious for a trainee to do most of the talking, her personal involvement might make her too aggressive in questioning and blow up the case.

The front door was a massive wooden showpiece, hand-carved with a mountain range design. James rang the doorbell, which seemed to echo in the cavernous interior.

A petite older lady answered the door, wearing a gray dress with a spotless white apron. Her once-auburn hair was streaked with gray and pulled back into a tight bun. She even wore a frilly lace maid's cap like Charlotte had seen only in the movies.

Fear snapped in the woman's dark eyes. "May I help you?" she asked with a strong accent that Charlotte couldn't quite place. Irish, perhaps, given the red hair and fair skin.

"May we speak to the lady of the house?" James asked.

"One moment. I'll go see."

The ornate door closed, and Charlotte shared a look with James. The sound of it clicking shut echoed in the pit of her stomach like doom. She might have been opposed to the visit originally, but getting this close—only to be denied entrance—was excruciating.

Yet she said nothing and stared straight ahead. You never knew when cameras or audio tapes might be rolling. If she were in the traffickers' position, she'd certainly take those precautions.

A staccato percussion sounded on the hard floor, and the door creaked open. "Hello, officers," said Madeline Stowers. "To what do I owe the pleasure?"

Long silver hair was loosely gathered at her nape in a stylish coif that was much too elegant to have been accidental. Self-consciously, Charlotte touched her hand to her own dyed hack job.

Maddie's face was beautiful and possessed the underlying bone structure of a model's, although a faint tightness suggested plastic surgery accounted in part for the firm, barely wrinkled skin. Her brown eyes were wide and her eyebrows thin and arched. A tasteful shade of rose-red glistened on her lips. She wore a black shirt with a deep V that belted at the waist and a black pencil skirt that highlighted her slim physique.

"Mrs. Stowers?" James asked.

"Call me Maddie." She glanced at their nametags. "Officers Tedder and Hanson?" Her slight frown did nothing to mar the smooth plane of her forehead.

Botox, Charlotte guessed.

"Yes, ma'am," James answered. "May we come in?"

It took willpower not to sneak a surprised glance his way. A bold move. He hadn't requested to enter anyone else's home.

A heartbeat of hesitation, and then, "Of course, do come in." Maddie stepped aside and waved them along with a graceful sweep of an arm.

Charlotte entered and picked up a familiar, powdery-sweet scent of black violets mixed with citrus. Maddie used the same brand of designer perfume that her late grandmother once favored. They passed through the foyer and entered the den. She felt her jaw drop, but she couldn't contain her split-second reaction to the opulence. This was a whole new criminal class from what she was normally accustomed to dealing with. Usually the ones she sought undercover lived in squalor in a crack house or some back alley.

The entire back wall was covered in plate-glass windows that afforded a stunning view of trees and mountains. Everywhere she looked, from the paneled, beamed ceilings and walls to the fireplace, the house consisted of custom wood, glass or stone. The only exception was the rustic touch of a twisting iron staircase that led upstairs.

The mountain outdoor element also continued indoors, so much so that even a water element was featured by a huge, man-made rock waterfall that poured into a custom inlaid pool edged with stone and set by the crackling fireplace. The faint scent of burning oak gave the place a ski resort vibe. Two rolled towels were set by the pool, an invitation to indulge in luxury.

"Please, come have a seat," Maddie said, leading them to a leather sectional sofa that could easily accommodate a dozen people. "I take it you're here to discuss some aspect of the fund-raiser? I'm surprised the sheriff didn't contact me directly, though."

"No, ma'am. That's not why we're here," James said.

Charlotte sank onto the sofa next to him while Maddie seated herself opposite, crossing her long legs and smoothing the front of her skirt.

"Sounds ominous," she said with a tinkling laugh. "It's usually so peaceful here. That's why Richard and I bought this place, to escape the noise and the crowds of Atlanta. Don't even get me started on the city traffic. The older we get, the more time we seem to spend here at Falling Rock. Excuse my manners. Would you care for some coffee?"

"Yes—" Charlotte began.

"No." James shrugged. "Okay, coffee would be great. Thanks."

Maddie turned her head and motioned to the maid. "Colleen, serve us coffee and a few slices of that lemon pound cake the chef baked this morning." She faced them again. "It's loaded with sugar, but delicious. Do try a piece."

Hard to believe the perfect woman in front of them ever ate anything but carrots and tofu. She must have an iron will to keep that figure with a pastry chef in the house, Charlotte mused.

James pulled a five-by-seven photograph of Jenny from his coat pocket. "Do you know this person?"

Maddie took the photo and examined it for several seconds. "No. Sorry. Is she in some sort of trouble?"

"She's been missing for two weeks," James said.

Damn, Charlotte had to give it to him. He might have been working in law enforcement for only a few months, but he had the poker face of an officer experienced at interrogating people.

"That poor girl," Maddie cooed, returning the photo. "I take it she's from Lavender Mountain?"

"No, metro Atlanta," Charlotte piped in.

"Is that so?" One perfectly tweezed brow arched, again with no accompanying wrinkles.

It was freaky, Charlotte decided. Unnatural.

"Why on earth are you looking for her way out here, then?" Maddie asked, directing her attention at James. "Does she have family in the area?"

"We're following a tip," he commented, giving nothing away.

"Hard to believe she's landed in such a remote area. I'd imagine strangers in our community would be easily noticeable, at least during this time of year, with the tourist season over."

"So you'd think," James agreed. "But so far, no one's claimed to have seen her."

"Then I'm afraid your tip must have been a bad one. Perhaps an attempt to steer you in the wrong direction?"

James nodded. "That's very astute of you."

Oh, yes, the man was definitely good at his job. Charlotte stood and casually stretched her shoulders. "That's an amazing view you have here," she said, stepping over to the windows against the back wall. Down below, she observed four muscled men dressed in jeans and sporting navy T-shirts. They'd obviously stepped up their security game. She squinted but failed to spot Sammy. Wherever he was staked out, he'd done a fine job of camouflaging his presence.

"It is lovely, isn't it? Ah, Colleen, that was quick. Thank you."

The maid set down a tray on the coffee table and then quickly left the room as Maddie leaned over to pour.

"I'd like to wash up first," Charlotte said. "If you don't mind."

"Down the hall and fifth door on your left," Maddie replied with apparent unconcern.

A quick glance at James's face showed a caution warning in his eyes. He might be a good officer, but this wasn't her first search. Well, technically, this was *not* a search. It was a mere observation of the property that could be legally obtained through a casual stroll.

She slowly walked down the hallway, grateful for the open doors. She passed three bedrooms, each huge with large windows and carpet that appeared to be inches thick, the kind that would feel like walking on pillows. The furniture was heavy wood, and the dressers were empty of any sign that someone actually slept there.

She looked up in the corners of the hallways and bedrooms, curious to see if there were any cameras. Nothing obvious, though they could be cleverly hidden and out of sight. But if she were caught spying on their camera, she could claim she'd mistakenly taken a wrong turn.

Charlotte stepped into one of the bedrooms. The carpeting was as plush as she'd imagined. She halted in the middle of the room, furrowing her brow as if she'd mistakenly entered. If nothing else, a decent undercover cop knew how to put on an act.

But her side excursion didn't help. The closet doors were shut, and even on the opposite side of the dresser bureau, there was no stray clothing or any strewn item to suggest a person used the room. No, the girls were more likely locked in a basement as Karen had claimed—although these bedrooms on the main floor might be used by potential clients to "try out the wares."

The mere thought stiffened her spine and strengthened her resolve to save Jenny. Charlotte left the room and located the bathroom. Gleaming white bounced from walls to ceiling with marble tiles, counters and flooring. As much as she admired the cozy opulence of the rest of the main floor, the white-on-white décor smacked too much of a sterile hospital to suit her tastes.

A camera in here would be inappropriate in all kind of ways, but anyone who kidnapped teenage girls for trafficking was not above installing a discreet bathroom camera. Charlotte leisurely washed her hands and let her eyes rove. Again, everything was meticulously clean and devoid of human personality. She opened cabinet drawers stocked with unopened toothbrushes and toothpaste for guests. The far-left drawer held a pewter hairbrush, but the few hairs in it were long and silver—Maddie's. Charlotte strained her ears, opening her senses to even the faintest whisper.

But only James's and Maddie's voices droned from the den. Disappointed, she returned to them. James fired a quick inquiring glance over his coffee cup, and she shook her head in an almost imperceptible move.

"Will you be in attendance at the fund-raiser?" Maddie asked. "We always invite the officers and their families, even young children. That is, if they're old enough to be awake in the later hours of the evening. It's a real family affair."

"Wouldn't miss it," he declared.

"Me neither," Charlotte said, sitting down by James. "Rookies are invited, too, I take it."

Maddie's smile never wavered, but a cold snap flashed for a second in her dark eyes. "Of course, dear."

So the platinum witch was one of those who viewed other females as competition. That, or Maddie had somehow guessed her true identity. Game on. Charlotte picked up her coffee cup and settled into the cushions, as if intending to make herself at home for a very long time.

"I hear there will be live music." Charlotte sipped the black coffee. "I can't speak for any of the other officers, but I plan on dancing until the music stops and the maids have to shoo me away at dawn."

"Lovely," Maddie said drily, shifting her attention back to James. "I heard about the commotion yesterday near Falling Rock. So shocking. Hope the officers involved are all okay?"

"We're both fine."

"Oh? It was you and—" Maddie leaned forward and scrutinized Charlotte's badge. "Officer Bailey Hanson."

Her name on the badge was a fake. A precautionary measure.

Charlotte lifted her chin. "We're still kicking. Obviously. Not so sure about the other guys, though. Any of your men show up hurt today, by chance?"

Maddie blinked. "As far as I know, they're just fine. You suspect one of them was involved in the incident?"

She made a mental note to ask Sammy if any of the workers outside looked as if they'd suffered injuries.

"It could be anyone," James said. "We've been talking to everyone in the neighborhood who's home."

Charlotte helped herself to a slice of the pound cake and bit into the buttery goodness. "Yum. This is delicious. Will you be catering the fund-raiser?"

"Of course. The menu's set. We'll have hors d'oeuvres and shrimp canapés and tea cakes. Plenty of champagne, as well."

Charlotte turned to James. "That should keep us all busy."

"What do you mean?" Maddie asked.

"All the catering and staff coming in and out of here will be monitored. We've set up camp at the gatehouse to record every vehicle and person that enters and exits Falling Rock. Can't be too careful. Kidnappers are on the loose." Charlotte set her plate down with a clatter. Let Maddie stew over that bit of information.

James stood. "See you soon, Mrs. Stowers. Thanks for the coffee."

Maddie stood, as well, smoothing down the front of her skirt again, then following them to the door. "My pleasure. We'll look forward to the event. Richard and I always enjoy this occasion. It's the least we can do to give back to this community. Lavender Mountain is our little home away from home. I understand that the proceeds from our event provides as much as twenty-five percent of your annual budget."

Charlotte almost snorted. Way to plug her political influence.

"The sheriff, and all of us, are most grateful," James said.

"I believe in giving back."

Charlotte hated the self-righteous tone of Maddie's voice.

"In Atlanta, I do lots of volunteer work, as well," the woman continued. "My favorite is working at the teen suicide hotline. So many young lives in crisis."

Charlotte's nerve endings tingled, and her mouth went dry.

James nodded. "Thank you for your service."

Maddie closed the door softly behind them, and Charlotte followed James to the cruiser. Inside, he turned to her. "What gives? I saw you tense up there at the end."

"The crisis hotline. My source about the Stowerses? Karen Hicks was suicidal and had called a hotline for help not long before she was kidnapped."

"Well," he said, starting the car, "it appears we've found our Pied Piper."

Chapter Nine

"Why are we stopping here?" Charlotte asked.

James mentally shook himself and stared at his father's cabin. Yet again, it seemed like the old homestead drew him even when he had no conscious plan to visit. Not that he'd admit that to Charlotte. It smacked of a weak character.

"Thought we'd visit Sammy. Check to see if any of the Stowerses' men have shown signs of injury. See if there's anything unusual."

She shrugged. "Beats doing nothing."

Her voice sounded as discouraged as his thoughts. For the last several days, all their knocking on doors and combing through the gatekeeper's records had yielded nothing other than an immediate complaint from the Falling Rock management corporation and the ire of the residents.

"My four-wheeler's still parked in the shed. Shouldn't take too long to go have a look."

Dispiritedly, Charlotte tagged along beside him as he pulled out the ATV. The case weighed heavily on her. For several nights, he couldn't help overhearing bits and pieces of Charlotte's conversation with her friend, Tanya. She'd tried to convey optimism, but after hanging up the phone, her face would be tight and withdrawn.

He knew that helpless feeling. When his own family had been in crisis, he'd been stuck in Afghanistan and unable to protect his sisters. Sometimes at night, he had lain awake on his cot, and worry had buzzed his brain like a storm of hungry gnats.

If she was anything like him—and he suspected Charlotte was—then the best cure was to keep busy, keep digging and poking even when there seemed no point. Even the tiniest clue could often make or break a case.

Charlotte zipped her uniform jacket all the way up and donned gloves and earmuffs. "You're not worried about blowing Sammy's cover?"

"Not particularly." He started the engine, and it sparked to life on the second try. "They already know we're watching them," he explained, raising his voice above the running motor. "Hop on."

She climbed on the back seat, and the contact of her body against his made him grit his teeth. Never had he once imagined being turned on by a partner when he entered into the life of an easygoing, small-town deputy. His dream of a quiet life wasn't panning out, but as he ran over a rut and Charlotte's body bounced against his back, James knew he wouldn't want it any other way.

He accelerated the engine. Trees and shrubs raced past his vision, and the chill mountain air invigorated his body and spirits. The land here never failed him— it was vast and constant, and every hill and hollow was imprinted in his DNA. His old army buddies questioned his decision to return to Lavender Mountain, but James knew this was his home, his land. The place he belonged.

He almost drove right past Sammy, who'd parked his camouflaged ATV behind a dense clump of evergreens. Only the sun glinting off the binocular lenses gave away his location. No surprise there. Sammy and Harlan and he used to hunt together, and each knew how to blend into the woods. James drew up beside him.

"Trying to blow my cover?" Sammy asked, but his eyes held their usual good humor.

"Doesn't much matter. They know we're keeping watch."

"Anything new happening?"

"Not a damn thing," Charlotte said, swinging one leg over the side and stepping down to the ground. "I want to nail Maddie Stowers so bad. She has the moral compass of a sociopath."

"The steel magnolia type, eh?" Sammy asked.

"In an evil way, yes. My theory is that Maddie often finds vulnerable, at-risk girls while working at a teen suicide hotline and then lures them into the trafficking ring. Either that or she preys on the homeless…whoever she can find who's vulnerable. Seen any unusual activity?"

"Nope. Just these men half-assed picking up broken branches and debris. Must be paid by the hour," he joked.

"Nobody staring out the window?"

James's heart pinched. She was desperate to know Jenny was alive and well.

"Sorry, Detective. Nothing."

James took the binoculars from Sammy's hands and stared at the crew. None appeared scratched-up or marred as though they'd experienced a near-fatal car crash days ago. But the Stowerses certainly had enough resources to keep hiring as many men as needed to maintain security. If one or two went down, they could easily hire more staff as replacements. Human trafficking was a lucrative business.

He recalled the immense house with its indoor heated pool and every other amenity for two people who lived there only part-time. No doubt their Atlanta mansion was just as opulent. And all of it earned off the misery of abused children.

Charlotte tugged at his jacket sleeve. "What do you see? My turn."

He handed her the binoculars and climbed back on the ATV. "Guess we'll go for a spin down the road a bit," he told Sammy. "Check out the area."

Charlotte sighed and returned the field glasses.

Again he reveled in the weight of her body braced against his as they rode, the ATV shaking and pitching in the deeply rutted dirt path. But as they rounded the curve leading away from Falling Rock, Charlotte yelled, "Stop!" waving an arm and pointing behind her.

James slammed on the brakes, and the ATV spun in a semicircle, sending up bits of mud and leaves. "What is it?"

"Over there, near the edge of the clearing. There are two men with shovels and a garbage bag. Do you think—"

"That they're digging a shallow grave?" He thought of the spilled blood they'd found earlier in the week. "Yeah. Could be. Or could they might be 'sengers."

"What's that?"

"I'll explain later." James stepped on the gas and reversed direction. "Let's find out which it is."

The two men abruptly stopped digging and eyed them warily. The eldest, sporting a long gray beard, hugged a garbage bag to his chest as he high-tailed it to a four-wheeler. The other guy, who looked young enough to be his son, or even grandson, dropped both his shovel and bag and also made a beeline for their mud-splattered vehicle.

"Halt!" James yelled.

Their old motor engine turned over once, then twice, before it started. James pulled in beside them, and the old man reached for a shotgun mounted on the hood.

Damn it. The old coot had a couple of seconds' bead on him. No way he could stop his ATV and withdraw his sidearm before he was already looking down the barrel of the mountain man's shotgun.

"Drop it!" Charlotte commanded. She half fell off the back seat, and then landed on her feet like a cat, gun drawn and aimed.

A blur of brown came between him and the old dude.

"Hell, no." The old man abandoned the attempt to grab his weapon and hit the gas. The old contraption lurched forward.

This was a chase the men had no chance of winning. "Get back on," he ordered Charlotte.

"Hell with that." She fired a warning shot, the blast echoing through the hollow.

The younger man glanced back, eyes round as a full moon. The ATV jerked to the right. The driver had enough smarts to get off the main path and try to lose them in the woods.

Charlotte dropped her weapon. "I had a shot at their back tire, but he switched directions on me at the last minute."

James revved the engine. "Get on. We'll catch them."

Quickly she climbed on board, and he gave chase. Had it been summer, the men might have been able to conceal their whereabouts, using green foliage as camouflage. But in the November barrenness, they were dead meat.

A shot rang out.

Son of a bitch. Did they really expect to get away with shooting two officers of the law in broad daylight? And then escaping on an old ATV that probably had a maximum speed of only thirty miles per hour? What the hell did they think they were doing? If they were guilty of illegally harvesting wild ginseng, as he now suspected, the pickers had way overreacted.

The trail narrowed. Did the men have a plan, or had they fled on a knee-jerk impulse? Soon there would be nowhere left to drive. Worst-case scenario, they were part of a larger group that was nearby and could be recruited to assist their fight. Or maybe there was a drying shed nearby that the men hoped to hole up in.

Both possibilities became moot as the men's four-wheeler crashed into a huge oak.

James drew out his sidearm as he raced forward. This time he'd be ready.

CHARLOTTE'S HEART NEARLY burst with anticipation. They'd get these men and force them to talk. With any luck, they'd provide a clue to help catch the traffickers.

Both men jumped off the ATV, the eldest clutching his shotgun. She and James did likewise with their pistols. But the yahoo mountain outlaws still weren't done fleeing, and the two ran in opposite directions.

So it was going to be one of *those* arrests. Lots of trouble and a real pain in the ass.

"You go after the younger," James shouted.

Of *course* he chose the armed man to chase, and it ticked her off. She was as capable as any male cop when it came to apprehending felons. No time to argue, though. Later she'd set him straight on that score.

Charlotte took off, legs pumping and heart pounding double-time with adrenaline. Fortunately, the past several days had been event-free, allowing her injuries to heal. Problem was, her target was just as hyped as she was.

From below, brambles sliced and shredded her pants legs while low-lying tree branches from above slapped her torso. On and on he ran. Whatever the guy had done, she'd make sure a fleeing arrest charge stick. That and whatever else she could slap on him.

The dude was fast and crafty, darting from tree to tree in a zigzag pattern. She briefly wondered if James had caught up with the old man.

"Stop!" she ordered.

He didn't look back or slow down. The jerk. He wasn't getting away. Not even if it meant her heart exploded from exertion. "You're just making—" Charlotte gulped oxygen into her burning lungs "—it harder on yourself." She drew a few more gasping breaths. "Give it up."

"Up yours," he shouted, flipping her the middle finger.

Nice guy. But she'd seen and heard worse. *Far* worse.

Abruptly the trail widened, and he stumbled into the open. He glanced back at her, eyes bewildered and panicked. Charlotte smiled and raised her gun. "Halt!" she called out. "Got a clear shot" —she panted, though her aim never wavered— "at you this time."

He hesitated, running a hand through his dark, shoulder-length hair, and then raised both arms high in defeat.

Charlotte approached, cautious. She didn't trust his sudden surrender for a second. Backup would be cool right about now, but she was used to working alone. She only hoped Sammy had heard the fired shots and had left his post to find James.

"On the ground," she ordered. "Facedown."

He dropped, and she was pleased to note the rise and

fall of his chest. Apparently, the run had tired him out, as well—but he might yet have some fight left in him.

"Hands behind your back, and spread your legs wide."

He grudgingly complied. "Bitch," he muttered, then spit.

"Careful. You might hurt my tender feelings." She stood over him and used her right leg to spread his legs out further. "Got any weapons?"

"If I did, I'd have used 'em on you by now."

Dude was charming. Defiant to the end. She tucked her gun into her side holster and withdrew a pair of handcuffs.

"That ain't necessary."

She bent to one knee and slapped a cuff on his left wrist. "I'll decide what's necessary."

Charlotte grabbed his right wrist, but he twisted and jerked away. He reached into his jacket pocket. Must have a weapon after all. She'd expected no less.

Quickly she rose as he pulled out a knife and flicked it open. Sunlight touched the silver blade, and it glinted with malicious promise. She had one second to prevent an attack that could leave her gutted. Another second, and she'd have to run and would turn from hunter to prey. *Not happening.* Charlotte lifted her right foot and then stomped with all her might on his right hand.

"Owww…son of a bitch!" His fingers loosened their hold on the knife, and he curled into a fetal position. "I think you broke it!"

She stuffed the knife in her pocket, then bent down again and cuffed his wrists together. "What you got here?" Inside his other jacket pocket was yet another knife. "Any more weapons? Tell me now, and I won't have to hurt you again."

"One more knife. Right pants pocket."

She retrieved the weapon and patted down his legs

before ordering him to roll over. Swiftly her hands ran down his arms, chest and hips.

"You need to git me to a doc," he said with a piti-ful moan.

The adrenaline left her system with a rush, and she sank onto her haunches several yards from his curled-up body. She reached for her walkie-talkie and then let out a moan of her own. Either she'd left it in the truck or had lost it during the chase. Just terrific. "Looks like we're in for a hike."

"Can't," he protested.

"You've got a broken wrist, not a broken leg."

His face flushed scarlet, and his eyes were bright with tears. Whether from pain or anger, she didn't know and didn't much care.

"Heartless bitch. I'm suing your ass. Police brutality."

"That's me. Coldhearted," she cheerily agreed. "Some perp twice my size tries to gut me with a knife, and I dare defend myself. Wonder who the judge and jury will rule for at trial?"

He scrambled to a sitting position, turned his head to the side, and spat again. "There's more than one way to get justice 'round here."

Anger blazed behind her temples, and she stuffed her fists into her jacket. What she really wanted to do was pummel some sense into the guy, but that was a line she'd never cross. In and out she breathed, willing her temper to cool. Dude hit a nerve for sure. This wasn't the first time she'd heard such a threat, and she didn't take it idly. One day her past might catch up to her. She'd return to her one-bedroom apartment some night, and someone would be there, waiting for her in the darkness.

"You want to sit around all day and exchange pleasantries, or shall we return to our ATV? I'm sure Officer Tedder has your partner in custody by now."

"Betcha Grandpa got away." A smirk twisted his thin lips.

Charlotte jumped to her feet. Why was she lollygagging? James might need her assistance. "Rest is over. Time to hit the trail."

"You go. I'll wait here."

"The hell you will." Charlotte leaned over and yanked at his cuffs.

A high-pitched wail escaped his mouth.

"C'mon, big guy," she said as he struggled to his feet. "Play nice, and I won't tell your grandpa and your future cellmates that I made you cry like a girl."

He opened his mouth, no doubt to call her another choice name, but then clamped it shut. "I'm coming," he said, his face scrunched in sullenness.

Frankly, he could pout all he wanted as long as he followed orders. Charlotte made a sweeping gesture. "You go first."

She followed a couple of feet behind as they made their way back through the underbrush. Only the crunch of their shoes and an occasional bird call ruffled the wooded silence. Where was James? With every step, her worry increased.

The crashed ATV came into view, still overturned and lying on its side. And still no sign of James. The cuffed suspect turned and grinned. "What'd I tell ya? Grandpa's long gone."

"Yeah, gone to jail," she snapped. But her uneasiness grew, pinching at her lungs and heart.

One of the large black garbage bags the men carried had fallen two feet from the ATV. What was in them—

drugs? Weapons? Body parts? Curious, she scooped it up and looked inside. The bag held…vegetables? She pulled out one of the plants and held it in her palms. It had a green stem about twelve inches long that was topped with five leaves. Long, stringy roots resembling white carrots were attached to the base of the stem.

"What's this? Albino carrots?" she asked.

He snorted. "It's 'seng."

She blinked. "Come again?"

"Ginseng. You ain't never heard of it?"

"It's an herb, right? But…what's the big deal? Why the hell did y'all run from us?"

A voice called from behind, "Because it's highly profitable and highly illegal."

Charlotte whipped her head around. James strode her way, grandpa cuffed beside him. Relief jellied her knees, and for one horrible moment, she thought she might faint. So this must be what Southern belles called a swoon back in the old days. She straightened her shoulders and frowned. Since when had James's well-being mattered as much or more than her own? She had a job to do here, one that required all her focus.

"Thought you'd got away," the younger guy muttered, clearly disappointed. "Did he rough you up any? I think this one broke my damn wrist."

James quirked a brow at her, amusement dancing in his eyes.

"He neglected to mention he sustained the injury while attempting to stab me," she said.

Her partner's amusement flashed to fury. His eyes were flaming blue orbs, and his whole body grew taut, filling the air with a crackling tension. He left grandpa behind, all his focus on the younger man.

Now the dude wasn't so cocky. He stepped backward and held up his cuffed hands. "I'm hurt," he whined.

James grabbed him up by the collar and pushed his body against a pine.

This was a side of James she'd never seen. "Wait." She tried to wedge herself between the two men. "Stop. I handled the situation. It's over."

James let go but kept glaring at the guy.

A little redirection was in order. She retrieved a pen and small notepad from her uniform shirt. "Okay. Junior claims to need a doctor, so let's get the ball rolling. Y'all have any identification on you?"

Grandpa shook his head. "Don't need it to drive my four-wheeler."

"Name, please." Her pen hovered over the notepad.

"Linton Harold Drexler the Fourth. And this here's my grandson." A grand name for grandpa.

"And yours?" she asked Junior.

"Ross Drexler, you—"

"Careful," James warned with a growl.

She scribbled down the information, then held up the plastic bag. "Ross told me they were digging up ginseng, and that appears to be what's in the bags they carried."

"Yep. If they hadn't resisted arrest, they'd be charged with poaching and trespassing, which usually only carries a small fine."

"You questioned them yet about seeing or hearing anything?"

"We ain't no snitches," Ross piped up.

"If you know something, you *will* tell me," Charlotte said through gritted teeth.

"Shut up, Ross," Grandpa said. "I done told ya digging for 'seng so close to them fancy-pancy houses were beggin' fer trouble, and I was right." He turned his back on Ross. "We heard some terrible screaming one day, and it ain't been sittin' right on my conscience, neither."

Charlotte swallowed hard. Sure, she was aware of the methods traffickers used to break down their captives, but she'd kept that knowledge tucked away in a don't-go-there zone. Now it was all she could think about. Jenny was one of the screamers. And jackasses like Linton and Ross heard them and did nothing to stop it.

"When?" James pressed.

"It's been since we found that patch last week. At first, I thought I was a-hearin' thangs, but several days passed, there weren't no mistakin' that a girl was screaming. Spooked me. We hightailed it outta there, and 'bout five minutes later, a shot was fired."

"But did you actually see anything?" Charlotte asked. "If we had a witness—"

Grandpa shook his head so hard that his beard whipped from side to side. "No, ma'am. We ain't seen nothin'."

"What about you?" James asked Ross.

"I ain't seen nothin'."

Charlotte sighed and gestured for James to follow. About six feet away from the men, she stopped by a copse of pines. "I'm surprised Sammy didn't hear the shots and drive over." She kept her voice low.

"He heard and radioed me. I told him to stay put, thinking these guys might have been hired to provide a distraction while the kidnappers transferred the captives out. If I'd known you were in danger…"

She waved a hand in dismissal. "I've handled worse. So how are we going to transport these two to the station?"

"Sammy's already taken care of it. A cruiser should be on the main path any minute."

Whew. She'd had enough exercise for the day without having a mile trek to James's cabin with two fugitives in tow. "Junior will be glad to hear it. He's been whimpering like a baby ever since I stomped that knife out of his hands."

Oops. Mistake to bring that up. James's jaw clenched again, and she sensed the anger seething from his entire body. "Old man give you any trouble?" she asked quickly. "I kept expecting to hear his shotgun fire."

"Nah, once he saw the writing on the wall, he gave it up quick. Sorry. I should have chased the younger one. Would have if I'd known he had a weapon."

"That shouldn't enter into your decision. We're partners—equals." She held up the bag. "How much is this stuff worth?"

"You can fetch anywhere from five hundred to a thousand bucks a pound for wild ginseng."

She whistled and glanced down at the strange-looking plants. "You're joking, right?"

"'Fraid not. They've been poached so much it's possible they'll become extinct in a few years."

What a damn shame.

"What's so magical about ginseng?" she asked.

"People claim it can cure anything from cancer to diabetes to weight loss."

James regarded the poachers, rubbing his chin. "Forget your occasional murderer preying on lone hikers walking the trail. Between the moonshiners, pot farmers and 'sengers, Appalachia can be a dangerous place. Atlanta's crime rate has got nothing on us."

"And now you've even got human trafficking."

"Not for long," he vowed. "Not on my mountain."

Chapter Ten

James settled into a chair in Harlan's office. The hot seat, judging by Harlan's scowl. That, and the fact his boss had told him to come alone and leave "that woman" behind, clued him in that this wasn't going to be a pleasant conversation. James mentally reviewed the ginseng poacher arrests he'd made yesterday with Charlotte. Everything had proceeded smoothly. This had to be about the trafficking case. Harlan leaned back and ran a hand through his hair.

"What's up?" James asked.

"I've just spoken to the mayor. There's been a backlash from our questioning at Falling Rock. Numerous complaints and a formal petition for the mayor to 'do something about me.'"

"Rich folks' complaints. We've done nothing wrong and the mayor knows it. Did Madeline Stowers and her husband lead the charge on the petition?"

"He didn't mention any names, but it wouldn't surprise me."

He'd be lousy at Harlan's job and the ensuing political pressure that came with holding a public position. Mostly he'd hate the necessary kowtowing to the rich and powerful that came with an elected office. But James had enough sense to realize his resentment of the upper echelon was partly a result of his own upbringing as a Tedder. People had always judged him by the black sheep in his family and it had left him with a huge chip—no, make that a *boulder*—to carry.

"Surely he understood the necessity for questioning everyone," James said.

"He did—but he's still not happy about the situation."

Anger flushed the back of James's neck. "Maybe the mayor should be more concerned about the safety of his officers and the welfare of the people in his city than he is with keeping up an all-is-well appearance about crime in the area."

"Was that little speech for my benefit, too?" Harlan asked brusquely. "Because if it was, I can assure you that I have my priorities straight."

He said nothing. Let Harlan make of it what he wanted. Bad enough to have this tension at work, but the fact that this man was his brother-in-law might make the next family get-together awfully awkward.

"I've been reviewing my conversation with Captain Burkhart, Charlotte's supervisor. Her claim that the traffickers operate here stems from an unreliable witness."

"But don't forget that she saw a young girl at the window."

"Exactly. *She* saw it—not you."

Heat lanced his gut. "You accusing her of being a liar?"

"Not deliberately. Hell, James, sometimes people are so determined to prove a theory that they actually invent things in their own mind as proof and believe it's real. Detective Helms has admitted to a personal involvement in the case and that's always dangerous. It can cloud your judgment."

Harlan was nothing if not stubborn. "What about the men who tried to run us off the road? You can't blame that on a figment of imagination."

"No. But it's possible the incident had nothing to do with covering up a human trafficking ring."

"What else could it be?"

"Let me put it to you this way," Harlan said slowly. "Ever since you found that woman in your cabin, trouble has followed. We know something is going on, but is it really what she claims it is? I'm concerned about Detective Helms's mental health."

James jumped to his feet. "Like hell you are. You're concerned about not making waves with the mayor and the Falling Rock residents."

"That's not fair," Harlan snapped.

A voice sounded from the doorway. "I can assure you, Sheriff, that I'm not unhinged. Although I'm not sure how one goes about proving their own sanity."

Charlotte leaned against the door, face washed of emotion. It was as though she'd donned a professional mask of indifference. But Harlan's words had to cut her deeply.

"You don't have to prove anything," James said hotly.

"Sorry you overheard it this way," Harlan apologized. He turned to James. "I'm afraid she does have to set my mind at ease. I can't risk your safety, or any of my other officers' safety, unless I'm convinced there's good cause."

"Can you give me until the night of the fund-raiser to prove my case?" Charlotte asked. "Just a few more days."

He nodded stiffly. "Sounds fair. In return, I ask that any inquiry you make into the alleged trafficking ring is done discreetly. This office can't afford to alienate the mayor and a significant portion of the people we're here to serve."

"Understood."

With that terse word, Charlotte turned on her heel and left.

Tension clouded the air between him and his boss. "May I be excused?" James asked.

Harlan waved a hand toward the door. "You two have until this Sunday to find enough proof of the trafficking to obtain a subpoena, or better yet, get this matter resolved."

"You've made that very clear." James strode to the doorway.

"Wait a minute. James…don't let your emotions blind you to the facts."

"Don't worry yourself on my account. And don't you let the bigwigs dictate what your office can and should investigate."

He retreated before Harlan could whip out another angry retort.

THE RIDE HOME had been tense and quiet. "I don't want to talk about it" was all Charlotte would say about the matter.

He stirred the camp stew and took the cornbread from the oven.

"I'm glad you know how to cook," she commented, setting out the plates and silverware. "Because I sure don't."

"You can thank Lilah. She always cooks more than enough for her family and then sends me the frozen leftovers."

"She's too good for Harlan." Charlotte clasped a hand over her mouth. "Oops. Didn't mean to say that out loud."

"Harlan's okay. We used to be best friends in high school. The two of us and Sammy used to go hunting and camping almost every weekend during deer and duck season. We did our share of sipping moonshine together under the Appalachian moon."

"Sounds like a real manly bonding experience. Did it bother you when he married your sister?"

"Took a little getting used to." He set the stew on the table. "Did feel strange at first when I got back from my tour of duty."

"And he offered you a job working for him?"

He returned to the kitchen for the cornbread as Charlotte ladled the stew into their bowls. "Yeah. Not sure how much of that was Lilah's doing, or whether or not he really needed me."

"You're a good cop. He's lucky to have you. Do you like the work?"

"Surprisingly, yes. Solving cases is like putting together the pieces of a puzzle."

A smile curled her lips. "I see you haven't had time to get jaded yet."

"The army already did that for me." His cell phone vibrated, signaling a text message. He picked it up from the table and swiped the screen.

Back off.

What the hell? The phone number didn't ring a bell. He'd run a check on it tomorrow, but odds were that it was generated from a burner phone.

"Problem?" she asked.

"Nothing to worry about." He turned off the phone and laid it down. What good would it do to tell her of the vague threat? And he certainly didn't plan on mentioning it to Harlan, either. He'd only point out that Charlotte

might have sent it, or that the threat could be about anything and not necessarily the trafficking case.

"I have to admit this is nice." Charlotte bit into a piece
of buttered cornbread and then took a sip of sassafras tea.
Her knee injury was almost completely healed. Luckily
she enjoyed the tea's strong, tangy flavor and dutifully
drank a glass or two a day.

"What's nice?"

"Being able to relax in the evening and have dinner
with a friend. Usually I grab fast food, when I remember
to eat, and scarf it down in front of the TV."

Friend? To hell with that. He wanted to sleep with her
the night through and wake up with her every morning
in his bed. Images of her spread on his couch in T-shirt
and panties the night he'd tended her wound interrupted
his train of thought. What had she just said? Something
about food. He cleared his throat.

"I can relate. If not for Lilah, I'd never get a home-
cooked meal."

"Ribs still hurt?" He'd insisted on X-rays and was relieved to discover none of her ribs were broken.

"Not too bad. The bruising looks worse than it feels."

He reached for the butter at the same moment as Charlotte. Their fingers touched. Heat traveled up his arm like
an electrical charge—hard, fast and almost painful. He'd
tried to be hands-off, but these nights alone with her had
taken their toll. Everything she did and said drew him
deeper into her spell.

She jerked her hand away from his as if the contact
had burned. Charlotte felt the fire, too. He read it in the
spots of color staining her cheeks, in the sharp inhala-
tion of her breath. James reached for her hand and held
fast. Her gaze moved slowly up from their clasped hands

until her teal eyes, darkened to the color of the forest, bore into his own.

"Charlotte," he breathed. His heart skittered as if he'd run a race for his very life. He pushed back his chair. Wordlessly she rose from the table and came to him, never breaking their handhold.

IT WAS AS if every ounce of her considerable willpower had flown the coop. She dropped into his lap, pressing her hands into the top of his shoulders.

And then he kissed her.

His tongue danced inside her mouth and she was drowning in a flood of desire. She needed him—all of him. His fingers raked through her hair and then pressed into her scalp, drawing their mouths even closer. His desire pressed against her left hip. James stood and his hands cupped her ass, pressing her more intimately into his erection.

"Wait. Stop." She withdrew from his kiss and took a deep breath. "This is too fast…"

He let go immediately, leaving her dazed and disoriented, as if she'd lost her mooring. Charlotte grasped the edge of the table behind her for balance.

James ran a hand through his hair. "If you're not ready, okay. I thought…"

"It's not that I don't want you," she quickly assured him. "It's just… I don't want you to think it changes anything. No matter what happens at the fund-raiser, by this time next week I'm back in Atlanta."

A momentary flash of some emotion—pain? Sadness?—swept across his normally stoic features. "I get that. But it's not like Atlanta's on the other side of the country. We could visit."

"No. You don't understand." How could she make him see? "Being undercover is nothing like a regular job with regular hours. If you visited my place at the wrong time, you could jeopardize my cover."

"So? I'll call first or we could meet elsewhere."

Charlotte stepped away from his intense scrutiny and paced the kitchen. "There's more. Sometimes an assignment requires me to be away for weeks at a time. That's why undercover officers hardly ever have intimate relationships. Or if they do, it rarely lasts."

"We could try," he insisted.

Damn, James was stubborn. She threw up her hands, exasperated. "Don't you get it? I'd be terrible for you, for any man. Harlan's right—trouble follows me. I never know when some ex-con with revenge on his mind might find me."

He held up a hand, warding off her objections. "I'm willing to tolerate a little inconvenience. And as far as danger, I can handle it, so stop borrowing trouble. We can take this one day at a time."

"Are you sure?" She anxiously searched his face. He deserved more than what she had to offer. He deserved a Lavender Mountain woman who could spend her evenings with him, share these cozy meals and be there to listen as he unwound at night and talked about his day.

She was not that woman.

"You're an all-or-nothing kind of man, James. With strong views about right and wrong. I don't want to hurt you."

"Let me worry about my own feelings." He crooked a finger and gave a lopsided grin. "I'm a big boy and can take of myself. Trust me?"

Like no one else. He'd never abandon her when danger went down, unlike Danny. And James cared about her.

She slowly walked toward him, drawn to his strength and to her body's urgent need to feel him inside her. To know him intimately. His hands rested on either side of her hips and he kissed her forehead, his lips tender and warm.

The tenderness completely undid her. Some small knot of reserve deep inside melted. Charlotte buried her head against his chest and shuddered.

"You alright?" he asked gruffly.

His voice rumbled against her cheek, the vibration setting off a corresponding rumble in her heart and a seismic shift in her soul. This wouldn't do. *"One day at a time,"* he'd said. For tonight, she'd find pleasure in his arms and not analyze her feelings. The trick was to focus on the physical, to imagine this as a temporary fling.

Charlotte raised her chin and found his mouth, eagerly succumbing to the passion. She pressed her body against his so hard that the table slid against the wall. He groaned, and the knowledge of his need fueled her own even more.

His hands were everywhere at once, down her back, against her ass, then roaming up the sides of her ribs toward her breasts. All while his lips trailed kisses down her neck and to the hollow of her throat. Impatiently she tugged at his belt. Without missing a beat, James undid the buckle and she pushed down his uniform pants.

He groaned again—or wait—was that her? Or both of them? Didn't matter. She cupped his most intimate parts and felt the velvet steel of his erection. "I need you. Now."

"Not yet."

He suckled her nipples and inserted a finger into her

core. When had he removed her pants? Her fevered brain hadn't noticed anything but the unbearable throbbing at the apex of her thighs, the need to be joined. "Now. Please," she whimpered against his mouth.

"Hell, yeah," he growled. "You're so hot and ready for me."

He took her hand, evidently intending to lead her to the bedroom. But that would take way—way—*way* too long. She couldn't, wouldn't, wait. Charlotte shook her head. "Here. Now."

"If you're sure you really—"

She smothered his mouth with kisses and wrapped her arms around his neck.

As if she weighed nothing, James hoisted her legs around his hips and flipped their positions so that she was seated on top of the table. He entered her quickly and she met his thrusts with an increasing urgency.

Harder, harder, harder...faster, faster, faster. Her body tensed and then exploded with pleasure and release. The muscles on James's back tightened and spasmed beneath her hands as he reached his own orgasm.

His head sank onto her shoulders and the sound of their labored breathing joined together. Her fingers gently traced lazy circles down his sides.

"I think I need to sleep," she said with amusement. "About ten hours or so."

He laughed and swept her into his arms. "I don't know about sleeping, but I'm all for going to bed early and often. No more sleeping in the guest bedroom for you." He waggled his brows.

Charlotte returned his grin, feeling more relaxed and carefree than she had since Tanya had called two weeks ago saying that Jenny was missing. "Lucky for you—" she began.

An angry buzz vibrated the tabletop.

"Not again." He stared at it, frowning.

"Better answer. It could be work."

"It is." He let her down and she hastily pulled her clothes together.

"Officer Tedder," he said. A moment's pause. "Okay, we're on our way."

Hope fluttered in her chest. "Any news on the traffickers?"

"Nope. Domestic disturbance."

"No one else is available?" Resentment quickly spoiled her afterglow, followed by the familiar weight of guilt. It was her own fault the sheriff's office was stretched thin.

"The surveillance at Falling Rock leaves us shorthanded. This shouldn't take long; the disturbance is just a small piece down the road."

Amusement tugged his lips as he surveyed the spilled camp stew that ran off the table and puddled on the floor. "This will be a mess to clean up later."

Charlotte put her hands on her hips and arched a brow. "Are you complaining?"

"No, ma'am. I wouldn't change what happened between us, even if it means staying up all night scrubbing floors."

His lopsided grin made her breath catch. Who was she kidding by thinking that sex with James could be a mere physical fling? That her life and heart could continue on same as before?

Tonight had changed everything.

Chapter Eleven

Blue strobe lights flashed across the night landscape, illuminating a disheveled clapboard house that had enough junk lying around the yard and porch to stock a small store. James hopped out of the car and headed for the door. "Stay behind me," he ordered.

Charlotte shot him the dagger look. "Like hell I will. And next time it's my turn to drive."

So much for postcoital afterglow. It was back to business as usual.

Screams reverberated off the house walls.

"You cheatin' sack of—"

"—crazy heifer. Put that poker down or I'll—"

"—who is she? I'll kill you first and then I'll kill her."

James shook his head. "I believe we can ascertain the root of the argument here. Which was no doubt enhanced by shots of moonshine." Idly he wondered if it might be some old batch of 'shine his father and uncle had produced. The irony of that never escaped his notice.

"You been called to this house before?"

"No, but these domestic disputes are amazingly similar."

Charlotte kicked an old tricycle out of her path. "Voluminous consumption of alcohol and a short fuse by one or both partners?"

"Followed by a cooling off period and teary reconciliation until the next round of drinks. You got it. Remember, these types of calls can turn out to be the most dangerous."

"Even undercover cops know that," she said, voice brusque.

James pulled open the screen and wrapped on the door. "Sheriff's office. Open up."

"See what you done did, woman?" a man shouted from inside.

"What I did? What *I* did? You stupid, lying—"

James turned the knob and discovered it was unlocked. He entered and took in the scene at once.

A heavyset woman in a floral print dress brandished a poker in her right hand. The man wore only a pair of boxers. Blood ran down his nose and he swayed slightly, off balance. But James's focus quickly passed the couple arguing and traveled to the couch where two young girls—probably ages four and five—huddled together beneath a Hello Kitty blanket.

"Ma'am, put down the poker," he said firmly. "Let's discuss this calmly."

"Ain't nothin' to discuss. I told him to git out and he won't leave."

"This is my house," the man bellowed. "You go."

James caught a movement from the corner of his eye—Charlotte reaching for her firearm. He flicked his wrist downward, motioning her to put it away. She raised a brow, hand hovering over the sidearm, but nodded and dropped her hand to her side.

"I'm ordering you to drop that weapon," James said, stepping between the two.

The woman lowered her gaze and stared at the poker blankly, as if she'd forgotten she held it. Her face was flushed and her eyes wild with rage.

Charlotte also stepped between the couple, facing the man and spreading her arms out wide. Together, the two of them provided a visual and physical barrier between the couple.

"There we go," James said, his voice softer. He stepped closer and took the poker from her shaking hands. "That's better. Could you do me a favor, please?"

"What the hell do you want? I ain't done talking to him yet." She tried to walk around him and James blocked her path.

"Ma'am, see your kids over there on the couch?" he asked. "Maybe it'd be a good idea to take them to their bedroom. You don't want them to witness this. You're a good mom and know this isn't good—"

"It's his fault," she muttered. "Pulls my chain every time."

"Officer Hanson, could you go with her and the kids? Sir, I need to you take a seat over there." He pointed to the recliner across from the sofa.

The man did as told, and Charlotte walked to the children, giving them an encouraging smile. "Everything's going to be alright. Your mom's going to tuck you in bed. Good deal?"

The youngest girl clutched her doll tighter and regarded Charlotte with solemn eyes that belied her age. The older one asked her mom, "You want us to go?"

The mother pursed her lips into a tight line and faced Charlotte. "I want him gone, ya hear?"

"We'll discuss that later," Charlotte said. She bent her knees and came eye-level with the youngest girl. "Such a pretty doll. What's her name?"

"Emily."

"Nice. What's your name?"

"Sarah Slackum. I'm four years old and live at 19 Pence Street." Sarah smiled at her mom. "I 'membered, Mama."

The woman teared up. "Ya done good, honey. Said everything like I told ya to do if'n ya was lost or the police asked ya questions."

James kept his focus on the man as the women left the room. "What happened here? Did she hit you in the face with that poker?"

"Damn sure did." He grasped the arms of the recliner and held tight.

The man had the nervous energy of an angry, caged tiger. He still needed to be talked down a few notches.

"How did this get started?"

"I come home late and she started accusing me of being with another woman. I've had it up to here." He karate chopped the air by his neck.

"Been drinking?" James nodded at the mason jar of applejack moonshine on the coffee table.

"A wee bit," he admitted. "But so did Edna."

"You need to go to the hospital?"

"Nah. This ain't nothin'."

"You want to press charges?"

The man snorted. "I'd hear no end of that at the factory. Everyone would make fun of me getting whupped by a woman."

"This a regular occurrence with you and your wife?"

"This ain't the first time," he admitted. "Ought to be in yer records somewhere about us."

"It's not good for the children. Ever considered getting counseling?"

"I ain't no alcoholic."

"That may or may not be. But I'm suggesting that you and your wife take anger management classes."

"But she hit *me*. Edna's the one that needs them there classes."

"Think about it for your children's sake. I'm reporting this domestic disturbance to a social worker. She'll talk to you and your wife about the classes and check out the children's safety. Be expecting a visit."

"What's he still doin' here?" Edna cried out, striding toward them.

Charlotte blocked her path and ordered her to sit on the couch. Surprisingly, Edna complied, putting her head in her hands. Her whole body shook with sobs.

"You'll be glad to know your husband isn't pressing assault charges," James said.

Edna dropped her hands and snapped her face up. "But it was his—"

James held up a hand. "You can't assault people. Ever. For now, let's just try to get through this evening without this situation escalating. Think of your children."

Silence at last descended in the room.

"For tonight, I think it's a good idea if you two are separated. Have either of you got somewhere you can go for a night?"

"I ain't a-leavin' my children," Edna said. "Make Boone go."

Boone rose. "Didn't plan on stayin' here's no way. I'm

staying with Grady." He grabbed a jacket and weaved his way outside of the house.

James followed him onto the porch. "How do you plan to get there? You can't drive anywhere in your condition."

Boone held up a cell phone. "I'm callin' my brother to come git me."

"We could give you a lift."

"Nah, Grady be here in less than five minutes. I'll wait here on the porch for him."

THEY WATCHED AS Boone climbed into his brother's pickup.

"Great job in there," she said, leaning her head back in the car seat. "Nice touch about contacting the social worker."

James nodded and started the cruiser. "I'll make sure either life gets more peaceful in that house, or the children are removed if they're in danger."

She cast a sideways glance, studying his strong profile. He'd be a great father one day—calm but firm, and loving. Tonight's call had been tense, but they'd worked together as a team, and every time she saw James in action, her respect for the man grew.

"I see how your department is a real asset to the community," she observed thoughtfully. Normally she measured success by the number of arrests made and the amount of contraband recovered. But there was another side of law enforcement, too. One where officers worked with more normal citizens and aided the vulnerable who needed them to intervene on their behalf.

"We try. The job has turned out to be a lot more enjoyable and interesting than I imagined it would be."

"What made you take it to begin with?"

"I was drifting after getting out of the army. Had become a bit of a recluse, actually. Then the opportunity came along and I took the job, thinking it would be easy, steady work."

"Must have been difficult reacclimating to civilian life after leaving the army."

"A little," he admitted. "I wanted peace and quiet when I returned home."

"Pretty rough over there?"

"I've seen and heard things that no man can easily forget. Ended up with a mild case of PTSD." He shot her an uneasy glance. "As my partner, I probably should have mentioned that to you sooner."

"I trust you, and evidently Harlan does, as well."

"Overall, I'm grateful for my experience in the army. It's defined who I am."

And he was a damn fine man—if a little bossy.

He might claim the job was coincidental, but there was more to it than that. "I don't believe you went into law enforcement only because it was convenient. You went in because you believe in justice, especially considering what's happened to your family."

He slanted her a thoughtful look. "Maybe. Glad to know I have your trust. I have a feeling you don't trust others easily."

"I don't." She drew a deep breath. What had Miss Glory said about opening her heart? James had opened his a crack, she could do the same. "My partner before you, Danny, ran out on me during a botched drug bust. Left me alone with a pretty scary suspect who had pulled a gun on us."

"What a son of a bitch."

"It gets worse. We…had a thing going for several weeks before this happened." There. She'd spit it out. What a fool she'd been.

"A double betrayal," he said, mouth grim. "That explains a lot."

The police radio crackled. "Fire reported at 101 County Road 14. Fire truck en route. Nearest officer please respond."

Charlotte rolled her eyes. "Is there a full moon tonight?"

"What the…" James picked up the mike. "Officers en route."

"Can't someone else take this call?" she asked. "We've done enough—"

"That's my cabin." He flipped on the blue lights and siren, hit the accelerator and spun the cruiser onto the road.

Charlotte held on to the door pull. "Your cabin," she repeated slowly. Coincidence? No. That old place had been standing for decades. This was a message.

She licked her suddenly dry lips. Guilt weighted her shoulders. She'd brought this on James.

They raced through the darkness in silence. Did he blame her for his old homestead going up in flames?

Her phone vibrated in her pocket and she pulled it out.

This is just the start.

Damn. The anonymous text left no room for doubt. The fire had been intentionally set. Charlotte slipped the cell phone back into her jacket pocket without comment. She'd tell James about it later. He had enough on his mind at the moment.

In record time, James pulled the cruiser onto the cabin property. At least a dozen other vehicles were parked helter-skelter in the yard and spectators had already gathered, watching as firefighters sprayed giant hoses on the inferno. Orange flames toasted the black sky and the fire's roar muffled the murmur of human voices.

There was no saving the family cabin. There wasn't even the possibility of saving any items inside, though she doubted anything of sentimental value had been left behind. Anger blazed inside her, as hot as the wall of heat emanating from the burning building. The perpetrators were probably long gone—if this was a professional job orchestrated by Maddie. If so, the bitch was probably standing at the window of her plush mansion, watching as fire glow lit the woods below.

But if the arson was a mere crime of opportunity by a pervert…her gaze drifted to the tree line. He could be hiding behind one of those trees, getting off watching the sight of his work. She glanced at James, but his focus was all on the cabin. His hands were on his hips, his face stoic. She longed to touch him, offer words of sympathy, but that would hardly do in public. Besides, she'd be of more use to him by finding the perp.

Charlotte slipped into the crowd and then hurried around to the back of the cabin. Only one lone firefighter fought the flames from the opposite direction. She jogged toward the woods, right hand resting on the holster of her gun.

A crash boomed from behind and she whirled around. The left cabin sidewall collapsed to the ground and the roof sank on top of it, shooting sparks like the Fourth of July. The smell of burnt pine stung her eyes and enveloped her nose and lungs. She swiped at her eyes and continued into the woods.

Leaves, twigs and pine needles crunched underfoot, loud as firecrackers in the sudden stillness. Only a few feet past the tree line and the noise of the fire and firefighters was already muffled.

Screech.

Her stomach cartwheeled and she raised her gun, spinning in a circle to discover where and what had sounded. Blood pounded in her temples.

And again, the cacophony arose. *Whoo whoo.*

"Just...just a barred owl," she whispered. Creepy thing was loud as a foghorn. "Nothing to fear."

But it took several seconds before her heart ceased its rapid pounding and her breathing returned to normal. Charlotte lowered her gun and searched the inky blackness for signs of anyone hiding.

Nothing was out of the ordinary. Barren tree limbs reached skyward and the tops of shrubs were laced with crisscrossed shadows from moonbeams. The wind whispered above and around her.

So why was she so sure that she wasn't alone?

Awareness prickled her scalp and snaked down her spine. Someone watched. She listened and strained to pinpoint a location.

"Charlotte? Charlotte? Are you out there?"

James. She exhaled in a whoosh and cautiously stepped forward.

Twigs snapped like a mini explosion from her left side. Footfalls vibrated the ground and at last she could make out the tall figure of a man running deeper into the woods.

"Halt," she called out.

The man kept running, just as she'd expected.

"Charlotte? Everything okay?"

"I'm fine," she reassured him. "Be right out."

She stepped out of the forest and quirked a brow at his stern face. "I was checking to see if our arsonist was watching all the excitement."

"Without backup? What were you thinking?"

His dad's cabin was in flames, so she bit off an angry retort. He had enough on his plate without her reminders that he wasn't her protector on the job. "You were busy," she said mildly. "Any leads about what started the fire?"

"They won't say yet but we both know what happened here. Especially since…" He clamped his mouth shut.

"Especially since what?"

"I wasn't going to mention it but I had a text last night saying to back off."

She shook her head in disgust. "Why didn't you tell me?"

"Didn't seem important. I mean, c'mon, it changes nothing. Neither of us will ever back down from pursuing this."

She marched past him, eager to leave the dark shadow of the woods and whoever had been out there hiding. "You still should have told me. If you were working with Sammy, I bet you would have, right?"

"Maybe," he agreed, falling into step beside her. "And don't think I'm finished. Promise me you won't run off on your own again without at least telling me what you're doing. That's professional courtesy at the very least."

"I can admit when I'm wrong. Sorry. I won't do it again."

"Excellent. I take it you didn't see anyone?"

Charlotte hesitated, but she could hardly withhold

information after she'd just chastised him for doing the same. "There was someone out there, but he took off running and I never saw his face."

"You could have been…" He broke off his chain of thought. "Never mind. You're here and safe."

"I had a text, too, on the way over. It said, 'This is just the start.'"

"The Stowerses are getting desperate and they know we're the ones investigating."

"I wonder how much else they know."

They trudged back to the fire, wrapped in their own thoughts.

The fire wasn't quite as bright and the flames were lower. It wouldn't take much longer before the firefighters had it completely extinguished.

"Sorry about your dad's cabin."

James shrugged. "Maybe it's all for the best. The place was a hard sell for buyers and neither Lilah nor I had any desire to move in."

"Speaking of Lilah, I see she and Harlan are here."

"And she's brought Ellie. At least you'll get to meet my niece."

The little family headed toward them. Lilah appeared solemn, but the toddler at her hip was clearly entranced by the fire, and stared at it with saucer-wide eyes.

"Hey, Ellie," James said, holding out his arms.

Charlotte ran a hand down Ellie's blond curls. "Such a pretty girl."

Ellie graced her with a cherubic smile before turning her attention back to James. "See the fire, Uncle Jim Bob," she squealed.

Charlotte snickered.

He winced. "Uncle James," he corrected her mildly, taking Ellie into his arms. "You okay, Lilah?"

She nodded, but her lips trembled slightly. "Yeah. A little sad, though. Me, you and Darla had some good times there."

They watched in silence as the hoses continued to beat down the flames. Most of the spectators drifted away, driving off in their vehicles. Harlan put an arm around Lilah's shoulder. "No point hanging around," he said quietly. "The cold air can't be good for Ellie's cold."

"You're probably right," she agreed.

They all walked together to Harlan's car and James strapped Ellie into her car seat.

"Sorry about the cabin," she said to Lilah.

Lilah wasn't her usual vivacious self, but she mustered a tight smile. "It represented our past. And it held as many painful memories as good ones. As for me, I'll keep my focus on the present."

Harlan glanced significantly at James. "Like I said—trouble," he muttered.

Resentment sliced through Charlotte, but she said nothing in protest. How could she? Harlan was right. She'd brought nothing but trouble to James.

Soon, she reminded herself, this would all be over. She'd leave Lavender Mountain and leave James. In time, he'd forget her and move on with his life—as would she. The thought should have been comforting, but it filled her with sadness.

Harlan dug into his jacket pocket. "I'd been on the way over to your house to deliver this." He held out a certified letter. "Captain Burkhart called me and said to make sure to find you. You've been formally summoned to a hearing tomorrow to discuss dismissal for job abandonment. Your suspension was over yesterday and you were supposed to have reported back to work today."

Damn. She hadn't paid any attention to the date. Atlanta seemed a lifetime ago. "Tomorrow," she repeated dully.

"We'll go together," James said, shooting Harlan a defiant look.

She stuffed the envelope into her pocket. "This isn't your problem."

"You're not going alone. End of argument."

Like hell it was.

Chapter Twelve

"The choice is yours. Report for work here tomorrow morning or be dismissed."

"I need more time," Charlotte pleaded. "Just a few more days and—"

"You're fired," Captain Burkhart said, smugness evident in his pronouncement.

She clamped her jaw shut and arranged her features to show no emotion. She wouldn't give him the satisfaction of knowing how those words hurt.

The man had never liked her. Whether it was because he was a sexist cop or because he'd taken offense for some other unknown reason, Charlotte couldn't say. But in the two years he'd been her supervisor, he'd made her job hell.

When she'd reported Danny and Roy's abandonment at the alley, he hadn't believed her. Instead he bought into her partners' lies that she'd been at fault for the life-threatening danger with the drug dealer. According to their false version of the story, she'd carelessly blown their cover and then fled the scene. Valiant men that they were, her partners claimed they stayed behind and pursued the drug dealer—at great risk to their lives.

Charlotte shook off the old memories and fought

for composure. The two other detectives at the hearing stared at her with a modicum of sympathy.

She rose and lifted her chin. "I used my suspension to pursue this case. My only fault is checking back in a day late. The punishment's a little stiff for the offense. All I'm asking is permission to use my annual leave for the next few days."

Burkhart slapped his hands on the desk. "Enough. We've been through this. You're insubordinate and I don't believe you ever intend to return to duty."

"Not until I have my arrests," she agreed.

"And now you'll never get one." He also rose from behind his desk. "You no longer have any authority as a police officer. Turn in your badge on the way out."

She bit the inside of her mouth, not wanting to lash out and set him straight. She might no longer be employed by the Atlanta PD, but Harlan could still deputize her to work in his jurisdiction until she'd arrested the Stowerses. Right now, she couldn't think about her future career. All that mattered was rescuing Jenny. After that, she'd have to come to grips with the mess.

"Richard and Maddie Stowers will be arrested by the end of the week. You can count on it," she promised.

Burkhart's face reddened. "Not by you. Let it go, Helms."

Hell, no. Easy for him to say. He didn't have a personal connection to the case. Nor did he have to interview trafficking victims and hear the pain in their voices and the horror in their eyes. She couldn't save everyone, but she could and would save Jenny.

She snatched up her purse and marched to the exit, slamming the door behind her. James was sprawled on a bench in the hallway. For the first time, she was secretly glad he'd insisted on accompanying her on the trip to Atlanta.

He quirked a brow. "Bad news, I take it?"

"I want out of here." The institutional-green walls and gray linoleum flooring, combined with the faint scent of industrial cleaner mixed with sweat and tobacco, were a sudden anathema.

"Couldn't agree with you more."

He matched her step for step as they left the building and climbed into her car. She turned on the engine and they headed into the late afternoon traffic.

"I'd hate to drive this every day," he observed from the passenger side.

She cast him a wry smile. "We're not even in rush hour traffic. Sure you don't want to drive like usual?"

"Nope. It's all yours."

Well, at least she'd won that battle today. Wordlessly she weaved along the crowded interstate, stewing over the long day spent at the hearing.

James interrupted her thoughts. "You can always appeal their decision, you know."

"And go through another kangaroo court?" She laughed dispiritedly. "Six years of stellar service—all down the drain on my first transgression."

"Sounds pretty stiff. You should fight it, or at least file a complaint about the severity of the judgment."

"Maybe." But she couldn't muster enthusiasm for the task. When had she stopped loving her job? It had happened so gradually. "I used to enjoy working undercover," she said. "It was exciting and it felt like I was making a difference. Stupid, huh? For everyone I arrested, it seemed like three more criminals replaced them by the next week."

"Would have been even worse on the streets if you didn't catch the ones you did."

"I suppose. But I get sick of the whole underground culture, too. And not getting to see my family as often as I want."

"Now you're free."

"Now I'm broke." A sudden worry assaulted her. "You really think Harlan will temporarily deputize me until the end of the week?"

He winked. "He's my brother-in-law, so I have some influence. Lilah could make life hell for him if he didn't help us out on this. Besides, you're a great cop and he knows it."

The words were a balm to her injured pride. Much as she'd grown to hate her job, she'd never been fired before, and the idea rankled. Maybe James was right. She should file a complaint and get her employment record cleaned up from this hit. Plus, it would have the added benefit of irking Captain Burkhart—always a plus.

It took forty minutes to drive the ten miles to her apartment, but at last she pulled into the parking lot and they headed up the stairs. While she was nearby, it'd be crazy not to pick up more street clothes, a fancy gown for the fund-raiser event and a few other little odds and ends.

They climbed the concrete stairwell and she dug the keys from her purse. A strong hand rested on her forearm. "What—?"

James frowned and cocked his head at the slightly ajar door. "You leave it unlocked?" he asked in a low voice.

She felt the blood drain from her face. "Maybe the landlord had to get in." Not likely.

James drew his gun and stepped in front of her. "I'll check it out."

"Not alone you won't."

He shot her an irate look. "Just stay back."

She unholstered her own sidearm and tried to squeeze her body in front of his. "Me first. It's my apartment and I know the layout better than you," she argued.

James muscled her behind him and slowly opened the door.

Books and sofa cushions littered the den floor. Every item on her bookshelf had been dumped and furniture was pulled away from the walls. James took a step in and she followed, her eyes sweeping from the kitchen to the dining room and balcony. The same mayhem from ransacking was everywhere, but no one was in sight.

That left the bedroom and two bathrooms to check. She carefully picked her way through the junk on the floor, sliding past James. He wasn't happy about that, but could hardly argue the point.

The hall bathroom was empty, all the contents of her medicine cabinet toppled into the sink. Which left the bedroom—the only room where lights weren't blazing. An unnatural stillness lifted the hairs at the back of her neck. If someone was in there, they knew she'd returned. She flattened herself against one side of the door, and James joined her on the other. She was about to enter, when he beat her to the punch.

He kicked the door and it slammed against the far wall. Charlotte flipped on the light switch.

Two men dressed head to toe in black, their faces hidden under dark ski masks, erupted from the closet. The two barreled toward them, so quickly she barely had time to catch her breath—much less shoot. One of the men chopped her arm holding the gun, and her weapon hit the floor by her feet. Strong arms grabbed her just above both elbows and then violently threw her to the side. She was airborne for two seconds before rolling clear across the bed. Her forehead smacked the bedpost and pain radiated through her head. Warm liquid trickled into her eyes and she swiped at them, seeking James in the melee.

Her attacker had fled, but James was wrestling on the floor with the other man. She had to help him. She located her gun and tucked it back into her holster.

"Go get the other guy," James grunted.

"No way."

"I got this," he insisted.

The need to help James warred with her need to catch the other intruder. They'd violated her sacred space. Every nightmare come true. If she didn't catch the fleeing felon, she would always worry that he would return one night. And the next time she might not be lucky enough to have a partner by her side.

"Be right back," she promised, racing to the stairwell.

The steps were slick with rain and she lost her footing, tumbling down the first flight. Ignoring the burning shinbone scrapes, Charlotte ran on and scanned the back of the property.

A silhouette in black crouched behind a garbage can. At first sight of her, the intruder took off running again, knocking over the dumpster can, spewing trash everywhere. But she was close enough—in shooting range—if her aim was accurate. Charlotte touched the gun she'd slipped back into her holster. *You aren't officially a cop anymore. You shoot the guy and you've got a mess on your hands.*

The moment's hesitation cost her a chance. He reached the street, blending with traffic and pedestrians.

She bent over, hands on knees, and took deep breaths

that burned her chest. *Get it together. James might need you.* Charlotte straightened and ran back upstairs, ignoring the jabbing stitch in her side.

PAUSING TO REASON with Charlotte had cost him the advantage in the fight. The masked man fought with the desperation of a cornered animal. Trying to wrestle him back down was like trying to bathe an angry wildcat.

"Who the hell are you?" James panted as they rolled on the floor.

No answer.

The scent of sweat and cheap aftershave filled his nostrils and lungs. He fought against the downward spiral that might tunnel into another flashback. *Keep it together.*

Pain seared his left thigh as the man landed a vicious kick.

Had he momentarily blanked out and weakened his hold? James groaned and grabbed one of the attacker's feet, trying to prevent another kick. Where was Charlotte? Fear pinched his gut. What if this guy's accomplice stopped running and went on the attack? To hell with this wrestling match. Charlotte's safety was his priority.

But he could accomplish one important victory—get a good look at who was behind the attack. If he was lucky, he'd find this criminal later. James released his grip and reached for the knit ski mask, ripping it off his face.

Startled gray eyes met his. James soaked in every detail possible—cropped brown hair, ruddy complexion, a hawk nose, thin lips. His gaze dropped lower and hit the jackpot—on the right side of his neck was a dagger tattoo. The mark looked to be a crude prison job with its lack of detail and grayish-black coloring.

The guy rushed the doorway and James gave chase. Halfway down the stairs, he spotted Charlotte coming toward them—alone and seemingly intact, but blood trickled down her face. Relief chased down his neck and spine. The man she'd been chasing was nowhere in sight, but she was now in the direct path of the gray eyes.

"Look out," he shouted.

Too late. The intruder never slowed, but he raised one muscled arm and knocked her out of his way. In horror, James saw her petite body absorb the pounding of concrete until she lay motionless at the bottom of the stairwell.

"Charlotte!" He rushed to her prone body and pushed the hair from her face. In the space of mere minutes, hell had unleashed its fury. She was pale, the whiteness contrasting with the crimson ribbons of blood on her face.

She groaned. "You okay? Did they get away?"

"Yes, on both counts. How bad are you hurt? I don't want to lift you if anything's broken."

She struggled up onto one elbow and drew several shuddering breaths. "I think I'm okay. Give me a minute."

"That's one nasty cut above your left eye." He pulled a handkerchief from his jacket and gently dabbed at the open wound.

She flinched and reached for his arm. "Stop. I'm going to try to stand."

He supported her weight on one side of his body and she sagged against him. "This is officially the worst day of my life," she joked. "Lose my job and then get the crap beat out of me. Now I get to return to my destroyed apartment and pick up the mess."

"Leave it. I'll lock up while you wait in the car. Where's the nearest hospital? You need stitches."

"I won't argue with you this time. We can stop at a doc-in-the-box on our way back to Lavender Mountain."

James quickly locked up her apartment. Slowly, they returned to the cruiser, his arm bracing her around the waist. "Think you might have sustained internal injuries?" he asked anxiously. Each time pain flickered in her green eyes, he sank lower into guilt. At last they reached the car and he carefully tucked her inside before entering it on the opposite side.

James keyed the engine and turned up the heat. Charlotte leaned back in the seat and flipped the mirror down. "Holy crap, I'm a mess. I promise I don't feel as bad as I look."

She faced him. "So what's wrong?"

"What's wrong? Everything. You're hurt and it's my fault."

"Don't say that." She pointed to the cut on her forehead. "That was caused by an unknown assailant. Not you."

"Yeah, an assailant who escaped me."

"We were surprised by an attack and neither one of us is to blame. I noticed you were limping. What happened?"

"Bastard landed a lucky kick." He gripped the steering wheel and stared out into the rainy darkness.

A warm, soft touch on his right hand startled him, and he glanced down. Charlotte's small hand caressed his tense fingers, which were white at the knuckles.

"I'm okay," she whispered, her breath clouding the air. "Those men did enough of a number on us without us piling on and beating ourselves up."

"Back there. I might have lost it for a couple of seconds in the fight," he admitted. "I'm not sure."

"Doesn't matter. My mind was a tilt-a-whirl a good thirty seconds after I crashed into the bedpost. As they say, shit happens. All we can do is our best."

But what if his best wasn't good enough? Some small part deep inside still felt broken from the war. It was getting better—much better—in large part because the insomnia had finally been laid to rest. The past nights he'd spent with Charlotte in his arms, he'd drifted into deep slumber. James loosened his grip from the steering wheel and held her hand, staring at their enjoined fingers. Every word, every touch from Charlotte was a balm to his spirit—that is, when they weren't arguing. A smile curled his lips. Fussing with Charlotte was still more fun and invigorating than normal conversation with anyone else.

The rain came down harder, a metallic din that thundered above and around them. Water washed across the car windows in sheets. It seemed as though they were separated from the rest of the world in a warm, safe cocoon.

Her hand traveled up his arm, and even through the jacket, the contact set his heart pounding as loud as the rain outside. She brushed her mouth across the edge of his bottom lip. "There's no need to hurry back. Let's wait out the storm together."

He kissed the top of her scalp. "If you're sure the stitches can wait."

"Kiss me and I'll forget all about the cut."

"I aim to please." His mouth met hers. What he'd intended as a tender gesture escalated at once into a roaring desire and he pulled away. "Not the time or place," he said with a frustrated laugh.

"Tonight, then."

The promise and passion in her eyes wiped away all pain and all misgivings. Somehow, someway, they belonged together.

Chapter Thirteen

The last three days before the Stowerses' fund-raiser event sped by way too fast. She and James spent most of their days outlining their plan of action for rescuing Jenny, and their nights...well, she'd never been happier. It was going to hurt like hell to return to her dreary apartment in Atlanta once this case was over. There was nothing there for her—no job, no lover and no friends. Her undercover work had consumed all her energy for far too long.

Charlotte checked the cruiser's pull-down mirror and smoothed back the few stray locks that escaped the bun on the back of her head. Her dyed ebony locks had faded a bit from repeated washings, and the gallon of conditioner she'd used had helped the damage, but it was still a disaster. The stitches above her left eye were removed yesterday, but no amount of makeup could cover the nasty bruise.

James laid a hand on the top of her bare shoulders. "You look beautiful," he assured her.

She smoothed a hand across the long green evening gown, thankful that its length would cover all her shinbone scrapes. Sure, she was being vain and embarrassed that James guessed her trivial concern. Crisply she closed the mirror and raised the sunshield flap to its original position. "Doesn't matter what I look like—all that matters is finding Jenny. And you look pretty spiffy yourself, by the way."

Did he ever. He filled out the tuxedo like nobody's business. The suit emphasized his lean, muscular build and lent an elegance to his high cheekbones and strong jaw. Her admiration must have been clear because his eyes darkened and his gaze shifted to her lips.

"Don't you dare kiss me," she warned.

Teasing mischief danced in his eyes. "Afraid you'll need to have me right here and right now if I do?"

"No, I just don't want you to ruin my lipstick."

"Liar."

She knew what he was trying to do—lighten the tension before they entered the Stowerses' mansion.

"Good thing our plan doesn't include having to actually dance. That bruise on your thigh looks rough."

Music spilled from the main level of the Falling Rock Community Clubhouse and every window was lit. It appeared so elegant and enchanting—if one weren't aware of the dark underside that funded such privileged wealth. If she had her way tonight, the Stowerses would spend the rest of their years in a dark, damp cell with no music. And even that wouldn't atone for all the lives they'd ruined. *I'll have Jenny home to you by dawn*, she silently promised Tanya.

James lifted her hand and kissed the inside of her palm. "We'll find Jenny and the others," he promised. "We've got our plans in place."

"Right." She inhaled deeply.

"One more thing."

She gazed once more at the glittering clubhouse, a hand reaching for the door, impatient to get started.

James placed a finger under her chin and gently turned her face to his. "I love you."

"Wh-what?" No, oh no. This wasn't supposed to happen. She'd let him get too close.

"You heard me. Does that really surprise you? I thought after last night…"

She swallowed hard. Last night had been magical. There'd been a certain tenderness along with the passion, emotions that she didn't want to examine at the moment.

"Don't love me," she whispered. The hurt in his eyes matched the hurt in her heart. "I bring trouble to everyone. Can't you see that?"

"I've told you before that I don't care. We can face anything together." He sighed and ran a hand through his hair. "Never mind. I shouldn't have brought it up now."

"You'll always be special to me…the best friend I ever had."

Friend? The word crushed his spirit. He wanted it to be so much more than that.

"James…" Tears threatened to ruin her carefully made-up face, and she couldn't control the tremble in her lips.

"Sorry. Really. You don't have to say anything." He cleared his throat. "Is your mike secured?"

Relieved to get the conversation back to the job at hand, she checked to make sure it was safely tucked into the front of the low-cut gown. "Yes. Ready when you are."

He nodded and opened the car door. "Showtime."

The wind chilled her bare skin and she hastily threw the gown's matching wrap over her shoulders.

They walked side by side to the front door, mingling with several other couples also on their way to the party. Everyone else looked excited and happy to be going to the annual fund-raising event, while a hard knot of misery twisted her stomach. She'd hurt James and she'd never meant to do so. He deserved a woman who would fill his life with good things—not her.

The door opened and they entered into the bright warmth. A live band played classical music that underscored the chattering of the houseful of guests.

Her eyes quickly swept the room of beautiful people dressed in formal attire. Serving staff milled about with glasses of champagne and shrimp canapés. She'd thought the Stowerses' house beautiful, but it was nothing compared to the present festive glory of the clubhouse.

"Thank you for joining us." Maddie appeared in the foyer dressed in a red low-cut gown that managed to be bold yet flattering. She ignored Charlotte and extended a hand to James. "Officer Tedder, if I remember correctly? Richard and I appreciate all you do in keeping peace and order in our community."

Yeah, I bet she appreciates us. Phony witch.

"I believe y'all are the last of the officers to arrive," Maddie said, still avoiding Charlotte. "Harlan said everyone's made it here except for one officer left manning the fort and another who's home sick."

That would be Sammy, who was guarding the back of the place, and Charlotte wouldn't be surprised if the Stowerses were aware of that fact.

"I don't believe you've met my husband before?" Maddie swept her hand toward the man at her side, who gulped a healthy swig of bourbon from a crystal glass.

Richard Stowers glanced Charlotte's way and discreetly looked her body over. But not so discreetly that it escaped her attention. A cheesy smile lit his puffy, albeit handsome, face, and he extended a hand. "And you must be Officer Tedder's wife?"

"Partner. Officer Hanson." She masked her displeasure at his handshake, which he held two seconds longer than customary.

His eyes narrowed in on her forehead. "Nasty cut you have there. What happened?"

As if he didn't know. As if the two of them hadn't sent those men to search her apartment for clues on how much she knew about their trafficking ring. Unless...unless Maddie were the brains behind everything while he merely enjoyed the fruits of her ill-gotten gains. Richard certainly didn't look or act the part of a criminal mastermind. His ruddy complexion, and the web of broken veins around his nose, suggested he either imbibed quite frequently or was an alcoholic.

His remark finally drew Maddie's attention her way. Brown eyes flashed at her, barely able to disguise anger.

Charlotte offered a cool smile to Richard. "I took a tumble down a flight of concrete stairs."

"Ouch. Guess it could have been worse, though," he said jovially.

Maddie's sharp chin jutted out even further than normal. "Colleen," she said peremptorily, summoning her housekeeper, who apparently served double duty at social functions. "Please take their jackets." Maddie faced them both with a chilly smile. "Enjoy your evening. Let's move along, Richard."

Charlotte removed her wrap, uncomfortably aware of Richard ogling the low-cut V of her gown before obediently tagging along behind his wife.

"Your purse, ma'am?" Colleen held out her hand.

She firmly pulled the sequin purse closer to her side. "I prefer to keep it with me, thank you."

Richard sidled up close to Charlotte and she drew back an inch. Annoyance stiffened her spine. The last thing she needed was to have this man clinging to her side while she searched his house.

James took her arm and guided her away. "Excuse us. We'd like to catch up to our friends by the buffet."

"Certainly." Richard took her other hand and pressed it into his coarse palm. "See you in a bit. Perhaps a dance later?"

Not if she spotted him first. Next time she saw Richard, she vowed it would be to handcuff the creep.

"Of course," she lied, accompanying James into the den, where a long buffet table was spread out the length of the entire room. Once they were out of earshot she quickly whispered, "Thanks for helping me escape."

James nodded. "I see my sister and Harlan. We'll talk a bit and then…"

Then, they implemented their plan. She nodded in silent agreement. With any luck, Richard would be too drunk to seek her out by the time they began the house search.

"Champagne, ma'am?" She accepted a slender flute from the waiter. He was tall and stocky and clearly uncomfortable in his ill-fitted uniform. No doubt he was also employed as a guard, same as the Stowerses' supposed gardeners. She exchanged a knowing glance with James.

"Be careful," he muttered.

The man just couldn't help himself when it came to unnecessary warnings. "Don't worry about me. I can take care of myself. Focus on your own—"

"Look at you all spiffed up in a tux!" Lilah rushed over and hugged James. "I haven't seen you in one of these since your high school prom." Her gaze swept to Charlotte and she clasped her hands in admiration. "Stunning."

"As are you," Charlotte said. Lilah's long blond hair was loose and she wore a lavender tea-length dress. But even more striking was her happy confidence. You'd think she'd grown up attending swanky parties every weekend. But as for Harlan…she stifled a grin. He tugged at his collar and looked as if he wanted to be anywhere but here.

Lilah's gaze fell to Charlotte's feet and she let out an exasperated *tsk*. "Too bad I couldn't talk you into high heels, or at least wedge pumps."

As if she'd attempt smuggling out Jenny and the other girls while tottering in high heels. She caught Harlan's warning glance—Lilah was in the dark about tonight's mission. Just as well. Let her have her fairy-castle, enchanting illusion for the evening. The less people that knew, the better their chance for success.

The band came to an abrupt halt.

"May I have your attention, please?"

Maddie and Richard posed in front of the band, and her cultured voice swept over the crowd. Conversations halted.

"As everyone is aware, we've gathered here tonight to honor our sheriff, Harlan Sampson, and all of the men and women employed by the Elmore County Sheriff's Department."

Richard raised his glass in the air. "Hear, hear!" he called out a tad too loudly.

Maddie slanted him a look.

"Bet she gives him hell later," James murmured by her ear.

"Not if they're locked in separate cells."

He clinked his champagne glass against hers and smirked. "Hear, hear."

Maddie continued. "It's because of their hard work and dedication that the Lavender Mountain community is such a peaceful haven."

A smattering of applause broke out.

"And now I'd like to ask Sheriff Sampson to come forward and say a few words."

"Damn," Harlan muttered.

"Speech," Lilah said with a grin, giving him a playful shove forward.

Now was the time to slip away. "I'm going to the ladies' room. Be back in a bit," Charlotte lied.

"Wait until after Harlan's speech and I'll go with you," Lilah offered.

"Sorry. It can't wait."

She cast a last look at James. His face was stoic, but she knew he hated her operating alone. Yet they'd both agreed beforehand that it would be less conspicuous if they searched apart from one another. She gave him a reassuring smile and strolled toward the side exit of the clubhouse, all while casually sipping the flute of champagne.

At the rear of the main ballroom she stopped at the buffet table and picked up a canapé, using the opportunity to check if she were being watched. Luckily all eyes appeared focused on Harlan's clipped speech. She dabbed at her mouth with a paper napkin and then whisked out of the room and into a back hallway with an exit door.

One last furtive glance behind, and Charlotte slipped

outdoors. Cool wind whipped through the thin material of her evening gown and she shivered, thinking longingly of her jacket. But soon enough, she'd be back inside. On the sidewalk, she passed a couple decked out in their finery, obviously out of town guests on the way to the party. The woman's voice was a tad too loud and the man practically carried her as she stumbled about in her high heels.

Charlotte waved at them cheerily. "Forgot my lipstick," she said. "See you in a bit at the party. The band's fantastic."

"Oh, damn." The woman placed a hand over her mouth. "I believe I forgot mine, too. I'm going back, Thomas."

Thomas rolled his eyes. "You look fine. Let's go."

Charlotte beamed at him, practically bestowing a conspiratorial wink. "You go on. Me and—" She glanced at the woman.

"Alyssa," she supplied. "Alyssa Renfroe."

"Alyssa and I will go in together and meet you in a few minutes."

"You sure?" he asked doubtfully.

"No problem."

He transferred the weight of Alyssa to Charlotte's arm, and she fought to keep her balance while propping up Alyssa. Their progression to the Stowerses' house was slow and arduous, but Charlotte was grateful for Alyssa. What a struck of luck. Now she didn't have to sneak into the house. Alyssa had unwittingly provided an alibi.

Once at the Stowerses' entrance, Charlotte didn't bother knocking and opened the door like she had every right to be there.

A tall, husky man entered the foyer and gave them the once-over.

"We forgot our… What did we forget?" Alyssa asked with a giggle.

"Lipstick." Charlotte smiled at the man and kept walking. "I'm staying in the east wing. Are you?" she asked Alyssa.

Her smooth forehead puckered. "I—I'm not sure."

"Don't worry. We'll find your room."

It took several minutes to make it down the hallway, but at last Alyssa came to a halt. "This is it," she declared. "I recognize my perfume bottles on the dresser."

"Great. My room's further down. I'll be back in a few minutes," Charlotte lied, relieved to be rid of her drunken burden.

She'd been down this particular hallway on her previous visit with James and didn't expect Jenny or the others to be kept so close to the party. But for the sake of thoroughness, they'd leave no room unexamined.

Every bedroom off the hallway was presently empty, but appeared to be used as a guest bedroom for the weekend. Each contained luggage, clothes hung in the closets and a few toiletries were set on the nightstands. Charlotte peeked out of the last room she'd entered to make sure the coast was clear before stepping back into the hallway.

"So sorry you are feelin' poorly, ma'am," Colleen said in her distinctive Irish accent as Charlotte started to enter the den.

Charlotte ducked back inside the nearest bedroom and flattened herself against the wall.

"Let me help you find your room," Colleen continued. "This way, please, ma'am."

She let out a deep breath and listened to the women make their way down the hall. Time to slip away.

Charlotte scurried out of the room, still clutching the

small sequined purse that was just large enough to hold
her cell phone and a small gun. The hallway made an L-
turn and she ventured on, but it was more of the same—
empty rooms.

Until she entered the last room on the right.

Someone was in there. A mattress squeaked and a
man and woman groaned. Uh-oh. Hastily she backed out
and softly shut the door. Had they heard her?

She waited a few heartbeats, prepared to make a lame
excuse if they came after her, but the mattress squeaks
never slowed.

Whew, bullet dodged. Charlotte retrieved her cell
phone and texted James.

East wing complete. Negative. No need to break in.
Go inside and say your name is Thomas Renfroe and
you are checking on your wife, Alyssa, who returned
for some lipstick.

A rough hand grasped her elbow. "What the hell are
you doing here?"

THE BAND RESUMED playing and James waited several
minutes before strolling through the crowd, biding his
time until he had an opportunity to leave unnoticed. A
teenage girl clutched the arms of an older gentleman
and her gray eyes were wide and...not exactly scared,
but apprehensive. Was the man her father or one of the
Stowerses' clients? He needed to check the west wing
of the Stowerses' house and then find Charlotte—the
quicker the better. But he couldn't ignore the girl, either.
He turned and scanned the crowd for Harlan.

His brother-in-law was surrounded by people congratulating him on his speech, but as if he had an extra sense for danger, Harlan raised his head and made eye contact. James cocked his head at the old-man-young-girl couple and Harlan nodded in understanding. He'd check it out.

"Look at her," a lady said close by. "Never thought I'd see a Tedder at an event like this."

Another voice murmured assent. "Heard Sampson's hired her brother now."

"Harlan's in bed with the dregs of our community," another chimed in. "Disgraceful."

Heat fevered his brain. They could say what they wanted about him, but not his sister. She was off limits.

James squared his shoulders and eyed the small clique. "Lilah Tedder is one of the kindest, smartest women you'll ever meet. Harlan's lucky to have her for a wife." He focused his gaze on the sole male among the group. "And if you've got a problem with me, let's discuss it now."

"No problem," the man said quickly. "Ladies, let's head to the buffet table for refreshments."

They made a quick beeline to move away and James took a deep breath. He shouldn't have confronted them. The last thing he needed was to make a scene. Their plan depended on acting as unobtrusive as possible. He meandered out of the room, relieved nobody paid him any mind. At the back door of the clubhouse, he exited onto the deck. No one was around. Quickly he walked through the backyard. If someone asked what he was doing, he'd claim he needed fresh air.

His cell phone vibrated and he read the text message. Great. Charlotte was safe. Soon as he finished searching the west wing, they were to meet by the kitchen.

Sure enough, he easily got past the man monitoring

the front door. The moment he was alone, James began his search, going into every room—a couple of bedrooms and baths, a fully equipped gymnasium including a sauna and a movie theater room.

The hallway was eerily quiet. The Stowerses had excellent acoustics in their place. Perhaps they'd built the mansion that way to contain the screams of desperate children. His pace picked up. No way he'd leave this place without every room searched. If Jenny was here, they'd find her.

His spirits sank with each empty room. But the most likely place the girls were hidden would be either on the upper level of rooms or in the basement. They'd expected this going in. James entered the den and searched for Charlotte. No luck. She might already be hanging around the kitchen area. He hurried to the door—but still no Charlotte. Stealthily he opened the door several inches, but the room was dark and quiet.

No Charlotte.

Unease tingled at the back of his neck. Where was she? He pulled out his phone and checked the time the text was sent—five minutes ago. She should be here.

He pushed away from the kitchen and reached for his phone. A familiar smell of roses startled him. "Charlotte?" He whirled around.

"The one and only." Her voice was light but her expression subtly strained.

"Where were you?" he whispered fiercely. "What happened?"

"One of the male serving staff grabbed me and asked what I was doing in that area. I tried to play it off as if I were lost and looking for the bathroom, but he wasn't buying it."

He stood between her and the doors, half expecting security to arrive and escort them out of the house. Or worse. "How did you get away?"

"I acted all embarrassed and haltingly admitted that I'd gone there in search of my married lover. Claimed we'd made a rendezvous, but I couldn't remember which room we were supposed to sneak into. Then I put on my best snooty air and said that Maddie and Richard were close personal friends and if he didn't leave me alone I'd have to report him."

"Quick thinking. Guess you learned it on the job."

"Sink or swim, as they say." She shivered and rubbed her arms. "I'm okay. Let's get on with it. We don't want to draw attention to ourselves in case guards are lurking about."

"Agreed." He kept his voice low as they walked by the pantry. "Kitchen appears normal but we can take another quick peek before heading upstairs."

"I want to see as much as possible before we search the attic and basement. Make sure no child is left behind when the raid begins."

People liked to tease him about his military rigidity, but Charlotte was just as thorough in her job process.

What a shame this gorgeous house was owned by such a despicable couple. How many years had the Stowerses managed to conceal their illegal activity and live this lifestyle?

A deep voice suddenly boomed from around the corner. "Did you see that drunk chick—Alice or something—stumbling around the house?"

"Her boobs were practically hanging out of her dress," another man replied, chuckling.

Quickly James took Charlotte's hand and they ducked into a side room as the men made their way past.

"That was close," she breathed at his side as they slowly eased their way back into the hallway and proceeded to the staircase. Sneaking upstairs would be even trickier than the basement. Anyone passing through the foyer would see them. Timing was everything.

A quick look back and then they bounded up the stairs together. Again, he was struck by the unnatural quiet as they left the den and walked the hallway. As mapped out earlier, he searched the rooms on the right while Charlotte worked the left. They made quick work of it. He glanced in the last empty room on his side and joined Charlotte for her last search.

A heavy padlock hanging on the outside door set him on edge. Even if it wasn't locked now—why was it ever necessary to lock someone inside?

Half a dozen cheap cots lined a stark room that was unlike the opulence of the rest of the living quarters. The beds were meticulously tidy, even though they were made up with only threadbare sheets and blankets. He entered and shut the door behind him while Charlotte flipped on the light.

A scratched armoire was the only other piece of furniture besides the cots, and Charlotte flicked it open. A few lone wire hangers dangled from the top dowel, but it was otherwise empty.

"Could be the maid's quarters," he said quietly.

"This isn't the Victorian era where indentured servants were forced to live in substandard hidey-holes."

She walked to the lone, narrow window and pulled back the tattered curtain. "And then there's this," she whispered.

He ran a finger down the pane's tinted liner. "Bingo."

Charlotte's eyes grew misty. "They're gone. Sold. I'm too late."

"There's still the basement." But his own spirits grew low.

The scrape of a shoe sounded far down the hall. With unspoken accord, they rushed to the door and positioned themselves on either side, backs flat against the wall. Charlotte flipped off the light switch.

A crescent moon struggled to shine through the tinted and curtained window.

Creak. Another step closer.

James hardly dared to breath, concentrating on the patterns of sound.

Creak, creak. Just one person. He carefully extracted the gun from his vest and closed his finger on the trigger, the metal cool and lethal in his hands. A rustle of movement beside him, and Charlotte extracted a gun from her beaded purse. Her face was pale but composed in the faint light.

A flashlight beam crisscrossed on the floor outside their door. He was closer now. With any luck, the man was only on a routine security check.

The footsteps reached the end of the hallway and stopped.

Silence as thick as the stale, dark air weighted down on him. He noted the rise and fall of Charlotte's chest, although she made no sound. What was the man doing on the other side of the door? James gave her a slight nod. *Be ready for anything*, he silently willed her with his mind.

The world exploded in a firestorm of splintered wood as the man kicked down the door and entered. The scent of sweat and cheap aftershave stabbed through the chaos of his mind. *The intruder at Charlotte's apartment.*

A metallic clatter ripped through the darkness, like the sound of automatic gunfire in Afghanistan. James shook off the memory. *Not now. Stay in the moment.* His eyes focused and he realized that Charlotte had knocked the gun out of the man's hand. That noise had only been the sound of it harmlessly hitting the floor.

The man raised a fist to her, ready to strike.

James lowered the boom. Raising his arms high, he thrust downward with his gun and knocked the guy on the back of the head. He never saw it coming and crumpled to the ground with a heavy thud.

"Go get some pillowcases and blankets," he told Charlotte, kneeling beside the injured guard. Handcuffs were in his pocket, but the first order of business was to gag the intruder. One loud yell and their gig was up. James rolled him flat on his back. Had he killed the guy?

He moaned. James hastily grabbed the sheet from Charlotte, rolled it into a cylinder and gagged him. "Get another sheet and tie his feet while I cuff his hands."

They worked quickly, and all the while he strained to listen for more footsteps. So far, so good.

"Here." Charlotte pressed the intruder's flashlight into his hands. "We might need it."

Curious, James flicked it on and shone it on the man's face, glancing at the dagger tattoo on his neck. Gray eyes glared back, defiant to the end.

"Got you now," James said with grim satisfaction.

Charlotte tugged at his tux sleeve. "Let's go find Jenny."

Chapter Fourteen

Charlotte gathered up the hem of her long gown and checked the hallway before entering.

Behind her, James spoke softly into his mike, filling Harlan in on their progress. "Bound suspect upstairs, heading to basement. Any news?"

Charlotte held her breath. What if they'd been spotted entering upstairs? Harlan might call off the whole mission if Maddie was breathing down his neck.

James winced. "Ten-four."

"Well?" she asked.

"Sammy hasn't seen any activity out back and the gate officer reported no young females have exited Falling Rock. We're on."

"So what's the bad news? I saw that look on your face."

"The usual. He says abandon the mission and don't attempt a rescue if there's more than one guard down there. And call backup if needed."

Charlotte bit her lip, hoping for James's sake there wasn't more than one guard so that he wouldn't have to break Harlan's orders. Secretly she and James had agreed to take on two guards if necessary.

And in her heart of hearts, Charlotte made her own

secret vow. She wouldn't jeopardize James's life if there were three or more guards—but she'd return alone and attempt a solo rescue operation, despite all the odds against success.

At the end of the hallway, James suddenly pulled her in for an embrace and gave her a quick, fierce kiss. "Be safe," he ordered.

Love and worry blazed from his blue-hot eyes. It took her breath away. But before she could even process her thoughts, James stepped around her and surveyed the area. "We're clear."

Together they hurried down the stairs. In the foyer, she pressed his hand. "Good luck."

This is where they parted ways again.

She hurried past the kitchen and started by the main entrance.

According to the architectural drawing, there was another entrance to the basement behind the main level utility room, third door past the kitchen. She swept inside and locked the utility room door behind her. To the right of the washer and dryer was yet another door. Quickly Charlotte hurried over and gave the knob a turn.

Locked. Of course it was.

She opened her purse and extracted the tiny pick and tension wrench that both fit in the palm of one hand. She and James had practiced for this eventuality, and he'd been taken aback at her skill. This wasn't her first time to pick a lock.

Assured no one was about to witness the break-in, Charlotte set to work inserting the wrench into the bottom of the keyhole and the pick at the top of the lock. She scrubbed the pick back and forth. A little twist here and there and—*ping*—the metallic click fell into place. She turned the knob and cracked the door open.

"—getting hungry," she heard a deep voice say. "We should go upstairs and filch some of their alcohol."

"Hell, no. Maddie would have a fit. Ain't worth it."

Damn, there were two guards at least. She listened harder, praying a third voice didn't chime in.

"Stop acting like a wuss. She won't know. Don't need two of us to guard one door. Them bitches are locked up tight. They ain't goin' nowhere."

A smile curled her lips. She wasn't too late. Jenny and the other girls were so very, very close. She and James had a shot at making this work. Charlotte dropped the wrench and pick in her purse and texted James on her cell phone.

I'm in. Only two guards. Girls locked in storage room inside basement.

Setting her purse behind the dryer, she lifted out her gun. It took all her self-control not to rush in with her gun blazing and demand their release. But she and James had a plan. For now—she waited.

JAMES RETURNED HIS cell phone to his pocket with a sigh of relief. That had taken a little longer than anticipated. On his end, the basement entrance door hadn't been locked so he'd already deduced that if the girls were downstairs, they were locked in one of the two storage rooms. If he were the Stowerses, he'd have taken those extra precautions.

Taking a deep breath, he threw open the door and stomped down the narrow stairs. "Halloo," he called out, slurring his voice. "Where's da bathroom?" he asked, belching loudly. "I need to—"

"Hey, you can't be down here," a man quickly answered.

"Whaddaya mean by that?"

A burly guy appeared at the bottom of the steps. "No guests allowed down here."

"That's b-b-bullshit." James staggered and clutched the handrail, as if he were too drunk to keep his balance.

"Sir, you have to go. Now."

With satisfaction, he watched the guard start up the stairs. "But, but I—I'm Richard's pal." James fell on his rear end and stumbled down two steps. He let go of the rail and waved his hands in the air. "Whoa. Them stairs are st-steep."

The guard scowled, climbed up to him, and grabbed his arm. "You have to—"

With all his strength, James pulled the guard down with both arms. The man gaped in surprise and James landed a swift punch to his gut before the guard regained his senses and realized what was happening.

The man doubled over in pain but had the presence of mind to keep his arms locked around James. Together, they tumbled down the stairs. James's mike and cell phone clattered to the ground.

"Hey, what's going on?" he heard another male voice shout.

Excruciating pain suddenly radiated from his right shoulder. The son of a bitch had bitten him. James kneed the man in the groin and the pain eased as the man stopped biting and let out a strangled yelp.

"What the hell?" the other guard shouted. James saw him reach for a gun that was belted at his waist. Where was Charlotte? Right about now would be a good time for her to make an appearance.

From his position on the floor at the bottom of the stairwell, he spied her flat green shoes and a swatch of green fabric advancing toward them. His avenging angel in emerald. He strained his neck upward and watched as she pushed her gun into the second guard's back.

"Drop your weapon," she demanded in a hard voice.

"Who? What? Ah, damn it." The guard bent his knees and placed his weapon on the ground. Charlotte kicked at the gun and it spun several feet across the concrete floor, out of grabbing reach.

James rolled his prisoner onto his stomach and jerked one of his hands behind his back. "Sheriff's office. Don't resist arrest. You'll only make matters worse for yourself."

"Okay, okay," he groaned. "Don't hurt me."

He made short work of slapping on the cuffs. "Say one word and you're dead," he warned before leaping to his feet. "You, too," he told the other guard.

Charlotte spoke, nudging her pistol into the suspect's back. "Get on the ground spread-eagle, hands out in front."

He complied without a word of complaint, and James quickly cuffed him.

"We need more gags," Charlotte whispered.

"We'll make do." He tore off his tie and gagged one of the prostrate men on the floor.

Charlotte glanced down, running her hands down her hips over the sleek gown and frowned. "I don't have anything... Wait." She raised her hands and tugged at the velvet ribbon holding the bun at the top of her hair. Her hair cascaded down and she held the ribbon in front of her, eyeing it critically. "Not as strong as I'd like, but it will do."

"Give it to me," he said.

"Get the storage key from him first."

James grabbed the man's chin. "Where's the key?"

"You won't get away with this," he grunted. "Guards are everywhere patrolling the grounds. Let me go and I'll cooperate."

Charlotte knelt beside him. "We don't need your cooperation, Ricky—that is your name, isn't it? You're the one who shot at me."

James patted down the man's pockets. "Nothing here."

Charlotte turned to the other prisoner. "I'll pat him down."

James pulled the ribbon tight between his fists, holding it in front of the guard's face. "Last chance to talk."

"Okay, okay," Ricky said, breathing hard. "But remember I cooperated later if I get arrested."

James said nothing, advancing the gag toward his mouth. There'd be no deals for scumbags like Ricky. He wanted everyone involved in the trafficking business to get the stiffest sentence possible.

"It's in my right shoe."

James exchanged a bemused glance with Charlotte, and then untied the man's sneaker and shoved it off his foot.

A small brass key dropped on the concrete.

Charlotte snatched it up with a trembling hand and they stared at one another, disheveled and breathing hard. "We did it," she whispered. Her green eyes shone with tears.

Bittersweetness gnawed at his heart. He loved Charlotte's strength and courage, but even more he loved her vulnerability and fierce loyalty. She might not love him, but he'd stood beside her when no one else would believe or help in her quest to rescue Jenny. That would count for something in Charlotte's book, and he'd take what he could get.

He took her hand and helped her to her feet. "Only one thing left to do."

She nodded and ran a hand through her hair. "Right. I just…should be prepared for whatever we find behind that locked door. It'll be an ugly sight."

"Maybe it won't be too bad," he said gently. "After all, they want these girls to look pretty for their clients."

Anger crackled in her eyes and she lifted her chin. "That's not happening again. Let's go finish our job."

Chapter Fifteen

Charlotte held her breath as she turned the key in the lock.

"Wait." James's hand held her back. "Could be a trap or another guard waiting. I'll go first."

She shook off his hand. "We'll go in together." Before he could argue further, she thrust the door open.

The room was almost pitch black, with only a faint trickle of light from a high, small window. The stale, moldy scent of damp air assaulted her nose. Her eyes adjusted to the darkness and she saw the faint, pale outline of three young girls huddled together in a back corner. Groping along the concrete wall, she located the light switch and flipped it on.

The large, square block room was devoid of anything except the girls and a half-dozen cots with thin mattresses. James drew his gun and circled the middle of the basement for any hidden surprises.

"Don't shoot us," one of the girls screamed. "We've been good."

"Don't scream. Nobody's going to hurt you. I promise." Charlotte approached them slowly as James put away his weapon. She blinked at the unexpected sight.

The girls were gussied up to look like living Barbie

dolls. They wore bright-colored, low-cut evening gowns, their hair was elaborately curled and styled, and their young faces were painted with red lipstick and heavy rouge. Their eyes were thickly lined in black kohl. In a gray room that held all the charm of a steel garbage can, they popped like discarded roses.

It took Charlotte several moments to realize the blonde in the middle was Jenny. She looked nothing like the last time she'd seen her with Tanya. Then she'd been fresh-faced, wearing blue jeans and a T-shirt, and sporting a wide, easy grin.

"Jenny. It's me—Charlotte. Your mom's been so worried about you."

Jenny hunched her thin shoulders and shrank back until she was pinned against the wall. "Don't tell her where you found me," she whispered.

"But, but…" Charlotte floundered, unsure how to proceed. This was hardly the grand welcome she'd expected.

A petite Asian girl with bobbed black hair eyed them warily. "Who sent you?"

James flashed his badge. "Sheriff's office. We're here to help you."

A whimper escaped the lips of the third girl, another blonde who appeared to only be about twelve years old.

Charlotte scrutinized the girl's features. She'd seen her photo listed in their book of missing children. "Lisa Burns?" she guessed.

Lisa's eyes grew even more terrified, but she left the other two girls and approached James and Charlotte on wobbly legs. "I'll do whatever you say."

"Hey, are y'all really cops?" the Asian girl asked. "Did you just come for Jenny?"

"We're here for *all* of you," Charlotte assured her.

The mistrust melted on her face and she ran to Charlotte, wrapping boney arms around her waist. "I want out. My name is Amy Chang."

"We'll get you out." Charlotte ran a hand over her smooth hair and eyed Jenny, who'd sunk onto a cot and curled into a ball. Leg cuffs bound her slim ankles.

"Promise?" Amy pulled away and swiped at her eyes. Mascara and liner ran down her face.

Lisa gasped and put a hand on her red lips. "You're all messed up now, Amy. They're gonna hurt you if we don't get outta here. We're supposed to be all pretty."

"Nobody's going to be hurt," James said. "You're safe with us."

"Safe?" Amy thrust out her right hand, wrist down. Deep scars crisscrossed the veins. "I almost killed myself six months ago. A few weeks ago, I got messed up one night, thinking crazy thoughts, and got scared I'd do it again. I called a teen suicide hotline. That's how I met Piper. She was so nice. Asked to meet me. Said she'd take care of me and keep me safe. I thought she was my friend." Amy's lower lip trembled.

Charlotte's heart squeezed until it ached.

"Stop it!" Lisa cried. "We're going to get in trouble. They'll come shoot us like they did Mandy when she tried to run away."

"Mandy?" Charlotte and James exchanged a look. The human blood on the leaves… That poor kid. She hadn't been as lucky as Karen.

"We should go," James said, casting a swift glance at the stairs.

Charlotte eyed the teary Lisa and recalcitrant Jenny. "Might be easier to call Harlan and have him come down here with backup."

"You still got your phone? Mine's probably busted."

"It's upstairs in my purse. I'll use my mike to contact Harlan."

"Good. Because mine fell in the tumble down the stairs."

Charlotte removed the small black disc tucked into her gown. "Officer Hanson to Sheriff Sampson."

Nothing. Not even a whisper of static. Charlotte blew into the mouthpiece. "Testing, testing."

"Damn it," James muttered. "I'll go search for my dropped phone under the stairs. There's an off-chance it's not smashed to smithereens."

Charlotte put a hand on Amy's and Lisa's shoulders, guiding them to the cot where Jenny lay. "Let's go talk to Jenny a minute."

They offered no resistance, as docile as lambs, and stood close by while she sat on the cot beside Jenny. Tentatively, Charlotte touched one of Jenny's delicate cuffed ankles. Besides being bound, she wore ridiculous sequined high heels. "Why the leg cuffs?" she asked. The others weren't cuffed.

"She tried to run away the first night," Amy volunteered. "She didn't even make it out of the house before they caught her."

Charlotte could only imagine the severe punishment for that defiance. No wonder she was so scared to try to escape again. "Jenny. Are you afraid to leave? You know me. I promise I won't let anyone hurt you."

Jenny's face was buried in a blanket and she vehemently shook her head. "No. I won't go."

"Why not?"

"Because." Sobs shook her body.

"Because why?"

Jenny suddenly sat up and faced her. "I've done…bad things with bad men."

"It's not your fault, sweetie."

"Yes, it is. I-I'm a bad girl. I ran away from home and then…they got me."

Charlotte wrapped her arms around Jenny and laid her cheek on the top of Jenny's head. "Shh. It's okay."

"But my mom… I don't want her to know."

"Tanya just wants you home. She misses you terribly and has been out of her mind with worry."

Jenny turned her head to the wall, refusing to listen. It was going to take lots of time and therapy to get this child over the brainwashing and abuse. And she'd been troubled to begin with. Tanya had finally admitted to her that Jenny had threatened suicide several times after her father had left home. But Charlotte didn't have time or therapist skills. Every second they spent in the basement meant the odds of rescue dramatically decreased.

Lisa suddenly screamed and cowered to the ground. Amy's mouth opened in horror. Charlotte's stomach cartwheeled as she jumped up from the cot and whirled around.

Footsteps creaked on the wooden stairs. Through the open step slats flashed a pair of shiny men's shoes and gray flannel pants. James heard it, too and ran to the stairs.

Richard Stowers stepped down and faced them, a gun drawn.

Charlotte blinked. This Richard was deadly sober. The affable albeit lecherous drunk from earlier at the party had transformed into a maleficent, hard column of a man whose eyes shone with a vicious intent. Or—more likely—this was no transformation, but an unmasking of his true self. The show of drunkenness might have been just that—an act to throw people off. It had certainly fooled her.

"Had a feeling I'd find you two down here," Richard said coolly. "Maddie might have underestimated y'all, but I didn't."

The utter calm of his voice was all the more terrifying for its unruffled focus. This was a man who could not be reasoned with or distracted.

James stepped in front of her and raised his gun. Charlotte maneuvered to his side. If they went down, they went down together.

"Drop it," Richard ordered.

"Hell, no. We appear to be at a standoff."

Amy let out a banshee wail that echoed in the chamber like an explosion. Richard turned his head a fraction to determine the cause of the noise.

This was Charlotte's chance.

She dived toward Richard's knees. He stumbled backward half a step. Time slowed and her whole body attuned to every nuance of detail—

The stiff fabric of Richard's pants.

Amy's wails.

James shouting her name.

The thundering of her own heart in her ears.

A whoosh of air as Richard raised his arm.

His furious dark eyes intent on killing.

The cylindrical chamber of metal pointed at her head.

She'd always known it would come to this one day. But she didn't shut her eyes and she didn't regret her decision. Her mantra was always to see a job through to the end. No matter what.

Another swoosh of air and Richard was falling. Charlotte swiftly rolled toward the back wall. Richard's gun fired. An explosion of smoke and noise assaulted her senses—but no bullet ripped into her flesh. She was unharmed.

James jumped on top of Richard and landed a solid punch to the man's gut. The gun fell out of Richard's hand and she picked it up, scrambling to her feet. "Stop fighting, Richard. Or I'll shoot."

The men stilled and eyed her, Richard gaping in surprise, and James with a grin.

"No need for that," James said. "Stowers is going to play nice now." He grabbed an arm and twisted it behind Richard. "Roll onto your stomach and put your hands behind your back."

"Damn you both," Richard ground out harshly. "It's not over yet. Do you hear me? This is *my* house. And those bitches back there are mine, too."

Charlotte's anger rose to match his. "They aren't bitches and they don't belong to anybody."

James slapped the cuffs on Stowers's wrists.

Richard bent his knees and managed a sitting position. "They've already been bought and paid for. This isn't over yet. You'll never make it out of here with those whores."

"Shut your mouth," James warned, grabbing a fistful of the man's starched shirt. "Unless you want me to gag you like I did your guards."

Richard glowered but kept his mouth shut as James frisked him for weapons. He pulled out a cell phone from Richard's pocket and tossed it to Charlotte.

"Give me that back," Richard cried out. "You've no right to search my house like you did. When my lawyer's through with you— Hey!"

James pulled off the tie from around Stowerses' neck. "You had your chance."

Charlotte smiled grimly as James gagged the guy. Actually, the threat of his lawyers was a problem, but she'd cross that bridge later and she damn sure wasn't going to let the bastard know she was worried.

"I expect nothing but commendations from law enforcement for breaking this case," she boasted.

James stood and raised a brow at her. "After all, we did hear the victims cry for help when we entered the house to escort a guest to their room. I'd say that gave us a right to investigate."

Nothing but muffled curses escaped from Stowers's gag.

"Go on and take the girls upstairs and let Harlan knows what's happening," James said.

"But I can't get Jenny to agree to leave, and her feet are cuffed anyway."

"Then you go ahead and take the other two while I deal with Jenny. If I have to carry her out of here screaming, then that's what I'll do."

"Okay. Lisa, Amy, let's get out of here." Charlotte walked over to Jenny's cot and ran a hand through her blond hair. "Officer Tedder's going to carry you out. You can trust him, okay?"

Jenny's entire body started to shake. "No! Just leave me alone."

Charlotte dropped her hand and stared at her, unsure what to do.

James sank to his knees by Jenny and cocked his head toward the stairs, signaling for Charlotte to leave.

Taking Lisa and Amy by the hand, Charlotte ushered

them across the basement. At the foot of the stairs, she glanced back once more.

James nodded. "I won't leave without Jenny," he promised.

And she believed him. He'd take a bullet before he broke that vow. Something fierce and warm and wonderful pulsed through her body. A feeling she'd never expected to happen again. She loved James. Loved and trusted him with a deep faith she hadn't imagined possible. She wanted to tell him, but now wasn't the right time or place. These girls desperately needed to get away.

"I know you will," she called out. Charlotte let go of Amy's and Lisa's hands. "I'll go first. Stay close to me and follow my orders."

The girls nodded in understanding, their eyes huge with fear.

They rapidly climbed the stairs. Each moment, Charlotte expected Maddie or one of her guards to appear at the open door. But the utility room was blessedly empty and she waved her hand at Amy and Lisa to follow her.

Charlotte gave them an encouraging smile, then turned toward the doorway and caught sight of her purse where she'd stashed it earlier behind the dryer. Quickly Charlotte dug out her phone and punched in Harlan's number.

They were so close to rescuing Jenny and the girls. All that was left was to find Harlan and get backup in place before arresting Maddie and Richard. Their guests were in for a real surprise tonight. This year's fund-raising event would be remembered for years to come.

Now if she could just get Harlan to answer the phone.

Chapter Sixteen

"It's time to go."

James strove for a firm yet gentle tone with the trau-matized Jenny.

"You don't get it. They'll catch us and kill us."

How must it feel to be sixteen years old and think you're forever doomed to a life of sexual slavery? To not be able to see help when it was in front of your very eyes?

He took her hand. "We're going. Whatever it takes, I'm going to make sure you leave here and never come back. I don't want to force you, but if that's what I need to do, so be it."

"No." She shrank further from him. "You can't make me and if—"

Enough. He'd wasted a good five minutes trying to gain her cooperation and it wasn't working. James quickly uncuffed her leg irons, then put one arm under her knees and the other across her back, lifting her ef-fortlessly. Jenny gasped and he placed a finger against her lips. "Not another word," he said sternly.

She blinked at him and slowly nodded. It hurt to use that tone with her, but her life was more important than hurt feelings. He crossed the room with the light burden in his arms, relieved tonight was almost over.

James started up the steps, but paused on the third rung. Sharp, staccato footsteps sounded above, from behind the door. Not the soft padding Charlotte made with her flats. The steps grew louder.

Jenny whimpered and turned her face into his chest, afraid of who it might be.

He wasn't so thrilled himself. His only options were to turn back and hide Jenny while he attacked their confronter—or push ahead at full speed and perhaps catch the guard off balance. Too late to retreat, he decided. Press on.

James plowed forward, but Jenny had a different reaction to the danger. She reached her hands out to either side, clinging to the walls in an attempt to slow him down. She twisted and squirmed in his arms, surprisingly feisty. The desperate always managed to draw strength when panicked.

A figure appeared at the top of the stairs—tall, dark and deadly.

"What's this?" Maddie asked with a hiss.

It looked like Maddie, same red outfit and elegant veneer, but her eyes were bereft of even a speck of human warmth. They crackled with aggrieved outrage. She didn't wait for an answer. "You're not going anywhere with my property."

She raised a pistol at them. "Turn around and go downstairs."

If Jenny wasn't in his arms, he'd take his chances—rush Maddie and knock her to the ground. But she was, and he'd do anything to keep her safe.

"Be reasonable, Mrs. Stowers. Your home's crawling with law enforcement and they'll be here at any moment."

Where the hell was Harlan? There'd been plenty of time for Charlotte to have alerted him. His skin flushed hot, then cold. Had something happened to Charlotte?

"Bullshit," she said flatly.

The profanity startled him. He'd thought her much too cultured and uptight to be coarse. "Nobody's coming to save either of you. Now move it."

He wouldn't turn his back on Maddie. Too dangerous. Instead, he slowly descended one step. The longer he delayed entrapment in the basement, the better.

Maddie slammed the door shut and waved her gun. "If I shoot, my aim's at the girl."

Jenny's nails dug through his shirt as she clung to him, her body tense and shaking.

"I'm going," he reassured Maddie. "This is between us. Leave Jenny out of it."

Another step down and still no hint of the cavalry coming to save them. He had to face this alone.

The scent of violets grew strong as Maddie closed in. The clamor of bells spun in his mind, a dizzying vortex of sound.

It was happening all over again. His skin burned as though he was back in Bagram, and his body felt lightweight and unbalanced. He stumbled on the last step and fell backward.

Get it together. Don't hurt Jenny.

He held tight onto her thin frame, absorbing the impact of the cement floor as they tumbled. "Stay behind me," he whispered to Jenny, grabbing her hand and pulling her behind him as he rose to his feet.

Maddie was closing in. He watched as she scanned the room and caught sight of the guards and her husband bound and gagged on the floor.

"Richard?" Her lips curled and her patrician nose flared. "You incompetent fool. What the fuck are you doing down here? You should have sent me to handle this situation."

She waved her gun at the guards, shaking her head in disgust. "I'll deal with the two of you later."

It was clear who was in control of the trafficking ring. And it wasn't Richard Stowers.

Maddie turned her back on the hapless men and focused her attention on the matter at hand. "It won't do you any good to hide behind the cop, Jenny. Did you really think you were going to get away? Come out and face me. Time I taught you a real lesson in obedience."

James slightly raised his arms to the side, shielding Jenny.

"Give it up, Maddie. Cooperate with me now and it will go better for you."

Her lips curled into a sneer. "That might have worked on these idiots—" she half-turned and waved her gun at Richard and the guards "—but your empty threats don't scare me one iota."

Jenny slipped beneath his right arm and shuffled forward.

"I'll be good," she said around the sobs that wracked her slender body. She dropped to her knees. "Please don't kill us."

"You'll be the first to die. It's you they've been searching for all along. You've been way too much trouble."

She means to gun us both down.

Death permeated the room, settling its dreaded weight on his shoulders. The last seconds of his life played out before him. Had Charlotte made it to safety with the other two girls? He hoped that would be some consolation to her when she discovered their bodies.

"Kill me. Let her go," he said in a last-ditch effort to bargain for Jenny's life. "She's your—" he stumbled over the next word "—*property*. Wouldn't want to miss recouping on your investment, would you?"

He stepped in front of Jenny again as Maddie wavered, clearly weighing the options. Would her greed win over her caution in leaving a witness to his murder? Once Jenny was sold and her ownership transferred to another person, Maddie would no longer have any control over what Jenny might say in the future.

Footsteps pounded down the basement steps and he turned.

Charlotte's voice floated down. "James? Backup's on the way. Where have you—"

She stopped short at the sight of Maddie's gun.

James squeezed his eyes shut momentarily and groaned. Why had she come back downstairs alone? That wasn't the plan.

Maddie frowned. "Hands up. Come on down and join the crowd, Detective Charlotte Helms. Yes, that's right. I know who you are."

Charlotte's eyes widened as she approached, hands held high. "How long have you known my real identity?"

Charlotte was playing his same game. Keep Maddie engaged, keep her talking, until help arrived.

If they were coming at all.

"Since day one," Maddie said crisply. "That bitch, Karen Hicks, tipped you off about our operation. I intend to make her pay for that, too."

"I don't know anyone by that name," Charlotte said.

James admired her loyalty. She'd go to her death and not reveal an informant's name.

"Liar! I thought when Larry fired you, you'd go away. Should have known better."

"Larry?" Charlotte's brows drew together and then smoothed.

"That's right. Your very own Captain Burkhart. He's kept us protected for years."

Damn. Burkhart was in for one serious ass-kicking— that is, if he ever got out of this freaking basement.

"Son of a bitch," Charlotte breathed.

Heavy footfalls rained down from the room above. Had Harlan arrived with backup—or was it more of the Stowerses' guards?

Maddie's fingers tightened on the trigger and her eyes narrowed.

A chill chased the length of his spine and a roaring pounded in his brain. Holy hell, she was going to kill Charlotte. He recognized the murderous intent in her eyes, the subtle micromovement of her hands before shooting. He'd witnessed it too many times in combat. With every ounce of willpower he possessed, James tamped down the spiraling sensations that threatened to tunnel him back in time and place. Right here, right now, he had to save Charlotte.

He launched his body in front of Charlotte.

Please don't let me be too late.

JAMES'S BODY FLASHED in front of her, blocking Charlotte's view of Maddie's madness.

The crack of gunfire exploded.

Blood. A thin stream of crimson arched upward and

then fell like droplets of red rain. James pitched forward, landing face-first on the concrete.

Charlotte swallowed the acrid, burnt scent of gunpowder. She registered the chaos of noise and movement coming from behind her back, and the screams of Jenny curled on the floor, hands over her ears.

Not James. Dear God, no.

She had to touch him, had to know he still breathed. Charlotte dropped to the floor and touched the back of his head, fingers curling over his short, sandy hair.

The whistle of a speeding bullet passed inches above her head. Unfazed by the danger, she moved her hand lower, down to the familiar, sensitive nape of his neck. Miss Glory had told her to open her heart, but right now her heart felt as if it were breaking. Her fingers probed and explored, finding the beat of his pulse.

He lived.

Hope renewed her mind and heart. They still had a chance to get out of this alive…and together. She homed in on the pandemonium surrounding them, crystallizing her focus.

"Drop it, Stowers."

It was Harlan. And he wasn't alone. A cavalcade of footsteps treaded the wooden floor, and from the corners of her eyes she noted dozens of black shoes and the hems of suit pants.

Maddie retreated a step. "You have no right to be here," she screeched. "This is *my* house. *My* property. *My* land."

Charlotte didn't have to look up and see Maddie's face to know that the woman was losing it. Her shrill voice trembled with panic and fury. Charlotte imagined that Maddie felt trapped as officers pressed in and surrounded her. A criminal mastermind like her might be unhinged at her lack of control in the situation. And that made her very, very dangerous.

Any moment, and Maddie could fire off a round of bullets, killing many of them before she was shot or taken down.

She had to stop her. Maddie's attention was on Harlan. Now was her chance. Charlotte lunged forward, latching onto Maddie's right ankle. Charlotte yanked at the woman's leg with all her strength.

Maddie shrieked and tried to kick her hand away, but Charlotte held on like a bulldog and pulled on Maddie's leg with both hands.

The elegantly thin Maddie crumpled to the floor, landing on her skinny ass.

Officers stormed from all sides, seizing Maddie's weapon and cuffing her.

"Do you know who I am?" Maddie screamed. "You can't do this. I'll sue you. I'll—"

Charlotte ignored her desperate ramblings and all the mayhem from above. She crawled to Jenny. The girl's stunned, wide-eyed stare was fixed on James's bleeding wound.

"It's my fault," she whispered. "All my fault. He kept trying to get me to go with him, and I wouldn't. And now he's d—"

"Shh. He's not dead," Charlotte assured her, patting Jenny's hand. "But he needs an ambulance, quick."

She left Jenny and hurried over to James.

He moaned and the sound was heavenly to her ears, much as she hated that he was in pain. She flipped him over onto his back and assessed the damage. All the bleeding stemmed from his right shoulder. It probably hurt like hell, but his heart and vital organs should be fine.

"Here, take this," Harlan said, handing her his jacket. "Medics will be here in a moment. I had them on standby. They said to staunch the bleeding as much as possible until they arrive."

She took the jacket and pressed it against the wound.

James groaned again and his eyelids lifted. Blue eyes shimmered with an equal measure of humor and pain. "Are you trying to kill me?"

"Trying to save you." She cried and laughed through tears. "Don't you ever jump in front of a bullet again. You got that?"

He grimaced and raised up on one elbow. "I don't plan on it."

"Hey, buddy," Harlan said, bending down on his knees. "That was a damn fool thing to do. Don't try to get up. Medics will take you out on a stretcher."

James clenched his jaw and raised to a half-seated position. "I'm fine."

"Like hell you are." Charlotte barely suppressed a snort. James was pale and had lost blood. "Just stay put and—"

"Are Amy and Lisa okay?" he interrupted.

"They're upstairs with Sammy." Charlotte turned and motioned Jenny over. "So is Jenny, or she will be, once she sees you're going to be alright."

James mustered a smile for the young girl. "Told you I wouldn't leave you behind."

Jenny threw himself at him, throwing her arms around his neck. "I'm sorry. It's my fault you got hurt."

Charlotte winced. That hug had to hurt.

James patted her with his uninjured arm. "You're not to blame. Not at all. I'm fine."

Charlotte placed a hand on Jenny's shoulder and drew her away. "He's hurt. Give him a little breathing room," she said lightly.

EMTs clamored down the steps as fast as they could with their bulky stretcher, and Charlotte exhaled a sigh of relief. She hated seeing James in pain. He needed to be stitched up, medicated, and then put to bed.

Maddie's voice rose again over the crowd. "You can't do this to me. Wait until my attorneys hear this..."

Charlotte watched as officers grabbed Maddie by both arms and forced her to move forward.

"Richard, do something," Maddie ordered.

The two guards and Richard Stowers were on their feet and their gags removed. They were also being read their rights.

"Shut the hell up, Maddie. It's over," Richard snapped.

Jenny hugged her knees to her chin, making herself small, watching Maddie's imminent approach. They'd have to pass close by on their way out. Charlotte moved to shield Jenny from the sight, but Maddie spotted her.

"You little bitch," she screamed, venting her ire at her former captive. "Everything was fine until you came along."

A change swept over Jenny's face. Her eyes flickered from fear to fury and she jumped to her feet, hands clenched into fists. "I hate you," she screamed, her voice even louder than Maddie's. "Hate you, hate you, HATE you."

Maddie blinked. The woman had probably never had a comeuppance before from one of her young, vulnerable victims.

Charlotte wanted to applaud. She'd much rather see her angry than scared. Jenny had spirit. With lots of counseling and her mother's love, she would have the strength to move on with her life.

And hopefully it would be a damn good life.

"Get the Stowerses out of here," Harlan ordered.

His officers hustled Maddie up the steps, her husband and their two guards close in tow. Maddie didn't say another word.

Charlotte put an arm around Jenny. "You'll never have to see that woman again," she promised. "We'll do all we can to see she stays in prison until she's a very old lady."

Jenny swiped at her eyes and nodded. "I want my mom now."

"Of course." Eagerness burst inside Charlotte like a dam. This was the moment she'd been waiting for ever since she came to Lavender Mountain.

Harlan handed her his cell phone. "Call your friend. She's waited a long time to hear this news."

Charlotte punched in the numbers with shaking hands. "Tanya? Hey, I called because...no, Jenny's not hurt. Just the opposite. Deep breath, hon. I have good news." Charlotte inhaled deeply herself, relieved the ordeal was almost over. She caught James's glance, and he smiled and gave a thumbs-up as an EMT bandaged his wound. For a moment, her lungs choked and she couldn't speak. "Tanya, there's someone here who wants to talk to you."

Wordlessly she handed the phone to Jenny.

"Mom? It's me." Tears, mixed with black mascara, streamed down her heavily made-up cheeks. "Can you come bring me home?"

There wasn't a freaking dry eye in the basement that

was still swarming with law enforcement officers—supposedly hardened men and women used to horrendous crimes. Harlan's chest rose and fell and he cleared his throat.

James was suddenly beside her. Stubborn man. He shouldn't be standing at all. But she nestled into his solid warmth. Leaving her job and coming to Lavender Mountain was the best decision she'd ever made.

She'd found Jenny, and so much more.

Chapter Seventeen

James shifted in his seat. The stitches on his right shoulder pinched uncomfortably under his shirt. Not that he'd admit that fact to anyone. Charlotte and Lilah had fussed over him for the last two days and he'd had enough.

"You okay?" Harlan asked, leaning back in his chair.

He groaned. "Don't you start with that, too. I came back to work to escape."

"Nothing but desk duty for you, at least for another couple of weeks." Harlan shoved over a mound of paperwork and gave him an evil grin. "This should be loads of fun for you."

"Yeah, right. Looks like you've let filing go for at least six months. What the hell does Zelda do around here?"

"Everything but filing. She hates it."

James rifled through the papers. Escaping the incessant nursing at home wasn't the only reason he'd returned to the office. But he dallied, reluctant to state his real reason. He changed the subject. "How are Amy and Lisa? Heard any word?"

"Lisa was returned to her home. Unfortunately, Amy tried to commit suicide again. But the good news is that she's been placed in an intensive psychiatric care facility. Hopefully they can put this behind them. How are Jenny and her mom doing?"

"Healing. Glad the nightmare's over, but struggling. It will take time. Charlotte plans on paying them a visit in a couple weeks."

Harlan scowled. "Never would have imagined a human trafficking ring had connections with Lavender Mountain. I'm trying my best to keep Elmore County crime-free, but by the time I clean up one mess, something new and unexpected pops up."

"No need to beat yourself up. The ring hadn't been here long."

Investigation had already revealed that the trafficking ring had been in Lavender Mountain for less than six months. The Stowerses were based in Atlanta, but they'd felt heat from the cops closing in, so they'd decided to cool things off a bit by temporarily switching their base to Falling Rock.

"After all, they'd been running this operation close to a decade in Atlanta," James continued. "There's always something new popping up, too. It's the nature of the job." And his brother-in-law was doing a damn good job. Credibility in the sheriff's office was finally returning after the disastrous tenure of the old sheriff. "What's the latest on the Stowerses' case?"

"Nothing new there. They're still awaiting trial in Atlanta. The real news is that Captain Larry Burkhart was arrested. Created quite the shake-up in their police department."

"Nothing worse than a dirty cop. After the way he treated Charlotte, I couldn't be happier to hear he's gone."

"I regret that I listened to his nonsense about Charlotte's mental stability."

"You should tell her, not me."

Harlan nodded and cleared his throat. "I intend to."

It was clear that Harlan wasn't looking forward to eating crow, but when he was wrong, he was man enough to own up to it.

"Speaking of Charlotte..." Harlan began. "What are her plans for the future? I'm assuming she'll be offered her old position, given that Burkhart was behind the firing."

"They called this morning. She told them she wasn't interested."

And hadn't he breathed a sigh of relief at that announcement? But Charlotte hadn't said she'd stay with him, either. It was an issue they hadn't discussed yet. But now that he'd recovered from his injury, there was nothing to tie Charlotte to this mountain—or to him.

Their living arrangements were in limbo and it made him uneasy.

Harlan tapped a pencil on his desk, a sure sign he was about to speak on a topic that made him uncomfortable. "You know our office policy. Since you obviously have some kind of—intimate relationship—the two of you can't work together anymore as partners."

"I'm aware. That's another reason I came back to work today." James opened the folder in his lap and took out its only contents—a single typed sheet of paper. "This is my official two-week notice, although if you need me to stay a little longer, I will. But I'm resigning."

He reached across Harlan's desk to hand him the notice, but Harlan didn't take it. James shrugged and let it fall onto the rest of his boss's paperwork.

"There's no need for this. You can both stay on, but work different shifts with different partners."

"The job isn't for me. I appreciate the opportunity, but I'd—"

"You've done damn good work," Harlan interrupted. "What don't you like about it?"

He knew his brother-in-law wasn't going to take the news well and he hated disappointing him. Harlan had given him a job when he'd returned from military duty, and he was floundering on what he wanted to do next.

"I'm pursuing an old dream. I want to go in business for myself as a carpenter."

"I always knew you were good with your hands…but are you sure about this?"

"Positive." He'd stayed up most of last night, resolving everything in his mind. Nothing like getting shot at point-blank range to make a man rethink his direction in life.

"I may be leaving, but you should keep Charlotte on. She's a fantastic cop."

"Agreed. Although I could find a place for both of you. If you change your mind, the door's always open."

James stood and they shook hands. "Guess I'll be getting a start on all this." He nodded at the stack of papers Harlan had unloaded on him.

"Count on me working you like hell for the next two weeks, buddy."

James grinned. "No problem. I'll see what I can do to get this stuff filed and organized—since you and Zelda obviously won't ever get around to it."

He turned to leave and had almost slipped out the door when Harlan spoke again.

"It's none of my business, but I hope you intend doing your part to get Charlotte to stay on here at Lavender

Mountain. Seeing as how you've left me shorthanded. Least you could do."

James narrowed his eyes and gave a slow smile. "I believe you may be as nosy as Lilah."

And with that nonanswer, he made his exit.

"YOU SHOULDN'T BE DRIVING," Charlotte scolded. "You worked late and then insisted on helping me clean up after dinner. Don't you need some rest?"

"Stop fretting over me. I'm fine." James backed the car out of the driveway and eased onto the dark road.

"Where are we going?"

"Nowhere in particular," he lied. "I was cooped up in the house for two days and then spent all day at the office. Thought it'd be nice to get out for a spell."

They settled into a comfortable silence as they traveled up the steep mountain road. A deep peace filled him since he'd turned in his notice. His career path was clear. At least that part of his life was in order.

Charlotte played with a lock of her hair. "I've been thinking—"

"Always dangerous," he teased.

She gave him a hard stare. "I'm going back to Atlanta this weekend."

His chest squeezed tight. "Why?"

"My apartment is a wreck. Remember? I need to clean it up and take care of my bills. You know, all the daily routine stuff that's gone undone."

His chest relaxed a fraction. "A temporary visit, then?"

"For now. The police commissioner asked if I'd meet with him."

His hands tightened on the steering wheel as he rounded a bend. "They really want you back."

"Maybe. Or maybe he wants reassurance that I won't go to the press about the way Burkhart ordered me to quit the case and then fired me when I refused."

The Atlanta news media was having a field day with the news that a high-ranking member of the police department had helped cover up a human trafficking ring.

"When are you leaving? Friday?"

"Bright and early."

Seemed like he was already losing her. Could she really be happy working and living in such a remote area? He didn't want Charlotte to settle. He wanted her to live out all her dreams. And if that meant living in Atlanta, he wouldn't stop her.

The confidence he'd felt earlier vanished. She hadn't told him yet that she loved him. He'd been so sure he'd seen it in her eyes down in the Stowerses' basement after he'd been shot. Had read a desperate concern in her eyes as she'd hovered over him once he'd been shot.

But he might be wrong.

Another silence descended—though this time not as peaceful. James continued up the mountain, then turned onto the familiar dirt driveway. Headlight beams illuminated the charred remnants of his old family cabin.

Charlotte glanced his way, brows raised. "You really want to see this place again? The last time we were here was so sad."

"Not all my memories here are bad ones."

"Right," Charlotte touched his arm. "You grew up in that cabin. I'm sure you had lots of great times."

He pulled around to the back of the yard. Yep, the old metal glider swing remained. He stopped the car and stuffed the keys in his pocket. "But my favorite memory of all is that this is where I first met you."

A delighted grin broke across her face. "Aww…that's so sweet."

"Come on." He got out and headed for the trunk.

"For a minute," she agreed, climbing out. "It's cold out here."

James opened the trunk and pulled out a thick quilt. "I've got you covered."

"Looks like you had this planned from the get-go."

"True," he confessed. He put an arm around her and led her to the glider.

"Did your mom make this quilt?"

"Grandmother. Mom wasn't into all the domestic stuff."

Charlotte sat down and he tucked the quilt around her legs before sitting beside her.

She giggled. "How could I forget the first time we met? That look on your face when you ordered me to stop running—so ferocious."

"Of course it was. You pointed a gun at me."

"Because I thought you were one of them and had come to finish me off."

A grin split his face. "Freezing cold and you had on nothing but an oversize camouflage shirt and black panties. All long, sexy legs, wild red hair and an attitude."

She jostled his side with her elbow. "Is that why you followed me everywhere and wouldn't leave me alone? You lusted after my body?"

"You were a mystery. One I had to solve."

"It's what makes you a good officer."

"About that… I turned in my two-week notice today."

Surprised widened her teal-green eyes. "Why?"

"It's not for me. I've been longing to go back to my old job. To work with my hands again."

"Doing what?"

"Carpentry."

He studied her face closely. Carpentry wasn't exactly a sexy kind of job, and it might take some time before he became established in the community. For some women, that could be a real turnoff.

"A carpenter," she murmured thoughtfully. "You're full of surprises. I should have guessed with the whittling piece at your house. If that's what makes you happy, then you should absolutely go for it."

His gaze drifted to what remained of the burnt pine structure. "My first job will be to tear down what's left of Dad's cabin and rebuild it into a new home."

"I love that idea, James." She paused a few heartbeats. "And I love you."

The tension in his shoulders relaxed. Charlotte loved him. They could figure the rest out later—together. He stroked her hair and ran his fingers over the delicate features of her face.

"Forever?" he asked quietly, hardly daring to breathe.

Her teal eyes sparkled and shimmered. "Yes. And I promise I'll never run away from you again."

Epilogue

Charlotte's breath caught at the stunning vista. A woman couldn't ask for a more perfect wedding day. Dogwoods blossomed on top of Lavender Mountain and the lush greenness of the forest contrasted with the turquoise sky. To think by summer's end she'd be living here, waking up each morning next to James and admiring this gorgeous view from their new home.

Her gaze sought his through the throng of well-wishers. He was deep in conversation with Sammy and Harlan. The threesome looked so arresting in their tuxes that her breath caught. Of course, James was the most handsome by far. How lucky was she?

As if attuned to her every nuance, James lifted his eyes and scanned the crowd until they settled on her. A slow, sexy grin lit his face.

Lilah was suddenly by her side. "Pretty impressive, huh?" she asked.

"He is," Charlotte murmured, gaze still locked on her groom.

Lilah laughed and slapped her arm. "I'm talking about the cabin, silly. Not my brother."

Charlotte wrenched her gaze from James and stared at his handiwork. The burnt remains of his dad's old place had been torn down, and a new home for the two of them was coming along at a quick pace. James had hired a crew and worked sunup until sundown, returning home every night sweaty and dirty, with a huge smile lighting his face. And he slept soundly at night, the insomnia a thing of the past.

"It doesn't have the grandeur of a Falling Rock mansion, but it'll do, right?"

Again she had to snap her thoughts back to the conversation at hand. "It's perfect."

Lilah hugged her. "I'm so glad you're marrying my brother. I haven't seen him this happy since before his first overseas tour of duty. You're good for him."

"And he's good for me. I was lonely and totally burned out working undercover." She hadn't even known how miserable she was until she met James and came to Lavender Mountain.

"I only wish Dad and Darla were here to see your wedding. And the new house."

"Me, too." She and James had talked about it just last night. His father would have been proud of James's accomplishments. "This work has been good for James. It's as if he's laying to rest the ghosts from his past with every board he cuts."

"What's this about ghosts of the past?" James was beside her, and Lilah waved goodbye, strolling over to Harlan and Sammy.

"Nothing. From here on out, it's nothing but new beginnings," she promised.

"No second thoughts about marrying a carpenter?" His voice was light and teasing, but his eyes hinted at worry.

"Not when you've built us this gorgeous house complete with custom cabinets and bookshelves." She winked. "Who am I to complain? You should be the worried one. I work crazy hours with Sammy and I've made plenty of enemies over the years."

"You're safe with me. Forever." James lifted her left hand, and her engagement ring sparkled in the late afternoon sun.

"I know," she whispered.

He lifted a strand of her red hair and smiled. "Glad it's back to its fiery color. It suits you." Then he kissed her. It started out as a quick press of the lips, but he deepened the kiss and she was lost in the moment.

Cheers and whistles from the wedding guests brought her back to reality. Before she could pull away, James whisked her into his arms and spun her around.

In a dizzying whirl, she saw them all there—her mom and dad and brothers, Harlan and all her coworkers, even Tanya and Jenny had come for the celebration. Finally, she was at home. At peace. In a place where she could plant roots and spend the rest of her life. Lavender Mountain was the haven she hadn't even known she was seeking.

Miss Glory had told her to open her heart, and at last she finally had.

* * * * *

LET'S TALK
Romance

For exclusive extracts, competitions
and special offers, find us online:

f facebook.com/millsandboon

◉ @millsandboonuk

𝕏 @millsandboon

Or get in touch on 0844 844 1351*

For all the latest titles coming soon, visit
millsandboon.co.uk/nextmonth